With Wine Comes War

JE Johnson

Contents

For the ones who stayed long after they knew better.
For the ones who swallowed their pain to keep the peace,
who wore silence like armor and called it strength.
For the ones who forgot how to ask for softness
because they were too used to the sharp edge of love.
This one is for the war you lost yourself in—
and the quiet, brutal way you crawled out.

—JJ

Trigger Warning

This novel contains depictions of physical violence, emotional abuse, PTSD, and self-worth struggles. It explores toxic relationships, alcohol abuse, gaslighting, and the aftermath of trauma. Please read with care if any of these themes are sensitive or triggering for you.

Chapter 1

ALEX

"Get off of me!" I screamed.

My arms thrashed at the figure pinning me down—Tanner, Roman...I couldn't separate them. Tanner's voice came out of Roman's face, then Roman's voice out of Tanner's. Hands closed around my throat.

"Roman, stop!" I tried to yell, but the words barely formed. "I love you." My lips shaped the plea, but nothing came out. He didn't hear me. His eyes were so dark they looked unrecognizable. His grip tightened. Pressure closed in. Air vanished. My chest burned, my vision fractured, and just before everything went black, my heart cracked open with the certainty that this was the end.

Then I inhaled sharply.

My eyes flew open to a quiet, bright room. The brightness should have stung, but it didn't. I felt weightless. Safe. Roman and Tanner were gone. My chest felt strangely whole, as though something broken had been lifted away.

I looked around. Nothing was familiar, yet I didn't feel alone.

Then I saw her—Mama.

"Mama?" She stood in front of me, radiant in a long white gown, her presence both real and impossible.

"I'm here for you, Alexandra," she said. "It's time for you to wake up, my daughter."

"Come with me," I whispered, reaching for her. I'd missed her so much.

She shook her head with a gentle smile that made my throat tighten. As her outline began to fade, I reached for her again, desperate to hold on.

"It's time to open your eyes, sweet girl. It's going to be okay." Her voice echoed through my mind—then she was gone, dissolving into the air.

I woke with tears slipping down my cheeks, dampening the pillow. A dull headache throbbed behind my eyes, the leftovers of last night's bottle of wine. Lately, I'd been waking from the same dream—Mama telling me it was time to wake up. Just like the hospital, when I finally opened my eyes after four days unconscious because of that drug Tanner slipped into my drink. The cops had called it a "designer date-rape drug"—a roofie laced with fentanyl. By all accounts, I should've died. But somehow, I didn't. Mama wasn't ready for me to go. Or maybe she thought I still had more suffering to go through.

No. Nothing is okay. None of this is okay.

I rolled over and dragged the pillow over my head. How can you tell me everything's going to be okay, Mama? You're dead. The thought tore through me as I hit the pillow with the heel of my hand. It felt like Ground-hog Day—same dream, same morning routine, same fury simmering under my skin.

I'd go to the gym, burn through the anger, and think of Tanner Ellington. As far as I'm concerned, he killed my mother. If he hadn't drugged me, I wouldn't have been in the hospital. She wouldn't have gotten in her car, wouldn't have been drinking before driving to see me. Maybe she was the only one in the accident, but he lit the fuse.

Jail would be too easy for him.

And every day, ideas for how to make him pay kept circling in my mind—sharper, clearer, more relentless as my anger grew.

My head was splitting.

I needed a new way to deal with the memories and whatever my life had turned into. I pressed my palms under the pillow and into my eyes, trying to dull the ache. Forgetting wasn't possible. The alcohol helped only until it didn't, but it was always easy to find. The only moments I didn't crave it were when I was moving—working out, running, or losing myself in the MMA studio.

Kickboxing used to be fun when my girlfriends were beside me. I missed Maggie and Abby—our Sunday brunches, our laughter—but I didn't have the strength to tell anyone what was going on. The gym was the only place where no one expected me to talk.

The morning I found Roman's gray hoodie in my closet hit me hard. That jacket had been wrapped around me at Lookout Park, his arms around me, his cologne still lingering in the fabric. For the first time in a long time, I'd felt safe. Cared for. I'm pretty sure that was the night I fell in love with him.

Poor Roman. I'd pulled him straight into the wreckage of my life. He deserved better than anything I could offer. I'd known from the start that I'd end up hurting him. He's better off without me.

Plus I didn't want to freaking talk to anyone.

I reached for my phone. Messages from Roman. Messages from my friends. I deleted all of them without reading a single word. A frustrated yell tore out of me, and I hit the pillow once before pushing it aside.

Six a.m. seemed as good a time as any to get up, now that I wasn't going to work...or doing much of anything at all. The gym would have to be my plan. I threw the pillow across the room, knocking over a stack of laundry I still hadn't put away, and dragged myself out of bed.

***

ROMAN

Erasing all the pictures I had of her from my phone would've been the smart thing to do. I swiped through them anyway—the one of us at the riverbank, the one at Maggie's house, the album from the beach trip with her family. I was going to drive myself insane staring at them. Everyone kept telling me to give her time to heal, but why wouldn't she stop being so stubborn and ask for help? I didn't do this to her. Tanner did.

I tossed my phone onto my desk and leaned back, covering my face with both hands. Agitated. Angry. Completely helpless.

The only connection I had to her now was Matt, who passed along what little he heard from Maggie. It wasn't much. Alex had stopped going to brunch altogether. She still showed up at the MMA studio for self-defense and kickboxing, but she didn't talk to anyone and left right after class. That's all the girls knew.

I let out a long breath, trying to steady myself. I needed to get my head straight and focus on work.

A knock came at the door. Amelia peeked in before stepping inside. I needed to calm down. She'd been tiptoeing around me lately, and that wasn't like her. Amelia was the most capable, upbeat assistant I'd ever had. Even when I gave her a hard time, she always handled it. Ever since everything with Alex, though, she'd been more cautious, treating me like I might break. I probably earned some of that. I'd been snapping at everyone.

"Hey, Amelia. What's up?" I muttered, trying to sound normal. It didn't land.

"There's a Detective Lewis here to see you," she said carefully.

I closed my eyes for a moment. This was the last thing I needed today. Detective Lewis was the officer handling Alex's case against Tanner. She'd been with Alex from the start, and from what Jack and Matt said—within the limits of what they could share—Alex trusted her. That counted for something.

"Sure. Send her in."

I sat tapping my pen against the desk, trying to keep my nerves in check. It was a habit I'd picked up ever since meeting Alex.

Detective Lewis walked in—a woman in her thirties with brown hair pulled back in a tight ponytail. Her expression was serious, but there was a sincerity in her eyes that gave me some ease. I stood, straightened my cuffs, and forced myself to meet her halfway to shake her hand. She had the presence of someone people underestimated at their own risk.

"Mr. King, I'm Detective Danielle Lewis," she said. "I'm in charge of Miss Kennedy's case."

"Yes, I remember," I replied politely. What I really remembered was her telling me to leave the hospital because Alex believed I had attacked her.

"Please, have a seat." I gestured to the chair opposite my desk and sat back down.

She began, "Mr. King—"

"Please. It's Roman."

"Of course. Roman." She nodded. "I'm sorry about what happened at the hospital and the misunderstanding, but I'm here to make sure this man is held accountable. We need to keep the case airtight so nothing interferes with prosecution."

That was exactly what I wanted. I leaned back, arms crossing to keep my pulse under control. "Tell me what you need."

She opened a notepad, balanced it on her knee, and clicked her pen. "There's some information we need to verify to ensure nothing becomes an issue later."

An issue that had to do with me?

"What kind of information? I thought I was cleared."

She shifted slightly in her seat, and the hesitation told me she expected this to land poorly. When she spoke again, her tone was more careful.

"Well...Ms. Kennedy believes one of the reasons Mr. Ellington did this to her was to get to you."

I pressed my lips together. Please tell me this isn't why Alex cut me out of her life. I can take care of myself. Does she really think I need her to protect me?

I looked up at the ceiling and let my frustration spill out. "Why would she think that?" My hands hit the desk harder than I intended. I'd been living in a constant state of irritation ever since she stopped answering my calls or texts.

Detective Lewis didn't flinch. She seemed to understand exactly where the reaction was coming from.

"Do you have any business issues with Mr. Ellington?"

Not with the monster currently sitting in a jail cell—unless he somehow knew I was the one who elbowed him in the nose at the bar.

"More so with his brother, Marcus." I forced myself back into control. I curled my hands into fists and placed them deliberately on the desk. "He's the one causing the problems."

"The district representative?" Her brows pulled together. She sat forward in her chair, clearly caught off guard. Did she know something more?

"Yeah. He's been pulling permits and holding them hostage until inflated fees are paid. It's caused delays on several projects."

"Was one of those projects in Burrow Township?"

My favorite project had turned into a nightmare.

"Yes. Although Tanner is just his brother's errand boy, it seems." I could feel my blood pressure climbing, the dull throb in my head growing sharper.

"Did Tanner know about Miss Kennedy's involvement in that project?"

How in the world would he have known anything about what Alex was doing? She only ran out of gas in that neighborhood. If I didn't calm down, I was going to lose it right here in my office.

"Alex didn't have any involvement in that project."

Detective Lewis looked genuinely confused. I pressed my lips tight, fighting the ache behind my eyes.

"She wasn't the realtor for Mrs. Ella Jackson? Negotiating the sale of her house?" she asked, glancing down as she took notes in her small black notebook.

"Look, I didn't meet Alex until after we started that project." I pressed my fingers into my temples, trying to steady myself. "She was angry with me because of it. She's the one who uncovered what the Ellingtons were doing. She went to Ella Jackson on her own and built that relationship. She didn't have anything to do with the project itself."

Detective Lewis shook her head. "Alex thinks this has something to do with Burrow Township. We're trying to sort out how. If so, the motive may have been intimidation—to get her to back off the project. She said he used your name. That's all we have so far."

That's why she thinks it was me? How does this guy know anything about me and Alex?

"She told us about your family's history with the Ellingtons—your father and their father. I'd like to hear it from you as well."

This was getting out of hand, and I didn't have the patience for it.

"Mr. King, are you alright? We can continue this another time."

I shut my eyes against the brightness in the room. I felt awful, but postponing this wouldn't help. I needed to get it over with.

I told her everything I could—what my father had explained to me, the recent dealings with the Ellington brothers, the fact that the so-called connection was nothing more than a disgruntled former employee and his politician son making life difficult. I couldn't believe Alex was carrying this guilt herself. Did she cut ties because she thought they'd come after me? Did they go after her to scare her off the project? My mind was spiraling down a dangerous track—one I didn't want to follow.

"Detective Lewis, why did Tanner say he was me?"

"Roman, I'm going to speak with the DA. He'll be reaching out. Tanner isn't giving any details. He's claiming he found her on the ground, unconscious. Depending on how the DA proceeds, you might be placed on the witness list."

"I'll do whatever is needed." If it meant putting Tanner away, I'd gladly testify. "Do you know how Alex is?" I asked, hoping she might know more than the others.

"She's doing the best she can," she said, offering a small, careful smile. "She's been through a great deal. I check on her weekly with updates. She still doesn't remember everything, but she has strong legal support and the DA behind her."

"Thank you," I said, standing. I rounded the desk and shook her hand. "Of course."

I walked her to the door. The moment she stepped out, I felt the urge to leave the building myself.

Amelia stepped in as the detective exited. "Is everything okay?" she asked.

No, it's definitely not ok.

"I wish I knew." The words came out strained. I wasn't in the mood to talk. One hand pressed against the wall, the other holding up my head.

"Would you like me to order you lunch?" Amelia asked gently.

My stomach turned. "No. I'm going upstairs for lunch. I need to get out of here for a bit." I checked my pocket for my phone and brushed past her on my way out.

I passed Harrison in the hallway and lifted a hand to stop whatever he might say. "Not now," I muttered, my voice too raw to manage anything louder.

He raised both hands in surrender. "Okay," he said, stepping aside.

Behind me, I heard Amelia quietly tell him, "I don't think your brother's feeling well. Can you be ready to take over his meetings if he doesn't come back today?"

Harrison sighed, irritated but resigned. "I'll do what I need to."

It wasn't a big deal. I just needed to rest for an hour. I stepped into the elevator and leaned my head against the cool glass as it carried me up to the penthouse.

Chapter 2

ALEX

Monday's self-defense classes felt pointless. I'd probably quit and sign up for one-on-one training instead. As long as I could put my hands on something real—on someone real—that would be enough to keep me focused on the case. It would also spare me one more day of the tense silence with Abby and Maggie.

I hoped I'd be more capable in real life than I was in my dreams. My life wasn't going back to what it was before; I needed to adjust to my "new normal." What a joke. I'd never been normal unless normal meant being a complete mess.

I turned up the radio in the car, trying to drown out the noise in my head. The ambient lighting wasn't even set to the right color for the day. Tuesday was red, but it was Wednesday. I swiped through the settings and changed it to green. My mother's color therapy was the only part of her I still had left, and I clung to it.

When I looked back up at the road, the wheel slipped in my hands, and I jerked it hard to keep from drifting off the lane. I needed to pull myself together.

The doctors wanted to put me back on antidepressants and anti-anxiety medication instead of helping me face the truth of what happened. I needed to understand why I thought it was Roman that night when it was Tanner. Roman hadn't even been there. The medications they tried to prescribe me for depression and anxiety fogged everything until I couldn't think at all, let alone process what happened. So of course I declined them.

Alcohol at least didn't require a prescription. I could always name the bar in my apartment "The Doctor's Office." Then, if anyone asked whether I'd been to the doctor, I could say yes without lying.

I pulled into Bruce's studio and noticed Abby's car already parked in her usual spot near the door. I knew I'd have to talk to them eventually. They were my best friends. But I couldn't handle the mention of Roman or the tidal wave of emotions waiting behind his name. And I really couldn't handle the pity in their expressions.

Time to get myself together and face whatever waited inside.

I grabbed my bag and climbed out, leaning against Betty for one last moment of steadiness before walking in. The girls were sitting on the bench changing shoes while laughing about something. I smiled and waved. As usual, the laughter faded the moment they saw me, replaced by those careful smiles I'd grown to dread.

I turned away, marched to the front desk, and greeted Bruce instead. The smell of chalk and sweat filled the studio—a sharp, grounding, scent—exactly what I needed. I set my hands and forehead on the counter in front of him, bracing myself for the effort it would take to be pleasant with the girls today.

"Hey, Bruce." The words came out more like air than speech, but he caught them.

"Hey, fighter. What's up?" He barely glanced up, too busy to entertain my theatrics.

"Can I talk to you after class about something?" I lifted my head just enough to look at him. That got his attention. He paused, narrowing his eyes.

"Of course. Is everything okay?"

No, but that was nothing new.

"Yeah. I just think Monday's class has run its course, and I was hoping to try something else." He nodded, like he'd already suspected it.

"Okay. We'll talk later."

I turned toward the girls and took a deep breath, trying to decide how to approach them.

I straightened, fixed my ponytail, and walked over like I was fine—almost even convinced myself by adding a little skip before sitting on the bench beside them. I bent down to change my shoes, giving them a sideways glance. They kept flicking looks at me then away again, as if direct eye contact might turn me them to stone. I pulled my laces tight and exhaled.

"See? This is what I've been trying to avoid." I motioned between us. "The awkward silences, the 'I'm so sorry' eyes, the emotional hugs. This..." I gestured wildly "...whatever this is." I leaned back against the wall and stared at the ceiling, silently daring it to collapse on me.

Maggie said, "Would it make you feel better if I called you Jerkface?"

Abby shoved her with a warning glare, but I laughed—actual relief loosening something tight inside.

"Yes. I'd love it if you called me that. Why are you two walking on eggshells around me?" My arms hung heavy at my sides.

Abby answered, "You won't talk to us."

I let out a tired breath. "Because I don't like the topics you want to talk about."

Could we please let it go—for a day, or a year, or forever?

"Don't you think it would be healthy for you to discuss them?" Abby asked, irritation showing.

I squinted at her from the corner of my eye. I understood why they were frustrated, but I just wanted the weight of everything to disappear.

I let out a short laugh. "Clearly I don't." I tossed my hands up and let them drop onto my knees, warming up my arms for the sandbag.

Maggie jumped in. "Fine, Jerkface. Let's go hit something!" She had always been good at redirecting.

"Now that I'm open to talking about," I said, nudging Abby with my shoulder.

I knew they were trying. And I knew I probably needed a professional. But the only professional I trusted was Dr. King. And she was Roman's mother—so she wasn't an option right now.

After class, I fist-bumped the girls on their way out and headed for Bruce's office.

I dropped into the small black chair in front of his desk, letting out a long sigh as I slumped down. I peeled the tape off my wrists, balled it in my hand, and tossed it into the trash by the door. It landed perfectly. Small victories mattered.

Bruce didn't waste time. "Okay—no more self-defense class. That's fine. You could teach that class anyway. So, what can I do for you?"

I sat up straighter, switching into business mode.

"I want to learn MMA fighting. I want private training."

He looked genuinely surprised. "Are you planning to compete?"

The thought had never even crossed my mind. I only wanted to be strong enough to never feel powerless again. I lifted an eyebrow, imagining all the ways I wished I'd been able to defend myself that night.

"No. I just need to push myself right now."

"I understand that." He leaned back slightly. "When football ended for me, I needed an outlet, and fighting worked. I didn't have anger issues," he said with a pointed look, remembering when I told him how furious everything made me. "I did it to keep my adrenaline up. I think I liked beating myself up, honestly."

That tracked. We both laughed. I glanced around his office—photos, trophies, all spotless, clearly maintained with pride. His success gave me confidence he could train me for anything I needed.

"Well, we know I have plenty of issues," I said, "but doing something physical keeps the noise in my head quiet. Physical pain mutes the mental and emotional mess. This is the only therapy I can handle right now."

He nodded in understanding—never treating me delicately. Then his expression shifted. He leaned back, arms crossing over his chest, his tough-coach demeanor softening into the sympathetic one I hated. My hands tightened on the arms of the chair, bracing myself for whatever was coming.

"I get that," he said. "Can I talk to you for a minute about the court case coming up?"

My stomach churned at the thought of seeing Tanner in court.

Just breathe, Alex.

"Okay," I whispered, loosening my grip on the chair. Business mode vanished, and I sank down into the seat again. I swallowed hard to push past the tightness in my throat.

Bruce held that look—the one that said he felt sorry for me—and said, "I know you don't like discussing this, but I'm going to be there. And if Tanner doesn't take a deal, I may have to testify. That part is fine. What isn't fine is this." He gestured at me. "You don't look okay, and I want to make sure you will be in there."

I didn't know how I was supposed to be any different in a courtroom. Bruce was the one who found me after Steve—the bartender at Sebastian's—saw the attack on the security monitor. The place had been packed that night. He'd called Bruce immediately, and Bruce didn't hesitate. He threw Tanner off me before things got worse. I owed him for that. But none of it fixed the part where my mind kept twisting Roman's face into the memory. Why had I believed it was him?

I kept my chin down, avoiding his eyes. "I can't answer that right now. I'm so angry. I want to rip his head off." My breathing spun out of control, and my heartbeat pounded so loudly it felt like it echoed in my ears. My grip tightened on the chair again.

"I know. I want to help you with that." He didn't tell me to calm down. Instead, he used the steady tone he saved for moments like this. He came around the desk and leaned against it. Then he nudged my chin up, redirecting my focus toward him.

"How?" The word shot out sharper than I meant. He didn't flinch. He simply leaned back and crossed his arms.

"I'm going to train you personally. And this isn't just about fighting—it's about control." He placed his hands on my shoulders, firm enough to pull me out of whatever storm I'd slipped into, holding my stare until I was fully present again. "Control over your mind and your body."

The idea of having control back—any control—forced me to listen. My thoughts steadied, and I blinked away the haze. He continued, "By the time you walk into that courtroom, I want you steady as ice. I don't want him thinking, even for a second, that he broke you."

It sounded like we were on the same page. I took a few breaths to settle myself. It wasn't fair to misdirect my anger at him.

"Do you really think that's possible?" I groaned, covering my face.

He snorted and nudged my shoulder—hard enough to nearly knock me out of the chair. "You're one of the most determined people who's walked into this place. Some of the pro fighters have asked if you're planning to go pro."

I burst out laughing, bending over as the absurdity hit me. He laughed too, patting my back as if guiding me out of the spiral.

"Finally, something I'm good at," I said. Fighting felt like the only part of me that made sense right now—the only thing pulling me through the mess.

He stopped laughing and shook his head. "I doubt that's the only thing."

"I guess we'll see. So...when do we start?" I clapped once, trying to build some enthusiasm. If I didn't feel like I'd been hit by a truck, I'd start right now. My back and shoulders begged for a hot shower and a bottle of wine. The cab on my counter would be waiting.

Bruce returned to his desk. "Can you train Tuesdays, Thursdays, and Saturdays?" He looked down at his calendar.

"Let me check my schedule..." I mimed flipping through a planner. "Just kidding. I'm free every day. I'll be there." Thank God for this. Without training, I'd probably drink all day. Maybe that was why my mom had.

He chuckled. "Great. We'll start Thursday. Are you still taking the kick-boxing classes?"

I stared at the hem of my shorts, picking at it while I mentioned. "Yeah. I still like seeing the girls. I'm easing back into things with them. A lot's changed and I still haven't processed how fast it all fell apart. Things were good...and then they weren't." My gaze drifted to a framed photo on his wall: Bruce, bruised and battered, holding a championship belt.

"Been there too," he said. "For what it's worth, you're doing good, considering. And if you ever need to talk to someone who's not emotionally involved, I'm here. Talking goes better when you're hitting something."

I gave him a look and laughed, imagining him as my therapist, but I wasn't ready to explain what truly drove me to train—not yet, maybe not ever.

"I might take you up on that." I gave him two thumbs up. "And thank you—for all of this. Don't go easy on me in training."

Keeping him focused was best. He didn't need to know what my real end goal was.

"Oh no. I'm not letting you walk in here and outwork me."

That's what I'm talking about.

"You may not have a choice," I said, giving him a small, mischievous smirk.

We said goodbye, and I felt lighter—steadier. It was exactly what I needed today.

I climbed into my SUV and leaned forward, crossing my forearms over the steering wheel and resting my head on them. I was drained, mentally and physically. I stayed like that for a moment, thinking through what came next. Maybe this training really would help me work through whatever was left tangled up with Roman.

I took a few deep breaths and decided to call the girls on the drive home. A three-way call sounded like a good first step. Maybe it was time to ease myself back into our Sunday brunches.

Chapter 3

ROMAN

Where am I? It's so dark in here. No light coming from anywhere. I tried to adjust my eyes, to focus on something—anything. What time is it? I rubbed my hands over my face and winced. My head felt like I'd been hit with a bat. I needed to get back to the office for those meetings.

I needed water. My mouth was dry as sand and my head was pounding. I squinted toward the window. The sun was gone; a low haze stretched across the horizon. Definitely later than a quick nap. Probably missed every meeting this afternoon.

I rolled onto my side and reached blindly along the table, hoping to find my phone without getting up. I needed to check my messages. Either it had been on mute or I'd been out deeper than I realized, because I couldn't find it. But the phone was ringing now, so apparently I'd needed the sleep—though it hadn't done anything for the headache. I pushed myself up, grabbed my head, and looked around until I spotted it.

"Hey," Harrison said when I accepted the call. "You okay?" He actually sounded concerned. I would've smiled if I had the energy.

"Yeah. Just a headache," I muttered. I dragged myself into the kitchen, grabbed a cold bottle of water from the fridge, and swallowed two gel caps. Then I pressed the chilled bottle to my forehead, hoping it would help.

"Alright," he said. "I just wrapped up your last meeting. I'm heading up. Put the code in. Or do you want me to use mine?"

I punched the code from my phone. "I got it."

"Man, you look rough," Harrison said as he stepped out of the elevator. The expression he gave me made it clear I looked worse than I thought.

"Thanks. I feel great now," I said, every word coated in sarcasm. Alex had clearly rubbed off on me.

He raised an eyebrow, not amused. Normally his comments didn't bother me, but nothing about my life felt normal lately. I went back to the sofa and sat down, rolling my neck to loosen it. The headache had pulled every muscle tight.

"I'm not good at this," he said, "but...do you want to talk about it?" His voice held actual concern. I wasn't interested.

"Not really. It's just a headache." I put my face in my hands, not wanting to see his reaction.

"Do you need to talk to Mom about your headache?" he asked, taunting me.

This wasn't helping.

"Harrison, are you trying to be annoying, or does it just come naturally? I just have a headache." I lifted my head in frustration, which only made things worse—a wave of nausea hit hard, and I bent forward with my head between my knees.

He must have lost his patience, because his tone shifted. "Just a headache, huh? You walked out of the office at noon and never came back. No calls, nothing. You left me and Amelia to handle four meetings because you wouldn't answer your phone."

My head throbbed at the volume, but I still let out a small chuckle. Listening to him scold me was almost amusing.

"How did they go?" He wasn't wrong—he'd stepped in for me. "I came up here to rest for an hour and just woke up ten minutes ago."

I leaned back slowly, resting my head against the couch. Harrison eased into the chair beside me.

"Amelia told me the detective came by. Did that have something to do with this? And your meetings went fine. They were just updates. Amelia took notes."

She really was the best assistant I'd ever had. Getting Harrison to step up made her even better.

"Thanks. And...I don't know. Maybe. This whole thing is a mess."

"I don't even know what to say," he admitted. "I thought you two had a good thing. I was happy for you. Even Mom seemed happy about it—and that's saying something."

"Harrison, I know you're trying, but that is definitely not helping. It feels more like salt in the wound." My head pulsed as I turned to glare at him.

"Alright, sorry. I told you I'm not good at this."

"I appreciate it, but I'll be fine. I'll see you tomorrow." I waved him off, hoping he'd take the hint.

"Okay. Call me if you need anything—but I probably won't answer." I let out a tired laugh because that was absolutely true. He wasn't built for emotional conversations.

After he left, I took a shower, hoping it would ease the tension, then went through all the calls and texts that came in while I was asleep. I leaned on the kitchen island, scrolling through them. Most were from Harrison and Amelia checking on me or asking if I was coming back to work. There was a message from Matt, too—Alex had actually talked to the girls at class today.

Good. Signs of normalcy.

I just wished I knew whether reaching out to her was the right thing. I didn't want to go through her friends—it might push her away from them again.

It was sad, honestly. I needed to get myself together. This wasn't helping anyone. Harrison might have been right.

I pushed away from the counter and headed toward my bedroom to change.

Time to call Dr. Mom.

***

ALEX

"Hey, Jerkface!" Maggie yelled into the phone the second she answered. I couldn't stop the smile that spread across my face. I had missed them more than I wanted to admit. Not talking to them had been harder than I expected. They wouldn't truly understand what I was feeling, and they'd try to fix it—but this wasn't something a girl's night or a Sunday brunch could mend. This was something twisted and heavy that I had to work through on my own.

"Hey Girls," I said, trying to sound like the old me while maneuvering my SUV back toward my apartment, weaving in and out of traffic. My attention should've been on the road.

Abby chimed in, excited, "There she is."

"Well...no promises I won't go silent again, but I'd like to come to brunch on Sunday."

"You mean return to brunch," Maggie corrected. "Sorry but we went without you."

I laughed, relieved they hadn't spiraled into some dramatic mourning of my absence.

"I deserve that. Abby, how's the baby bun?"

Her pregnancy should have been a bright spot for me—another god-child to love.

"We're doing well," Abby said. "We just miss our threesome. And what do you mean you can't guarantee you won't go silent again?"

"I don't know, Abbs. There's a lot going on. I've been overwhelmed." I tried keeping the tone light. "I miss our threesome too. Oh—and I won't be doing Monday classes anymore. Just Wednesday kickboxing. I'm starting private training."

There was a pause before Maggie spoke. "You planning to do MMA for real?"

"No, not competing. I just need to learn how to manage the chaos a little better. An outlet."

Abby snorted. "Good luck with that."

Really? Well...maybe she wasn't wrong.

"What are you trying to say Abby?" I asked with a light tone while rolling my eyes because I already knew the answer.

"Oops. Did I say that out loud?" Abby replied in a teasing voice.

We all laughed, and for the first time in three weeks—since everything happened—my shoulders loosened and I felt like myself.

Maybe enough time had passed that I could start slowly reaching back out. Tomorrow I might swing by the real estate office to check on Shay and Grant. I needed to see how they were managing without me. I felt guilty dumping work on Grant and abandoning Shay. But I needed space to figure out what came next.

Tonight, though, I felt like I might actually sleep.

***

I jolted awake, drenched in a cold sweat as the alarm blared beside me. I grabbed my phone to shut it off, heart still racing. What in the world was that? Usually it was my mother appearing in the same echoing dream, telling me to wake up. I'd gone to bed feeling steady last night. But whatever that dream was...it wasn't steady. I'd been with Roman—then his face shifted into Tanner's. I was grateful the alarm dragged me out of it.

I threw the covers back and hurried to get dressed. I needed the gym and get out of my head.

I pushed hard that morning—ran, lifted, even swam laps. It was never empty enough for laps, but today it worked. The sauna helped most of all. Heat wrapped around me, melting the tension even as my thoughts drifted back to the dream—specifically the part involving Roman. Was that my mind trying to return to something familiar? Something safe? I couldn't let myself get distracted. He didn't need more chaos in his life, and I needed to stay focused on the case.

I leaned back against the wooden slats, letting the steam work through me, willing every toxic thought to drain away.

Finding something to wear felt like its own chore. With nowhere to be, all my work clothes looked foreign. I sat on the closet floor, staring at them before grabbing ripped skinny jeans off a hanger. I pulled on a white T-shirt, slipped into my white Adidas sneakers, and tied my hair into a ponytail. I grabbed a bottle of water from the fridge, threw my crossbody bag over my shoulder, and I was finally ready to step out.

When I opened the door, I nearly stumbled. "What in the—" I cut myself off and glanced both ways down the hall. No one in sight.

A huge, vibrant bouquet sat directly in front of my door. The concierge must have brought it up. I picked it up and carried it inside, setting it on the counter. The flowers were stunning—bursts of color, with a few African daisies woven in. They reminded me of the bouquet Roman had once given me. They even matched my apartment, which made my heart think I knew exactly who sent them.

I grabbed the small envelope, planning to read the card in the car. Curiosity won. I opened it.

Not Roman.

"Alex, I hope these flowers find you well and make you smile. Amelia."

Well...great. I felt like a complete jerk again. Amelia and I had just started to become friends. I was pretty sure the door was still open, but she was Roman's assistant, and the two of them were close. It didn't feel like the best idea for me to ease back into her orbit right now. Still, I owed her a thank-you.

I called her.

She answered in her usual bright tone. "King Construction. Roman King's office."

My heart skipped, and my stomach flipped just hearing his name. I sank into the driver's seat, resting my head against the headrest as a single tear slid down my cheek. I wiped it away quickly and tried to get myself together.

"Hey, Amelia...it's Alex," I managed, hoping she wasn't upset with me for everything that had happened with Roman.

"Hey, Alex! How are you?" Her upbeat energy was refreshing. I'd had enough sympathetic tones. With Amelia, I was honestly more nervous about being lightly scolded.

"Not too bad. I just wanted to thank you for the beautiful flowers." There was a hint of sadness in my voice—I hoped she heard the gratitude beneath it.

"I'm glad you got them," she said. "I don't like sending flowers when everyone else does. Then they just blend in. I like to stand out."

I laughed, because at nearly six feet tall, she always stood out. And she wasn't wrong—my place was full of wilted arrangements. Her bouquet felt alive.

"They're beautiful. They definitely stand out among the graveyard of flowers I've got going on."

"That's hilarious—and you're welcome." She didn't even give me time to add to it before she continued, "Hey, want to have lunch with me one day this week?"

I hesitated, then nodded to myself. "Yeah, I'd like that. I'm trying to be...'normal.'" I even did little air quotes she couldn't see, but she probably heard the attempt in my voice. I needed to rebuild some kind of routine, and spending time with Amelia might ease some of the tension tied to Roman.

She laughed softly, then whispered, "Little secret: lunch sustains life and normal doesn't exist. Just be you."

I smiled. That right there told me we could actually be real friends someday.

"Can you do life-sustaining lunch tomorrow?" I asked, feeling almost shy.

"Of course. How does noon sound?"

"Perfect." I said it just as I pulled into the parking lot of Johnson Realty.

I walked into the office expecting Shay to be at the reception desk. I'd completely forgotten we had a new receptionist.

As I approached, she beamed. "Good morning! How can I help you?" She was adorable—like a younger, brighter version of Shay, if that were even possible. She couldn't have been more than nineteen or twenty, with a perfectly straight blonde bob and hazel eyes. For a split second the old me wanted to sit her down and ask about her goals, her future, her growth in the company—then I remembered I didn't actually work here anymore. A frustrated breath slipped out before I could help it.

I reached out my hand. "Hi, I'm Alex Kennedy. We haven't officially met yet." Her eyes widened.

"Are you the Alex they talk about all the time?" She looked nervous. What on earth had they told her about me?

I raised an eyebrow. "Well, that depends. Is it good talk or bad talk?"

"It's really good. You're like a celebrity."

I burst out laughing and leaned over the counter to read her name tag. "Felicity, right?" She nodded. "Don't listen to a word they say about me. I'm not a celebrity. I'm just a normal person like you—"

I screamed as someone lifted me clean off the floor and spun me around. Ryan set me down but didn't release me, pulling me into a hug so tight I could barely breathe.

"It's so good to see you," he said. Ryan was the friend I never thought would settle down—good-looking and fully aware of it. I'd been genuinely happy when he started seeing someone before everything fell apart for me.

"This place is not the same without you," he added just as Landon and Shay came running down the hall, shouting my name.

I turned back to Felicity with a smile. "It was nice to meet you. I'll see you around."

"Nice meeting you too," she said before the phone rang again.

I hugged everyone and let them shepherd me into what used to be my office. It had been turned into another conference room, but nothing of mine had been touched. My personal photos were still on the desk and shelves. Grant must have refused to let anyone take over the space, certain I'd come back someday.

I ran my hand over the desk and picked up the picture of my family. My finger traced the outline of my mom's face. I held the frame for a moment, imagining what she would say to me right now. Would she somehow find the right encouragement, or would she default to telling me this was as good as it gets?

I pushed the thoughts away and set the picture back down.

"Where is my old man anyway?" Grant was in his sixties, a complete silver fox, though to me he'd always been more of a father figure. I settled onto the sofa—far away from my old desk—so no one would assume I was back to work. I'd already taken enough of a stroll down memory lane.

Landon said, "He's out showing one of those estates to your Italian clients."

The Santoros—my wealthy wine-making clients from Italy who were planning a vineyard in Ohio. I winced thinking about how much I'd dumped on Grant when I suddenly took an indefinite leave.

"Really? Has anything been cleared up with the zoning?" I crossed my legs and relaxed into the cushions, hands resting in my lap.

Shay said, "On Friday, Grant got a message from a construction company saying the commercial zoning had been restored."

"Construction company?" I asked, though it came out sounding more like I already knew the answer.

Shay continued, "Yeah, we thought it was strange too. But Grant said he's been working with King Construction on a project, and they pulled some strings for him."

I burst out laughing. "Was I really that secretive?" Did no one besides Grant realize I'd been seeing Roman King of King Construction?

Ryan blinked at me. "What do you mean?"

"Do you guys know who owns King Construction?" They all exchanged blank looks and shook their heads.

"No. Should we?" Landon asked, clearly confused.

Landon was the kind of person I wished I'd met before marrying Luke—handsome, kind, successful, but not arrogant. But one of my rules had always been to never date someone I worked with, and that rule had saved a lot of friendships.

"Roman," I said, lifting my hands with raised brows. Even saying his name did something to me—half warmth, half unease.

Ryan's eyes widened. "Oh wow. We never met him, so we didn't connect the dots."

"Never?" I asked. Maybe I really didn't mix business with pleasure more than I'd thought.

Shay said, "We were supposed to meet him that night at your place...but he had a late meeting."

My excitement dipped at the reminder, shoulders lowering slightly.

"You mean the night everything fell apart?" The room shifted into a heavy silence. I didn't need that spiral today. "Let's not dwell on it," I said. "I do enough of that for everyone."

"How are you and Roman doing?" Shay asked quietly.

I simply said, "We aren't." And before anyone could respond I shifted the attention. "But how are you and Owen?"

Owen and I had almost crossed a line once—after the closing of a big deal between their investment company and ours. When I realized he might want something more than casual, I shut it down immediately...and then quickly learned Shay had a crush on him. I nudged her in that direction instead.

Her whole face lit up. She sat straight, hands clenched with excitement. "Wonderful. We're official. We're talking about the future, but we're not rushing anything."

I hugged her. I was truly happy for her—and grateful the spotlight was off my own nonexistent love life.

"Honey, I'm so happy for you. How's training going with Grant?" I had planned to train her myself, but nothing in my life had stayed on track lately.

She bounced in her chair. "I already have my first house under contract!"

I screamed—because oh my gosh, that was huge.

"I knew you'd be amazing at this. Get ready to put your name on my office door!" We squealed together.

Ryan groaned dramatically. "Hey, what about my name?"

Ryan was ambitious—charming, driven, and absolutely not meant to be someone's employee for long.

"Please. You don't want an office. You want your own agency."

He laughed and rolled his eyes. "Yeah...you're right." He shrugged, trying to hide a smile.

"Ryan, how's the new girl?" Time to see if he'd changed his ways.

"Which one?" he said, giving me that familiar smirk. I'd hoped he liked the last one. But some people weren't meant to settle down.

"Oh no, again? What did you do this time?" I tried not to laugh, covering my mouth.

He looked down to hide a smile, pretending to be offended.

"Wait—why am *I* automatically the one who did something?" he asked, brows raised.

I gave him my "tell the truth" stare.

He finally grinned. "Okay...fine. I may have found someone else before the breakup actually happened."

A nicer way of saying he cheated. I shook my head. Definitely still Ryan.

"You know how I feel about that kind of behavior." I smacked his arm.

"Ow. I know, I know—but I couldn't help it. She was hot."

"That is not an excuse. Don't let someone think you're committed if you're not. Cheating is the lowest of the low." I pushed his shoulder lightly.

"I know. Trust me—I could hear your voice in my head scolding me."

They all knew where I stood on cheating Years of being lied to and betrayed by my ex-husband had carved that stance into stone. I took a slow breath, steadying myself before the memories could pull me under.

"Good. I hope it was my super–bitch face." I tried to make it, but Ryan was one of my closest friends, and it was impossible to stay annoyed with any of them for long.

He pulled me into his side. "It scared the crap out of me."

I slipped out of his hold and turned to Landon next. "So, Prince Charming, what's new with you and Piper?"

All three of them lit up at once.

"I asked her to marry me!" Landon blurted.

I widened my eyes innocently. "Did she say yes?" I knew she had, but I couldn't resist teasing him.

He gave me a flat stare. "Very funny. Of course she said yes."

I hugged him tightly.

"I better be getting an invite to that wedding."

"Absolutely. I was thinking of asking you to be my best man. Didn't want to risk some guy throwing the whole thing off by chasing the bridesmaids."

We all laughed, and Ryan shoved him, fully aware who he meant.

"Not a chance. I'm the best man," Ryan fired back.

Watching them playfully argue was the highlight of the past three weeks—weeks that felt strangely distant, like they'd happened in another lifetime.

The door creaked open, and Grant stepped inside. "I'd recognize this party anywhere," he said, his eyes locking on me.

I jumped to my feet and rushed into his arms. He looked as polished as ever—tall, with perfectly groomed gray hair, a well-kept beard, and the tailored Italian suits he favored. His cologne was familiar and grounding, a comfort I hadn't realized I needed. There was always a hint of an accent when he spoke, one he never confirmed but couldn't quite hide.

"Alex, where have you been? You need to come around more often."

I nodded, blinking rapidly as tears threatened. I was tired of crying, but it kept happening anyway.

"I will. I just needed some space." I grabbed a tissue from the desk and dabbed at my eyes.

"I understand. By the way, there's a couple in my office you need to see."

I told the others I'd be back and followed Grant down the hall to his office.

Chapter 4

ROMAN

"Hey, Mom."

I didn't want to put this on her, but I didn't know who else to turn to.

"Hey, honey. Harrison said you left the office with a headache and never came back. Is everything okay?"

Thanks a lot, Harrison. I looked up at the ceiling and let out a breath. We were a little old for tattling.

"I think we need to talk," I said, slipping a hand into my pocket while I debated whether this was even a good idea. Mom had helped Alex because I'd asked her to, but this might be too much. What Alex didn't know was that Mom didn't see patients anymore—she'd burned out years ago and spent time in a rehab program overseas. I'd been young then, too protective, too angry, and the thought of losing someone I loved still triggered that same edge. Alex had brought all of it to the surface again.

"Do you want me to come over?" she asked.

I needed fresh air. The drive would help.

"No, I'll come to you. It'll be calmer at your place than mine." Too many memories here. My eyes drifted to the sofa—our last night together, the moment we told each other "I love you." The memory made my head throb again. I forced myself to look away and headed to the bedroom.

"Alright, I'll see you soon, honey."

I hung up, tossed my phone on the bed, and splashed some water on my face before leaving.

My stomach growled the entire drive. Irritability was setting in, and I realized I hadn't eaten since breakfast. When I walked into my parents' kitchen, Mom was already plating food for the three of us.

"Did I sound hungry on the phone?" I asked. Either she could read minds or my timing was perfect.

"You used to get headaches when you stayed out all day playing and forgot to eat," she said. "I figured the reason might be the same now. You've been through a lot these past few weeks, and I'm sure your mind has been elsewhere." She leaned up to kiss my cheek, and I tilted down so she could reach. That was Mom—she always knew before I did.

"You got it right," I said, kissing her cheek in return.

"What happened at noon that set you off?" she asked as I sat at the table. I didn't answer yet—I took a bite first. Growing up, dinner was always just the four of us, and I'd forgotten how centering it felt. Tonight she'd made homemade spaghetti and meatballs, one of my favorites. Her sauce was perfect—tangy, and the parmesan melted into it exactly the way it always had.

A small smile pulled at me as a childhood memory surfaced.

Then my father cleared his throat. The sound jolted me. "Hi. Sorry," I said, realizing I hadn't even noticed him sitting there.

He patted my shoulder. "No problem, Roman. Just make sure you're taking care of yourself. What happened today that led to all this?" He motioned at me while I sat at his dining table slurping pasta—something I rarely did here unless it was a planned weekend dinner.

"My lunch visitor was Detective Lewis," I said. "She's working with Alex on the assault case. She wanted to let me know that if it goes to court and Tanner doesn't take a plea, I might be called to testify so they can establish motive." I didn't mention the part Alex had told the detective her thoughts on why Tanner had done it. My parents didn't need that added fear. They already knew she'd mistaken me for her attacker in the hospital because of the drugs. That alone was hard enough.

Dad asked, fork halfway to his mouth, "Do they think they have a strong case?"

Mom cut in before he could finish the bite. Her tone was sharp, and clipped. "Regardless of that. Roman, let's go to my office and talk. There's no point in speculating about a hearing that hasn't happened yet."

That tone wasn't like her. I wasn't sure what caused it.

I stood and followed her out of the kitchen, taking my plate with me. I glanced back at Dad. He didn't look rattled, but the tension in the room was impossible to ignore. I stepped into Mom's office, casting one more glance behind me to make sure Dad was still intact after her rebuke, then sank carefully onto the couch across from her. I set my dinner on the coffee table and lay back for a moment. I was tired in every possible way.

"What was that about back there?" I asked.

She scoffed. "Did you come here for more stress or less? And eat a little more before we start."

She had slipped fully into mom-mode. I sat up again. I wasn't getting an answer to my question, and honestly, eating was probably the right move.

"Good point," I said, hoping it would smooth out whatever irritation she was carrying. Her demeanor returned to normal as I finished the rest of my dinner.

When I set the empty plate aside, she asked, "Tell me what's really bothering you."

I wiped my mouth with a napkin, settled back into the cushions, and exhaled.

"Am I really this pathetic now?" I asked.

She looked like she was trying not to laugh. I couldn't blame her. I felt ridiculous—sitting here talking to my mother about a headache like I was twelve. The sofa cushion gave under my head, and I briefly wondered if she'd worry if I wrapped myself in the throw blanket and fell asleep right here.

"Pathetic? That's a strong word," she said. "And not an accurate one."

I rolled to face her.

"Well, how would you describe my behavior?" I asked. "I forget to eat, I look at her pictures all day, I try to figure out how to contact her without it being strange, and I drift off at work." I took another breath. "Harrison looks like the competent one right now."

That was a sobering realization. I gripped the edge of the blanket, fully tempted to pull it over myself and disappear.

She laughed lightly and offered reassurance. "Oh, honey. This is what real, genuine feelings feel like. Do you understand what I tried teaching you before? Did you ever feel like this when something ended with any other woman?"

I closed my eyes and mentally flipped through every name, every brief connection, every woman who had passed through my life. None of them came close to what Alex meant to me—not even Caitlin, the woman I once thought I would marry.

"You know I didn't," I admitted. "But this is miserable. Would it be the worst thing if I tried to get in touch with her?"

She asked gently, "The worst thing for who?"

I didn't have an answer. For her? For me? I couldn't just sit here and pretend the last three weeks hadn't happened.

"Good question..." I shifted. "Let me ask it a different way. Do you think I should contact her? Do you think it would be alright if I did?"

"Roman, I think it's fine—as long as you're prepared for her response. It could be anything. She might be polite, or upset, or distant...or she might not respond at all. Are you ready for that?"

I laughed once under my breath. "I've had three weeks of practice." I leaned forward, elbows on my knees, head in my hands.

"Well," she continued, "how are you planning to reach out?"

That brought me back to reality. I briefly pictured throwing a rock through her window with a note attached—an idea that would absolutely land me a visit from the police. Not the direction I needed to go.

"I don't know," I said. "I was thinking...maybe email. Ease into stalking." I joked. Maybe.

She laughed. "That's probably a good idea."

At least she didn't think I'd completely lost my mind.

When I left their house, the headache was gone. I didn't drive straight home, though—I needed to clear my head. So I went to Alex's favorite place: Lookout Park.

It didn't unsettle me the way it had the first night she brought me here. Now it felt like the only place I could still feel connected to her. I parked in the same spot, the city stretching out below. I opened the sunroof, turned on Pink Floyd, reclined the seat, and looked up at the sky.

The night was ink black, the stars bright and steady above me. The breeze moved through the car, winding around me, easing the tension from my body. I remembered how being here with her had felt overwhelming. Maybe I'd been too focused on her then to appreciate the place itself.

Now I was focused on her again, but in a different way.

I finished typing the email.

And I hit send.

***

ALEX

I stopped at the door to Grant's office and gripped the fabric of my pants to steady myself before greeting the Santoros. Something about this felt heavier than a simple hello. When they saw me, they each pulled me into a warm hug and gave the familiar European kiss to both cheeks. Being around them felt strangely comforting—like reconnecting with old friends.

Lucia Santoro smiled, her thick Italian accent lilting like music. "Alexandra, it is so wonderful to see you again. You look beautiful. Time away has treated you well."

Time away.

As in: grieving my mother.

The reaction rose before I could stop it—a tight wave of nausea gathering at the base of my throat. I knew she meant it kindly, so I forced the feeling down.

"Thank you, Mrs. Santoro—"

She took my hands gently. "Lucia, please."

"Lucia," I repeated with a small smile. "I've been trying to stay busy."

Pretending never came easily to me. She seemed to read that in my expression and nodded with quiet understanding before returning to her husband's side.

Alessandro's accent always carried a certain weight, deep and commanding, but he'd never directed anything but kindness toward me or Grant. "We wanted you to know Grant and your friend Mr. King have resolved the zoning issues. We decided to put an offer on the property that feels most like home."

Mr. King.

Right—they met him at the hospital, but I didn't realize they'd kept talking. The property they were referring to was the villa-style estate on ten acres—rolling land, perfect for vines and tasting rooms. I'd suspected they would choose it before the zoning complications. I assumed the deal was dead.

"That's wonderful," I said. "I can see rows of grapes already and more wine tastings than I can count."

It took energy to sound enthusiastic, but they deserved it. In truth, once the vineyard was built, it would probably become one of my favorite places.

They both beamed. "Bellissimo. Grazie."

I couldn't handle any more polite conversation. I flashed Grant a small wink, said my goodbyes, and slipped out. The reminder that Roman had known about those zoning issues hit me on the way out. I still didn't know how he'd pulled it off—and right now, I couldn't afford to think about it. I needed air.

With nothing else planned for the day, I headed downtown to walk along the river. Watching the boats drift by settled me. They moved slowly, almost dreamlike. It wasn't as peaceful as Lookout Park, so I slipped my earbuds in and let music drown out the city.

As I wandered, I passed the swings Roman and I were supposed to sit in the day it started pouring. The memory warmed me just as much as the sunlight did. I sat down, closed my eyes, and let the breeze lift the swing in an easy rhythm. The wind skimmed past my ears, and the chains squeaked in a steady pattern as I rocked back and forth.

But after a minute, the sensation shifted—tilting and weightless, like my mind had stepped outside of my body. The dizziness pulled me straight back to the plane ride to Florida, when Roman and I flew down to vacation with my family. That moment when he guided me through trust rather than fear—hands tracing my arms, my shoulders, my face—an experience unlike anything I'd known. It had been the first time I understood what it meant for someone to treat you with intention, care, and patience.

I laughed softly at the memory—then immediately snapped my head around to make sure no one heard me.

The irony hit me like a punch. Roman taught me what love felt like...and I broke his heart.

The Roman King I know could have never done something so terrible.

So why won't my mind release the image of his face in a moment he wasn't even there for?

It was partly his fault for introducing me to all this empathic nonsense. Maybe that played a role in what was happening in my head. He said he could feel what I was feeling during that trust game, and I guess he didn't like how much of me he picked up. He told me he loved me, but now I kept wondering—were those his feelings or mine mirrored back at him? I wished he had never mentioned any of it. Now I didn't know what was real, what belonged to me, or what my mind had twisted into something else.

Thank God for my classes. Physical energy made sense. It was tangible—impact, resistance, muscle, breath. Black and white. A little painful sometimes, but at least it was real and it was mine. The noise in my head was what I couldn't handle. Wine handled it, though, and right now that felt like enough.

I stopped the swing with my feet, lowered my head to steady myself, then got up and walked home.

I made dinner, texted the girls for a bit, and set plans to hang out with Shay and the guys this weekend.

I poured a glass of wine and turned on some music. It actually felt good—talking to friends again, making plans. Tomorrow I'd check on Ella and Darius too. Walking away from them had weighed on me; I worked hard to earn their trust, and I didn't like that I'd disappeared right when they needed someone steady. Their neighborhood was being torn down for high-rise greed, and I'd made it my mission to make sure Ella and her grandkids were protected. Grant was handling things, but I had dropped a lot on him without warning.

I set my phone on the table and leaned back on the sofa, letting my eyes drift closed while the music washed over me. If I focused hard enough, maybe it could drown out the lists spinning through my thoughts and leave only the good memories—what Roman and I shared before everything came crashing apart.

After a few songs, I finished my first glass, refilled it, and settled deeper into the cushions. I pulled the velvet blanket over my legs, enjoying the warmth. Since I was finally relaxed, I figured it couldn't hurt to clean up my email. Most messages lately were from work or the MMA studio advertising new class schedules. Plenty of junk to delete.

I grabbed my phone, swiped it open—and froze.

There was an email from King Construction. The subject line was simple: "Hi." My heart jumped. I reminded myself I was meeting Amelia for lunch tomorrow, so maybe it was a reminder she sent from her work address.

I should have checked the sender more carefully. I would have seen it wasn't Amelia.

It was Roman.

I wished I hadn't opened it. I didn't know if I was ready. My whole body felt like a live wire, my nerves sparking everywhere. My thumb hovered next to the delete button, but I couldn't press it. Something in me wouldn't let me.

The message wasn't long.

From: Roman

To: Alex

Subject: HI

I just wanted to let you know that Detective Lewis stopped in to see me. I really hope you're doing well, Alex.

Roman

Some days I wished Tanner would take a plea so this entire nightmare could finally end. Other days I wanted him to face the maximum sentence and every consequence that came with it. But right now, all I could think about was whether I should answer Roman's email.

I took a long drink of wine, letting the warmth settle my nerves before deciding.

A small hello couldn't hurt. It might even help.

So I typed back: "HELLO."

Almost immediately, a reply appeared.

From: ROMAN

To: ALEX

Subject: HELLO

Guess where I am?

RK

My heart took off the second I saw his reply. I stood so fast my blanket slid to the floor, and I hurried to the window, pressing my palms to the cool glass as I looked down. From twelve floors up, with the night settling over the city, I couldn't see anything. But a part of me still hoped—feared—that he wasn't down there waiting or planning to come up.

I told myself he couldn't have meant he was nearby.

I refilled my wineglass, trying to steady my nerves, and glanced at my door to double-check every lock. Then I sat back down and emailed him again.

From: ALEX

Reply to: ROMAN

Subject: RE: HELLO

Hmmm, give me a hint

AK
From: ROMAN
Reply to: ALEX
Subject: Peaceful
Stargazing
RK

I took a deep breath and sank back into the couch. I hadn't been up there in weeks. How could I have forgotten that place? Why would he go there alone?

He once told me it unnerved him. He even lectured me for going there by myself.

And now he was the one sitting there in the dark.
From: ALEX
Reply to: ROMAN
Subject: Scary
Interesting. Have you run into any serial killers yet?
AK
From: ROMAN
Reply to: ALEX
Subject: LOL!
I should apologize for that. I get it now.
RK
From: ALEX
Reply to: ROMAN
Subject: Riverfront
Guess what I did today?
AK

That was easier than I expected—just simple, steady back-and-forth without emotion pressing in on either of us. I leaned back, let my shoulders loosen, and took another slow sip of wine.
From: ROMAN
Reply to: ALEX
Subject: Hmmmm
Hint?
RK
From: ALEX
Reply to: ROMAN

Subject: Peaceful
Swing
AK
From: ROMAN
Reply to: ALEX
Subject: Thinking of me huh?
I miss you too.
RK

Okay, that was enough. I didn't want to keep emailing after drinking. I'd end up saying something I couldn't take back, and the last thing I needed right now was a surge of emotions I wasn't ready to confront.

My hands had started to shake. I watched the wine ripple in the glass, the surface moving in slow waves that pulled my focus in like a trance.

I couldn't do this anymore.

From: ALEX
Reply to: ROMAN
Subject: :)
Goodnight.
AK

Chapter 5

ROMAN

I was terrible at letting things like this go. I sat there staring at my phone, biting down on my lip, nostrils flared, trying to stay in control and not say something I'd regret.

I was tired of all of it. I knew she missed me. I knew she couldn't possibly still believe I'd hurt her. So what was she afraid of? Me? I'd only ever shown her love. None of this made sense—not for her, not for me.

I wanted the last word.

I dropped the phone onto the cushion and dragged my hands through my hair, back and forth, trying to pull myself together. A strangled sound escaped me before I finally picked the phone up again. I took a breath, forcing my thoughts to settle, and tried to figure out how to respond to what felt like a dismissal.

From: ROMAN
Reply to: ALEX
Subject: Y Goodnight?
Please just talk to me. How can I make you see it wasn't me?
RK
From: ALEX
Reply to: ROMAN
Subject: I don't know
I just don't know.
AK

I wasn't as composed as I wanted to be, and I had no intention of giving up—not when there was still something there, at least for me. I wasn't a quitter.

I just hoped I wasn't drifting into territory that would make me look like anything close to a stalker.

***

I slept better last night just knowing we'd communicated, even a little. The gym helped too—my workout actually felt productive for the first time in weeks.

When I got to my office, I flipped on the lights. Everything was exactly the way I'd left it—papers scattered, folders half open, the usual proof of yesterday's chaos. I settled into my chair and started straightening things up before calling Amelia in so I could get the notes from the meetings I'd missed.

She walked in, not nearly as cautious as she'd been lately. "Good morning, Mr. King. You're looking much better today." She handed me the files with a bright, almost knowing smile.

"Yeah, I'm feeling much better. Thanks. Can we go over the notes from yesterday?" I took the folders and began scanning them for anything urgent.

"Of course." She sat in the chair across from me, crossing her legs, posture perfect almost exaggerated.

"I sent an email this morning with everything attached. And I pushed your first meeting back an hour in case you needed extra time." She said it like it was obvious—like she already knew I'd need the margin. I smiled. She was right: she always emailed the notes. But having them in my hands grounded me in a way the screen didn't. Plus the blue lights weren't good for people who got headaches.

"Thanks for that. You always seem to know what I need." I leaned back in my chair, arms crossed, waiting for her to take the compliment the way she usually did.

"It's part of my job description—to anticipate your needs. Didn't you know that?" she said, handing me a second stack of files. The one's for today's meetings.

I laughed and shook my head. "Since HR wrote that job description, I may never have even looked at it. Thought maybe you made it up."

We both laughed, and she settled more comfortably into her seat while we went through the notes from yesterday.

If there was anyone I could talk to about those emails from last night, it was Amelia. She and Alex got along well, and she had a perspective I didn't.

"Hey, are you free for lunch today?" I asked, leaning forward with my elbows on the desk. "We haven't done that in a while, and I'm trying to get back into some kind of routine."

A flicker of discomfort crossed her face. "I actually have a lunch date today. Can we do it tomorrow?" She looked almost nervous, like she was waiting for my reaction.

A date?

Was she seeing someone? She rarely talked about her personal life at all. Hearing her say the word sounded almost...foreign.

"Really? Anyone I know?" I asked, raising an eyebrow as I clasped my hands on the desk.

She smiled—tight, uncomfortable. "I'd rather not say, if that's okay?"

I nodded. With Amelia, private was normal.

"Sure, no worries. We'll plan on tomorrow then. What time are you heading out for lunch?" I walked to the mini fridge and grabbed a bottle of water. I held one out to her. She shook her head, so I put it back.

"Noon. Same as always," she said with a shrug.

Another detail I probably should've noticed sooner. She took lunch at the same time every day. You'd think that would've stuck. Apparently not.

"Alright. Enjoy. I'll see you this afternoon. My first meeting's off-site, so I'll get ready and head over."

She smiled and left. I opened the water and drank half in a few gulps, still trying to stay hydrated after yesterday's headache. That was the most reserved I'd seen Amelia around me. She must genuinely like whoever she's meeting. Good for her.

I checked my phone and saw the alert for my first meeting—Grant Johnson, Alex's broker. We needed a plan for helping the Burrow Township residents relocate. I'd never been to their office before, and aside from Grant, I'd never met any of Alex's coworkers. This was going to be another window into her world.

The building surprised me—beautiful, set in what felt like a small park. Peaceful. It made sense why Alex had chosen this place. I walked inside and approached the receptionist.

"Hi, I'm Roman King. I have an appointment with Grant Johnson." I reached out to shake her hand. The usual reaction—wide eyes, nervous stare—met me as she slowly extended her hand like she wasn't sure if I was safe to touch.

Before she could respond, a hand landed on my shoulder.

"Roman. Right on time," Grant said. Her mouth snapped closed as I lowered my hand. "Let's head to the conference room."

He guided me down the hallway. A few heads lifted from desks as we passed—curious eyes following us. Clearly, they didn't get many visitors, and even fewer they recognized.

When we stepped inside, I stopped short.

This wasn't a conference room. I looked over all the photos of Alex with friends and family lining the shelves. Framed on her desk. Everything arranged in such a way it looked as if she never left. I stood in the center of the room with my hands in my pockets, careful not to touch anything. I didn't want to sit, didn't want to get close enough to see or smell anything that might still feel like her. Seeing her face everywhere was enough.

I lifted an eyebrow at Grant, silently hoping he'd reconsider and take us somewhere else.

Grant looked at me with sympathy. "Alex hasn't been in to work since the accident, but she hasn't picked up her things either. I can't seem to let her go, so we're keeping it as is until she tells me for sure whether she's coming back."

"I know how you feel." I glanced at the photos again before turning back to him.

"Have you seen her or talked to her?" I asked, sounding more hopeful than I felt.

"She stopped in yesterday for a quick visit." Good. She needed these people.

"We emailed, but that's it. She hasn't wanted to see me or talk to me." I confessed.

Grant gave a weary nod. I hoped this wasn't turning into a full conversation about her—I didn't have it in me today.

"I don't know if this helps or makes things worse," he said, "but she was the happiest we've ever seen her when she was with you. Hopefully she remembers that and gives herself a break."

Helpful, yes. Also painful. And just because it was true then didn't mean it was true now. My comfort level was dropping fast.

"Thanks. Good to know." It did spark a small sense of hope—or maybe she really was punishing herself. Either way, we needed to steer this back to the actual purpose of the meeting.

Grant picked up on my mood and moved on, talking about the Burrow Township residents he'd been working with. After a beat I realized I was still planted firmly in the middle of the room—my hands clenched in my pockets. He gestured toward the sitting area—the green velvet sofa and the two green-and-gold chairs. I took one of the chairs, and he sat on the sofa beside me.

I leaned back, ankle over knee, letting my hand pass briefly over the fabric. It pulled a memory I didn't want, so I forced myself to focus as he updated me on the neighborhood.

"They're more comfortable working with Alex, but Ella assured everyone that if Alex trusted you, they could too. She also mentioned she hasn't heard from Alex either."

"That surprises me. She was determined to help them. I figured she'd at least stay in touch." The idea that she'd pulled back from them too didn't sit right.

"I think we should talk to Alex. See if we can get her re-engaged with Ella." He said.

"How? She won't talk to me."

"Let me think on it. The two of us can come up with something, I'm sure." He smiled, patted my shoulder, and excused himself for another meeting.

Overall, it went better than I expected. I managed to stay focused on the work instead of everything this room reminded me of.

As I stepped into the hallway, a young woman stopped me.

"Mr. King? I'm Shay—Alex's friend."

The name rang a bell. I gave her a polite smile and shook her hand.

"Hi, Shay. Please call me Roman. It's nice to meet you."

Alex had talked about the people here, but I hadn't met any of them. Shay looked younger than I expected. If most of Alex's coworkers were around her age, it explained a lot about where she spent her time—and what her life looked like when she wasn't with me. I forced a small smile and pushed that thought away.

"You too," she said. "I just wanted to meet you since we didn't get the chance that night."

Her expression shifted—heavy, pained. Everyone here felt the impact of what happened to Alex. She looked like she was holding back tears. "Alex told us yesterday that you two weren't together anymore... I'll be she ended it, right?"

Not a conversation I wanted, but Shay seemed sincere.

"Shay, we all have our reasons for the choices we make. She had hers. We have to respect that."

I turned to leave, but she grabbed my forearm. I glanced down at her hand, drew a breath, and braced myself.

"Please wait," she said. "I know she still loves you. She's one of the kindest and most generous people I know—except when it comes to herself. Don't give up on her. She deserves to be happy."

I had no words. I nodded and walked away, chest tight and a lump rising in my throat.

I left the building as fast as I could.

If Shay was right, Alex wasn't fooling anyone but herself.

***

ALEX

Morning routine complete.

I sat on the edge of my bed, phone on speaker while it rang, tying my shoes. Ella's voice soothed something inside me almost immediately as she answered the phone.

"Miss Alex, how you doin', sweetie?"

Hearing her voice felt like stepping into warm sunlight. Making friends in a neighborhood where most people would rather threaten you than help you wasn't the smartest thing I'd ever done, but somehow I'd found one of the truest friends I had.

I finished the last loop, grabbed the phone, and carried it to the kitchen. I set it on the island while I pulled a bottle of water from the fridge.

"Oh, you know Miss Ella," I said, leaning against the counter, "I'd say I'm doing better than fair today." It was a saying my dad always used.

She laughed, and I stared down at my nails, chewing one nervously while I sorted through what I needed to say—how to make amends for disappearing when she needed me most.

"I'm so happy to hear from you. What can I do for you?"

Only Ella would ask how she could help me when I was the one who was supposed to help her.

"Ella... I haven't been a very good friend. I promised I'd help you, and then I ghosted you."

The pressure in my chest tightened, emotion rising fast.

"Now don't you say that," she corrected gently. "You did no such thing. You left us in very capable hands. Mr. Grant is wonderful. He's no 'White Girl Rambo' like you, but he ain't scared of those people either."

I let out a small laugh, pushing back the tears. Darius had given me that nickname after the knife incident—not exactly my proudest moment, but at least it had become a joke.

"Grant is my mentor and taught me everything I know," I said. "But the reason I'm calling is because I'm still your friend, and I'd like to come see you today. Darius too. I have a lunch meeting, but after that, if it works for you?"

I chewed the inside of my cheek, waiting.

"Yes ma'am, you come on over when you're done. Darius and I will be here."

She sounded excited. Relief washed over me.

"Wonderful. I look forward to seeing you."

"Same, sweetie."

Another weight lifted. I let out a long breath, hung up, and slipped the phone into my purse.

Amelia and I were meeting at Benita's—the little bistro across from her office. She only had an hour, and the last thing I wanted was to end up eating anywhere near King Construction where I could risk running into Roman.

I spotted her crossing the street as I parked. The second I stepped out of the car, she squealed, sprinted toward me, and wrapped me in one of her signature full-body hugs. Being swallowed whole by a six-foot goddess wasn't exactly my aesthetic, but it was hard not to smile.

She held me by the shoulders and gave me a once-over, head to toe.

"Girl, how do you manage to look this good in workout clothes?"

I shot her the you-have-lost-your-mind look. I felt like a mess—Lululemon leggings, sneakers, no makeup, hair pulled back just to get it out of my face.

"You're crazy," I said, crossing my arms over my stomach. "I'm sorry about the outfit. I have a meeting after this and then kickboxing. No time to go home."

Meanwhile she looked like she'd been poured into that burgundy sheath dress. Four-inch stilettos. Makeup flawless. Hair perfect. Standing next to her outside felt like I was some kind of charity case. I prayed we'd get inside quickly before anyone saw us together.

She didn't hesitate—she linked her arm through mine, unbothered, and pulled me toward the entrance.

"How do you like that class?" she asked once we ordered and sat down.

"I love it," I admitted, taking a bite of my sandwich. Once I swallowed, I added, "It was brutal at first, but now it's... weirdly relaxing."

I remembered that first day—two back-to-back classes, stuck to the floor afterward like a crime scene outline. Now I felt almost invincible.

She laughed. "Maybe I need to sign up."

"I'd love that," I said honestly.

She flexed her bicep dramatically, and we both cracked up.

Lunch was good—easy, comfortable—until my throat closed and I couldn't breathe.

A familiar scent drifted through the room. One glimpse from the corner of my eye confirmed it: Roman.

His cologne hit first, and my heart took off like it was trying to break free of my ribs. My eyes shut on instinct. Not this. Not now.

If I didn't move—if I stayed perfectly still—maybe he wouldn't see me.

I gripped the edge of the table until my knuckles went white. The attack flashed across my mind, sharp and fast. My hands started shaking.

Amelia's voice cut in. "Alex, what's wrong?"

Roman hadn't seen us—he was absorbed in his phone as he walked in. Amelia was mid-story before she noticed the way I'd gone rigid.

"Nothing," I whispered, still barely breathing. I swallowed hard, forced a slow inhale, but my gaze drifted toward him anyway. I couldn't stop it.

Amelia followed my eyes, turned back, and—of course—acted like it was nothing.

She shrugged and muttered under her breath, "At least he's eating again."

My head snapped toward her. "What do you mean by that?"

I kept my voice low, but the edge was unmistakable. Amelia's brows shot up, and she leaned back, arms crossing over her chest like she was reevaluating me.

"Woah. That sounded a whole lot like caring." She tilted her head, studying me far too closely. "He's had a rough few weeks too, Alex."

The way she said it felt like I was being scolded. I forced myself to breathe, normally again.

"Sorry," I murmured. "Didn't mean to snap."

Get through the next minute, that's all I needed to do. Then I could decide if lunches with Amelia were going to be a recurring thing or a one-and-done situation.

"You two should really talk," she pressed gently. "If you want me there, I'll go with you. This... whatever this is between you—this is hard to watch."

Nope. Not having that conversation here.

I gathered my trash and stood. "Let's do this again sometime. And think about that kickboxing class. We could hang out more."

I kept my gaze on the table, not her.

She nodded. "Maybe. But I bruise easily."

I didn't buy it—but fine. We could always do something else.

"We could do mani-pedis instead," I offered.

She lit up a little too brightly—performative, like we were both politely pretending everything wasn't suddenly twisted up between us. For the first time, it hit me: our friendship might depend on whether I could handle her closeness to Roman. Even when I no longer had him.

"Yeah," she said lightly. "That's definitely more me."

Her eyes flicked sideways—toward him—right as Roman turned.

And our eyes collided.

He stopped. I stopped. Everything inside me surged forward like it recognized him before my brain caught up. His gaze held mine steady, unwavering, and my breath stalled. My mouth parted just slightly before I snapped it shut.

Amelia, sensing disaster, cut in fast. "Well, Alex, this was fun. Let's do it again."

I didn't answer. Couldn't. My eyes were locked on Roman and the faint lift at the corner of his mouth.

"Don't you have an appointment you need to get to?" she prompted.

I nodded, still staring straight at him. "Yeah... thanks."

Amelia offered him a quick hello and slipped out. I reached for my purse, ready to bolt, but the strap snagged on the back of the chair.

I muttered under my breath, yanking at it. "Of course this would happen."

***

ROMAN

I stopped scrolling and slid my phone into my back pocket, handed the cashier my debit card, and stepped aside while she bagged my order. When she gave it back, I dropped a few bills into the tip jar, thanked her, and turned to leave.

And then it happened.

My eyes found hers instantly — as if my body already knew where she was before my mind had time to catch up. It hit me with the force of a physical jolt. I froze; caught in those green eyes I hadn't seen in weeks. Eyes that used to look at me like I was hers. Eyes that now made my chest tighten in a way I wasn't prepared for.

This was harder than I expected. Much harder.

Someone said my name — Amelia, I think — and I barely acknowledged her. My attention snapped right back to Alex. So, this was Amelia's secret lunch date. It made sense now why she didn't elaborate.

I watched her fight her purse off the chair like it had personally offended her. The sight pulled at something deep in my chest — the fierce woman who could level a grown man in the gym was locked in a battle with a purse strap in a crowded bistro.

And she was losing.

I bit down on the inside of my cheek to stop myself from reacting to how endearing it was. I should've looked away. I should've walked out. Instead, I stood rooted in place, drawn to her like there was no other option.

"Hi, Ms. Kennedy."

My voice came out low barely controlled— carrying every ounce of restraint I had left. The sound of her name on my tongue did something to me I couldn't hide. Her eyes snapped to mine again, and for a moment time stretched thin and unsteady between us.

One look, and everything I'd been holding back was bubbling to the surface.

"Hello, Mr. King." She said it with a small shake of her head, and then, "I have to go," before bolting for the door.

Something inside me tipped. I'd been patient. Considerate. Careful. But watching her run from me again snapped whatever restraint I had left. I wasn't chasing a stranger. I wasn't forcing anything. This was the woman I loved — the woman who had loved me every bit as fiercely. And somewhere beneath all her fear and confusion, I knew she still felt it.

I stepped outside in time to see her reach her car. My lunch slipped from my grip, forgotten. Instinct moved my feet before I could think; I caught her arm and turned her toward me.

I searched her eyes fast — a reflex, a check — needing to be certain. There was no fear there. Just surprise... and something else. Something I hadn't seen in weeks but had prayed wasn't gone.

Before doubt had a chance to interfere, I closed the distance.

I kissed her with all the urgency I had been holding back — not rough, not demanding, but with the full force of everything I still felt. One hand curved around her waist, drawing her against me, the other sliding into her hair to hold her close. The moment she melted toward me; the air left my lungs. Her body leaned in as if it remembered exactly where it belonged.

Emotion surged through me in waves — relief, longing, the unmistakable shock of finally touching what I had been aching to touch again. When she lifted her hands to my chest and curled her fingers into my lapel, it was like being pulled back into a truth I'd been starving for.

I traced the outline of her lower lip with a slow, deliberate sweep — a question, not a command — and she answered by opening to me, her breath warm and uneven against my mouth. The connection hit hard and consuming, like a current snapping back into place.

We were standing half in the road, the world moving around us, but all I could feel was her — the heat of her heartbeat against mine, the way her hands trembled with the same overwhelming urgency I felt.

I wanted more. I wanted all of it. But I also didn't want to misread the moment or take this further than she was prepared for. As much as her response unraveled me, I wasn't about to push past whatever line she needed to keep.

Still, she hadn't pulled away.

She held on.

And that alone nearly brought me to my knees.

I broke the connection gently, still feeling the vibration of it as I guided her back toward her car. I opened the door for her because it felt like the only thing grounding me after what just happened. She slid into the seat, breath uneven, eyes unfocused in a way I recognized far too well. I wanted nothing more than to lean back in and finish what I started, but I stepped away.

I picked up my dropped lunch, dusted off the bag, and walked toward the building. Halfway across the street, I turned. She was still sitting there, gripping the steering wheel, her shoulders rising and falling with unsteady breaths.

Yeah. I knew exactly what that kiss had done to her.
And I knew exactly what it was doing to me.

Now it was time to deal with Amelia.

I stopped right in front of her desk, narrowing my eyes while I sorted out whether I was irritated or just blindsided by the whole situation.

"I'm going to need about twenty minutes for lunch today. Hold my calls, please."

She didn't flinch. "Okay, Mr. King."

"Don't 'Mr. King' me right now." My voice was edgy and sharp, but I didn't back off. "You could've told me you were having lunch with Alex."

Her expression didn't crack. Not once. And for the first time in a long time, I had the unsettling sense that the person behind that desk wasn't my assistant at all—but a woman with her own opinions about my life, and very few hesitations about sharing them.

She slammed her palms against the desk and stood tall enough that I instinctively stepped back toward my office door.

"Why? So you can spiral again like you did the last time her name came up?" Her tone wasn't raised, but it carried a sharpness that sliced straight through me. "You skipped work for a headache and made me handle the fallout. I'd rather deal with the version of you who knows how to lead a team than this unraveling version who can't even pick up his phone."

I blinked. Once. Slowly.

She wasn't finished.

"You and Alex are both running in circles, pretending you can outrun the obvious. It's exhausting. For everyone. You need to talk to each other." She pointed toward my office like she owned the place. "Soon."

I shook my head—not in disagreement, but in pure disbelief—and walked straight into my office. I didn't let myself laugh until the door clicked shut behind me. Then I leaned back against the wood and doubled over, one hand braced on my thigh.

Whoever that was... it wasn't the Amelia I knew.

I set my lunch on the desk, still grinning when the ping of a new email cut through the room.

Everything in me stilled.

From: ALEX

Reply to: ROMAN

Subject: Ambush

I feel like you're messing with me.

AK

I had an easy response to that.

From: ROMAN

Reply to: ALEX

Subject: You too huh?

Ditto!

RK

Chapter 6

ALEX

I sat there in a daze for what felt like forever after I sent that email. My fingertips drifted over my lips, chasing the fading warmth he left behind. It was still there—the imprint of his mouth, the slide of his tongue, the way my breath tangled with his like he was the only thing keeping me upright. That is not the action of a man who wants to harm me. So why is my mind still twisting the truth? Were those drugs strong enough to leave permanent shadows behind? I have to figure this out before it swallows me whole.

This short drive suddenly felt impossibly long. Every red light, every second of silence, amplified the confusion in my chest.

And honestly—did he really think he could just show up and kiss me after everything I've been through? That kiss stole the air from my lungs and the ground from beneath me. My body had gone soft, unguarded, leaning into him before my brain could catch up. I didn't even remember getting into my car afterward. It was like my instincts were moving faster than my memory.

I forced the moment out of my head long enough to function. I gripped the steering wheel and rested my chin against the top of it, breathing evenly until the trembling settled and the world felt steady again.

When I finally pulled into Ella's driveway, the quiet felt different—thick, watchful. I climbed the four cracked cement steps, feeling each uneven rise under my shoes. The rickety screen door creaked under my hand, and I slipped inside the small porch without letting it slam, mindful of every sound.

I knocked gently on the inner door with the tips of my fingers. The whole neighborhood felt unnervingly still. My pulse kicked up as my eyes tracked the shadows around me. Too many bad memories lived on this street—being threatened with a knife right here on the porch, the cops showing up every time I breathed in the wrong direction, and of course the night everything changed at that club.

No wonder I'm paranoid. Every time I show up here, trouble seems to follow.

Maybe they think I'm weakened now. Maybe that's why it's quiet.

I hope it stays that way. I just want to see Ella and Darius without looking over my shoulder every two seconds.

I was surprised when Darius answered the door, even though Ella had told me he'd be there. He was usually running around somewhere whenever I stopped by. Today, though, he stood in the doorway waiting for me, his expression warm in a way that eased some of the tension I'd carried from the car.

"Hi, Ms. Alex. It's good to see you. I'm sorry to hear about your mom."

His voice was steady, kind, and it hit me deep. I swallowed the tightness, willing the ache behind my eyes to stay put.

"Thank you, Darius. It's good to see you too."

He stepped aside, giving me space to enter. I hesitated for a second before leaning in for a hug—light enough for him to choose whether he wanted to reciprocate. He did, looping one arm around me in a shy but genuine gesture.

From the kitchen came Ella's unmistakable voice.

"Boy, you get out of the way and invite that girl in. Where are your manners?"

Darius and I both laughed as I kept my arm around his back long enough for us to step farther inside. The house smelled like sweet tea and something simmering—warm and homey.

"Hi, Ella. I promise you, he has perfect manners," I called as I moved toward her.

Before I could say anything else, she pulled me into one of her signature hugs—tight, comforting and familiar. I hugged her back, then we all headed for the living room.

I tucked one foot beneath me, settling onto the couch, focusing on Ella. "How's Grant working out for you?"

She smoothed her floral skirt over her knees, giving a satisfied little nod. "Really good, and the rest of the neighborhood likes him too. He just doesn't have your spunk."

I huffed a small laugh. Spunk. That was a generous way of describing what is more accurately poor impulse control and a willingness to run headfirst into danger. But hearing her say it so fondly may have smoothed things over in my head.

"Thank goodness. We don't want to overwhelm this place," I teased.

But my mind was already shifting. I couldn't leave this all on Grant forever. Not if I still cared. Not if they still needed me.

I turned toward Darius, placing my hand gently over his. His hand tensed under mine at first—surprised—but he didn't pull away.

"Darius," I said softly, "tell me something about you I don't know. What would you like to be doing with your life?"

His eyebrows knit, unsure where the question came from. But I meant it. Everyone had dreams tucked somewhere. His mattered. And I wanted to see what sparked in him when he said them out loud.

He looked at Ella in surprise, like the idea that someone cared about his future had caught him completely off guard. I recognized that look far too well. I wore the same one the first time Grant asked me what I wanted for my life. It was the expression of someone who'd never been asked before.

"Well... I never really thought about it," he admitted. "It hasn't come up."

I tightened my hold on his hand, steadying my voice. "Are you in school? Or thinking about going back?"

He shook his head with certainty. "School isn't really my thing. And I can't afford college. Even if I could, they don't have anything I want to learn."

"School isn't for everyone," I said gently. "I didn't go to school for what I actually do either. My degree wasn't what changed my life—my license did. There are a lot of ways forward that don't start in a classroom. So... what interests you? What would you want to do if you could try anything?"

His eyes drifted toward the window, the muscles in his jaw working like he was measuring the risk of telling the truth.

"I really like construction," he finally said. "Building things. I'd like to get into that, but I don't know how. I don't know where to start."

My heart lifted. Construction. Of all the possibilities, this one landed right in the middle of something I actually understood—and something I could help with.

"That's amazing," I breathed, unable to hold back my excitement. "And I think I know someone who could get you started."

The second the words left my mouth, I wanted to grab them out of the air. My stomach dropped. My pulse jumped. Because the someone I knew was the exact man I was trying so hard not to think about today.

"Who?" Darius asked quickly, hopeful.

I reached out to steady myself more than anything, laying my hand on his arm again, choosing my words with care.

"Don't get upset," I said, "but... it's the company working on the construction here."

His entire expression snapped shut. The hope vanished. He pulled his arm from under my hand and shot up from the couch, shaking his head hard.

"No way," he said sharply, backing away like the suggestion itself was dangerous.

I smiled. It surprised me how much Darius and I had in common. Ella didn't look thrilled with his outburst, but I caught her eye and gave a small shake of my head—no need to let this turn into a household scolding.

"Darius," I said cautiously, "I'd feel the same way if I were you. And I did. When I first learned he was involved, I was furious. But he didn't know anything about the corruption, and he's not going to force anyone out without making sure they have somewhere safe to go. He's working with good people to find better housing for you and your neighbors... and if he can recover the money the Ellingtons took, he wants to disperse it to the families who were affected."

The tension in his shoulders eased, and Ella's expression softened too. This was something I had planned to tell her today.

Darius studied me, his tone measured. "Sounds like you like this guy."

Like wasn't even close to the word.

"I like him enough to help get you a job with his company," I said, trying to keep my voice steady. "I trust him."

Did I? The flutter in my stomach said yes—at least enough to make this moment matter. There was a spark of something new in my chest that I was mentally clinging to.

"That would be amazing if you'd do that for me," he replied, glancing at Ella, then back at me.

"Consider it done," I said, lifting my hands as if sealing the promise in the air. It hit me a beat later—this meant I would have to speak to Roman. My pulse kicked up, but I told myself to breathe. I could handle it.

Turning to Ella, I added, "I'll stay in touch with Grant so I can keep track of everyone's progress. And one of my friends—Matt—is looking for ways to move this neighborhood into his district."

Her face cooled instantly, and the warmth in the room thinned. My stomach dipped. What did I say wrong?

"What do you mean his district? He's not another politician, is he?"

I lifted my palms, calming the moment. "Yes, but he's also an attorney—and he's married to one of my best friends. Their kids are my godchildren." The thought of the babies softened my voice without permission; I couldn't help it.

Ella watched me closely before she relaxed. "Judging by that sweet look on your face, I'm guessing he's not like the other one. Do you really trust him?" she asked, still laced with worry.

I nodded and pulled out my phone to show her pictures of the kids—only realizing too late that Roman's photos were still mixed in with them. I swiped through pictures of him quickly as I angled the screen where she could see better and talked about the kids until Ella's smile returned.

The rest of the visit felt lighter. I even got to meet Darius's little brothers—Isaac and Dante—two bright-eyed athletes fresh from day camp. Sweet kids, twelve and fourteen. Ella was doing everything she could to keep them focused on sports and away from trouble.

We said our goodbyes, exchanged hugs, and I headed out for kickboxing, feeling—finally—a little more like myself again.

***

ROMAN

I had a smile etched onto my face for the rest of the day—an unfamiliar, almost foreign lift in my mood after three weeks of nothing but tension and worry. Between the emails and that kiss flashing through my mind, I could barely keep air in my lungs. My shoulders loosened for the first time in days as I stretched my arms over my head to shake off the stiffness of a long day at my desk.

I turned toward the window. The sun was sinking low, painting the river in streaks of gold and deep rose. The haze that usually muted the view was thinner tonight, revealing sharper colors, clearer reflections—everything brighter than it had any right to be. It felt symbolic somehow, like the day itself was easing into something more hopeful.

My hopes of seeing her name pop up in my inbox again had a pull stronger than anything work could offer me, but email wasn't going to be enough—not for long. I already knew that. I'd have to find a way to see her, to prove I'm not the confusion in her without pushing too hard. For now, though, I'd take what I could get.

I made it through my six o'clock meeting—barely—nodding at the right moments, offering input just enough to stay convincing. No one had any idea I was counting down the minutes, tapping my finger next to my laptop while my mind chased possibilities of what to say to her next. I'd already talked myself out of the rock-through-the-window idea... probably for the best.

"Yes, that all sounds great. I look forward to working on the specs, and I'll have Amelia email everything to you," I said, hoping it was the appropriate response. If it wasn't, Amelia would tell me.

I caught her staring at me as I closed my laptop and slid it into my bag, desperately trying not to look like a man ready to bolt. "What?" I asked, giving her a look as even as I could manage.

"Nothing, honestly." Her tone carried that sharp edge of amusement she didn't bother to hide anymore. "I was impressed you managed to contribute coherently to a discussion about the riverwalk, considering how distracted you are." She raised her brows, a match lit behind her eyes, then snapped her notebook shut and moved toward the door.

"I'll have all the notes organized and emailed to you by tomorrow afternoon. Good night, Roman. Enjoy your evening." She didn't look back, but I could have sworn she was fighting a smile.

She wasn't wrong. I'd been completely useless for anything but thoughts of Alex. And as much as Amelia liked to poke at me for it, her bluntness somehow kept me on task.

I tossed my bags onto my kitchen counter and opened the fridge, letting the cool air wash over my face while I debated what I even had the energy for. My housekeeper, Mary, had lined up several meals—each packaged, labeled, ready to heat. A luxury, honestly, because cooking after a day like this wasn't happening. Heating something up was pushing it.

I grabbed the container marked lasagna and the beer beside it. The top hissed when I popped it open, and I took a slow pull, the cold settling into my chest before I set it down and put the dinner in the microwave.

Standing there, listening to the low hum of it heating, it hit me just how empty all of this felt—coming home to no one, eating meals someone else prepared, filling silence with anything that kept me from thinking too much. Still... better silence than the wrong person. The memory of Caitlin, and the day I ended everything, tried to push its way in. I exhaled deeply and shut it down before it could get traction. Another sip helped.

I sat at the kitchen island and ate mechanically, barely tasting any of it. My hand kept drifting toward my phone, muscle memory tugging me toward something I knew I should leave alone. I pushed the feeling down, but it kept circling back until the frustration spiked.

I stood, placed the plate in the sink almost aggressively, and opened another beer. Half of it was gone before I lowered the bottle. Then I returned to the stool, picked up my phone, and let myself slip back into the only thing my mind wanted—her.

From: ROMAN
Reply to: ALEX
Subject: "TRUTH OR DARE"
RK

The body of the message didn't say anything else. I left the rest in her hands. Whatever happened next—whether she responded or didn't—was entirely up to her.

I took my phone and walked to the sofa, dropping on the seat next to me. The living room felt too still, too aware of every thought I was trying to outrun. I opened the drawer of the chairside table and grabbed the stereo remote, needing something—anything—to keep my mind from circling the same anxious loop.

The classical station came on immediately. The one she and I used to listen to. The familiar strings drifted through the room, and my chest loosened for a moment. We were always so in sync—same tastes, same instincts, same quiet corners of the world we gravitated toward.

I sank into the cushions, letting my head fall back. Thoughts of her started to pull me under.

I couldn't help smiling as I remembered the night we danced under the stars—her body in that red dress tucked against mine, wrapped in my hoodie. Her breath warm at my neck, the scent of lavender from her hair threading through the air. The memory felt alive, like it was still imprinted on my skin.

A slow ache built in the center of my chest as the memory shifted. I adjusted my position on the sofa, trying to ease the tension coiling through me. Every part of me remembered what it felt like to be that close to her. To want her. To be wanted by her. The first time we were together replayed in a flash of sensation rather than visuals—her voice, the way she whispered my name, the weight of emotion behind every touch.

I closed my eyes. Maybe if I had known how intricate her heart was—how layered, how wounded, how unguarded and guarded at the same time—I would have slowed down. Maybe I would've protected myself better. But it's far too late for that now.

She's anchored so deeply under my skin it feels elemental. She's inside every breath, every thought, every space I've tried to wipe free of her. Sometimes it's hard to tell where her gravity ends and mine begins.

And tonight... waiting for her reply... it felt like the entire world had narrowed to the sound of a classical melody and the hope that she still felt even a fraction of what I did.

I went through some work documents, talked to my mom and Harrison then switched from beer to bourbon to relax. I was trying to keep myself occupied so I wouldn't be tempted to check my emails every ten minutes. It's sad that this is what my nights have turned into.

I leaned my head back on the couch and decided to try some visualization techniques my mom taught me when I was first dealing with my empathic anxiety. First you need to be clear about what you really want. If she responds to the email with dare, should I dare her to call me? What if she says, truth? What do I want to know– if she's happy? Of course she's not happy. I saw her face at the restaurant, she's fucking miserable. Broken hearts don't make people happy and if she is happy then she's some kind of sadistic praying mantis or black widow and I'm truly screwed because I'd rather have her and let her kill me then be without her.

I hadn't done anything to make her stop loving me. Those drugs couldn't possibly last this long, could they? If they are then Tanner is truly a sick monster and he needs to go away for life.

As I was slipping farther down this torture spiral, feeling myself drift off to sleep, I heard an email notification. My eyes slowly opened, and I reached for my phone. The lights were low in the penthouse but the reflection from the phone might as well have been a beacon from outer space. The subject said, "FAVOR."

I can do favors.

From: ALEX KENNEDY
Reply to: ROMAN KING
Subject: "FAVOR"

I know this is off the topic of Truth or Dare, but I need a favor. Can you meet me tomorrow for lunch or just meet before my training tomorrow? Its business related, but it's also a personal favor.

Sincerely,

Alex Kennedy

Realtor

Ok, this shit's getting weird, these visualization techniques my mom turned me onto a few years ago have worked almost every time I've put them to practical use. But honestly, I don't think Alex and I could stay away from each other if we tried no matter what kind of drugs are in her system. Or manifesting technique.

From: ROMAN KING
Reply To: ALEX KENNEDY
Subject: Re: FAVOR

Yes Ms. Kennedy, I'll check with my assistant, Amelia, and see where we can fit you in tomorrow.

Kind Regards,

Roman F. King Jr.

From: ALEX KENNEDY
Reply to: ROMAN KING
Subject: Re: FAVOR

Thank you, Mr. King. As always, I look forward to hearing from Amelia. I can be open for a meeting anywhere between 8:00 am and 2:00 pm.

Sincerely,

Alex Kennedy

Realtor

I forwarded the email on to Amelia so she could deal with that in the morning. I know I have a full schedule of meetings tomorrow but I'm sure Amelia can sort it out.

From: ROMAN
Reply to: ALEX
Subject: Back to Truth or Dare
I'm still waiting on your response to Truth or Dare
RK
From: ALEX
Reply to: ROMAN
Subject: Re: Back to truth or dare
How about one of each?
AK

I wasn't expecting that response. This is probably a dangerous game to be playing with someone who seems as emotionally fragile as Alex, but she can handle it, right? Plus, I'm only trying to get information out of her to see if she still thinks it was me.

From: ROMAN
Reply to: ALEX
Subject: Re: Back to truth or dare
TRUTH: How are you?
DARE: Tell me you honestly think I did this and you can't get past it and I will go away.
RK

Now I'm holding my breath.

From: ALEX
Reply to: ROMAN
Subject: Re: Back to truth or dare
TRUTH: It's hard. My reality is really messed up.
DARE: I can't! I don't know what to think.
AK

If she'd just let me see her or talk to her, I know we can get through this together.

From: ROMAN
Reply to: ALEX
Subject: Re: Back to truth or dare
Then I dare you to just call me. You don't have to tell me anything.
RK

Ten minutes. Still nothing.

I guess that was the final line for her. Maybe I pushed too far. Maybe she's done.

I rinsed out the bourbon glass and set it in the sink, shut off the music, and slid the remote back into the soft-close drawer — wishing I could slam it just once just to shake off this restless energy.

***

ALEX

That was a dangerous dare.

I set the phone down and walked to my room, every step feeling heavier than the last. This was going to take time... if I could even bring myself to do it. I moved through the motions as slowly as possible: changing into pajamas, brushing my teeth, pulling my hair back. It felt like stalling, because it was.

Back in the kitchen, the corkscrew felt absurdly heavy in my hand, like some kind of shield as I eyed my phone from across the room. It sat there harmlessly, but my nerves acted like it had teeth. I opened another bottle of wine, satisfied the phone wasn't going to leap at me, and poured myself a generous glass of cabernet.

I breathed in the deep swirl of cherry, dark chocolate, and that faint hint of tobacco that made this blend so grounding. My buzz was already strong from earlier, but I needed every bit of insulation I could get. Anything to dull the memories still trying to mix Roman with the fear of that night. Maybe it was the wine that made the call seem potentially possible now.

But what if I slurred?

I should test my voice.

And the second I heard myself talking to no one, I winced.

Wonderful. Talking out loud to make sure I sound sober... which is the clearest sign that I'm not. I sat up straighter on the sofa, set the glass down, and covered my face with my hands, breathing deeply while I debated how on earth I was supposed to make this call.

Thinking too much about it was going to destroy my courage entirely. So I picked up the phone, pressed send, and braced myself as the ringing crawled up my spine and almost made me sick.

When he answered—his voice low and warm—tears instantly blurred my vision. The wine wasn't numbing anything. It was unlocking every-thing. I felt him everywhere inside me at once: the ache, the connection, the pull I couldn't ignore. I hit speaker and set the phone down so I could swipe the tears away before they betrayed me further.

"Hi Alex," he said. "I didn't think you'd really call."

His voice sank right through me. I steadied myself, drew in a breath that felt shaky and thin, and forced myself to answer.

"I wasn't sure I was going to," I admitted, trying to sound composed. "But I just hate to lose, I guess."

I rolled my eyes at the absurdity of this game, took a long sip of wine to smooth out the roughness in my voice, and prayed he couldn't hear the lingering emotion there.

He let out a brief, warm laugh. "It's really good to hear from you. You sound... good."

He was being kind. I felt anything but. My voice felt raw, my chest tight. He, however, sounded exactly the way I remembered: steady, unshaken, and impossibly calm.

"Thanks," I managed. "I'm a little tired, but that's all. It's nice to hear your voice too. How have you been?"

I still didn't know how to talk to him anymore—what parts of myself I was allowed to reveal, what he still felt, what I was supposed to do with the storm inside my own mind. But I hoped he bought the "tired" part.

It was easier than admitting the truth: I was unraveling just hearing him breathe.

"Ummm... a little upset, actually." His tone tightened, the earlier hint of humor revealing itself for what it must have been—deflection. Maybe even hurt. This was never going to be easy.

"Probably at me, huh?" I tried to mask the uneasy laugh that threatened to break through, but I didn't want to set him off further, so I took another sip to bury the sound.

"Yes, Alex. How could you ever believe I could do something like that to you? Even with everything in your system." His voice cracked with emotion. "Everyone told you it wasn't me—the officers, Bruce, Steve. Why can't you believe them?"

I stood to refill my wine, then emptied the last of the bottle into my glass. If I was going to get through this, the numbness would have to carry me.

"I was drugged," I fired back. "I couldn't see. He took me into the room you took me to the night we met. I asked if it was you, and he said yes—he said *your* name. What was I supposed to think? My mind wasn't my own." My throat burned as I swallowed another mouthful.

He came back with equal force. "Are the drugs still affecting you, or are you just pushing me away?"

That one landed in my chest like a stone. I took another swallow, letting the wine burn the ache more.

"I don't know." The laugh that escaped was slurred, unsteady. "It's a good question." I lifted the glass toward the phone in a delirious half-toast. "Nothing a little wine won't fix, though."

His voice dropped, torn open. "Why are you doing this to us? If you're hurting the way I am... why?"

His pain wrapped around every word, and I could feel it—too sharply, too deeply. Tears slid down my cheeks, but the wine kept me from sobbing outright. I wasn't prepared for how raw he sounded. I wasn't prepared for how much it would undo me.

"You don't deserve me," I whispered, barely audible. My head bowed, my tears falling onto the screen like tiny drops of confession. "You deserve someone better."

It felt like the words came from somewhere far away, like I was watching myself speak from outside my own body.

"I'm like a storm, a black cloud that ruins everything it touches," I said, breath trembling. "Why would you ever choose that?"

I blinked hard. The room spun once, slow and disorienting. The honesty slipped through before I could catch it, and a wave of self-loathing washed over me. Somewhere, in the fog of my mind, it echoed one of my mother's old speeches, and I lifted my glass slightly toward the ceiling—an unsteady, heartbreaking tribute to the heavens.

"Alex, what are you talking about a black cloud?"

Black cloud. Number thirteen. Black cat crossing your path. Take your pick. They all applied. I sank deeper into the pillows, the room tilting just enough to remind me how much wine I'd already had. I took another long sip, before I forced myself to answer him.

"Seriously... look at the disaster trail behind me. One stupid moment of running out of gas... then the fight at the bar with T-T-Tanner... and then my worst nightmare. And it—" My voice cracked. "It took my mother. All that was my fault." I confessed in a stuttering fog.

Hold it together. Just a little longer. After that I could pass out and forget every word I'd said.

"Alex, none of that was your fault."

His voice steadied me, threading through the static buzzing in my head. It wrapped around me in the way only his voice ever did, and for a second, I hated how much comfort it brought. I didn't need comfort. I needed distance.

"Were they awful turns of events? Yes. But you couldn't control any of that." He added.

Why couldn't he just be angry? Why couldn't he let me push him away the way I kept trying to?

A broken sound slipped out of me before I could stop it. Then the tears came harder, spilling fast and hot. I pressed my fingers to my lips, trying to quiet the emotion, but my breathing hitched and the effort dissolved.

The conversation wasn't mine anymore—my thoughts weren't mine anymore.

The wine had taken over.

"I know somewhere inside you're right," I whispered, though it barely sounded like me. "But I can't convince my head. My heart feels so shattered I don't think I deserve anything good. Every time something good shows up, it gets taken away. It feels like I'm not meant to keep anything."

I was so drunk the words slid out unfiltered. I just wanted it all to stop so I could curl up and disappear. All I meant to do was ask him about helping Darius. That was supposed to be it.

"Please listen to me," he said softly.

I didn't want to listen. I pulled my nightshirt up over my face, trying to smother the tears, but the sound that came out of me was loud and broken, spilling past the cotton like it wasn't even there.

"I'll do whatever it takes to fix this." He said. "I still care about you, Alex. And I know you feel the same. You have to find a way to climb over whatever this is."

Why would he say that? Why would he still feel anything? I curled into myself tighter, the room spinning, the ache inside me twisting like a knife. I didn't understand him. I didn't understand myself. I was trapped in a version of pain that felt permanent—something I was choosing because it kept the anger focused on Tanner. If I let that ease, if I let myself want Roman again... I'd hurt him all over again.

"Roman... I'm sorry. I have to go." My voice shook. "I'll see you when Amelia schedules the meeting, alright?"

Please just say yes. Please don't make this harder.

"Alex, wait—let's have the meeting now. Whatever the favor is, tell me."

I couldn't. My chest felt bruised from crying. My throat hurt. My vision blurred around the edges. "No. I'll see you tomorrow, okay?"

There was a pause. A soft, aching exhale.

"...Fine," he murmured, and it sounded like something inside him gave way.

We hung up.

I drained the rest of the wine—didn't taste it, didn't care—and stumbled to my room. I crawled under the covers, clothes still on, and cried myself to sleep, heavy, hollow and exhausted in a way only alcohol could carve out.

***

ROMAN

I felt like hurling the phone across the room. I didn't know what else to do. How was I supposed to get through to her? I started pacing the floor, tension rolling through my shoulders in sharp, restless waves. Maybe I really was losing it.

She sounded drunk. That rattled me more than anything else. I hoped she wasn't slipping back into old habits—back into bars or numbing herself until she couldn't feel anything at all. She'd only just begun letting people in again.

I dropped onto the sofa and leaned back, covering my face with both hands. The frustration pressed hard against my ribs.

"I wonder if she still runs on the weekends," I muttered to the empty room, already picturing the route, the stretch of morning light over the river, the coffee shop she always stopped at afterward. My mind leapt to the absurd solution before I could stop it: showing up there. Not to corner her. Just to... be where she was. Somewhere she wouldn't feel ambushed.

It was ridiculous. And yet—at this point, I didn't know what else to do. I'd never admit these thoughts to my mom. She'd have my head if she knew the emails had led to me actually stalking her.

At least I got her to talk tonight. Even if it was messy and painful. I hated that she'd stopped speaking to my mom on account of me. They'd connected so easily, and I knew it helped her. I didn't want to be the reason she lost support she actually needed.

I sat up slowly, grabbed my phone, and swiped it open to our message thread. The sight of her name sent hope mixed with dread. She probably wouldn't see it tonight, not in the state she was in, but at least I could set the tone before tomorrow's meeting resurfaced every awkward corner of tonight.

ROMAN: *Alex, I'm sorry for earlier. I didn't mean to upset you. I just want you to know my mom is still here if you want to talk to her. I know she helped you, and she thinks the world of you. I won't interfere. She's never told me anything except to give you space. If she knew how much I've pushed, she'd probably drag me across the coals. Sleep well. Love, Roman.*

I drew a long breath and hit send.

I grabbed a bottle of water from the fridge and shook two Advil into my palm. The chill from the bottle seeped into my fingers as I leaned against the counter, staring down at my phone like it held the blueprint to the rest of my life.

I kept thinking about all the plans I'd made—the ones I'd mapped out so cleanly before Alex ever crossed my path. I had everything written in a five-year plan tucked in the nightstand by my bed. Every now and then I'd pull it out, smooth the pages with my thumb, and remind myself of what I was working toward.

A thriving business.

A wife I adored.

Kids laughing in a backyard.

A dog racing across the grass.

A home with peace in every corner.

Simple. Predictable. Steady.

But life hadn't followed my outline. Not even close.

I twisted the cap off the water and drank half of it in one go, letting the cool rush settle the heat behind my eyes. Somewhere in the back of my mind, I could almost hear God laughing at the arrogance of that perfectly planned life—as if the universe hadn't been intervening in every text, every email, every impossible moment Alex and I kept colliding in.

I set the bottle down and let out a slow breath.

Maybe tonight I'd read that plan again before bed.

Maybe it would remind me of who I thought I would be... And why my heart stopped caring about that version of me the second she entered my life.

Chapter 7

ROMAN

I woke with the weight of a future I couldn't see anymore pressing hard against my chest. For a moment, I just stared at the ceiling, feeling the kind of heaviness that doesn't come from sleep but from everything you try not to think about. The frustration built fast enough that I pushed the covers aside and headed into the closet to pull on workout clothes.

If my mind was going to start the day with Alex, I needed to turn it into something useful.

The pool was quiet—still, reflective, the way she liked it. I slipped in and pushed through lap after lap, letting the cool water drag the tension out of my muscles. For a few minutes, it almost worked. The rhythm gave me something steady to hold on to. I lifted my face from the water, took a breath, and rested my forearms on the pool edge.

"Why am I doing all her routines," I muttered under my breath. "She does all this to quiet her mind and it's clearly not helping her."

I hoisted myself out of the pool and sat on the edge, working a knot out of my calf. Part of me wanted to believe that following her habits might bring me some answers...get in her head a little. Another part knew it was ridiculous. When it came to Alex, nothing seemed to help either one of us, and getting into her head was probably not a sane idea.

Moving to the hot tub was a great idea, however. I eased into the heat, closing my eyes as the jets worked at my muscles. For a moment, I let myself try to focus on work, on the day ahead—on anything other than the fact that in a few hours, I'd be seeing her again.

After showering and heading into the office, I stopped at Amelia's desk to check in.

She looked up quickly, sliding her cell phone into her drawer with a smile she tried to hide, but I saw it.

"Good message, I'm assuming?" I asked, leaning on the desk.

The smile disappeared. She gave me a glare sharp enough to cut glass. "It's none of your business."

I pushed away with my hands lifted. "Alright. Noted."

She didn't respond—just handed me a stack of messages and pointed to her screen. "I emailed your schedule. Ms. Kennedy is at two o'clock."

I let out a slow breath. "Got it."

I made it to my office without shutting the door too hard. I wasn't sure why Amelia was acting irritated, but it felt like everyone was on edge lately, myself included. I opened my calendar, scanning the day's appointments, when the door flew open so hard it bounced off the stopper.

Harrison strode in, shut the door behind him, and dropped into the chair across from me without saying a word. He just stared—evaluating, waiting.

After a long minute, I frowned. "Can I help you?"

He continued his silent assessment, elbows on his knees, eyes narrowed.

"I'm checking your mood," he finally said. "I have a date tonight. I'd prefer not to get stuck here until midnight because you decide to lose it again."

I stared at him, unimpressed. "That's your concern?"

He shrugged. "You've been unpredictable lately."

"And you've been irritating since birth," I shot back, waving him toward the door. "Go. I'm fine."

He stood, still watching me like he wasn't convinced, but he didn't push further. He just opened the door, paused, and said, "Try not to make today a disaster."

I rolled my eyes and went back to my calendar, though my thoughts weren't on work—not really. Not with two o'clock coming.

Not with her coming.

"Glad you're feeling better." He tossed the words over his shoulder and flashed me a middle finger before he pulled the door shut.

I shook my head and picked up my phone.

"Hey Matt, we still on for one o'clock today?" I asked when he answered.

"Yeah," he said. "And I've got some good news about Burrow Township. And I know Grant's doing a great job, but we really need to see if we can get Alex back on this. She's got the time to focus on it, and the residents trust her."

He sounded hopeful, and it hit me again that I wasn't the only one missing her.

"I've got a meeting with her today about something business related," I said, rolling my pen between my fingers. "I'll see what I can do. Maybe reach out to Grant too—see if he can nudge her. She went to see them the other day, so she's getting there, I guess."

"I like that she's reaching out to you," he said.

I wasn't sure I deserved that much credit. It felt more like I'd forced the door open and she'd just not slammed it in my face.

"Well, she's keeping it strictly business," I admitted. "She asked for a favor. I don't actually know what it is yet."

"Baby steps then," he said. "We've been trying to get her over to the house to hang out with the kids. She never did that sleepover. The kids don't understand why she canceled or why she hasn't come back. They're too young for us to explain. But still—baby steps. She's making progress with the girls. With Abby pregnant, maybe that'll pull her in more."

His optimism seemed to help ease my worries.

"We can hope," I said. "But it's going to have to be on her terms, in her time. This court case isn't going to help. I'm supposed to get a call from the DA this week about possibly testifying if it goes to trial."

Maybe he'd let something slip—anything.

"Yeah, I heard," Matt replied. "I'm trying to steer clear of that topic since I'm part of her counsel. It's hard not to bring you into more, but we can't risk anything that might complicate the case, not with the political ties involved."

So much for inside information. I tapped the pen against my notepad, watching the ink point hover over my calendar.

"I get it," I said. "I'm not going to ask for anything you can't give. Just one thing—do you have a tentative start date?"

"Should be in about two weeks if he doesn't plead out."

I circled the rough date on my desk pad and set the pen down.

"Let's hope for the best," I said. "She doesn't need any more weight piled on top of what she's already carrying."

"Amen to that. I'll see you after lunch."

We hung up, and I called Amelia into my office.

She stepped in with her tablet in hand. "Yes?" Her tone was clipped, and she looked annoyed. I had no idea what I'd done, but I didn't have time to unravel that mystery.

"What's after my two o'clock?" I asked.

She checked her screen. "An update meeting on some local projects. Nothing to do with the zoning work. And your four o'clock rescheduled to tomorrow morning at ten."

So the rest of the afternoon was wide open. That could work in my favor if things went well with Alex.

"Amelia, reschedule the afternoon meeting and have them email the updates." I paused, watching her carefully. "Also, what are you doing for lunch today? Are we still on?"

I leaned back in my chair and held her gaze, making it clear I expected an answer that wasn't another dodge.

"Yes, we are," she said. "I'll send an email to take care of that three o'clock. I'll just order something in. Is there anything specific you want?"

I wasn't sure what I'd do without her, but I intended to figure out why she'd been acting off the past few days.

"Whatever's fine," I said. "And... thank you for putting up with me lately. I know I've been a lot to handle."

Her expression softened. "We'll get back on the same page." She gave a faint smile as she turned. "I'll meet you here for lunch."

She closed the door quietly behind her, and I let out a breath. Maybe some of her mood was my fault. Hard to blame her.

I cleaned up the notes on my desk and grabbed the folder for my next stop. I hated on-site meetings, but every so often I needed to walk a project myself to make sure everything was being done the way I expected. Today was one of those days. Stewart, the lead investor, wanted to go over the architect's plans for the renovation of the five-hundred-unit complex. Not exactly my favorite way to spend a morning, but necessary.

I headed out, already counting the hours until two o'clock.

***

ALEX

Fantastic. Red, puffy eyes staring back at me in the mirror like someone had swapped me with a Cabbage Patch doll that had been living in an attic for twenty years. I'd slept maybe three hours total. My head throbbed, my stomach rolled, and my face looked like it had given up on me entirely.

I splashed cold water onto my skin, hoping the shock would tame some of the swelling, grabbed my gym bag, and headed out. The pool stretches helped, but barely. My arms felt like I was dragging sacks of wet sand with every stroke. Yoga wasn't the peaceful reprieve I hoped for either—every pose trembled, burned, and reminded me how much wine I'd poured down my throat last night.

The sauna finally loosened the tight, aching knots the alcohol and dehydration had left behind. I sank back against the warm wooden slats, letting the dry heat draw it all out of me, sweat by sweat. I needed this. I needed something to push the nerves from my bloodstream before two o'clock.

The shower revived me enough to wrap myself in my robe and attempt an actual breakfast. Eggs. Water. Something nourishing.

As I ate, I considered calling Dr. King again. Maybe that was what I needed. Or maybe I should wait and see how my meeting with Bruce went. I didn't want to undo one person's help by introducing another's. But maybe... maybe they'd work together. Maybe they'd align. Or maybe I was overthinking all of it to death.

Probably that.

I cleaned up the kitchen and went to change, but instead I stretched across the bed, staring at the ceiling, mentally ticking down my schedule. Meeting with Roman at two. Training session at four. Bring clothes. Be prepared. Don't unravel.

I hated the idea of walking into his building dressed casually when everyone there looked like they stepped out of a high-end designer catalog. And yet... why did I care? Why did it still matter what I looked like around him? Around any of them?

I draped my arm over my forehead and exhaled. The meeting was coming whether I was ready or not. My heartbeat sped up just thinking about standing in front of him again.

God help me.

I slipped into a black fitted pantsuit, black heels, and my usual simple gold jewelry. Professional. Controlled. Untouchable, if I could manage it. Hopefully I'd keep this meeting strictly business and deflect any personal questions Roman might try to slide in—because after last night, I doubted he'd let things go easily.

My makeup did a decent job hiding the evidence of crying, and my hair—miraculously—looked cooperative. I flipped it back over my shoulder, studying myself in the mirror. I didn't look half as wrecked as I felt.

The unsettling part was that I had no plan this time. I was about to walk in there and say, "This kid needs a chance. I'm asking you to give him one." No slides. No presentation. Just a favor from a man who still had too much influence over my pulse. I wasn't sure if he would give me something out of goodwill, or if this would turn into the perfect opportunity for him to see what he could get out of it.

Bad idea. All of it.

I closed my eyes, took a long stabilizing breath, and reminded myself: This is for Darius. Not for you. Not for whatever gravitational pull exists between you and Roman King.

I wished I'd already started Bruce's stone-cold mental training—it felt like stepping into this meeting without armor.

Deep breath. Get out of the car. Get out of your head. Go. I forced the thoughts into action.

I walked from the garage to the elevator without engaging with a single person in the lobby. I didn't need polite smiles or curious looks. Amelia had emailed me instructions on bypassing reception; thank God, because my first encounter with those women was frosty enough to freeze lava.

The elevator chimed on an intermediate floor, making me jump. As the doors slid open, I spotted a familiar face—Harrison. My pulse thudded against my ribs. I instinctively stepped back, trying to blend into the wall, offering a cautious smile like maybe—just maybe—he'd pretend he didn't see me.

No such luck.

"Hey, Alex. What're you doing here? Come to give Roman more shit? If so, I'd prefer it if you didn't."

His tone wasn't cruel—just blunt, the way only a protective brother could sound. Still, the words hit harder than I wanted them to. What had Roman told him? My stomach dipped, both guilty and annoyed at myself for caring.

"Hi, Harrison," I managed, clasping my hands to keep them from fidgeting. "No. I'm just here to see if he has any job openings for a friend."

He gave a short, unimpressed snort.

"I hear you're jobless. Is it for you?"

I pressed my lips together to keep the smile from forming. It was actually funny, in a warped way, but I wasn't about to give him more ammunition. And despite his edge, something about his protectiveness felt... comforting. Like someone was guarding Roman's heart since I clearly hadn't.

"No," I said gently. "It's not me. I have enough to deal with without adding a job on top of everything."

I lowered my eyes, trying to steady myself as memories of my mother's funeral raced through my head.

The elevators soft hum in the silence that followed my admission brought me back to the space.

He shifted, leaning a shoulder against the wall. "Yeah... I'm sorry about your mom. I hope you're doing alright."

My eyes squeezed shut for a moment. The kindness in his voice cut deeper than the bite he'd thrown earlier.

I swallowed, opened my eyes, and nodded.

Inside, my pulse fluttered with nerves—the meeting upstairs waiting for me, Roman waiting for me, all of it pressing against my ribs like I'd stepped into a place full of old ghosts.

And I still had to walk straight into the heart of it.

"Thanks, Harrison."

He gave me a soft, sympathetic nod, one that lingered just long enough to make my throat tighten, before turning down the hallway in the opposite direction. He didn't look back. I watched him go for a second, absorbing the unexpected sting of that small dismissal, then turned toward Amelia's desk.

She was finishing a call when I approached, her posture straight, her tone polished... but the moment she hung up, her eyes flicked past my shoulder toward where Harrison had disappeared. Something guarded settled across her face.

"How did that ride go?" she asked, her voice quiet, genuinely concerned.

I rested both palms on the edge of her desk, head dipping as I stared down at my heels. "He doesn't seem too happy with me right now."

"Yeah," she murmured, "Roman's left him with a few extra tasks lately while he's been dealing with things..." She stopped short of elaborating.

My head snapped up. "How so? What things?"

***

ROMAN

As much as I don't enjoy coming to these job sites—the nails that always find their way into my tires, the hard hats that never fit right, the scaffolding, the dust—I can't deny how much I love the transformation. The before-and-after photos are the only thing that makes all this chaos worth it. This place, especially. A rundown apartment complex with a slumlord who ignored every leak, crack, and broken fixture as long as the rent checks kept coming.

At least we didn't have to relocate tenants before starting renovations. The building was in such disrepair that we could've condemned it, but underneath the neglect, the structure was solid. The foundation, the framing—everything that mattered—was still intact. That meant potential. That meant a chance to rebuild without wiping the slate clean.

Today was all about design review—seeing what the architects drew up and deciding where we needed to break ground first. I may have gone to school for architectural design, but I learned more on these sites than I ever did in a classroom. Standing in the grit and noise, watching real construction unfold—this was where the education happened.

I really needed to revisit the idea of a training facility at the office. If I could bring in talent from within instead of relying so heavily on subcontractors, it would streamline everything. Better consistency, fewer headaches, fewer unknowns. I'd have to talk to Amelia about setting up a meeting with my senior builders and architects. It might be time.

Charlie—my foreman, the only subcontractor I trust without reservation—stood with Stewart and me under the canopy the crew had put up. We unrolled the plans across the fold-out table, the edges pinned down with steel clamps to keep the wind from flipping them. The designs looked strong. Clean layout, efficient flow, realistic budget. Everything was on schedule, which meant I could head back to the office for lunch with Amelia... and mentally prepare myself for my meeting with Alex.

That weight had been sitting on my shoulders since sunrise.

When I returned, Amelia had set lunch up in the conference room. An hourglass sat in the center of the table, tall and narrow, sand already trickling down in a steady, quiet stream. I paused in the doorway and stared at it, eyebrows raised before I continued to my office. She didn't bother to acknowledge me.

I hung my suit jacket on the hook behind my office door, dropped my keys and phone on the desk, and ran a hand through my hair. I didn't want distractions. I needed clarity, and as much as I hated admitting it, Amelia was usually the one who helped me find it.

When I walked back into the conference room, I gestured toward the hourglass.

"What's this about?"

Her expression didn't change—not amused, not even annoyed.

"Well," she said, folding her hands, "this is a therapy session."

A therapy session?

I blinked at her, uncertain whether I should be confused or worried.

"And I'm expecting a raise." she announced. "You've got a list of issues we can't fit into a single hour, so I brought a timer."

I couldn't help it — I laughed as I dropped into the nearest chair.

"You know you're the best, don't you?"

She didn't miss a beat. "Yes. Now pay accordingly."

I ran through the conversation I'd had with Alex the night before — every jagged edge of it — and Amelia leaned back, assessing.

"For someone so tough on the outside," she said, "she's surprisingly fragile."

"She's scared of falling apart... or of taking me down with her, maybe." I searched into the depths of my mind for answers.

"Has she reached out to your mom?"

"Not that I know of. I told her she needed to."

Amelia paused, thinking hard. When she finally spoke, the question hit me square in the chest.

"Do you think it's a good idea to tell her she needs therapy?"

"It was only a suggestion." I rubbed the back of my neck, replaying my wording, trying to remember if I'd pushed too hard. "I wasn't trying to make her feel worse."

"Well, to someone in her state, it might sound like you're calling her crazy."

I'd made that mistake before.

"You really think so?" I murmured to myself, running through the list of reasons I thought professional help would actually benefit her.

"Hey there, daydreamer," Amelia poked at the device in the middle of the table sifting it's last bits of sand. "Time's almost up. You have a meeting at one."

I snapped out of my thoughts. "Sorry. I was just... thinking."

She lifted her brows. "Want to share?"

I shook my head. I wasn't giving her the satisfaction of being right. "Nope."

She laughed softly, and I helped her clear the table before heading back to my office to get ready for my one o'clock with Matt.

***

"Hey Matt, let's sit over there." I motioned toward the dark leather sofas, and we both settled into the cushions.

He started right in. "I want to talk about Burrow Township first. Grant's been helping us locate property in my district to relocate the residents. He's sent me a few homes, but I don't have the time to vet any of it... and neither does he. I'm worried we're not giving this everything we should. This is where I think we bring Alex back in. If she focuses on something meaningful, maybe it'll help her stay grounded and keep her mind off the case for a while."

"I'll bring it up when we meet today. She's asking me for a favor, so maybe she'll be willing to reciprocate if it doesn't involve anything personal."

Maybe distraction really was the only way back to her right now.

Matt tilted his head. "Roman... whether she knows it or not, everything she's doing still involves you. She's keeping you close even while she's pushing you away. Same with the girls—she didn't quit their classes. That isn't accidental."

"You might be onto something. She also had lunch with Amelia yesterday. Maybe subconsciously the people around me are enough for her right now... just not me directly." Except for this meeting.

Matt nodded. "Your mom's a psychologist, right?"

I huffed a laugh. If only I'd inherited that level of patience.

"Yeah. I've picked up the habit of analyzing people without meaning to."

"Seems like a useful skill where Alex is concerned."

"Except it's also unnerving. Trying to figure out what's going on in her mind is like walking blindfolded into traffic."

He smiled. "It's not just Alex. Maggie is one of the most stable people I know, and even I wouldn't want to crawl around inside her head. Don't make Alex the benchmark for complicated."

Comforting... or not. Hard to say.

I walked Matt to the elevator, feeling like I finally had some direction in how to approach this meeting. At five minutes till two, my phone buzzed.

HARRISON: *She's here. Just a heads up. Pull it together.*

ME: *Thanks. (middle finger emoji)*

I set my phone on the desk and braced a hand on the doorframe before opening it. The moment she came into view, everything in me tightened. She looked polished, composed... stunning in a way that didn't look like effort, just steady strength wrapped in a perfectly tailored suit.

For someone carrying so much, she wore her battles like armor—sleek, impenetrable, and deceptively calm. It struck me how easily she concealed the storm I knew was still inside her.

Stay professional, I warned myself—along with the rest of me that reacted on instinct the second she entered my line of sight.

"Ms. Kennedy, are you ready?"

She didn't even look at me. Just walked straight past, clipped heels tapping once on the hard floor before softening against the carpet inside my office. Her scent drifted after her—subtle, familiar—pulling every memory of her straight to the surface.

I couldn't help the faint smile that hit me. I shut the door behind us, steadying myself before this meeting turned into something it wasn't supposed to be.

Chapter 8

ALEX

I went straight to his mini fridge and grabbed a bottle of water, twisting the cap off like my life depended on it. Half of it was gone in three gulps—an attempt at cooling the nerves that were snapping through me like live wires. When I finally turned around, he was sitting on the edge of his desk, arms loose at his sides, that maddening smirk tugging at his mouth.

So much for the stoic, unflinching professional version of myself I *swore* I'd walk in here with.

"Sorry, I should've asked," I said, lifting what was left of the bottle in some awkward peace offering before taking another swallow.

He laughed—low, warm, and entirely too tempting. Even that sound had a way of sliding under my skin. Completely distracting.

"No, help yourself," he said. "It's not like you haven't been here before."

I know. And yet somehow it felt different—stranger, charged—like walking into the memory of a place instead of the place itself.

"It just feels... off," I admitted. "Like the first time, even though I know exactly where you keep everything. I probably should've asked if you wanted one while I was in there."

This was unraveling fast. My composure was leaking out of me like air from a balloon. And the way he was watching me was only making things worse.

He blinked away the intensity in his gaze long enough to say, "Why don't you have a seat, and we can get to it."

Get to it.

The words hit lower than they should have. An invisible current ran through me, hot and unsettling, and my palms grew damp around the bottle. Why was my body reacting like this? A few days ago, I couldn't breathe near him without flinching.

Now I couldn't breathe without wanting him.

I sat in the chair across from him, but we bumped lightly as he moved around his desk. Even that brief contact shot a shiver through me—sharp, uninvited—and it pooled low in my stomach before sinking deeper, sparking something I wasn't prepared for.

While I scrambled to get my thoughts in order and silence whatever part of me had just woken up, he cut straight in.

"What's the favor you came here to ask me?"

My breath caught. Because my mind offered the wrong answer first—wild, unfiltered, completely inappropriate. A flash of memory. A fantasy we'd joked about once. The desk. His hands. Mine.

Oh God. What was happening to me?

Heat pulsed under my skin, unmistakable and climbing fast. I lifted the bottle again just for something to hold onto. Roman's stare shifted—focused, knowing—and for a second, I wasn't sure who was feeling what first.

Was I reacting to him...
or was he reacting to me?

"Do you need me to turn the air down a bit?" he asked, amusement roughening his voice.

He was enjoying this while I was losing control.

I smiled and shook my head—there was no sense pretending this wasn't happening. Whatever was between us always had a way of announcing itself the moment we shared air.

"No, it's fine," I insisted, setting the bottle down before it slipped from my hands. "The favor is... I wanted to ask if you have an apprentice program."

The look on his face said everything. Shock, confusion—almost identical to Harrison's in the elevator. So I rushed to clarify.

"Not for me," I added quickly. "I know someone who wants to learn construction and building. I told him I'd talk to you."

I straightened in my chair, crossed my legs, and set both hands on my knees—mostly to keep them from fidgeting.

"As of right now, no," he said, still studying me. "But Amelia and I are putting a committee together to build exactly that—an in-house contractor program." Then he leaned forward slightly. "Who's the person you want me to consider?"

"Darius Jackson," I replied. "Ella's grandson."

His brows shot up. "The drug dealer?"

I raised a hand, dismissive. "Not a dealer. That was the police trying to stir things up. He was the one who stepped in when that kid pulled the knife on me."

Some of the tension in Roman's posture eased, though suspicion lingered in the crease of his brow.

"Well," he said, "what makes you think he'd be a good fit for my company?"

His tone had shifted—interview mode. And nothing turned me off faster than feeling interviewed, especially when he had the nerve to sit there sweeping his tongue across his bottom lip like he didn't know exactly what that did to me.

I locked my eyes on his—because his mouth was absolutely out of the question.

"He's a natural leader," I said. "Smart. Focused. And he lit up at the idea of real work—especially construction. It's hard to feel good about yourself when no one will give you a chance."

Roman didn't look away from me once, and the way his attention settled on me—direct, absorbing—making the air feel thicker and harder to pull into my lungs.

Finally, he stood. I exhaled as the connection broke, like someone had just untied a knot I didn't know I was holding. He walked to the window, stared out for a breath, then crossed to the fridge, grabbing a bottle of water, and tipped it back in the same way I had earlier.

The mirrored gesture almost made me laugh—until he crossed the room and sat on the edge of the desk right in front of me.

Too close.

My breath snagged. I looked away and subtly slid my chair back, creating just enough space to think.

But it didn't help.

I could still feel him—focused on me with that unspoken pull neither of us had ever learned how to control.

He looked intensely at me and said, "You're right. People do feel better about themselves when you give them a chance."

I knew that little jab was meant for me, but I pretended not to notice. My hands stayed clasped in my lap, and I kept my posture steady even though everything inside me was rattling.

"Mhm." I mumbled. "so does that mean you'll do it? Or at least consider it?" I asked, trying to sound grounded rather than winded by the energy rolling off him.

He nodded once and said, "Yes, on one condition..."

Here it comes, I thought. His inevitable attempt to get something from me in return. My pulse ticked faster, but I held my expression neutral.

"We'd like you to take over the relocation of the residents," he continued. "Grant can't handle it with everything else he's dealing with, and it's out of Matt's scope of knowledge. I met with Matt before this. He said they've located some possible properties, but they can't do much more than that."

I hadn't anticipated that. The request hit deep, tugging at the guilt I'd been carrying for leaving that neighborhood hanging. I drew in a slow breath.

"I'll do it. I'm in. I obviously have the time, and I think I've let everyone down enough." I pushed the words out before I lost my nerve. I didn't want to stay a second longer than necessary—not after the overwhelming intensity of yesterday and the way my body reacted the moment I stepped into his office today.

"I guess I should meet with Matt and Grant to see where I need to catch up," I added.

"That's a good place to start," he said simply.

Perfect. Good enough. I was almost out the door. I scooted to the edge of my chair and rose carefully, keeping distance between us like it might save my sanity.

"I have to get going. I have training in forty-five minutes, and I still need to change." I sidestepped him, slow and deliberate, avoiding even the faintest brush of contact. My heart was pounding too noticeably. If he felt it, if *I* felt *him*, I wasn't sure what would happen.

I thought I had made it. I thought I was going to escape unscathed—until he spoke again.

"Before you go..."

Shoot.

I froze mid-step, staring down at my hands—traitors trembling in full betrayal—before I forced myself to turn back toward him.

And then I saw the look on his face—the focus, the tension, the unmistakable pull—and my breath caught. He wasn't smirking now. He wasn't teasing. He was watching me the way he always used to when he was trying to read every breath I took—as if one shift in my expression might unlock the answers he couldn't stop reaching for.

My pulse thudded against my ribs. Heat crept up my neck, that same invisible pull stretching tight between us. The air felt heavier again, charged with something that never seemed to leave us alone no matter how hard I tried to outrun it.

Roman stepped forward, not enough to touch, but enough to feel. Enough that the faint trace of his cologne slid around me in this slow, familiar sweep that made my lungs work twice as hard.

"I need to ask you something," he said, his voice low and steady—far steadier than mine would've been. "And I want you to answer me honestly."

My throat tightened. Every warning bell in my head started ringing, but my heart—traitor that it was—leaned in anyway. It always did with him.

"What is it?" I asked, hoping the words didn't sound as thin as they felt.

He studied me, eyes tracing my face in, making my skin prickle with awareness. "You said something on the phone last night... something that didn't sound like you. I need to know if you meant it."

My stomach dropped. The wine-soaked confession. The self-loathing. The broken edges he wasn't supposed to hear.

I took a shaky breath, fingers curling into fists at my sides.

"Roman... I was emotional. And drunk. And exhausted. I wasn't thinking clearly."

He shook his head once, his gaze hitting me like a warm strike of pressure against my chest—intense, searching, impossible to hide from.

"You were thinking clearly," he said softly—but not quietly, not gently. "You were just letting yourself say what you've never allowed yourself to feel...out loud."

That invisible thread between us tightened another notch, drawing heat up the back of my neck and over my skin.

"Did you mean what you said about yourself?" he asked. "About not deserving anything good?"

My heart stuttered. My shoulders tensed. And every instinct in my body told me to run.

But he waited and the room felt too still to lie.

"Yes," I simply answered.

***

ROMAN

"Now I have a request." I crossed my arms and leaned back against the desk, legs extended, making it clear I wasn't moving to stop her. She kept her distance, that cautious few feet like it was the only thing holding her upright. The apprehension on her face was unmistakable—an uneasy smile, the kind that flickered and vanished.

"I'd like you to have dinner with me tonight," I said. "I'm not going to make excuses. I want to talk about us." My hands dropped to the edge of the desk, gripping it hard enough to keep myself anchored in place. If I stood, I knew I'd reach for her. "I'm being honest. I just want to talk."

She pressed her hand over her mouth and looked around the office, searching for an escape route that didn't exist. Her fingers started tapping the side of her leg—restless, uncertain.

"Training is over at 5:30..." She drifted into a ramble. "...then I need to take a shower and get ready. I don't know how I'm going to feel afterwards." She stared at the floor, picking at imaginary lint on her pants, then drew in a slow breath. "But I guess you can pick me up at seven, if that works?" She finally lifted her gaze, lashes framing eyes I'd been drowning in for weeks in photos on my phone. "I know I owe you at least a conversation."

Her voice softened at the end, barely holding together. It took everything in me not to close the distance and pull her in. But she'd said yes, and for now, that was enough.

"Thank you," I said quietly. "I'll pick you up at seven. I can just meet you at the valet?"

"That would be great," she agreed. "I'll see you then."

I walked her out to the elevator. She gave Amelia a quick smile and a small wave, and then the doors slid shut between us.

"So, how did it go?" Amelia asked as she stood and leaned over her desk.

"It was very productive. We all got what we wanted." All meaning me, Alex, Matt, and the entire Burrow Township community.

"How was it?" Harrison appeared at her side, bracing his forearm casually against the desk.

"It was good. She's going to help with the neighborhood. She also asked if I'd give someone a job. It fits exactly with what I mentioned earlier..." I shifted my attention to Amelia. "...about training people so we can start building an in-house team. We need to get that moving next week. Do I have anything else today?"

"No, that was the last one." She exhaled as if she'd been waiting for the day to end as badly as I had.

"Good. I don't have anything either. Let's go have a drink," Harrison suggested.

Not happening. I had a date to prepare for.

"I'm not in the mood to go out," I said, keeping it vague.

"Fine, then we go up to your place." Harrison turned toward Amelia. "You free right now?"

He winked. She immediately shook her head, eyes widening like she wanted to disappear under her desk.

"You are now," I declared, already heading toward the elevators.

"Looks like we're having happy hour at Roman's." Harrison said as he punched the button to call the elevator.

Amelia sighed, grabbed her things, and followed us into the elevator. I had never actually hung out with her socially. This was about to be... interesting.

Once inside the penthouse, I poured her a glass of white wine while Harrison uncorked the bourbon and grabbed a single glass from the cabinet.

"Pour me one too," I said as I handed Amelia her drink. "Not like it's my place or anything," I muttered.

Harrison grinned. Amelia smothered a laugh behind her glass as she took a seat on a stool at the kitchen island, keeping to herself.

"You're quiet... anything you need to tell me?" I asked.
She had a surprisingly guilty look on her face.

"Not that I know of... just didn't expect this today," she muttered.

Harrison chuckled as he handed me a bourbon neat, just the way I like it.

"Well, I'm not good with these weird awkward moments, so I'm just going to say it—"

Amelia practically shouted as she cut him off. "Um, yeah, there is actually something."

She shot a sharp look at Harrison before continuing. "Roman, you clearly haven't been yourself at the office, and I was wondering if you needed me to take on more responsibility as far as meetings go…"

I looked between the two of them, trying to figure out what this was.

"Also," she added quickly, "I'm going to need a list of names for everyone you want included in the meeting about the new training-contractors division."

Another pointed glance toward Harrison, who turned away to hide the smirk spreading across his face as he tossed back the rest of his bourbon. He walked to the bar laughing and poured himself another.

This was supposed to be happy hour. Why were we talking about work? Is that really all I know about Amelia?

And what on earth was going on between these two?

"Is that really what you want to talk about?" I asked. "What do you do when you're not working? I hope you're not spending your time at home worried about me. And Harrison—what were you about to say that set her off like that?"

Harrison was still laughing as he topped off Amelia's wine. He leaned toward her as if he might kiss her, and she pulled back immediately, shaking her head.

She glared at him. "Stop it."

Now I was fully confused.

"What Amelia would rather you not know—for some reason—is that she and I are dating…"

My eyebrows shot up.

No way.

I plopped down on the island stool and rested my chin on my hand in shock as Harrison continued. "I mean it's probably more embarrassing for her than me but you know I'm an open book and not one for hiding shit even at the office. Don't like to keep secrets. If I feel like kissing her or smacking her ass at the office I don't want you running to HR or something." Well I think the shock on my face is mimicking Amelia's right now. I was not expecting this, that's for sure.

Amelia's face flushed a bright red as she mumbled, "Sorry I didn't tell you about that, but unlike your brother I like to keep my private life private. And no, there won't be any PDA in the office." She was staring daggers at Harrison. She crossed her arms while holding her wine. I figure he's in deep shit right now.

I couldn't help but laugh. "I guess opposites really do attract." Harrison leaned in again to kiss Amelia's cheek and this time she didn't lean away. They actually looked really happy and good together despite her death stare.

"When did this happen?" It had to be something new. I sat up and patiently waited for the answer. She was looking to Harrison for confirmation.

"Six months ago." She said while looking at Harrison. *What? Seriously?*

"Are you kidding me? I'm that clueless? Harrison, why were you taking me out to bars trying to pick up women?" This just blows my mind.

"I wasn't. I was trying to get you laid. Caitlin really left you in a bad way." Caitlin is my ex-fiancé that the family apparently did an intervention on to get rid of for me. "Amelia was there, you just didn't see her. You either had your face buried in your phone or you were looking for *Ms Kennedy...* "He threw up air quotes. "...who I didn't know about yet." He glanced quickly to Amelia. I shook my head, thinking if I had known that's what all those nights out had been about, I would've never gone out with him. Not saying some of the women I met weren't worth the one night I spent with them, but no one really had the potential to go the distance until Alex. Now, I'm starting to rethink that as well.

"Yep, Amelia is right, you're an ass...!" He shoved me before I could finish. We all started laughing.

"She didn't call me that, jerk." He whined.

"Listen, you two, I have to get ready for dinner. I have a date." Amelia and Harrison both looked at each other a little worried.

Harrison grunted, "Don't you dare come back to work tomorrow with a *'headache'* thinking we're going to take all your meetings for you." I hope it doesn't come to that either.

***

ALEX

I walked into the MMA studio with no idea what I was signing up for, but I had a feeling Bruce was about to enlighten me. I changed in the locker room, then went over to the counter. He was still talking to a couple of attendees, all of them glancing my way. He tossed something at me. I caught it—a mouth guard, thankfully still in the package. Good. At least they weren't sharing those like the boxing gloves. I tore the plastic open.

He looked down at my feet and pointed toward the cubbies. "Shoes off."

I put them away and climbed into the ring. The mat was cool against my feet, coated in a faint layer of chalk that clung to my skin.

He glanced down again, eyebrows shooting up. "Seriously?"

"What?" I asked, already annoyed. I'd just had a pedicure. What could possibly be wrong?

"You really want to put those feet through this?"

"Put them through what?" I sat cross-legged and tucked my feet underneath me like a kid hiding contraband. "What's going to happen to them?"

He shrugged. "I don't know. They might not look like that afterward."

"I have an entire team of people who take excellent care of my feet," I told him, wiggling my toes at him. "So don't worry your pretty little head about it."

He laughed. I laughed. Ice officially broken.

For the first fifteen minutes, we sat and talked—expectations, goals, and the one thing he insisted on:

"No feelings. Just moves and counter moves."

I leaned back on my palms. "You know this court hearing is in two weeks. That gives me six days of training. It would take me a lifetime to control my emotions."

Especially the ones Tanner triggered. Just thinking about that courtroom rattled me. I knew exactly what I wanted to do to him, and none of it involved calm breathing or mindfulness.

Bruce laughed under his breath. "Then let's have those emotions without tying them to a person. Bring them back to movement. That's where your mind needs to live right now." He said as if he could see my thoughts.

As if anything could replace the image of Tanner. I closed my eyes anyway, staring up at the ceiling, trying to force him out of my head.

"I'm pretty sure my emotional scale has two settings: irritation and full-blown rage. So does that mean I only get two moves?"

He shook his head like he'd already accepted his fate.

"You're going to have to stop talking if you want to learn anything. Focus. Mimic."

Fair enough. I sat up and clapped my chalk-dusty hands. A little cloud drifted between us as we got started.

What I appreciated most was that he didn't hold back. He pushed me. It got me out of my own head. He taught me basic moves that demanded every ounce of my attention. Focusing on where my body needed to go was the only thing that kept my emotions from taking over.

Then he taught me a submission hold that was both terrifying and incredible—one where you could dislocate a shoulder and knock someone out if you held it long enough. He demonstrated it slowly, guiding my arm up and back. The stretch in the tendons lit me up, and panic spiked. He felt it instantly and let go.

When it was my turn, he called one of the other fighters into the ring. I practiced step by step, keeping everything slow. That move was going to need repetition. And maybe a volunteer. Or a victim. Honestly, at this point I wasn't picky.

If dinner with Roman went badly tonight, I already knew my test subject.

I rolled out of the ring and stretched my whole body like a cat, every muscle throbbing. I was already sore and fully expecting bruises by morning.

It was around six when I finally got home. I grabbed a glass of wine on my way to the shower and turned on some music. After rinsing off the sweat and chalk, I slipped into a pair of high-waisted khaki linen pants and a plain white tank. I pulled my hair into a ponytail and leaned into the mirror long enough to swipe on mascara and lip gloss. Good enough. I was too drained to care.

I took another sip of wine and slid my feet into flip-flops because bending down required strength I didn't have. At 6:45, I poured half a glass more and tried not to think about how stupid this dinner was. My phone buzzed—Roman, letting me know he was early.

Great. Butterflies and nausea at the same time. I tossed back the rest of my wine, grabbed my purse, and headed to valet.

The valet opened the car door while Roman stayed seated, staring straight ahead. When he finally turned to me, he smiled like he was hiding a laugh.

"Hi." He breathed.

The smell hit me before anything else—bourbon, warm and unmistakable. No wonder he didn't get out of the car. I suddenly wondered if I should be the one driving.

"Hi. Wow. What kind of bourbon were you drinking?" I asked, setting my purse on the floorboard and buckling my seatbelt.

"Why do you say that?"

"I can smell it on your breath."

He smirked with a wink. "Wanna taste?"

Oh, for God's sake. If he was drunk, this night was over. My body leaned away on instinct, arms crossing, shoulders flattening against the door. A different part of me—a reckless part—wondered what it would taste like off his tongue, but that wasn't the point.

"Do I need to drive?" I asked, pulling my arms in tight like I needed armor.

"No, I only had one. Heaven's Door. Very smooth—you'd like it." He leaned back casually.

I probably would like it. Especially if I tasted it from his mouth. I shook that visual out of my head before it ruined me.

"Where are we going?" I turned forward again, needing to break the tension.

"Somewhere casual. Hope that's fine."

He wore jeans hugging those ridiculous thighs and a fitted tee stretched across his chest. Absolutely zero help for my concentration.

He drove us to a restaurant on the river. The hostess led us to a covered deck overlooking the dark water, our table tucked away in the back corner, isolated. Perfect. Or dangerous. Hard to tell.

The server came over.

"I'll take a Tito's and soda with a lime. Tall. Double," I said. "...Please."

My shoulders dropped like I'd been holding my breath for an hour. The anxiety stayed lodged in my chest.

Roman's eyes widened a little, and he told the server, still watching me, "I'll have your best-selling IPA on draft."

The server glanced between us with something like concern. She wasn't wrong. This could go nuclear.

I lifted the menu high enough to break the connection between us. Roman groaned.

"Can you put that down and look at me for a minute?"

I could've sworn I moaned under my breath. When I finally lowered the menu—after deciding on fish tacos with tater tots—I set it down and crossed my arms on top of it.

"That's better. I don't want to talk to a menu," he said, clearly frustrated.

The moment our drinks arrived, I took a long pull from the straw, letting vodka settle the shake under my skin.

He started.

"First, thanks for coming."

I bit my lip, searching for the least complicated answer. "You're welcome. I feel like I owe you this much, I guess."

I pushed back in my chair, crossing my arms again, holding my drink like a shield while bracing for whatever he was about to unload.

"You don't owe me anything. I just figured you might want to. Just three weeks ago we were 'in love,' and then suddenly you weren't because you thought I attacked you."

My arms dropped as he crossed his, and I set my drink on the table. This defensiveness—his and mine—was suffocating. I leaned in closer so I wouldn't have to raise my voice. I didn't need an audience for this train wreck.

"When did I say I didn't love you?" I whispered. "That was never the problem."

"Then I just don't fucking get it, I guess," Roman shot back. "You know I didn't do this, and you say you love me, but you don't want me? Please explain that, Alex." His voice edged above normal volume, and I immediately scanned the tables around us. "What am I not getting here?" He threw his hands up, exasperated.

Since when did he become so combative?

"I don't know what the drugs did to me, Roman," I hissed under my breath, trying to keep this from turning into tonight's entertainment for the restaurant. "It's been especially difficult because of all this empathic shit you threw at me. I really don't think I can focus on us right now—or any relationship for that matter. I don't know how long it'll take me to figure it out." I tried to slow myself down, keep the momentum from rolling me straight into tears. "Right now, I'm focused on the court case. I'm working on controlling my emotions around that, and I can't do both."

My pulse kicked. My throat tightened. The vodka wasn't helping anymore.

"Bruce is helping me," I added, quieter and calmer now. "It's kind of like meditative fighting. And I'm planning on calling your mother tomorrow..." I hesitated, watching him. "I need to start seeing her again. If you can really keep your distance—like you said."

He stared at me, lips parted, stunned. Caught completely off guard.

"Why couldn't you just tell me that?" His voice dropped but the edge remained. "Why can't I be in your life to help you through it? And what do you mean Bruce is teaching you meditative fighting? I thought you were taking self-defense and kickboxing?"

"There's so much confusion in my head," I said, and the words scraped up my throat. "I still see you in my dreams as the one attacking me. Sometimes it's Tanner, but sometimes it's you."

He leaned forward, shoulders tight and jaw locked, clasping his hands on the table like he was trying to keep himself from exploding. The agitation came off him in waves—sharp, hot, impossible to ignore.

"Alex, you know there's nothing I can do about that?" His voice tightened, irritation rising by the second. This drink had to be a triple, or his empathic energy was hitting me full force. My insides shook under the weight of it—his agitation vibrating straight into my bloodstream.

I exhaled hard, trying to get him to come down from whatever cliff he was climbing. "Look, I'm just worried I won't be able to focus on this case. Bruce is teaching me MMA-style fighting—private lessons."

"You're going to be an MMA fighter? Don't you think that's a little overboard for self-defense?"

Of course he wouldn't understand.

"No, I don't." My volume jumped without my permission. I threw my hands up, and when I crossed my legs, my knee slammed into the table, nearly knocking over my drink. The sharp sting shot up my thigh. "God." I rubbed the spot, both irritated and embarrassed.

"Alex, look—I'm sorry. I shouldn't be yelling, and if this is what you need to do, then fine. But can we please talk about this?" He lowered his voice, but the strain was still there. "Cutting me out of your life isn't going to change anything you're dealing with."

Heat rose under my skin—anger, sadness, fear, the alcohol, all of it twisting together. His irritation was bleeding into me, and mine right back into him. This was exactly the emotional crossfire I'd been afraid of.

Then—thank God—the waitress appeared with our food, breaking the tension long enough for me to shut my mouth before something reckless slipped out. I didn't answer him. Didn't trust myself to.

I was starving, so we ate in silence. Forks scraping, glasses shifting, the deck creaking under distant footsteps—every sound felt magnified, sharp. I ordered one more drink, even though I already knew it was a terrible idea. He ordered water while looking right at me, straight through me, his gaze heavy enough to pin me to my seat.

Apparently, I was determined to follow this bad decision all the way down tonight.

***

ROMAN

"So... is that it?" I leaned back in my chair, the hollow question lingering between us. "Is there no hope, no future for us?" I finished the rest of my beer, set the bottle down harder than I meant to, and reached for water instead. She was clearly self-medicating; one of us needed a clear head.

"Roman, I don't know..." Her voice was calmer after getting food in her, and she took a normal sip of her drink instead of inhaling it. "I can only tell you where I am right now. I'm not capable of an 'us.' I'm not good at predicting the future, so I don't want to give anyone false hope. Nothing's changed about how I feel. The confusion is still so prominent." She buried her face in her hands and shook her head like she was trying to shake herself awake.

That was enough. I flagged the server down and paid the bill immediately.

"I'm ready to leave. Let's go."

She tossed back the last of her drink and stood, wobbly on her feet from the ridiculous amount of vodka she'd downed. Instinct took over—I grabbed her hand without thinking. I glanced at her, waiting for her to pull away. She didn't. So I kept walking, guiding her to the car because she clearly needed it.

When we got inside, I asked, "Your place or mine? I'm staying with you tonight regardless of which one you choose. Maybe I'm a glutton for punishment, but you're drunk and I'm not leaving you alone."

She scoffed like I'd said something absurd. "This is the stupidest shit I've ever heard in my life. We're not together anymore. Y-y-you s-s-sound c-c-crazy, like a s-s-stalker." She threw her hands up, smacked her knuckles on the roof, and burst into a slurred laugh. "Ouch."

I huffed out a laugh of my own. Hell, I was a stalker at this point. That's exactly what she'd driven me to.

If people could see the headlines now:

HEAD OF KING CONSTRUCTION PATHETICALLY STALKS WOMAN WHO REPEATEDLY TELLS HIM TO FUCK OFF!!!

"You still haven't told me where we're going," I said. "If you don't answer, I'm going to pick one myself."

She stared straight ahead, clearly trying to think hard through the haze of vodka and exhaustion.

And I waited, the engine idling, my patience hanging on by a thread—but still hanging on.

"Fine, your place."

Thank God. Her hands dropped to her thighs, and I couldn't help the small smile tugging at my mouth. I'd missed her dramatics more than I'd admit out loud. And right now she was so unsteady, so wound up, it made me want to anchor her. This mess was partially my fault—at least that's how it felt.

"Alex," I said softly, turning her face toward me with both hands so she'd actually look at me. Her skin was warm under my palms, flushed from vodka and emotion. "My feelings for you haven't changed either. I still love you. I'll feel the same tomorrow and the next day and every day after that."

I meant it. Every syllable. Maybe if she saw it in my eyes—really saw it—something would break open in her. Maybe she'd remember. Maybe she'd say it back.

Instead she muttered, "And I thought I had issues," and rolled her eyes like I'd just confessed to being a cult leader.

I huffed out a laugh because... well, fair. I didn't have issues until I met her.

After I parked, we made our way to the elevator. And then something shifted—so sharp and sudden I felt it in my chest. The air between us changed, charged, as though the whole room inhaled along with us.

Before I could figure it out, the elevator doors opened and she shoved me inside with surprising strength, pinning me against the glass wall. Hard. Her hand landed near my shoulder, her body angled toward mine—not seductive, not playful, but full of tangled emotion that wasn't aimed at me but still hit me dead-on.

"Alex," I said carefully, raising both hands in surrender to show I wasn't a threat. "I need to press the elevator buttons."

She froze. Blinked. Her expression slipped from anger to confusion, same as at the restaurant—like she'd lost the thread of her own reaction and was trying to claw it back.

She stepped away. I keyed in the code and stood beside her—not too close, not too far—because I had no idea what the hell kind of fighting Bruce had been drilling into her, and I wasn't keen on becoming a practice dummy.

When the doors opened, I stepped aside and motioned her forward. She walked in slowly, arms wrapped around her torso, holding herself together like she was keeping something from spilling out.

"Would you like some water?" I grabbed two bottles from the fridge and set them on the counter, watching her carefully.

"No," she murmured. "I think I just want to go to sleep."

Her uneasiness still lingered in the air, but for the first time in weeks a strange, heavy relief settled in me. She was here. Safe. I knew exactly where she was tonight, and that felt like oxygen.

"I'll take you to the guest room," I said gently. "There's an extra toothbrush in the bathroom. Towels too, if you want to shower."

I walked her down the hall and opened the door for her. She stepped inside, small, exhausted, fragile in a way she'd never let anyone see if she were sober.

"Thank you," she whispered.

I nodded once, kept the rest of the words I wanted to say lodged in my throat, and shut the door before I could make any more demands of her tonight.

I stood there a moment, listening—just long enough to see the light go out under the door. When it did, I exhaled, pushed off the wall, and walked back to the living room.

Now came the part where I had to sit with my own tangled thoughts and decisions.

Because as much as I wanted her here... I had no idea what she'd feel when she woke up, hungover and disoriented, in a place that wasn't familiar anymore.

And that worried me more than anything.

I made a bourbon and sank into my oversized black chair, the one that always fit my body like it was built for me alone. I let my head fall back. My arms draped over the armrests, the cool glass resting loosely in my hand. The silence in the penthouse settling around me. It gave me room to sit with everything I'd just done.

The bourbon's warmth slid down my throat, but it didn't quiet the worry circling in my chest.

I couldn't take her home. Not like that. Not when she could barely stand, barely think or hold her own emotions together. Leaving her alone would've kept me up all night wondering if she slipped in the shower, or cried herself into another panic attack, or drank until the world spun out from under her.

But now I had a different problem—one waiting behind a closed guest room door.

How was I supposed to handle tomorrow morning? How would she react when she woke up here— reminded of every emotional blow we traded tonight?

She could walk out without a word.

She could snap.

She could shut down.

She could shut me out for good.

And I'd have no one to blame but myself.

I took another slow sip. I'd made the choice I could live with—the one where she was safe.

Chapter 9

ALEX

O h my God—what kind of dream is this?

Pain and pleasure?

I'm making love to Roman in my dreams again, and honestly... it's always the best. But why does my body hurt so bad? And my head? Dreams aren't supposed to come with physical pain, are they?

I try to stay focused on the good parts, the familiar warmth of him, and I actually moan out loud.

"Good morning."

His deep voice hums through the dream, slow and sexy—so clear it's like he's right beside me. The dream feels so real... and then I feel actual hands cupped over my breasts.

Wait.

I can feel that.

My eyes fly open and dart downward—strong arms are wrapped around me. Real arms. Real warmth. Real Roman.

I squeak—completely involuntary—and panic shoots through me. My anxiety spikes, my muscles ache everywhere, and the soreness makes me fear the worst. I wiggle out of his hold instinctively, and he releases me, giving me space.

"Good morning," he repeats, and the vibration of his voice is somehow soothing, even though my pulse is hammering in my throat. I swallow and close my eyes, breathing deep. I can handle this, I tell myself. I can. I've survived worse.

"Good morning," I mumble back, mostly to myself. My hair hurts. My skull hurts. My dignity hurts. Everything hurts.

I force a smile—even though he can't see my face—and then something clicks.

We're both naked.

I'm on the edge of a full-blown meltdown.

I whip my eyes open and look around wildly, heart racing—

And realize the truth all at once:

It was just a dream.

A damn vivid dream.

I'm alone.

Fully dressed.

And lying in a beautifully made bed that absolutely does not belong to me.

So where the hell am I?

I got up and circled around the bed, spotting my shoes beside my purse while I tried to piece together what happened after we left the restaurant. Wait—I *did* go to dinner with Roman last night. And I definitely over-indulged. I'd only meant to take the edge off, not get completely wrecked.

My eyes moved around the room. The black-and-white decor clicked instantly. One of Roman's guest rooms.

Great. Perfect. Exactly what my anxiety needed.

I wandered into the bathroom and turned on the shower, letting the steam fog the mirror while I tried to slow my breathing. I didn't have a dream about Tanner last night—not one. The only dream I had was Roman. That has to mean something... *right?*

"God, how did this happen?"

A knock at the bathroom door froze me in place.

"Alex..." Roman's voice murmured through the wood.

I held my breath and stayed silent, hoping he'd take the hint and walk away.

"Honey, I brought you a T-shirt and some sweatpants, and a bottle of water—and something for a headache if you have one. Clothes are on the bed. Water and pills are on the table."

Silence followed, and I finally exhaled.

I really need to talk to someone about this... all of this.

I slipped into the clothes he left out. I was swimming in them, but they were soft and warm and unmistakably him. The scent hit me immediately. I gripped the fabric tighter around my torso, trying to steady the chaos within.

I took the Advil with the water, brushed my teeth, ran my fingers through my hair, and forced myself toward the living room.

Time to talk about whatever happened last night.

If I can get the words out at all.

***

ROMAN

Breakfast sounded like a good idea. I pulled out the ingredients for pancakes.

She walked out with a sheepish grin I caught from the corner of my eye, then headed straight for the sofa and collapsed face-down. My instinct to touch her, reassure her, steady her—it was all immediate. I walked over and eased down beside her.

"What happened last night?" she groaned into the pillow.

"Nothing," I said softly. "You got drunk, and I didn't want to leave you alone." I brushed my hair back and waited for her to lift her head, hoping she'd feel safe enough to talk.

"Really?" She pushed herself up, confusion all over her face.

"Alex," I said steadily, "do you honestly think I would ever take advantage of you in the state you were in?"

Her eyes wavered. "Roman, I still don't know..."

"Still don't know what?" I asked, feeling my frustration coil tight in my chest. "Still don't know if it was me or Tanner? Somehow, I don't think that's true anymore."

I shouldn't have said it—not like that. But our history, everything we've been to each other... it's impossible not to push just a little, hoping she'll finally see it.

She stood abruptly and brushed past me, heading for the kitchen.

"What's for breakfast?" she muttered, glancing at me quickly before bending over the marble island, palms pressed to the cool stone.

I followed her, placing my hands on the counter on either side of her. Her breath hitched the moment I leaned close.

"Blueberry pancakes, Alex," I whispered into her ear. I let her name drift out on my breath, then let my lips graze the warm skin at her neck. Her soft gasp shot straight through me. I steadied myself, placed a chaste kiss on her cheek, then moved around to the stove before I lost every shred of restraint.

"Do you need to go to the gym?" I asked as I plated the pancakes, trying to keep things level, normal. "It's kinda late for you, isn't it?"

"I may go later to swim or just sit in the sauna." She was still talking to the counter instead of me.

"Do you want to stay here?" I offered gently. "The hot tub would help your muscles."

Her face tightened in uncertainty. I knew I was pushing again, but I couldn't seem to stop. I set her plate in front of her, turned to refill my coffee, and finally grabbed food for myself.

"I don't have any clothes," she said. "I'd at least need to go home and change."

This is both good and surprising. I wish I didn't have to work today but I could come up for lunch. Maybe she can stay another night. I don't want to push my luck any further, but, fuck, who am I kidding? I wanted to go to sleep and wake up next to this woman every day. *I'm going to fuck this up.*

***

ALEX

Sexy as hell—and he can cook.

I peered up at him, watching the way he moved around the kitchen with effortless confidence, and the thought hit me like it always does— how stupid it feels not wanting to be with a man like this. Except that's not even the truth. Wanting him isn't the issue. Wanting him is easy. It's everything that happens after the wanting that terrifies me.

I keep waiting for the shift...the snap...the moment everything slides back into fear and confusion again. One good dream shouldn't feel like a miracle, but it does. I should take it as a win, but what if it changes tomorrow? What if I wake up and see Tanner's face again instead of Roman's? What if all of this progress evaporates the second I'm relaxed enough to believe in it?

Agreeing to stay here tonight is probably a terrible decision. Why am I doing this to him—to myself?

But then the other voice—the stubborn, hopeful one—whispers: One more day won't hurt. One more day might actually help.

Maybe seeing him in small doses like this, without the chaos, without alcohol, without fear bleeding into every thought... maybe that's what I need. Maybe this is helping. Isn't it?

I exhaled slowly, sinking into the thought.

Tomorrow is another MMA session, then a night out with the work crew. A normal night. A real night. I don't know if I'm fully ready for the club scene— even thinking about it makes my stomach flicker—but I need my friends. I need something that doesn't revolve around trauma or therapy or Roman.

Just Shay and the boys. That's it.

I haven't been to this place in months. Mostly because my ex spends too much time there, and since Matt and Jack won't even talk to him anymore, I'd have no warning if he happened to show up. The thought of running into him unexpectedly makes my nerves crawl, which is ridiculous because he's not dangerous. He's just... part of an old life I'm trying to bury.

Still...

My chest tightens at the idea.

Tomorrow will be fine. It has to be.

Tonight...

Tonight I just need to survive my own heart without letting it rewrite history.

As soon as Roman went to shower and get dressed, I used his absence to clean the kitchen—anything to pull my mind away from the gut-twisting memory of my ex.

My phone buzzed.

One glance and I nearly dropped it.

You've got to be kidding me?

No. Absolutely not.

Please tell me my empathic connection hasn't expanded to include that asshole too.

Delete. delete. delete—

LUKE: *"Hey gorgeous. How are you? Your family wouldn't let me see you at the hospital."*

ME: *"Can you blame them?"*

LUKE: *"I was hoping we could talk."*

Oh no. No more talking.

Not to him.

Honestly? Not even to Roman at the moment.

ME: *"Nope, not a good idea. Doubt there will ever be enough time behind me to talk to you again."*

LUKE: *"Alex, that's not very nice. It sounds like you could use someone to take care of you. Heard you quit your job. You're not homeless or anything are you? I'd hate to see you living on the street because you lost your mind over this."*

ME: *"Bye Luke."*

I threw my phone toward my purse with a muted grunt and clenched my fists so tightly my nails bit into my palms. I squeezed my eyes shut, breathing through the heat rising beneath my skin.

I opened them slowly—just in time to see Roman walking toward me from the hallway.

Oh, God.

That man.

A smile broke across my face before I could stop it, warmth sweeping through my chest in a way I couldn't fight even if I wanted to. My gaze traveled over him instinctively—his tall, lean, powerful body wrapped in a perfectly tailored suit, the restraint in every line of him, that faint five o'clock shadow that made him look like temptation incarnate.

My head tilted.

My tongue swept across my top lip.

And I realized I was staring when he cleared his throat, the sound vibrating through the room and straight down my spine.

"What's wrong? Why did you just throw your phone?"

His dazzling smile locked onto me, and whatever answer I had evaporated. My brain went blank.

"I'm sorry... what?"

Great. This was going to be a long day.

"Just wondering if your phone did something."

He pointed to where it lay on top of my purse. Luke's name flashed through my mind again, souring everything.

"It was my ex."

The sigh that slipped out of me felt like surrender.

"What was your ex?"

I couldn't tell if he was being playful or genuinely confused.

"My ex texted. He wants to talk."

He smiled, but it didn't reach his eyes. His head tipped in a polite little nod, but the tension around his mouth gave him away.

"Oh."

Just that. No questions. No probing. It surprised me.

"Okay, well... I guess I'm ready." I forced a breath into my lungs. "It'll only take me a minute to grab some things. Are you sure I can't just get an Uber and drive myself back?"

I hated not having my car. I liked having control—always needing an escape route.

"I actually like this little bit of control you're allowing me to have."

He said it gently, with a warmth that wrapped around the edges of his tone. "It makes me feel good to take care of you. And I know you can take care of yourself—trust me. It's just a guy thing. Or... my thing."

He said control.

My stomach knotted.

Luke had said the same thing more times than I could count.

Was it genuinely protective?

Or manipulation disguised as care?

I was glad Roman didn't push the topic of Luke. That would've been torture. And truthfully... being treated this sweetly felt good. Too good. That was the problem.

I didn't know how to let myself enjoy it without wondering if it was softening me at the exact moment I needed to be hardened. Focused. Ready.

I needed to stay sharp.

Anger and frustration were the only reliable fuel I had to keep my head in this case—keep Tanner exactly where he belonged.

His brother could pull strings for him. I knew it. And every part of me was bracing for that possibility.

If I let myself get tangled up in this fragile, hopeful thing with Roman again, I could lose sight of everything. And I couldn't afford it.

So today...

Today I would torture myself a little. Lean into the frustration. Use it.

Because if I let my heart soften, even for a moment, everything could collapse.

***

ROMAN

It took a lot of self-control not to ask her what her ex had texted. From everything I'd heard—from her and her family—that guy was trouble. The last thing I needed was more anger slipping through. The way she'd reacted last night was already concerning.

We pulled into her valet and she ran inside to grab a few things. While I waited, all I could think about was where everything had gone wrong. If Tanner had never laid a hand on her, things between us would've been solid. No question. The thought of what he'd done to her made my jaw tighten. I smacked the steering wheel and shoved a hand through my hair, trying to stop the rush of it. I was just grateful she was giving me any time at all.

My phone rang.

"Hey, you up yet?" Harrison sounded way too cheerful.

"Yeah. Why?"

"Just checking to see if you need aspirin."

Of course. He thought he was hilarious.

"Nope. I had breakfast this morning."

"Did you now? How many times did you have breakfast?"

Absolutely not doing this with him.

"Blueberry pancakes, Harry."

He groaned. "You're so boring lately. You used to be more forthcoming. Alex ruined our brotherly date recaps. Now I get nothing."

Right then she opened the passenger door. I raised my brows at her while she tried not to smile.

She leaned toward my phone. "Hi, Harrison."

For a moment, the car went still—me and Alex staring at each other like neither of us knew how to look away.

"Well," Harrison said, "this is a surprise. Is this a carryover from last night?"

She hit mute and whispered, "Can we not get him involved? He already has a problem with the way I'm treating you." She emphasized it with air quotes.

I unmuted. "I'll call you later."

He said goodbye, and I hung up.

She was still wound tight; it was written all over her.

"He's not the only one," I told her quietly.

Her shoulders tensed. "Maybe I should just stay home."

She reached for the door handle, and instinct took over—I caught her hand before she could pull away.

"Nope. You're mine today. If I only get today, I'm going to cherish every moment." I lifted her hand to my mouth and pressed a soft kiss to her knuckles before letting go.

"You'll be at work all day, so that's not too many moments." She clasped her hands in her lap, rubbing her thumb over the spot where I'd kissed her. I noticed every second of it.

True. But I wasn't settling for just today. I could feel the shift happening between us, and I wasn't about to let it fade.

"Then you owe me time tomorrow, too." I kept my tone easy, a hint of a smile tugging at the corner of my mouth as I looked at her sideways.

"Sorry, I'm busy tomorrow. I have training and then I'm going out with Shay and the boys." Her voice had a nervous edge to it.

Good. She was getting back into her routine. But that didn't stop the pang of irritation that came with knowing she'd be out without me.

"Where?"

She rolled her eyes and stared out the window. "It's not your scene."

A bar. Had to be. Definitely not Sebastian's after what happened there with Tanner. Still, I wasn't dropping it.

"Try me." I smiled.

"Dejavu." She looked back at me with a smirk.

Of course. The loudest, most chaotic club in the city. I hated that place. Harrison loved it. I made a mental note to see if he and Amelia would go.

"Love that place." I lied without blinking.

She rolled her eyes again—this time with full irritation. I hated that version of the eye roll. Loved the other one...the one she gave me when she wasn't doing much thinking at all.

"Is that right?" she asked, annoyed.

"Yes. Do I have anything to worry about if I go?"

"Like what?"

There it was—another eye roll. I bit my tongue to keep from commenting on it.

"Like some random guy putting his hands on you?"

The second it left my mouth, I knew I shouldn't have said it—not after everything she'd been through.

"I hope that doesn't happen."

Her expression dropped, and the regret hit hard. If I went to that club and saw anyone touch her—dancing or not—it would be a disaster. I'd need Harrison there just to keep me from doing something stupid. This entire situation was starting to feel like a bad idea for both of us.

At least now I knew who her friends were.

"Your friends seem nice. I met them the other day at the office. Shay's a sweet girl who cares a lot about you."

I was clinging to the subject change like a life raft. Talking about the incident wasn't something I wanted to revisit.

"Shay's the best," she said warmly. "I look forward to getting back in the office again and working with her. Especially on the Burrow Township Relocation Project."

"I think they'll all appreciate that."

Good. Her friends kept her grounded. I'd take note of that.

We rode the elevator up to the penthouse, and I said, "I'll meet you in the lobby at noon. We'll go out for lunch, so you don't think I've locked you in the tower."

She giggled, and I pulled her in, kissing her cheek as the doors opened. I gave her a light tap on the rear as she stepped out. She shot me her most irritated look... then smiled as the doors slid shut.

Progress.

Chapter 10

ALEX

Well, him announcing he's going to show up on my night out takes the relaxation right out of it. What is with him? He's more into self-torture than I am. At least that'll give me plenty of frustration to work off when he inevitably annoys me at the club, but I didn't factor in all the strangers I'll be worried about. People I don't know. People who could hurt me.

Whatever. That's tomorrow. Today, I need to focus.

First step: get to the gym and sweat the alcohol out of my system—and shake off that irritating text from my ex.

The gym was more relaxing than I expected after what I put my body through yesterday. I did some cardio on the treadmill, swam laps, and then soaked in the hot tub. Roman was right about one thing: this hot tub is magic. It melted the tension right out of my muscles. I stretched my arms across the edge, leaned my head back, and tried to sort through everything sitting heavy on my mind—the court hearing, the evidence, what I'm up against.

I've spent days digging through old cases online, trying to understand the reality of what Tanner could actually be charged with. And the more I learn, the more it makes my stomach twist. The police and my attorneys keep telling me the same thing: nothing is guaranteed. Not even if he's found guilty. I'm not considered a credible witness because I couldn't identify my attacker, and because I thought it was someone else. Roman, to be exact. The man I love.

Two weeks of obsessing over every detail, every possible outcome, every angle—and one truth keeps rising to the surface: I'm not learning MMA for self-control. Self-control is just a side effect. I'm learning MMA because I need a way to make sure Tanner gets exactly what he deserves.

And there's only one plan that works.

It has to be executed perfectly.

No one is going to allow me to just step into a ring with Tanner, not with everything going on.

So I'm going to need help. Someone willing to make this happen. And the rest of the plan requires getting my attorneys to set it up.

That part might cost me more than money.

After the gym, I let Roman's shower work its magic on me. I mean... honestly, would this life really be so bad?

And there it is—focus gone again.

Get your head out of the clouds, Alex. You've got things to do.

First call: Grant. I need to get back in the office and actually help him. I've dumped so much on his shoulders, and the guilt hit me the second his name flashed across my screen. He picked up immediately.

"Alex, good morning, honey. What can I do for you?"

The warmth in his voice went straight through me. I missed him—missed being able to spill my guts and get either incredible advice or a compassionate scolding. I flopped down on the leather sofa, kicked my feet up, and tucked one arm behind my head like a pillow.

"Hey, Grant. I think the real question is: what can I do for you?"

"Oh yeah? What's going on?"

"I hear you need help with a relocation project."

"Well, you'd be correct. Anything else you think you could help with?"

I sighed, already knowing the answer. I could feel the office tugging me back.

"As a matter of fact... yeah. I think it's time to get back in there. But I'd like to sit down with you and Matt Stevens and get fully updated. Can we schedule that?"

I dragged myself upright and pushed my hair out of my face.

"Would you like me to transfer you to your assistant and let her check your schedule?" he asked, sounding way too cheerful.

Oh right. I hired Shay to be my assistant—right before everything in my life went sideways.

"Yes, I would love that. And Grant... thank you for not writing me off."
I got up and started pacing, nerves firing in a slow, irritating wave.

"I could never do that. I knew you'd figure it out somehow."
I wish I could believe that as easily as he did.

He disconnected as the call transferred to Shay's desk.

"Grant Johnson's office." Shay's bright chirp made me smile before I could help it.

"How about we start answering with 'Alex Kennedy's office' from now on?"

I had to yank the phone away from my ear as her high-pitched shriek stabbed straight through the speaker.

"Are you serious? Why didn't you tell me!?"
Maybe because I didn't even know yet.

"I literally made the decision yesterday—after hearing what an asshole I've been for dumping everything on everyone."
My pacing picked up, and the faster I moved, the hotter my irritation burned at myself.

"Well, tomorrow night we celebrate you coming back to the office!"
The excitement in her voice was palpable.
"Sounds good to me, but Roman has decided he's going to be there."
Another scream.

"Oh my God, you got back together?"
Wow. What? I did not say that.

"No, we didn't. But he can't seem to leave me alone, and I didn't want him just showing up unannounced. At least this way I'll know he's coming."
My nerves spiked and I dropped into the nearest chair, head falling between my knees as I forced a breath in.

Shay rushed to fill the silence. "Not my business, but... the guy's hot. And he's nice. I don't see the problem."

I let out a dry laugh, snapping my head back up. "Damn, everyone is Team Roman. It's fine. I have my reasons."

She sighed softly. No one knew the full story—why this thing with Roman wasn't simple, why loving him and fearing him could coexist in the same body.

"Okay, I won't ask again. I'm just glad he's coming so I can ogle him."

"Oh my God, Shay. What would Owen think?"

Honestly, I couldn't blame her. Roman was a ridiculous level of handsome.

"What? I can admire a fine piece of art without touching it."

We both cracked up.

"I'll see you tomorrow night. Are we meeting at my place?"

She hesitated. "We're going to have dinner at seven and then head over," she said carefully—as if I might feel excluded.

"I'll just meet you at the club. I have training from five to six-thirty, then I need to go home, shower, change... I won't have time for dinner. I'll Uber over once I'm ready."

Not a big deal. At least, that's what I told myself.

"Can't wait." She sounded relieved.

"Now for business," I said, shifting back into work mode. "I need you to check my schedule and Grant's and see if we can meet with Matt Stevens next week for an hour."

We said goodbye, and I hung up to make my next call—Roman. I needed to set up an interview time for Darius, and the safest way to keep everything strictly professional was to run it through Amelia.

"Roman King's office."

"Hi, it's Alex."

"Hi, Alex. What can I help you with?"

"Does Roman have any time next week to do an interview?"

"With you?" she asked, confusion thick in her tone.

I laughed under my breath.

Why does everyone think I'd ever ask Roman for a job?

"No. With Darius Jackson. He wants to learn construction."

"Oh! Okay. I just sent out an email about building a training facility, but that won't be ready for months."

"Hm." I tapped my fingers on the arm of the chair, thinking. "Do you have any ideas where Darius could get started in the company now?" He needed direction—fast. I didn't want him getting sucked back into the pull of that neighborhood.

"Let me talk to Roman. At the very least, we can bring him in, show him what we do, get him familiar with the different divisions while the training program is being built. You know—see if he's genuinely interested."

"That would be great. Thanks, Amelia."

I set my phone down and kept working through the list of calls I needed to make—Matt, Darius, and a few others. I'd just started another note when the elevator doors slid open and Roman stepped out.

"I couldn't wait for you to come to the lobby," he said as he walked toward me, that intensity in his eyes dialing up again. "I needed to see you and make sure you were still here."

Control freak much?

"I'm still here. I've been busy. I've got two more phone calls to make and some searching to do in Matt's district. I might drive over there next week and scope things out."

It actually felt good to have something productive to focus on again.

"You seem pretty excited about this. I'm happy for you."

He leaned against the counter beside me and brushed his knuckles over my shoulder—light, familiar.

"Yeah... I feel bad about how I left everyone."

I shifted just enough that his hand fell away. His brows rose, then dropped, and he slid his hand into his pocket.

"Even me?" he asked, straightening a little, his body pulling back an inch like he wasn't sure he wanted the answer.

A light flicked on in my mind.

"That reminds me—I need to call your mother and schedule a session."

I grabbed a bottle of water from the fridge and spun back to face him.

He laughed. "So talking about me reminds you that you need therapy. I love that."

He came over as I grabbed another water and handed it to him. His fingers grazed mine—barely—and heat shot through me. I ignored it.

"Where do you want to go for lunch?" he asked, settling the moment before it started to unravel.

"Mexican food?" I blurted, wanting to move past the whole therapy comment before he turned it into something else.

"Sure. Anything you want," he said, but there was a thread of condescension under it—maybe because I didn't answer his question about him... or because he thought I agreed about needing therapy because of him. Honestly, I probably need therapy because of me.

"Thanks for the water," he said, leaning in to brush a light, almost familial kiss over my cheek.

"Let's go eat. You can finish your calls after." He said, efficiently dismissing the conversation. "Amelia said you talked to her about scheduling an interview for Darius."

He really was good at smoothing over awkward moments—even the ones he created.

"Yes. But I'm trying to figure out what he can actually *do* right now. Amelia said you haven't set up the training division yet."

"No, not yet," he answered, thoughtful. "But maybe you can use him to scout areas with you. And once the training division is active, he can move straight into it. I'll put him on my payroll now so he can start helping you."

"That would work but..."

I crossed my arms, staring at him. "What would he do for *me*? I don't want you paying Darius when he'd basically be working under me. And I don't want to feel like I owe you."

We'd definitely be talking about this later.

Roman didn't flinch. "Just get him familiar with real estate. See what ideas he has for locating his new neighborhood. You said he has leadership skills—let's see where he can actually lead you."

Yes. Perfect.

A slow smile crept across my face. "I think that's a great idea. I'll email Amelia and set it up for next week."

***

ROMAN

Amelia came in to go over my schedule for the day. I figured this was as good a time as any to rope her into tomorrow night.

"Amelia, I have a favor to ask you and Harrison for tomorrow."

She looked up from her computer, head tipped, waiting. "Okay... what's that?"

I scrubbed a hand over my jaw. No way to make this sound sane. "Alex is going to a club tomorrow night, and I want eyes on her. I wish she'd just go with me, but she's still being stubborn. A place like that... I don't trust it. I don't trust *her* judgment right now. I feel like she could get herself into trouble."

"So you don't want her meeting any guys?"

Of course not.

"That's not the point," I muttered. "She's making me completely irrational."

Amelia laughed. I didn't.

"Well," she said, leaning back, "the day she saw you at Benita's, I made a comment that I was glad you were eating. She freaked out—wanted to know why you weren't. She's worried about you too, even if she'll never admit it."

I blinked. "Yeah... I don't know what that was about. But she's going to start seeing my mom again. That seemed to help. And if she wanted to cut me off completely, she wouldn't be in my penthouse right now, or go back to therapy with my mother. Right?"

"What?" Amelia's eyes went wide. "She spent the night? And she's staying again tonight?"

She looked genuinely alarmed. "Roman... is that a good idea? The two of you are torturing each other."

"I know," I admitted. "It feels like some sadistic mind game."

"Sorry," I added with a half-laugh, because it really was the only way to describe this mess.

"No, you're completely right. You're both going to need therapy." I kept laughing as the door opened.

Harrison walked in and dropped into the chair beside Amelia. "This doesn't sound like work in here. What did I miss?"

"Roman wants us to go clubbing with him tomorrow night," Amelia said. Harrison's eyes lit up instantly.

"Uh, hell yes. Which one?"

His enthusiasm made me wish it mattered. They all suck.

"DejaVu," I answered flatly.

"I love that place. First club I ever took Amelia to."

I looked over at her, surprised.

"You like clubs?"

She smiled and nodded.

Learn something new every day.

"That's why I've never had to worry about running into you out anywhere," she added with a smirk. "We don't go to the same types of places."

Obviously.

"Yeah, I wouldn't have pegged you as a club girl," I admitted. Truthfully, I hadn't pegged her as much of anything—until she started dating Harrison.

Harrison turned to me. "Hold up—why are you going clubbing?"

Amelia snorted. "He's babysitting Alex. And she doesn't want him there."

Harrison threw his head back. "Oh, this'll be fun. What are you going to do when she's grinding on some guy?"

Amelia shot him a look, and he held up his hands. "What? I need to know if I'm breaking up a fight. My brother's a hothead—I'm trying to plan ahead."

He wasn't wrong.

"Actually, that's why I invited you," I said. "To keep that from happening."

"Okay, cool," he replied. "But honestly? I think you should ignore her and have your own fun. We both know she doesn't want to see you with anyone else. She thinks she's got some kind of hold on you. Flip it on her. You're both a mess—might as well lean into it."

My little brother is a terrible influence. But he's entertaining.

Amelia shook her head. "Wow. All of you are messed up if you think this is a good idea."

I winked at her. She really had no idea what she signed up for, dating one of us.

"Alright, enough," I said, waving them toward the door. "I actually have work to do."

Amelia stood. "Have fun at lunch with Alex in the penthouse."
She rolled her eyes at Harrison and walked out.

"I'll go talk to her out front," Harrison added with a point of his finger in Amelia's general direction, already scheming. He was absolutely about to interrogate her about Alex staying with me.

"Good. Bye," I called after them as they finally left.

Harrison might actually have a point about making Alex see that she doesn't want me with anyone else. Then again, Amelia might be right too—we're already a bit messed up, and pulling a stunt like that could just pour gasoline on an inferno.

Jesus, what am I doing?

Maybe I should just let her go. If she comes back, it was meant to be. If she doesn't, I can move on.

Yeah, right. That's not helping at all. What we need is less drama, not more.

Once Amelia was back at her desk, she sent a call from Grant Johnson through.

"Good morning, Grant."

"I don't know what you did, but she's coming back to the office and taking over the project."

Thank God she called him.

"I was just honest with her and told her you and Matt needed help," I said as I straightened my desk for the rest of the day.

"Well, it worked. And I know she's going to put a hundred percent into it."

I laughed lightly. "She actually told me she was all in."

That was good news. Really good news. I'm glad she made that call.

***

"Did you go to the gym today?" I asked as I slipped my arm around her shoulders and stepped into the elevator. It happened without me thinking, but she didn't pull away this time. I let it sit there like it was always supposed to be.

"I did—and I took your advice. I soaked in the hot tub after. It really did the trick. I'm a lot less sore than this morning."

Damn. I wish I'd been there for that.

"Good. Glad you finally listened to me." I glanced down at her with a smirk.

She rolled her eyes, and it scraped right across my nerves.

"What's with the eye rolling?" Great—there's the irritation in my voice.

"Sorry, it's an allergic reaction to arrogance."

Perfect. Sarcasm at full strength. At least she sounded better.

"You know what the cure for that is?" I asked. She crossed her arms and gave me that "just say it" look.

"I can only imagine. What?" she muttered, rolling her eyes again—dramatically this time.

"You over my knee, and my hand connecting with that bare ass of yours."

Her laugh came quick, but it wasn't the soft one I liked—it was sharper, edged with something I couldn't quite read.

"You think that's punishment? You should see what Bruce puts me through. A spanking would feel like a relaxing massage." She laughed harder, and I couldn't help but join her.

"I'm not looking to punish you," I said honestly. "But I do enjoy smacking your ass."

And immediately regretted saying it when I remembered the bruises training was probably causing. The last thing I wanted was to be part of that—joking or not.

Then she smiled...slow, sultry...and licked her lips.

"Maybe we can do that later."

Oh, hell.

How do I cancel the rest of my day?

I was supposed to be steering this, and suddenly I was the one trying to keep up.

This was new.

And dangerous.

Or...crazy hot.

When the elevator doors opened, I grabbed her wrist and practically rushed her to the car.

"Look," I said once we were inside and my hands were wrapped tight around the wheel, "I'm going to play whatever fucked-up head game this is—until you're ready to tell me what's actually going on."

She looked out the window calmly. "I don't know what you mean."

Bullshit.

Something was definitely going on.

"You don't get to make up any rules either."

She turned sideways in the seat, fixing me with a look that was part challenge, part warning—like she was daring me to push back.

"What rules? How can there be rules in a fucked-up game? That's kind of the point."

She smiled, but it wasn't playful. It had an edge to it—almost sinister.

"So mind games turn you on, huh?" I muttered. God, she's crazy.

She slumped back, staring at the ceiling.

"Right now my head is a mess," she said flatly. "All it wants to do is fight and be angry. I wish all this bullshit was over so I could stop obsessing about it. And I'm scared that even when it's over...it won't really be over. I have nightmares."

Her voice cracked. Her hands came up to cover her face.

I reached across the console, gently pulling her hands down. "Why didn't you tell me?" I asked, hearing the plea in my own voice.

She tore her hands from mine, slapping my touch away through tears.

"This is why. Because I start crying, and I feel pathetic, and it makes me feel like Tanner won—like he broke me. That's how you distract me, Roman. I don't like feeling like this. When I'm angry, I can focus. I can aim all of it at him and make sure he goes to jail. I'm terrified his brother's going to get him off somehow."

She practically shouted that last part, shaking.

"Damn it, Alex," I whispered. "You should've talked to me about this. Or at least talked to my mom. All this anger...it's not good for you."
Jesus. And I'm sitting here feeding it.

"I know that" she snapped back. "I'm channeling it. I'm a decent fighter. I don't want to compete, but it's amazing what the body can do when you put your mind to it."

At least she was putting it somewhere. Maybe.

I finally pulled out of the parking lot and drove to a small Mexican restaurant I liked on the edge of town. We slid into a booth across from each other and—miraculously—talked about nothing important. Just small things. Easy things. Light things.

I was grateful she was letting me in again...even if it was only by inches. But she was still holding me at arm's length. She'd built a wall higher than before, and I had no idea if I'd ever get through it.

Maybe she needs more therapy than my mom can even give her.
Maybe I can't fix this.
Maybe...I lose her.

"What do you want to do tonight?" I asked, leaning back to watch her.

"I know what I *don't* want to do." she said.

"What's that?"

"Drink."
Yeah. That seemed to get us into trouble.

"Okay, I'm good with that. Want to watch a movie?" I wiggled my eyebrows at her. The last time we watched a movie, things went...very well.

She chuckled. "No, I don't think so. What if we walk down by the river? Maybe swing or ride the carousel?"

Perfect. Out in the open. No confined spaces. No scenes to make.

"Let me check the weather."
We both laughed. Getting caught in the rain last time had turned into

something unforgettable, but we never actually got to swing. Maybe it would help settle her mind.

After we finished eating, I drove back to the building. We rode the elevator to my office floor. I kissed her cheek as the doors opened and sent her up to the penthouse.

Amelia caught me the second I stepped past her desk. "I've been trying to call you."

I patted myself down—keys, wallet...no phone. I must've left it inside.

"Why? What's going on?"

She looked flustered. "The detective and the DA have been calling. They're waiting for you in your office."

My stomach dropped. I hurried inside. Detective Lewis and a man I didn't recognize were whispering when the door opened.

"Hi, Detective."

"Mr. King," she said. "This is DA Ralph Martin. He's prosecuting Miss Kennedy's case. We've been trying to reach her. Her attorneys told us to check with you. Hold on—she's calling right now." She lifted her phone. "Alex, we're in Mr. King's office—"

"She hung up," Detective Lewis said, startled.

I slumped into my chair and stared up at the ceiling. Just when things were calming down.

I took a breath. "My guess? She's already on her way here since that's where you told her you were. We might as well wait so you can kill two birds with one stone. I'm assuming this isn't good news."

The detective's expression confirmed that.

A moment later, Alex stormed in—arms crossed, eyes wide, looking absolutely unhinged. Whatever calm she had at lunch was gone.

"There's something wrong, isn't there?" she demanded. "I *know* there's something wrong."

I stood, came around the desk, and pulled out a chair for her, bracing myself for whatever was coming next.

She shook her head and growled, "I don't want to sit." I knew better than to try and calm her down right now, especially with that feral look in her eyes. The one of a trapped animal ready to attack.

The detective stood up and said, "Alex, you know I prepared you for everything that could happen." She was nervously shaking her leg and biting her lip looking between me and Detective Lewis. Then she nodded and the detective continued. "An unfortunate thing happened. He's out on bond until the hearing. His brother managed to pull some strings. It doesn't mean he's going to be able to get off."

The DA chimed in and added, "He isn't taking a plea deal. He claims you assaulted him first. Luckily the cameras in the room picked up on the fact he assaulted you in the room."

"Where is he?" Alex looked deranged at this point.

What the hell is she planning to do, go hunt him down? I don't think so.

The detective calmly stayed, "We can't tell you that because we don't want you to screw up your case by going after him." Alex's nostrils were flaring, and her eyes were wild.

"I'm not going after him. I just need to know someone is keeping an eye on him. I know he was following me and watching me before he attacked me. I could feel it everywhere I went, even in the parking garage of this building. I thought it was my fucking ex-husband until the attack." All prior calm is officially gone and now she's yelling.

She never told me about this. Is this why she was upset about the messages from her ex? Why did she think he was stalking her?

I interrupted, "Alex, you should've told me. I have cameras in there. I'll have security check and see if we can go that far back." I didn't think we could, because once they are checked each day they're erased, but I could at least look into it.

"I felt paranoid. I never actually saw anyone, and the police won't help you if you just have a feeling. Besides, you know how I felt about the police." Tears were streaming down her face.

Detective Lewis tried to assure her with more information. "I'll make sure he has a detail, plus there's a protective order that he can't come within 500 feet of you. Your attorneys went to get that immediately after they heard."

Just great. Two steps forward and ten steps back. Now she's really going to be a headcase, but with good cause.

***

ALEX

Get a hold of yourself. This is why you're training. You need to calm down so you can think.

I reached for the chair Roman had pulled over and sat. I lowered my head, breathing deep, trying to settle the hurricane building momentum. When I lifted it again, the blood was still pounding in my skull, but I forced all of it — fear, rage, panic — into the one thing I could control right now: the next question.

I gripped the arms of the chair to anchor myself. One more breath. Wipe the tears. Pull the mask back on.

And there it was — the snap — that cold, composed anger sliding into place. The part of me born for war. The part that would make damn sure Tanner ended up exactly where he belonged.

"What does this really mean? Is he free to go wherever he'd like, then?"

All three of them exchanged looks. Roman smiled faintly, almost knowingly, while the detective and DA registered the whiplash of my mood swing.

I know — it's a gift. Let's move on. I thought anxiously.

Detective Lewis answered, "Yes, he can move freely. His passport was confiscated, and like I said, he can't come within 500 feet of you or he goes to jail. If he does, you *do not* engage him. You call me immediately."

Don't engage him? I'll kill him if he comes near me. That's the part that terrifies me — the way those thoughts leap forward, blinding me of rational thought.

"What do I do now?" I snapped. "Just look over my shoulder? Be paranoid twenty-four seven? Not sleep? Keep the lights on? This is bullshit."

"Alex," the detective said gently, "I know this isn't what we hoped for, but you knew it was a possibility. The best thing you can do is stay somewhere safe where you're not alone. Maybe with your dad or a friend."

Roman hadn't taken his eyes off me once.

"She can stay with me."

Of course.

Here we go.

Like he'd been waiting for the moment.

This felt almost rehearsed — perfectly timed.

Manipulation at its finest.

"This is exactly what I was trying to avoid. Why am *I* the one who has to hide and lock myself away? *He's* the predator. I guarantee I'm not his first target, and I won't be his last if he's allowed back on the streets." I gasped for a breath. "I hate that you all want me to play the victim. I was unlucky once — but I'm not unlucky now, and I will never be a victim again. So please stop looking at me like that."

My hands were shaking hard enough that I had to wring them together just to keep them still, but my mind felt steady — sharp, even.

The DA said, "Alex, we're sorry this happened. We just want to make sure you're safe and that he goes away for what he did. We know you didn't assault him that night."

I laughed, tipping my head back and dragging in a breath.

I shifted in the chair, twisting one way and then the other as if trying to get comfortable in a body that had no intention of calming down. Finally, I crossed my legs to hold myself steady.

"Did you know I assaulted him on a different night? Does he know Roman's the one who broke his nose?"

The thought alone made my blood boil. My fingers curled around the arm of the chair until I could almost feel Tanner's throat beneath my hands instead.

The detective said, "Yes, we're aware — and he knows exactly who did what that night. The only problem is we don't have a witness from that night to confirm what he did to you."

I narrowed my eyes. "So what you're saying is everyone saw what *I* did, but no one saw what *he* did? He has witnesses?" I questioned.

The DA shook his head. "Just to be clear, no one has come forward on his behalf about your involvement. It seems you're pretty well liked in that place."

Liked?

I nearly snorted.

If they believed even half of what Tanner said about me — that disgusting rumor he spread — then "liked" wasn't the word I'd use.

"Then how does anyone know who did what?"

My voice cracked with frustration.

"There were cameras in the bar," the DA said. "His attorney subpoenaed them. They didn't catch what he did to you—only that you handed your purse to a girl beside you before you turned around. Does she know what happened?"

I dropped my head and slowly shook it. Of course this would happen. Of course the worst part would be the part no one saw.

"I'm going to put everyone through hell, aren't I?"

Roman's hand settled on my shoulder. "Alex, anyone who testifies for you is doing it because they care about you. I'll take whatever comes my way—gladly—if it means that piece of shit ends up in jail."

That wasn't what I wanted. I didn't want anyone dragged into this because of me.

"Can we just call Shay right now? I don't want her getting subpoenaed." My voice lilted on the word.

The detective asked, "Does she have time?"

"Yes. She's my assistant at the Realtor's office."

Lucky her. She gets all the bullshit I can't seem to stop generating.

Shay answered on the first ring. "Alex Kennedy's office."

I let out an exhausted sigh. "Hey, Shay. Are you busy?"

"Not for you, boss. What's up?"

I hated how that made me feel—like I was about to hand her something awful.

"I'm at Roman's office with Detective Lewis and District Attorney Martin about my case. They saw you on camera a few weeks ago and need to ask you a few questions."

She burst out, way too energized for the situation, "I've been waiting for this." She said and my heart sank. "I remember that night like it was yesterday."

I'd give anything for her to forget it ever happened.

The DA stepped closer to my phone. "Miss...?"

"Pierce," I said. "Shay Pierce."

He continued, "Miss Pierce, can you tell me what you witnessed that night?"

I closed my eyes and pressed both hands over my face, bracing myself. Then I dropped them and stared into nothing, waiting for Shay to recount the moment I'd give anything to rewrite.

Shay began to give her version of the events of that night. "We got in line to get a drink, and Alex turned and said—word for word—'That better be your hand on my ass.' I held both of my hands up so she could see it wasn't me. Then we each took a shot. After that, she gave me her purse to hold. She didn't say what she was planning. I told her I'd be more than happy to get kicked out with her if it came to that."

I dropped my chin and pressed my lips together so I wouldn't react, but I could feel my pulse hammering. I had no idea she remembered anything from that night we never talked about it. I wished she hadn't.

Shay continued, "She asked the guy if he grabbed her ass. He said yes—and then told her he was looking forward to grabbing other parts of her later. That's when she reached down and squeezed his parts and asked him how he liked it. Then she told him to keep his hands to himself."

My stomach rolled. I'd repeated that night only to detectives and my attorneys. Hearing it out loud like this made me want to crawl out of my skin.

The detective asked, "Did Alex tell you what she said, or did you hear it?"

"I was close enough to step in if she needed help," Shay replied. "I heard every bit of it. Especially him calling her a bitch and a prude because she didn't appreciate being touched. And, oh—his pathetic screaming right before he called her a psycho bitch." Her voice tightened, like she was gearing up for round two with him right now.

For a second, it almost made me smile. Then the DA said, "Miss Pierce, will you testify to that in court?"

I put both hands over my face as tears slipped free. This nightmare wasn't slowing down—it was growing teeth.

"Absolutely," Shay answered without hesitation. "He belongs in jail for what he did. She's not just my boss—she's my friend. I know what kind of person Alex is, and she'd never do something like that unless she had a damn good reason."

After that, the DA said he'd be adding her to the witness list. We hung up, and they left.

The room suddenly felt too small, too bright, too loud—even in total stillness.

Everything is spinning out of control. Twelve days until the trial, and with all this chaos happening, I have no idea how I'm supposed to keep my head straight.

I need help and some direction before I unravel completely.

Next call...Roman's mom.

Chapter 11

ALEX

As soon as the penthouse doors opened, I dialed Dr. King. She answered with that calm, warm tone she always uses—soft around the edges but perceptive enough to catch the urgency in my breath.

"Alex, how wonderful to hear from you."

"Hi, Dr. King." That's how she knows I'm not calling as Roman's... whatever I am. It's business. Or emotional triage. Or both.

"This is a professional call, I'm assuming?"

"For a minute, yes—if that's alright?"

"Of course. What can I do for you?"

"Can I see you tonight? Roman's going to bring me."

I didn't even mean to say that part out loud. It just stumbled out of me.

She paused only a second. "Alright. Did something happen?"

"Well... some things happened today. And the last three weeks have been hell, so I think I need to talk about all of it."

"Of course. How about six? Then you can stay for dinner at seven."

Perfect. I exhaled for what felt like the first time all day. "That would be wonderful. I'll tell you everything when I get there. I'm still processing."

After we hung up, I ran a hot bath, lit candles, put on meditation music, and dumped half a bottle of lavender oil into the water. I sank under until the water cooled and my fingers pruned. When I got out, I wrapped myself in Roman's robe hanging behind the door—warm, oversized, and carrying the faint scent of him—then crawled into bed for a nap. I set a timer. If I didn't, I'd sleep straight into next week.

The alarm ripped me out of a nightmare, and I gasped like someone had shoved me into cold water. Tanner this time—hands around my throat, shoving me back into that room.

I shot upright, grabbed my neck on instinct, and blinked hard until the penthouse came back into focus.

So much for a restorative nap.

I shuffled to the closet, praying I'd magically find something nicer than what I packed. No such luck. A thin navy sweatshirt, jean shorts and flip-flops. I could change at my place if Roman thought I needed to look more formal for dinner with his parents.

And so much for avoiding alcohol today.

Just remembering the detective, the DA, the words "he's out," made my pulse spike. My hands shook as I crossed the room.

I walked straight to Roman's bar.

A very stocked bar.

Grey Goose. One shot.

Cabernet. One heavy pour.

He won't mind. And if he does, he can take it up with the part of me that's barely hanging on.

I settled at the kitchen island, laying out my laptop, planner, and phone like I was trying to create order in a life that currently had none. I texted my brothers—both offered to let me stay with them, but even they admitted Roman's place was the safest. Matt's phone went straight to voicemail. I didn't call Dad. I wasn't ready to hear the fear in his voice.

I checked emails. Shay had already sent my new calendar. God, she's efficient. She deserves a raise and hazard pay for being attached to this disaster of a week. I texted Matt to look at his inbox, then made a three-way call to Abby and Maggie.

Abby answered first. "Oh shit. What happened?"

Maggie jumped in. "Whose ass am I kicking?"

Their voices cracked something in me, and for a second, I almost laughed—until reality shoved itself back into place.

"Tanner's out!" I blurted.

Dead silence.

Abby calmly said, "I know. We weren't allowed to say anything until you talked with the detective and the DA. Jack's been in court all day, so he couldn't call you."

Of course they knew. They're married to my attorneys.

So why did it piss me off so much that they didn't tell me?

Maggie jumped in carefully, "Matt went straight to the courthouse to get the protection order in place. Where are you? Are you safe? Is someone with you?"

I let out a laugh, but it sounded broken. "Wow... there's actually something you two *don't* know?"

Abby sighed. "Do you know how hard it was for me not to call you? Jack would've divorced me."

"Yeah right," I muttered, though I could picture her pacing holes into the floor. "But I get it. I'm at Roman's. I guess I'm staying here until the court stuff is over. My brothers and everybody else think it's the safest place. I'm seeing Dr. King tonight too. I need to talk through some things."

I lay my head on the marble countertop. Maybe if I roll it back and forth hard enough, I'll forget everything that's happened.

Maggie pounced. "Well, *halle-f'ing-lujah*. Seriously—why were you pushing him away?"

Here we go again. I groaned and dragged my forehead across the counter like a slug.

"Maggie, we're not back together. I just can't do that right now."

She scoffed. Abby took over, diplomatic as always.

"You can call it whatever you want, Alex. We're just happy he's there."

"Same," Maggie added.

I confessed the first distraction that came to mind. "LUKE texted me this morning."

Both of them reacted exactly as expected.

Maggie snapped, "Did you punch him through the phone or at least send the middle finger emoji?"

Abby practically growled, "Oh absolutely not. What did that loser want?"

"Just to say hi. Thought I'd want to talk. Total delusion." I shook my head. Leave it to my friends to drag me laughing out of a panic spiral.

They said in unison, "And what did you say?"

Someone yelled "Jinx," and they both giggled.

"I told him no and said bye. That's the entire conversation."

"And he *let it go*?" Abby sounded stunned.

Yeah. Luke wasn't someone to let things go. I still don't understand why he let the divorce go through as easily as he did.

Maggie asked, "Why haven't you blocked him?"

"Good point. Right now seems like a good time."

I scrolled, blocked, deleted, done.

She moved on. "Do you and Roman want to come over for dinner Saturday?"

I winced. "We actually have plans. We're going to Deja Vu."

Silence.

Then Abby snort-laughed. "Roman's going clubbing?"

Exactly. They all knew the truth: Roman is many things, but a nightclub regular is not one of them.

"Well, we weren't both going until he found out I was. But now I guess we're going together," I said, dripping with sarcasm, and dropped my head back onto the counter.

"Were you going with Shay and the boys?" Maggie asked.

They both knew my work crew—my go-to group for going out since Maggie and Abby were full-time moms now, and their husbands weren't exactly fans of my nightlife.

"Yes. They have dinner plans, and I've got training that'll run into their dinner, so I was just going to meet them after. Then we got the fun news that Tanner was getting out, so now... here we are."

I topped off my wine while we wrapped up the call and said goodbye.

Roman walked in right as I hung up. He made a small comment about my drinking, and for some reason it hit me harder than it should've. Everything suddenly felt too heavy, too immediate, too much.

I swallowed hard, trying to get words out, but they caught in my throat.

"Do you want to stop at your place and grab some things?" he asked gently.

I nodded, completely checked out. Staying at my dad's without Mom there? Not an option. The thought alone made my chest tighten. I just kept nodding as he pulled me into his arms and walked us to the elevator.

Then I looked down at myself—navy sweatshirt, jean shorts, flip flops—and looked at him: immaculate suit, pressed shirt, polished shoes. I burst out laughing.

He started laughing too. "What's so funny?"

"Me next to you."

"I'm lost. Not a clue what you mean." He said confused.

"It's fine. I'll change when we get to my place."

"What's wrong with what you're wearing?"

"Seriously? Look at you and look at me." I waved my hands up and down like a deranged game show hostess trying to get him to see the contrast.

He shrugged. "First, my parents don't care what you wear. Second, the only reason I didn't change is because I didn't want to let you go. If I had, I'd be in shorts and a tee shirt right now."

Great. Now I'm so needy the man couldn't even change his clothes.

"Sorry," I muttered. "You should've told me you needed to change."

"It's not a big deal. Let's just go grab your things."

We went up to my apartment. I pulled out a suitcase and loaded it with clothes while Roman stood clueless as if wating for instructions. I told him what to grab from the bathroom and tossed him a bag.

Watching him pack my toiletries felt strange—necessary, but strange—and the whole moment sat heavy in my chest, like I'd just crossed an invisible line I wasn't ready to admit was real.

I felt twelve again—standing in my bedroom while Maggie and Abby helped me pack to "run away" and live with them after one of Mom's drunken episodes. Dad already knew I'd be staying with Maggie's family for a couple weeks; he'd talked to her parents ahead of time. Both their families were fully aware of my situation and always on standby.

Mom went to a rehab facility in North Carolina, and Dad stayed with her for a couple weeks. That particular episode still sits heavy in my memory: watching the EMTs working on her, doing CPR and everything they could before loading her into the ambulance after she fell in the bathtub and shattered half the bones in her face. Somehow, she survived it. The doctors were stunned—couldn't believe her body held up under that level of abuse.

My brothers and I used to joke that we would sell her to science or trade her liver for ours because hers seemed indestructible.

Turns out that wasn't true at all, was it?

By the time we had everything loaded into Roman's car, my mind was full of her—both the hard memories and the good ones. I guess I haven't really let myself process any of it. It's not only about Tanner and what he did. Dad lost his wife. My brothers lost their mother. I almost didn't make it either. And no matter how badly she spiraled, she was a good mom when she was present. All our friends loved coming to our house. We just never knew when the switch would flip. I'm pretty sure I inherited that trait, it just manifests differently.

No point coming apart over that now. I'll make myself crazy. Though maybe I've already crossed that line.

We drove to his parents' house in silence—not quiet, but silent. No words spoken, but my mind was loud, so loud I honestly felt like jumping out of the car while we were still on the highway.

And now comes the fun part.

Alex, pull it together.

But the tears were already pressing up behind my eyes. The pressure in my chest was building. This wasn't something I could shove down or compartmentalize. It was coming whether I wanted it to or not.

Chapter 12

ROMAN

When we pulled into my parents' driveway and I opened her door... everything inside her broke loose. Every emotion she'd held back for weeks exploded all at once. My mother took one look at her and sprinted down the steps, gathering her up before I could even get a word out. And then came the sound — raw, violent grief tearing its way out of her. You could hear it echo off the brick. My mom sat on the ground holding her, rocking her, letting her unravel against her shoulder, and I stood in the doorway trying not to fall apart myself.

She'd been right — I never could've helped her through that. Not like that. Whatever people think I can feel... it's nothing compared to the weight she's been carrying alone.

I left them and went looking for my dad. I found him out back under the porch, nursing a scotch like he'd known something was coming.

"What'll you have, son?" he asked.

"A double bourbon. Neat."

He lifted his brows. "That bad, huh?"

I dragged both hands through my hair. "You have no idea."

The screen door was cracked open, and when Mom finally led Alex through the house toward her office, you could still hear her crying from the porch.

Dad winced. "I guess I can imagine it now."

"Yeah," I sighed. "It's been one bullshit thing after another. The guy they arrested? He was released on bond today. They told Alex she needs to stay somewhere secure. Everyone's scrambling to keep eyes on him. They served a protection order, but it freaked her out. And he's claiming she assaulted him. They've got video of me breaking his nose, and they're calling her friends to testify. So... yeah. It's been a hell of a day." And then I took a breath.

Dad set a hand on my shoulder.

"That poor girl doesn't deserve any of this," he said quietly. "And I hope she stays here with you. I can't think of anyone better to protect her."

I nodded, but part of me still wondered why everyone else was so damn certain I was the safest place for her to land.

The bourbon went down easy, and we sat there in silence, listening and waiting.

***

ALEX

I don't even know how I got off the ground, much less into the house. I couldn't stop crying. I couldn't catch my breath. My chest seized from the heaving, and I was close to hyperventilating. Dr. King never once let go of me. The longer she held me, the more it reminded me of my mom... and the harder I cried.

When the sobbing finally eased into quiet shaking, she handed me a glass of water and waited without a word. When the tears stopped, I wiped my face with the tissues she'd set out and pulled in several long breaths, trying to stitch myself back together.

"I could literally kill him with my bare hands right now." The words ground out through clenched teeth. My eyes stayed fixed on my own fingers. I'd never felt rage like that — not ever. I looked up at her through a haze of red, afraid if I made direct eye contact she'd see exactly how unhinged I felt.

She looked me over and said, with a small knowing smile, "I have no doubt that you could. And from the looks of it, you've been training to do exactly that, haven't you?"

Was I? I wasn't sure. But if he came near me right now, I guess we'd find out. At least she didn't seem scared of me. That helped.

"Maybe," I said, shrugging slightly, "but probably only in my mind."

"How's the training going? What kind is it?"

She was redirecting me on purpose — and it worked. I needed the shift.

"I started with self-defense and kickboxing," I said. "Then I felt like I hit a wall, so now I'm taking private MMA lessons."

"Are you thinking about competing?"

I actually laughed, a tired, small sound. "No. Not at all. Bruce is teaching me how to use it almost like meditation."

"That's wonderful."

Not what I expected, but the approval loosened something in me. I sank back into the sofa, kicked off my flip-flops, and folded my feet beneath me.

"Really? I wanted to ask you if it would even be a good idea — learning that from him and seeing you at the same time. I didn't know if that would... clash."

"Tell me what he's teaching you."

She leaned in a little, focused, calm, waiting.

So I explained how Bruce was trying to get me to channel everything — the emotion, the panic, the noise in my head — into moves and countermoves. How the entire point was detaching the anger from a person, so when I walk into court, the questions and answers would trigger the motions instead of my fear. So I could tune Tanner out completely.

She smiled. "I like his approach. I think you should keep doing exactly what he's showing you. And I'll help you handle the pain."

Relief washed over me. "That sounds like a good plan." Finally. A direction. Something to anchor to besides panic.

Then she asked, "Was this the first time all of it really hit you?"

So much for the distraction.

"Yes," I admitted weakly. "I felt it building all day. I knew if I came here it would come out. I feel safe around you." I swallowed hard. "But today was... different. He got out on bail. And now I feel like the prisoner."

"Why do you feel that way?" She shifted forward, gently probing.

I lifted my head, exhaled toward the ceiling, and let it fall out.

"Because I'm the one who has to stay somewhere 'secure.' There's a protective order, he can't come within five hundred feet, and I'm still the one looking over my shoulder. My friends and coworkers got dragged into it. Roman was caught on camera breaking his nose. Tanner is claiming I assaulted him first. It's just—"

My voice cracked.

"—it's too much. All of it. And I feel like I'm collapsing under it."

She smirked. "Is anyone testifying for you against their will?"

I knew what she meant. People wanted to help... but the fact they *needed* to help still made me furious.

"No. In fact, they seem excited to help."

"I doubt anything major will happen to Roman for what he did. He's not going to lose his job. At most he'll pay a fine. Don't waste energy worrying about him. He's more than willing to testify for you, and I already told you—we can handle the Ellington situation."

The Ellington situation. That phrase again.
I still wasn't sure what exactly needed "handling."

I tried, "But—"

She cut me off with a gentle, firm shake of her head.

"No buts. You aren't responsible for any of what these people have chosen to do for you. That weight isn't yours to carry. So take it off the list. Now tell me—what else about this case is bothering you?"

I opened my mouth, then shut it. I couldn't give her the real answer. The plan I was forming stayed locked behind my teeth.

"You know he can't hurt you in there," she continued. "In court, you get to say everything you need to say. Everything he did. Everything you felt. And he can't do a thing to stop you."

Her confidence in me — in my strength — settled something inside my chest.
The power he stole... she gave some of it back.

I let out a slow breath. My shoulders eased.

"That was amazing," I admitted. "How did you do that?"

She and her son had that way about them — that strange, unnerving ability to see into you and anchor you at the same time.

She smiled. "Perspective. This is consuming for you because it's your pain, your trauma, your fear. And you care so much about protecting everyone around you. But none of this responsibility belongs to you. Let the people who love you help. Now... have you decided where your safe place is?"

I dropped my gaze, then lifted it back to her, embarrassed by the answer even though everyone else seemed so sure of it.

"With Roman and everyone seems to agree."

It felt forced — like the entire world had voted on where I should be. Like the only person who couldn't protect me was me.

She nodded warmly. "I agree. Are you feeling more comfortable around him?"

Not really. But I wasn't going to say that to his mother.

"I think we've got a weird head game going," I admitted. "It's just... hard. I don't know if anyone told you why I stayed away from him."

She reached out and gently patted the back of my hand. "I heard you thought it was Roman who attacked you. Is that right?"

I nodded without meeting her eyes.

"And how do you feel about that now?"

"Better. My dreams are good when he's in them. Not like before. The nightmares are still vivid... but now they're only of Tanner."

"Just be good to each other," she said softly. "Your mind was playing tricks on you. It doesn't matter how many times I tell you Roman would never hurt you — you have to regain that trust internally. Brain trauma is still trauma. It takes time. Being around him seems to be helping. Don't label it. Don't sabotage it. If it works, it works. If it doesn't, it doesn't. That's all any of us can do."

Her voice softened even more.

"If you start to feel uneasy about him, call me. Or talk to him. He'll understand. And so will I."

We wrapped up everything that was weighing on me about the case and made another appointment — one dedicated to my mom. That was a different wound entirely.

***

ROMAN

After the last sip of the double bourbon, I finally felt a little more relaxed. Dad and I didn't talk much—we just sat there, both of us silently hoping things would settle by the time Mom and Alex reappeared.

The screen door slid open. I glanced over and saw them coming toward us, both smiling. Mom's arm was around Alex's back, protective and steady. The sight made something in my chest unclench.

I stood and asked, "Can I get either of you a drink?"

Mom answered for both of them. Alex still wouldn't look at me. "Yes, could you pour us each a white wine, please, Roman?"

I nodded and headed for the bar, keeping my focus on the bottles so I wouldn't stare at her too long. I poured two glasses and brought them over, expecting them to join us.

They didn't.

They went to the seating area by the pool instead, settling in like they'd done it a hundred times. I watched them talk, watched Alex laugh—really laugh—for the first time in weeks. It made me smile despite everything.

I turned toward my dad. "Why do you think they didn't come sit with us?"

I tilted my head toward them.

Dad smiled knowingly. "That's their thing."

Their what?

"And what thing is that?" I asked, brow tightening. How did I not know anything about an entire... *thing* they apparently shared?

"After Alex's sessions, the two of them would come out here with a glass of wine and talk for an hour or so," he said casually.

Right. I vaguely remembered Alex mentioning she'd hang out with my mom afterward. Still—seeing it with my own eyes was different. Comforting, even.

She bonded with my mom.

God, how I wished she would bond with me like that again.

"Well... that actually clears some things up," I muttered.

Dad and I picked through the pretzels and mixed nuts on the bar while we waited for their "girl time" to run its course.

Eventually they wandered back over. Mom kissed my cheek, said "Hi, honey," and disappeared inside to finish dinner. Dad followed to help.

Alex sat across from me, holding her almost-empty glass with both hands. She stared into it like it held some answer she desperately needed. Her eyes were red and puffy—no makeup left.

She didn't look at me, and for a moment I let the silence sit, hoping she'd lift her head on her own.

She didn't.

So I broke it gently. "Do you want another drink?"

She extended the glass toward me with a small, strained smile then a polite nod.

I brought back two fresh pours and handed her one before cautiously taking the seat beside her. I slipped an arm around her shoulders and took a sip of my wine.

She softened instantly—leaning into my side, settling her head on my shoulder like her body remembered the habit before her mind could protest. I let out a long breath, the scent of her relaxing me as I pressed a kiss to the top of her head. I rested my cheek there, the way I used to when things were... simpler.

Though honestly, were things ever really simple with her?

Sitting in comfortable silence until Mom brought dinner out felt... good. Strangely good. Not an ounce of awkwardness between any of us. We didn't bother setting a table—this wasn't a formal night, just an impromptu meal wherever we landed. After we ate, Dad and I cleaned up, grabbed an after-dinner drink, and I finally couldn't take it anymore. I had to know.

"Okay, who knew about Harrison and Amelia—and have you both been spending time with them together?" I demanded, half joking, throwing my hands up while looking between them.

Alex glanced up at me, brows raised, just as curious.

Mom answered first. "Yes, we knew about them, and we've spent time with them."

Dad added, "I suggested they not say anything because you and Amelia work so closely together. She's a professional—she would've kept that to herself for as long as it took. I'm sure Harrison outed them." His tone carried a hint of annoyance.

I barked out a laugh. "He did. She wasn't happy about it either."

Dad nodded. "I can imagine."

Mom smiled softly. "She's lovely. And she's been a wonderful influence on Harrison."

"Have you all been having dinners without me?" I asked, jokingly, sounding way more like a petulant child than a grown man.

Dad gave me a look. "Very mature, son. We can have as many dinners as we want with whomever we want. We're having dinner with you right now—without Harrison." He flicked his hand at me like he was swatting away a fly.

"Point taken," I muttered. "So now we can have family dinners with everyone—Amelia included, right?" I flashed a grin and shot Alex a wink. She sighed and looked away, but I wrapped an arm around her anyway. No escape.

I leaned in and whispered, "You can still come to dinner even if we aren't together. I think my parents want to adopt you." I kissed her cheek, and she blushed and giggled. God, I loved that sound. I'd include her in this family no matter what.

But she'd definitely had more to drink than usual, so I nudged things along. It was already nine. We wanted to walk down by the river, maybe swing or ride the carousel. I didn't know if she'd still be up for it, but I wanted to try. Keep her mind busy. Then get her to bed—because after today, she needed real sleep.

When I pulled into my spot and turned off the car, I looked over. "Do you still want to go for a walk?"

She met my eyes and nodded with this sudden, bright enthusiasm.

"Okay, do you need to change your shoes or anything?"

"No, I'm good. I'm looking forward to swinging. But I should warn you—I've had a bit to drink."

Yeah, she was definitely slurring, and the giggling wasn't helping. It was contagious.

She hopped out of the car and flung her arms out like she was announcing herself to the universe. "I'm ready."

Then she started skipping toward the exit.

I had to jog to catch up with her.

***

ALEX

"Skipping? Really?" he groaned, like it physically hurt him to witness it.

"Yeah, you should try it." I started skipping again, purely out of spite, and Roman grabbed my hand and yanked me back. I stumbled straight into his chest—solid, warm, and immovable.

"I don't think so. Not in these shoes."

Right. He was still in his suit and dress shoes from work. He probably was in actual pain. The realization tugged at me—he never got the chance to change because he didn't want to leave me alone.

I looked up at him, hesitant. Maybe we should skip the whole adventure.

But he smiled, and tugged gently on my hand, that small, steady warmth spreading through my arm and—God help me—straight into my heart.

Adventure it is.

When we reached the river park, it was quiet and peaceful with only a handful of people around. The lights farther down by the bars left the swings and walkway empty—ours alone. We glided in silence for a few minutes, letting the calm settle over us like a blanket.

Roman slipped his arm around me. "How're you feeling?" he asked.

I leaned into him, breathing in the steadiness he always carried. "Much lighter, actually." And it was true. I needed that release more than I'd realized. I looked up into his warm brown eyes and smiled.

"I was worried I was witnessing a complete mental breakdown or something. I've never seen anything like that before." His tone carried worry, but not judgment. Just honesty. I let it float past us so we could stay in this soft, peaceful little bubble.

"Well, me either. I guess it was a breakdown of sorts. Not the kind that gets you locked away, but... maybe the kind that clears the ground so you can rebuild on it."

Rebuild my life, rebuild myself. The moonlight rippled over the murky water of the Ohio River—somehow still beautiful. A silver lining, maybe.

"So," he said after a moment, "and you don't have to answer this... but do you think we can rebuild us?"

A slight panic feeling surged. I wasn't ready for that. Not tonight. Not in this soft, fragile headspace. My gaze drifted to a small boat sliding across the water before I answered.

"One thing at a time, okay?"

It was on my mental list—just not a task I could check off yet. He nodded and looked out at the river with me. He didn't push and somehow, that made the weight on my shoulders lift even more.

I rested my head against him. I didn't know what would happen with us, not yet—but for the first time, he finally felt separate from Tanner in my mind. And that was something.

"The first thing I need to focus on is getting back to the penthouse without falling asleep."

It flew out of my mouth so fast it even surprised me. He laughed, and the sound actually made me happy.

"I can just carry you home."

Home.

That one word could unravel everything. My mind shot straight to my mom, and suddenly my eyes were burning. Definitely the alcohol—had to be. I shook my head quickly and hopped off the swing, heading toward the penthouse before he saw my face crumple.

He hurried after me and caught my hand.

Chapter 13

ROMAN

Not sure what I said to trigger that reaction. We'd been swinging, and all I did was offer to carry her back if she couldn't make it without falling asleep. Maybe it was the word "home." Maybe it was anything to do with us. Whatever it was, I decided to let it go. She'd been through enough today. If she wanted to talk, I'd listen. If she didn't, I wasn't going to push her. I brushed the overthinking away for the rest of the walk. Honestly, all I could think about was getting into a hot shower.

Back at the penthouse, she collapsed onto the couch and patted the cushion beside her. I wanted out of these clothes more than I wanted air, but if I disappeared to change, she'd be asleep before I got back. So I slipped off my jacket, draped it neatly over the chair, unbuttoned my cuffs, and rolled them up. Then I sat down beside her and waited—letting her decide what happened next.

"Thank you. For everything. I never knew there was so much I needed help with until I met you."

She slurred through the words, sounding exhausted and a little unsteady. It should've felt like a compliment, but something in it made my stomach pull tight. Like she was about to say something I wasn't going to like—something that would hit me the way my own worries about her hit her.

I took a slow breath before reassuring her.

"Honey, you've never needed my help. I just wanted to be there for you." I pulled her closer so she knew she could trust me—really trust me.

She looked up at me through glassy eyes with this soft, crooked smile. "Yeah, I'm a real tough ass bitch, ain't I?"

She rolled her eyes—at herself, not at me. Definitely an inner monologue slipping out.

"Alex, maybe it's time for sleep."

I started to stand, but her hand landed on my knee, firm enough to stop me.

"No. I have things to say, and I think you should listen."

Her eyelids were heavy, like she could drift off mid-sentence, but her tone said she wasn't backing down.

I tried to gently redirect her, but she wasn't budging.

"Okay," I said quietly. "I'm all ears."

She stared straight ahead, expression blank—like she wasn't even looking at me but somewhere way past me.

"So, I think about spending my life with you," she said. "But I don't want you to be miserable because I'm such a trainwreck disaster."

Hearing her talk about the future with me should've felt incredible, and it did—until she twisted it into something it wasn't. The idea that I could ever be miserable because of her was insane. I was miserable without her. But she was worn out, half-asleep, half-drunk, and fully overwhelmed. Answering that right now wouldn't help either one of us.

So I kept my mouth shut and let her keep talking.

She continued, "I was so happy you never gave up on me, and I still think I might run again... but I also want you to chase me until I figure it out. I know that's really messed up, and you don't deserve to get strung along like that, but it's how I stay motivated to do what I feel needs to be done. I don't think you're going to like it..."

Her voice lifted on that last part, and it sent unease straight through me.

"...so I just want you to be prepared."

Prepared for what?

I had no idea where this was going anymore. She didn't even seem fully aware of what she'd let slip, and something in me knew she hadn't meant to say it out loud.

I tried to coax the truth out of her—liquid courage usually loosened her guard.

"Babe, you have me at a disadvantage here. What do you think I won't like? I've kept up so far. And look... this isn't the kind of relationship I ever pictured, but it's not something I'm willing to walk away from. You should know that."

She smiled, then shook her head like I'd missed the point entirely. "I can't tell you right now. You'll know when I do."

That didn't clarify a thing.

How was she planning something she couldn't even articulate?

This had the distinct feel of alcohol steering the wheel.

"Well, that makes perfect sense," I deadpanned.

She burst into laughter, then let out a long yawn—her tell-tale sign she was seconds away from shutting down for the night.

"How about we go to bed," I suggested quietly, "and in the morning I'll make you breakfast. After that, we can talk about our living situation for the next two weeks."

She nodded and held her hands out for me to lift her up.

I walked her back to the bedroom before realizing her bags were still in the car. I grabbed one of my t-shirts for her, then watched her try to get changed. When I moved to help, she shoved my hands away—stubborn even half-asleep and unsteady. So I let her be and went to take a quick shower so I could get out of these clothes.

When I returned, she was already asleep, curled into the blankets. I climbed into bed beside her, easing my arm around her waist. I traced my fingers down her arm, brushed her hair back, and pressed a slow kiss to her cheek. The tension drained out of me almost instantly.

She was here.

With me.

And for the next two weeks, I had the privilege of keeping her safe.

I knew I'd have to work to help her rebuild trust after everything she'd been through—and after how fast life had forced her into this arrangement—but none of that changed the truth.

I loved her.

Not the idea of her.

Her—exactly as she was.

And after tonight, I knew without question that a life with me was the life she wanted too.

***

ALEX

Woah… that was a good dream for once.

Relaxing on a beach, sunlight on my skin, a bottle of water in my hand, a book in my lap.

Did that mean I already needed another vacation? Probably. But there was too much waiting on my plate to even pretend that was an option.

I stretched out across the mattress and felt nothing but empty sheets beside me.

He was gone.

But on the nightstand sat a bottle of water and two Advil—set there intentionally, left for me. He knew me better than I wanted to admit, and something about that settled in my chest in a way I wasn't ready to examine yet.

Then last night came rushing back.

Everything I'd said.

Everything I'd almost said.

I took a slow breath and tried to brace myself for whatever questions might come later. I had no answers—not yet—but I could at least prepare to pretend I did.

But the first priority this morning was simple: a shower.

I rolled to the edge of the bed and stood carefully, moving slow so my head didn't throb. I took the pills, washed them down with half the bottle, and waited for the room to stop tilting before heading to the bathroom.

I saw my bags by the bathroom door, grabbed them, and headed in. The shower was exactly what I needed—hot water melting the tension from my muscles while I tried to come up with a reasonable explanation for everything I'd blurted out last night.

The smell of coffee and bacon drifted in as I stepped out and dried off. I wrapped his robe tight around me and practically floated to the kitchen. Roman was at the island, leaning over his laptop, coffee already poured, bagels and cream cheese set out, bacon still warm on a plate. It looked like he'd reached straight into my mind and put breakfast together.

He looked up. "Good morning. I thought something greasy might help soak up the alcohol. I hear that's supposed to work."

I walked straight to him, slid my fingers through his hair, and kissed him softly. If luck was on my side, that might distract him from anything I said last night.

"You have no idea how much this helps."

He wrapped his arms around me, pressed his face into my neck, and let out a long breath—one that sounded a little frustrated, maybe even conflicted.

"I'm glad," he said, though it felt like he'd cut off whatever he really wanted to add.

I sat beside him, and we ate quietly while soft classical music drifted through the room.

"So, is there anything you want to do today?" he asked without looking up from the news on his screen.

"Well, I have training from five to six-thirty tonight, and then we're still going clubbing, remember?" I waited for the groan. He didn't disappoint.

He rolled his eyes and dropped his head back. "I was trying to forget." Then he grabbed me by the waist and tugged me onto his lap. "I'm kidding. But now we all go together, right? I also want to watch you train today." He added surprisingly.

"Who's all? I thought it was just the two of us." I slipped out of his hold so I could see his face.

He smirked. "Ahh, well... you heard last night that Harrison and Amelia are a thing now, right?" I nodded. "They very generously accepted my invite to the club yesterday—before everything went sideways."

"Okay, so you want to go clubbing *and* watch me train? Is that what I'm hearing?" I smirked, because we both knew he didn't actually want to do either.

He nodded but it looked painful.

"Should I be worried about either of those things?" he asked, already sounding uneasy.

"What exactly would worry you?" I rubbed his arm to calm him a little. I didn't want him stressing over things that didn't need to be stressful.

"I don't know... when you're training, are you just being taught, or is someone actually fighting with you?"

Oh. There it is.

"As honestly as I can say this without overexplaining it," I replied, "Bruce is teaching me, and he's not just standing there pointing and talking."

A look of unease crossed his face as he contemplated me and Bruce. Six-foot-five, nearly three hundred pounds, former MMA fighter. I understood the reaction.

"Is he the one you're getting the bruises from?" he asked with a grimace. I grinned.

"Sometimes I spar with the other fighters. No one hits me full force—because that would be lethal," I said, and his whole body tensed, "but they are tough. They know why I'm doing this, and they're supportive."

He exhaled slowly. "I should probably sit there and keep my mouth shut, shouldn't I? But also... maybe don't say things like 'that would be lethal.'"

I smiled, even though I knew all of this was hard on him. He shifted in his seat again, clearly not comfortable with this.

"And at the club..." he hesitated, "I'm not sure I'd love the idea of you dancing with someone I don't know."

I didn't want anyone touching me but him.

"Then you'd better dance with me all night," I said, biting my bottom lip at the thought of being pressed up against him on a crowded, overheated dance floor.

His eyes darkened instantly.

He looked at me and murmured, "You know I can feel you when you look at me like that?"

I immediately switched gears before things could escalate. "I'd like to go see my dad today. I haven't told him what's going on yet, and I'd rather do it in person."

He softened. "Do you want me to go with you?"

"I really do. Safety in numbers, you know? And... can we visit the girls today too? I want to see the kids. I've been a bad aunt." I missed them so much after the last month of chaos.

"Are we going to have enough time for all that?" he asked.

"If we get moving soon, we will."

I ducked into the bedroom and pulled out black leggings, a white tee, a thin gray sweater, and white tennis shoes. I packed a gym bag just in case we didn't make it back before my training session. Then I headed back to the kitchen, calling Dad first to let him know we were coming. After that, I dialed Maggie and Abby on three-way.

"Hey, Jerkface, what's up?" Maggie greeted. Music to my ears.

Abby chimed in, "Girl, you good?"

"All good. I'm just in the mood for a visit. I'm heading to Dad's in a few, then I want to see all of you and the kids." Lately, every call felt like a crisis, so it was nice to say things were good and actually mean it.

They both got excited, and Maggie asked, "Are you coming by yourself?"

"No, Roman's coming. He's basically my bodyguard for a couple weeks, so I'm dragging his ass everywhere."

Abby swooned. "Yeah, well... that's an ass worth dragging around."

I shook my head, laughing. Abby was never shy about admiring Roman.

"So do we have juicy info for brunch then? Or does he have to come with you?" Maggie asked.

"He will *not* be coming to brunch. Absolutely not. I've got things to talk about."

"Oh, hell yes. I need some serious gossip," Abby said, sounding exactly like one of her reality-show obsessions. She used to host watch parties for that stuff back in school.

I laughed. "I'll call you when we leave my dad." The girls were exactly what I needed right now.

I took a sip of coffee. It was delicious. I grabbed the coffee bag from the pantry and checked the label. Some kind of Colombian dark roast in a foreign language— figures. I heated the leftover bacon and spread cream cheese on a toasted bagel. Absolute perfection. And Roman was right: the grease was a miracle cure for this hangover nonsense. I was practically inhaling it.

He walked out of the bedroom in jeans and a black tee that clung to him exactly the way God intended. He looked stupid hot. Meanwhile, I was shoveling bacon into my mouth like a feral raccoon. He came over and wiped a smudge of cream cheese from the corner of my mouth. I almost licked his fingers.

"Good lord," he muttered, laughing. "We really need to get out of this house today. Come on."

He kissed me, grabbed a bottle of water, picked up his keys, and spun them around his finger. "Ready."

"Let me clean this up first." I can't leave a dirty kitchen. I rinsed everything, wiped down the counters, and then we headed to my dad's.

Dad was in the front yard with Sadie when we pulled up. She hobbled toward me, tail wagging, and I scratched her head gently. She couldn't play like she used to due to age and injury a couple years back so I had to be gentle. I hugged Dad, then watched him shake Roman's hand.

"This is a nice surprise," Dad said. "I was worried about the two of you."

Roman and I exchanged a quick look and a smile before following him inside. When we told him what was going on, he freaked out for a second—and then immediately shifted into relief that I was staying with Roman. I knew he liked him, but I didn't realize he was worried about us not being together. Does literally no one think I can handle myself?

"Sorry I haven't been by," I told him quietly. "I've been having a hard time with Mom's death." Saying it still sliced straight through me. Being in that house still felt like walking through a ghost.

"I know, sweetheart," he said. He looked better too. He said the boys had helped him clean up the place.

"I wanted to tell you I'm going back to work. Sitting around just gives me too much time to think about what I've lost, and it's not helping."

"I think that's a good idea," Dad said. "Now don't be a stranger."

I hugged him, and then we headed to Maggie's.

As we pulled into the driveway, Abby was walking down the street with Jack and Jax.

When I got out of the car, Jax screamed "Aunt Ali!!!" and launched himself down the sidewalk like a tiny missile. He jumped straight into my arms, wrapped his legs around my waist, and squeezed my neck.

"Where you been?" he squeaked in that sweet little-boy voice that always melts me.

"Resting," I told him, hugging him tighter. "So I have enough energy to play with you."

"I want sleep at you house."

My heart clenched. I hated that I'd canceled their sleepover. I was absolutely rescheduling.

"That's what I want too, buddy. We'll talk to Mommy and Daddy about it, okay?" He nodded eagerly and went right back to playing with my hair like he always did.

Abby grinned. "Hey girl, looks like your buddy still remembers the sleepover."

"He sure does," I said, rubbing Abby's baby bump out of habit. This time she didn't nudge my hand away. "Maybe we can still have it at Roman's place. Plenty of room."

I glanced over my shoulder at Roman, who was smiling at me like he didn't mind one bit being volunteered.

Jack and Roman followed us up to Maggie's front door. Abby pushed it open and yelled, "Is everyone decent?"

The kids came screaming down the hall like they'd been caffeinated. Jax wriggled out of my arms to greet his friends. Sophia Grace and Cameron hugged me, and Jax proudly announced we were still having a sleepover.

Cue even more screaming.

Maggie and Matt came racing in behind them, both looking like they were trying to wrangle feral goats.

"You need to finish your lunch!" Maggie yelled over the chaos.

God, I missed this. This house. These people. This beautiful mess.

Maggie threw her hands up. "Hey, y'all, can you round up the troops so they can finish eating?"

"On it," I said.

I grabbed all the kids by the hands and led them into the kitchen. I sat the three of them at the counter, got them settled, and fixed a plate for Jax too.

***

ROMAN

It was sweet watching the kids with Alex. They adored her—absolutely lit up around her—and she seemed to soak up every bit of their energy. I made a mental note to talk to Matt and Jack later about letting the kids do their sleepover at my penthouse with both of us, once all this chaos settled. No point making them wait longer for their "Aunt Ali." She was so good with them...almost made me wonder if it ever hurt her that she didn't have kids of her own. That was a conversation for another time.

While the girls were inside getting the kids fed, the three of us stepped out back to talk about the case.

"How's Alex doing?" Matt asked, genuine concern written across his face.

I winced just thinking about last night. "She had a session with my mom yesterday and honestly...it scared the crap out of me. I thought she'd had a total breakdown. But she said it helped. She actually seems better—if that's even possible after what I watched."

"What happened?" Jack pressed. Matt leaned in too, both of them waiting.

"What happened was a tidal wave," I muttered. "She'd been holding everything in. You know that eerie calm she gets? That quiet-before-the-storm look? When we got to my parents' house yesterday, she snapped. Everything came out at once. I figured you should know, whether she mentions it or not. It was intense—but I think she needed it."

Matt nodded. "That might actually help her with the case. Getting all that emotion out instead of bottling it. Did the DA reach out about her deposition?"

"Yeah," I said. "As soon as I know her schedule this week, we're going together to get them both done."

I paused before asking, "Have either of you heard anything about Tanner?" I looked between them—if Alex was staying at my place, I needed to be aware of anything that might affect her safety.

Jack lowered his voice, leaning in. "His attorney is trying hard to spin this. We need Alex to stay calm during the hearing. I know she can... I just worry she'll get defensive when she's questioned."

Yeah...she does get defensive. Snarky as hell. It's part of the fire I love about her—but it's also the fire that could make this whole thing harder.

"She said something strange to me last night, but to be fair, she'd had a bit to drink. She told me she was planning to do something I wouldn't like—but she didn't know what that 'something' was yet."

The confusion on Matt's face mirrored my own.

"Well," he said, "let's chalk it up to drunk talk for now. She hasn't mentioned any plans to either of us."

He looked to Jack for confirmation, and when Jack shook his head, I felt a small relief—though not enough to quiet the nagging worry that there was more beneath the surface than she was letting on.

When the girls came outside with the kids, all three of them immediately attached themselves to Alex. She was magnetic—every one of them orbiting around her, even when she sat down.

Watching her with them made me smile. I didn't even notice Abby walk up beside me until she spoke.

"So, Roman... have you ever thought about having kids?"

Alex's face went almost white, but there was a flicker of curiosity behind the surprise as she looked at me, eyebrows raised. I heard the question, but I didn't take my eyes off her.

"I hope to have children in the future, yes," I answered, giving her a quick wink before turning my attention back to Abby—just in time to see the relief soften Alex's whole expression. "Abby, speaking of children, how are you and baby number two doing?"

She laughed. "I'm getting fat, and I'm almost always hungry."

You never agree a pregnant woman is getting fat. Ever.

"You look great, if you don't mind me saying."

She flushed a bright pink.

"There it is—that superpower of yours again," she teased.

The guys exchanged a look while the girls laughed, and I shrugged, lifting my hands as if I had no idea what they were talking about.

We had lunch on the patio around two and stayed until it was time to take Alex to training. She told me she'd packed clothes to change into, and a minute later she ran inside the house and came back out in what she called her "fight clothes."

All she had on were tight black spandex shorts, a black sports bra, and a lightweight zip-front jacket. She'd swapped her shoes for flip-flops, and I wasn't sure what to make of that until she caught me staring.

She wiggled her toes and said, "I fight barefoot."

Sounded painful.

We said our goodbyes in the driveway. Abby and Maggie promised to work out a sleepover or at least a playdate, depending on what Alex could handle before the hearing.

We only had one more weekend before the court hearing, and I didn't know if Alex would be up for a kiddy sleepover right before that. Still, today seemed like exactly what she needed. She was happy—really happy—and that smile hadn't left her face once.

"Something you want to share?" I asked.

"Don't those kids just make you so happy? They radiate so much joy, and I feel so good around them." She was beaming.

"You're definitely more at ease around the kids than anyone else." I reached over, laced my fingers with hers, and lifted her hand to my lips, placing a light kiss on her knuckles. Might as well kiss them now before they're battered and bruised again.

She looked at me with this soft, almost awed expression. "They're so carefree, not a worry in the world, and nothing bothers them. It's amazing."

When we pulled into the parking lot, she looked ready to jump out of the car, but I gently put my hand on her arm. I couldn't shake what she'd said last night.

"Hold on a minute before you run in there. I'm still a little concerned about something you said last night."

"What did I say last night?" she asked. I couldn't tell if she genuinely didn't remember or if she was dodging.

"Well... that you were planning to do something you thought I wouldn't like." I watched her eyes closely, trying to see if she was hiding something.

Her smile faltered for just a second. She looked like she was trying to recall it. Maybe it really was just drunken rambling.

"Hmmm, I'm not sure what that might be," she said slowly. "Could be any number of things, I guess. Like what I'm about to do in here today." She smirked. "I'm good at worrying you. I wouldn't try to analyze it too much—it was probably just the alcohol talking. I say some weird stuff when I've been drinking, and last night was one hell of a night."

I agreed.

Chapter 14

ALEX

We headed into the gym where Bruce and Roman talked for a bit before we got started, then Roman sat on a bench in front of the ring. One of the other fighters went over to sit with him and they seemed to be hitting it off.

I was working out with Bruce today then I would finish sparring with one of the smaller guys. Every time I was taken down, I could see Roman wince and I tried not to seem amused because I figured that would upset him. When I fought back as hard as I could and held my own with both of them, I could see a look of surprise on his face. I felt strong today. I think Roman being there motivated me to show him how much I've learned and how strong I've become so he won't worry so much.

I wiped the sweat off with my towel and grabbed my things. I thanked everyone for helping me like I always did. Roman and Bruce shook hands, and we headed back to the penthouse.

"What were you and Felix talking about?" I asked as I wiped my face with the towel again.

He huffed out a little laugh and said, "He was telling me that I didn't have to worry about you, because you could take a hit and give one."

I laughed. He told him I could take a hit?

"How did you feel about that? I bet you weren't too thrilled hearing those words." I tried not to smile but it totally got the better of me.

He shook his head. "Yeah, I don't really want anyone hitting you for any reason, but at least you seem to have a lot of friends here, so I doubt I need to worry about you in the ring. I wasn't happy watching you take those hits. I don't need to go back again." He had his elbow on the door while driving with one hand.

That sucks. I was hoping he would keep coming.

"Roman, thanks for coming, anyway. I felt a lot stronger with you there. I don't know if I was trying to prove to you that I can take care of myself or if you just make me feel like I can do anything, but I really liked it that you were there." Maybe that would help to get him to come back– if he thought I needed him there.

"I don't know if I can watch that on a weekly basis." He couldn't even look at me when he said it. He was staring straight ahead looking rather distraught.

"I understand. I won't ask you to come again."

My shoulders sagged, but I understood. It bothered him, and I couldn't expect him to feel something he didn't. He supported me enough. I didn't need to make him stand there and watch while I came home with fresh bruises.

Back at the penthouse I pulled him into the shower with me so I could multi-task.

"Ok, what time are Harrison and Amelia coming?" Roman reached over grabbing my arm and tugged me to him but I kept pushing him away. I needed to get this taken care of.

"In about an hour." He seemed annoyed as he reached for me again and I backed up under the cascading water farthest from him.

"Then we need to eat something before we leave. We can just heat up some leftovers. Do you know what you're wearing?" He moved closer to me sliding his arm around my waist moving me out of the waters stream and I wiggled from his grasp, giving him a warning glare. He dropped his arms, picking up the soap instead and started rubbing it all over his body. My attention shifted from what to wear to climbing him like a tree.

"Ummm, no, I haven't thought about it, I've been hoping it gets can-celed." Me too, I thought as he looked up, letting the water run over his face and I watched the soap run down his body. The anxiety now turned to desire.

"Is it really that big of a deal what I'm going to wear?" He said, his eyes were still closed as he washed the soap from his hair.

"Probably not, I just wanted to make sure I wasn't underdressed or something. It's really hard to keep up with you." I stepped into his space, reaching out to touch his abs. I ran my fingers over his taut muscles as they tensed under my touch.

"Alex..." He said breathlessly as I reached up and touched his face, remembering all the things I loved about him.

"I'm remembering you. All of you and how much I love you." He pulled me into his arms and tears started to fall from my eyes mixing in with the water. I missed this closeness so much. I wrapped my arms around his back and caressed him, committing every muscle to memory. I nuzzled my face into his chest trying to control the tears that I knew he would feel anyway. He held me tight against him. It had been over a month since I'd felt him in all the ways that made me whole. Was this the breakthrough I needed to heal? God, I hope so.

Roman's hand went to the back of my head where his fingers slid effortlessly through my wet hair, and he gently tugged my head back. When I opened my eyes, his penetrative stare filled with desire and love was all I needed to know this was right.

"I love you." He said then his mouth was on mine. The desperation of the kiss forced my lips to part and his tongue to enter dancing with mine. I dug my nails into his shoulders trying to hold him as tight as I could with the water spraying in all directions. He pushed me gently but urgently against the wall and I lifted my leg hooking my ankle over his hip as his hand came down, wrapping under my thigh pulling me closer to him, pressing into me.

With my back against the tile and my hands braced around his neck for balance, I felt him guide himself against me—slow at first, testing my readiness—until the warmth of him pressed right where I ached most. A low sound rumbled from his chest, deep and hungry, and the need inside me unfurled so sharply I could barely breathe.

"I need you... more," I whispered, my voice breaking with urgency.

He answered with a single, decisive thrust—swift and sure—pulling a cry from me that loosened something heavy in my chest. Weeks of agony, fear, tension... it all tore free with each movement, each breath, each surrender. The world narrowed to the rhythm of us—his body anchoring mine, my hands clutching for something solid as the storm in me finally had somewhere to go.

"Alex..." he shakily murmured against my ear, his voice strained and reverent. "I've missed this... missed you."

Guilt fluttered through me, raw and sharp. "I'm sorry," I breathed, but he slowed—searching my face like he needed to see the truth in my eyes.

That wasn't what I wanted. Not now. Not when the last pieces of the past were finally breaking loose.

"Don't stop," I whispered. "Please. I need all of you."

Something shifted in him at that—not unkind, but powerful. Intent.

He turned me around, lifting my hands then pressing them to the wall, steadying me. His palms slid to my hips, firm and claiming, guiding me exactly where he needed me. He eased my body forward, angled me just right, and when he drew me back to him, the breath left my lungs all at once. The world dissolved into sensation—sharp, consuming, overwhelming—each movement pulling me closer to the edge I'd been holding back from for far too long.

The release came fast and hard, shaking through me like a current. I heard him groan behind me—felt the way he held on, the way he unraveled with me—and for several long seconds, neither of us could speak. Stars burst behind my eyes. My knees wavered. I might have slipped if he hadn't caught my waist and pulled me with him as he lowered onto the bench beneath the spray.

I curled into him, still trembling. His arms wrapped around me like he wasn't willing to let even an inch of distance settle between us. His forehead rested against the back of my neck; my head fell back against his shoulder, spent.

"Please don't ever leave me again," he whispered—raw, terrified, honest.

I turned toward him and framed his face with my hands. The fear in his eyes softened the moment I spoke.

"Never," I said, steady and certain. "I'm yours."

***

ROMAN

After the shower it was back to getting ready. "I need to find something that will at least look as good as whatever you're planning to wear." She yelled from out in the bedroom as I was getting ready in my wardrobe.

"Are you serious? You always look fantastic. I'm sure whatever you plan to wear tonight will put me on edge. I thought we talked about this. You can wear whatever you want honey." I stuck my head out of the door to see if she was really that concerned about this, but I didn't see her. She must've been in the other closet. God, I wish she would get over this clothing competition bullshit.

She laughed and said something with a little less angst, "Actually, I can't wear whatever I want. Not after what happened. I had to throw that dress out that I was wearing that night." I never did get to see that dress on her. I wasn't really looking at it when they put her in the ambulance. I tried to shake that thought out of my head and refocus.

"What's going on babe? Are you worried about being around all these people tonight?"

"I don't know. Maybe. I think I just really need to do this. Face my fears and all. Don't you think?" No, I don't think it's that great of an idea at all, honestly, but I doubt she wants to hear that if the goal is to face her fears.

She walked out of the closet, and I followed her, watching as she put on a pair of skintight black leather pants and a very shiny silver top. She was so toned and muscular from all the training, too. Her long dark hair was cascading down her shoulders and however she was wearing her makeup was making her eyes really glow. They were so green I'd probably be able to see them from across the room– and that damn red lipstick and sky-high black heels. I'm glad I called for backup tonight to help me keep an eye on her. I knew she was going to love who I invited.

"What?" She said as I blinked myself back into the room.

"Sorry, Um, yeah you look stunning babe."

"I couldn't bring myself to wear anything even a bit revealing after what happened that night at Sebastian's. I know they told me nothing happened and thank God for that, but if a camera hadn't been in that room things may not have turned out the way they did, and that short dress would've been partly to blame."

"What do you mean, nothing happened? I don't know who they are, but you were brutally attacked and drugged. That is not nothing." I didn't know if she was trying to downplay it for me or for her but that was not nothing and if I ever see that guy again, I will rip his fucking head off. I kissed her reassuringly and went back to my closet to finish getting dressed. I put on some black slacks and a black button-down shirt and black shoes. I hope that all this black will make me look incognito in this place tonight.

Chapter 15

ALEX

*H*oly moly he looks hot in all black.

 When Harrison and Amelia arrived, I felt a little spark of excitement seeing Amelia walk in. She looked amazing in a tight blue dress paired with spiky silver heels, somehow seeming even taller than usual, if that was possible. Harrison wore a blue button-down shirt with black pants, almost as if they'd planned to match. I thought it was cute, and for a moment my mind drifted to the idea of dressing for holiday pictures. Surprisingly, the thought didn't unsettle me nearly as much as I would have expected.

 We poured ourselves a drink while everyone finished getting ready. Amelia and I drifted off to the side, chatting for a few minutes before it was time to head down to the car.

 She asked just above a whisper, "How're things? Are you good with this arrangement for a couple of weeks?"

 "I think I am. We've figured some things out. I mean this is not the ideal situation, but I can think of worse." We both turned, looking in the direction of the men.

 Roman caught us staring and said, "Is there something we should know over there?" We shook our heads and giggled.

 "Amelia, I should probably warn you about something," I said quietly. "I've been to this club before. I used to go all the time, but after my divorce I stopped because my ex still hangs out there."

I hesitated, chewing on my lip. "He's been talking like we're going to get back together. That's not happening, but he's never been great at accepting no."

My eyes flicked toward Roman for a second before I looked back at her. "I haven't mentioned any of this to him, and I'm trying to decide if that was a mistake. If my ex starts something... do you think Roman's the type who'd actually take the bait?"

"He asked Harrison and me to go so he doesn't get into a fight." She smiled and gave me a quick hug.

Well, there you have it, Roman King, Mr. Responsible.

"Good to know," I said under my breath. "Because my ex is the kind of guy who would start something just to cause a scene... especially if I'm involved."

I took a slow sip of my wine, my eyes drifting toward Roman across the room. For a moment, I seriously considered suggesting we skip the whole thing.

Amelia gave my hand a gentle squeeze. "Would you mind if I mentioned it to Harrison?" she asked softly. "He could give Roman a quiet heads-up so you don't have to be the one to bring it up."

I hesitated. I wasn't even sure it was necessary, but a little warning probably couldn't hurt.

"Sure." When I start to think something is truly a bad idea, I'm usually right.

In the car on the ride there we had another drink, and I texted the group from my office to let them know where to go and that we'd meet them there. The line outside was already wrapped around the building. I was feeling anxious, maybe because I was still a little paranoid about Tanner being out and what happened to me the last time I was in a crowded establishment, but also because I could potentially run into Luke.

Roman put his arm around me like he knew exactly how I was feeling right now. This time, however, everyone was here keeping an eye on me, and I wasn't going to drink anything I didn't pour myself or watch being poured. I wasn't going to take my eyes off my glass all night.

Walking into the club with the four of us felt a little like making an entrance. Roman headed toward the door first while Harrison stayed just behind Amelia. She rested a hand on my shoulder, and Roman kept hold of my hand as we stepped inside.

Amelia leaned toward me. "You alright?"

"Mhm." I guess she could feel me shaking. I hadn't been around this many people since that night. I didn't think it would have this effect on me. I've never had an issue like this before and it seems to be getting to me now.

Is this what PTSD is like?

When we reached the VIP area, I stopped short.

The whole section was packed with familiar faces. My friends from the real estate office were already there, and standing just behind them were Maggie and Abby with their husbands.

A laugh slipped out before I could stop it. I had no idea how everyone managed to pull this off, but seeing them instantly melted the nervous energy I'd been carrying all evening.

I moved forward, wrapping Maggie in a hug, then Abby, making my way through everyone as greetings and teasing comments flew around me.

By the time I pulled back, Roman had stepped in behind me, his arm sliding around my waist and drawing me close.

"You said safety in numbers, so I figured you wouldn't mind this crowd." The overwhelming emotion almost brought tears to my eyes.

"Thank you, this is amazing." I squeezed his hand and dropped my forehead to his chest, letting out the breath I was holding on the way in. Now I can relax.

The waitress opened a few bottles of champagne and poured us all a glass except for Abby— who was drinking water— and Maggie got everyone's attention by tapping on the side of her glass. "I'd like to celebrate being out and away from the kids tonight, first." We all laughed and clinked glasses together. "But I would also like to let Alex know that this is her tribe, and she is never alone. We're all here to support her in the coming weeks."

Now why did she have to do that? I'm going to have makeup all down my face.

To hold the tears in I threw back that glass of champagne and said, "Thanks for that Mags, you Jerk!" Everyone laughed and we tapped each other's glasses again.

Abby and Maggie grabbed my hand and yelled, "Come on girls, we're going to take advantage of this night out." All the girls went out to the dance floor while the guys stayed back at the table for a bit talking and drinking.

The dance floor was loud and warm, the music vibrating through the floor as we laughed and moved with the crowd. Being out there with my girlfriends felt incredible, the kind of carefree energy you only get when everyone's in the same mood and the night is still young.

For a while, I let myself disappear into it—dancing, laughing, letting the music carry me.

At one point I glanced up toward the VIP balcony. The guys were leaning along the railing watching the chaos below.

I couldn't quite make Roman out through the shifting lights and bodies, but somehow I knew exactly where he was. Even from across the room, I could feel his attention on me.

And strangely... I liked it.

Somewhere along the way, my head had finally caught up with my heart where Roman was concerned.

I only looked away for a second but when I turned back around, they were gone.

I spun slowly, scanning the room, trying to see over the sea of people, but being short had its disadvantages in a packed club. Bodies moved everywhere—arms up, hair flying, lights flashing—but none of them were the ones I was looking for.

The feeling was one of loss and a brief sadness washed over me. I know he didn't leave but not even being able to see him was something I was ultimately bothered by and starting to wonder if this was love or something more complicated.

About thirty seconds later, a pair of hands slid onto my hips and warm lips brushed the side of my neck. A low hum vibrated against my skin.

"Mmm." I smiled instantly knowing who's hands were holding me tight.

I reached back, wrapping my arms behind me and pulling his solid body tight against mine. For a fleeting second I wondered if he minded the sweat from all the dancing.

Maggie shouted over the pounding techno beat, "Get a room!"

I shot her a wink. She burst into laughter just as Matt slipped up behind her and did the exact same thing, earning the same reaction.

Roman and I stayed out there for what felt like forever. I loved dancing with him, loved the way his hands stayed firm and steady on my hips like he already knew exactly how to move with me. Our bodies found the rhythm without effort, falling into each other as the music pounded through the floor beneath us. The bass was so loud it felt alive, vibrating up through my heels and into my bones.

We moved together like we'd done it a hundred times before, even though we hadn't. There was something easy about it, something almost dangerous in how natural he felt against me. Every turn of my body seemed to draw me closer instead of pulling me away. His touch never wavered, and the heat of him mixed with the crush of the crowd and the pulse of the music until it all blurred together.

After a while, the room around us started to disappear. The lights, the people, the noise—it all faded into something distant and shapeless. It felt like it was just the two of us in the middle of all that chaos, moving in sync, caught in our own private current.

Finally, the heat won out and we left the dance floor for some libations.

As much as the drinks were free flowing, I didn't feel like drinking too much tonight and I already had a decent buzz going. I was still a little uneasy about my surroundings even though I was completely safe in this group. The only thing they didn't have in the VIP section was a bathroom.

"So, how's it going for you so far? You feeling good??" He had his arms wrapped around my waist and his hands firmly placed on my thighs, probably trying to assess how tight these pants really were. I had my arms wrapped around the back of his neck.

"I'm good, just trying not to have to use the restroom till the last minute. How the hell am I supposed to get these on and off?" I huffed out a laugh as he shrugged and shook his head.

"No idea babe, but I'd be happy to help." He gave me a sexy wink and a quick squeeze of my behind. I leaned in and kissed him, thinking we might have to say goodnight soon.

A restroom break would've been a simple task before but now it seemed I needed a chaperone just to use the restroom, so Abby and Maggie went with me as an entourage followed behind, comprised of Amelia, Roman and Harrison.

I laughed, grabbing Abby by the arm to pull her close so I could whisper in her ear, "I better be important, or all this is a big waste of time."

She looked at me confused and I explained, "I just feel like everyone is being, maybe, a little overprotective."

She looped her arm through mine and informed me, "Honey this is for all of us, not just you. Do you think any of us are going to be allowed out of their sight ever again after what happened to you?" She cocked an eyebrow at me before answering her own rhetorical question. "Hell no, and I'm fine with that."

I wrapped my arms around Abby and Maggie as we made our way through the crowded hall and Amelia joined us in the line for the over-crowded restrooms.

When we came out of the restroom, finally, laughing about how long it took me to get these leather pants off.

"I really want to thank you girls for tonight," I said, pulling them each into a hug. "I feel so loved."

I glanced across the room and spotted Roman and Harrison leaning against the wall with their arms crossed, looking completely unimpressed while a couple of girls tried their best to get their attention—with absolute-ly no success. It made me smile to know that I didn't have to worry about Roman the same way I always worried about Luke.

Abby, Maggie, and I headed back down to the dance floor while the others stayed upstairs. It was getting late, and even though we were having a blast, the girls needed to get home to their kids soon. One last dance together seemed like the perfect way to end the night.

The three of us laughed as we flailed our arms and jumped around to the pounding techno music while strobe lights flashed across the crowd.

Suddenly Maggie's eyes went wide.

Abby reached for my hands, but before she could grab them, someone wrapped their arms around my waist and pulled me tight against them, grinding their hips into me from behind.

My stomach dropped.

It wasn't Roman.

The strange, creeping feeling crawling up my spine—and the look on Maggie's face—told me that instantly.

I spun around.

Luke. The Ex

My hands started trembling as I tried to push away from him, but he grabbed my wrists.

"Come on," he slurred. "Just one dance."

I shook my head, trying to pull my hands free without jerking away and hitting someone in the crowd. The smell of alcohol on his breath hit me immediately, thick and sour, and I could hear it in his voice.

He was drunk. Very drunk.

And I knew exactly how bad that could get with Luke.

This wasn't good.

Maggie and Abby rushed toward us.

"Luke, just let her go," Abby said firmly. "She doesn't want to dance."

She reached for my hand, but Luke pulled me out of her reach.

My eyes widened as my heart started pounding. I felt trapped, but the last thing I wanted was Abby getting pulled into this.

I gave her a quick shake of my head, silently telling her to stay back.

"Abby, mind your own damn business. This is between me and Alex."

He shot both of them a dirty look.

How things had changed. Or maybe it was just him.

There was a time when all of us were friends. Luke had been close with Matt and Jack when we were all married, but somewhere along the way the drinking started. Nights out got later, and none of us were part of them anymore.

That's when the mean version of Luke showed up.

The sad part was I probably would have kept trying to make the marriage work. That's what my dad had done with my mom all those years. You stay. You fix it. You don't quit.

But Luke had been the one who walked away.

One day he just announced he wanted a divorce. No discussion. No trying to work things out. Nothing.

And that had never been like him. Luke was a control freak. Letting me go that easily had never made sense.

I should have been grateful. Everyone else certainly thought I should be. Who stays married to someone who drinks too much, cheats, and tears you down every chance he gets?

Apparently someone with very little self-worth.

I'm still working on that. Although the MMA classes were helping... and part of me wasn't entirely opposed to testing what I'd learned tonight.

If anyone deserved a demonstration, it was Luke.

"Luke," I said firmly, "there's nothing between us anymore. I already told you I don't want to talk."

Even saying it, I could still feel the strange pull he used to have over me. But Maggie and Abby were right beside me, and the last thing I wanted was to make a bigger scene and drag the guys down here.

Luke pulled me closer when I tried to push him away. His grip tightened around my wrists, the pressure starting to hurt.

"Yeah, you blocked me," he slurred. "What the hell was that about? Do you still think I'm stalking you?" He leaned closer. "Look, I need to talk to you. Can we just go somewhere and talk? It's important."

The girls exchanged worried looks, but this wasn't the time to unpack whatever he thought was so important.

I leaned closer so only he could hear me.

"Blocking you was a not-so-subtle hint," I whispered. "One I wish you had taken."

Then I took a breath and remembered the drills from self-defense class.

Twist both hands inward and down.

Break the grip.

Before I made the mental decision to do it, someone came up behind me and sternly demanded. "Get the hell off my woman." I rolled my lips to keep from laughing because it was Harrison. I mean thank God it wasn't Roman.

Harrison asked in a tone I'd never heard from him before– protective. "Alex, is this guy bothering you?" With that Luke let go of my wrists and stepped away looking between us skeptically. Thankfully I didn't need to use force. I rubbed the lingering feel of his hands from my wrists.

I moved closer to Harrison to feel more grounded and said, "Actually he is but it's nothing I can't handle." Maggie reached out to grab my hand and I pulled it in, shaking my head. I wanted them to back away and stay out of this. I strategically inched us off the dance floor, so no one gets hurt.

Luke looked up at Harrison then quickly directed his steely eyes back to me, "You're with this guy? I saw him here last weekend with a different chick. Another tall blond. You either like the cheating type after all or all your men prefer tall blondes to short. Plain. Brunettes." He made sure to enunciate each word that described me. "Especially when they cheat with big busty blondes huh? I knew you were secretly a freak."

His demeanor changed quickly from wanting to talk to insults. The insults were the Luke I remember. His eyes averted to Amelia who was on her way over. The heat rose through my body, and I was doing everything I could not to let the anger get the best of me. He was just goading me. My chest was tightening as the fire ripped through my veins. Did he know this would happen or did he just get off on torturing me with humiliation? Most likely it was the alcohol but no more excuses.

"Oh, you mean her?" I reigned in enough control to stand my ground and pick this fight back. "She's his girlfriend you jerk. He's my *boyfriend's* brother." Yep, I said it out loud in front of everyone. "I suggest you just go find some poor sucker to believe your bs and leave me alone." Ok, I guess having backup is making me feel better after all. I rubbed my wrists again and crossed my arms to try and control the feel of my heart beating out of my chest.

Luke laughed pointing just past my head. "I'm guessing that's your boyfriend now on his way to save the day?"

I snapped my head around. *Shoot*, Luke was one of those people who liked riling people up to fight and Roman looks pissed— I don't see this ending well.

***

ROMAN

I turned toward Harrison and gave him a look that needed no explanation—a sharp, carved-out stare that said exactly what I was asking of him: *Don't watch me. Watch her.* Keep Alex out of this. Make sure she doesn't take one step toward this mess.

She didn't need one more thing stacked against her before that hearing. Not one more ounce of chaos to weigh her down.

Harrison subtly shifted, moving to her side, angling his body so she was behind him while he kept a wide stance between her and the brewing fight. Only when I saw her tucked safely out of the line of fire—his arm out like a barricade, eyes locked on her like she was his only assignment—did I let myself face the bastard who'd started this.

And then I drove my fist straight into his face.

The impact cracked through my hand, a sharp, jarring vibration that shot up my arm. The guy dropped instantly, hitting the illuminated dance-floor tile with a sickening thud. His friends lunged at me—shoving forward in a disorganized scramble—but Matt and Jack were already on either side of me letting the guys know not to interfere.

I grabbed the scumbag by the front of his shirt and yanked him clean off the ground. The club's neon lights—violet, ice-blue, silver—flashed across his face, and for a split second I saw Alex's bruises in their place.

It made my vision tunnel.

I hit him again.

His head snapped back. Blood spattered across my shirt and dripped down my wrist. The coppery scent mixed with the club's fog machine and sweat, creating a thick metallic haze in the air. The crowd around us backed up fast, forming a loose semicircle, phones out, music muffled under the roar of people trying to decide whether to watch or flee.

My fingers tightened in the fabric of his shirt until my knuckles blanched. With my other hand, I pummeled him—relentless, heavy blows that sent pain shooting through my hands. I felt something crack. Maybe his nose. Maybe one of my bones. Didn't matter. Rage drowned out everything—sound, light, logic.

A hand clamped down on my shoulder.

I snapped my head toward it, ready to swing.

But it was Matt.

His expression was stern but calm, the deliberate stillness of someone trying to pull me back. Jack stood beside him shaking his head slowly—silent and grounding. Just like a couple of attorneys.

It cut through the haze.

Just enough.

I released the guy with a sharp shove to the back of his head, sending him staggering forward on his hands and knees. He scrambled away, wiping blood from his face, cursing under his breath but too scared to turn back toward me.

"Excuse me," a deep voice boomed from behind us. "All of you are going to have to leave. Management's orders. No fighting in here."

The bouncer stepped past me—massive, broad-shouldered, wearing a black earpiece and an expression that said this wasn't his first rodeo. But then he extended a respectful hand toward Harrison, shaking it firmly.

Right. Connections. A lucky break.

If not for that, we'd probably have police here instead of bouncers escorting us out.

Fine. Let them throw me out. I'd take that over cuffs any day.

I grabbed Alex's hand the moment we got upstairs to retrieve our things. Her palm was shaking. Mine was too—but from adrenaline. She watched me like I was a live wire, ready to spark. And I didn't blame her. I wasn't letting her out of my sight until she was in the car—away from witnesses, away from cameras, away from the risk of screwing up her case more than I already had.

Once we were inside the car, she ripped her hand from mine and pressed herself back against the door—putting distance between us.

Honestly?

Smart.

The anger was still radiating off me like heat from asphalt. My jaw clenched so hard my teeth ached. If I didn't relax soon, I'd crack a molar.

She let out a slow exhale, her shoulders sinking as she watched me carefully—like she wasn't sure if I was going to explode again or breathe through it.

I slid closer, cautiously, gently placing my arm around her so she could pull away if she wanted.
She didn't.

"I think we should just chill out and do low-key stuff until this case is over," I murmured against her hair.
Maybe I was saying it for her.
Maybe I was saying it for me.

Her head fell onto my chest reluctantly, and I rested my cheek against the top of her head. For once, I was the one inhaling her calm—trying to pull it into me, trying to let her steady me the way I usually steadied her. But even then, I could feel her anxiety vibrating through her body.

"You two can do whatever you want," Harrison muttered, irritation dripping from every word. "Amelia and I will stay far away from all of you."

He glanced between us, but when his eyes met mine, he held the stare a beat longer—checking me.
Asking silently, *Are you good? Are you in control?*

He knew this side of me better than anyone.
He'd been on the receiving end of my fists when we were younger more times than I cared to admit.

I gave him a nod.

But the truth?
I wasn't sure I was okay at all.

Not even close.

Chapter 16

ALEX

As soon as we stepped into the penthouse, I hurried straight into the bedroom, desperate to get these clothes off. The leather pants felt like they were glued to my skin, stiff and unforgiving after hours of wearing them.

I tugged at the zipper, muttering under my breath.

Roman's arms suddenly wrapped around my waist from behind. The surprise made me jump, which only twisted the pants tighter around my hips.

"Oh, for the love of—" I groaned. "Help me get these off, please. They're so tight."

He chuckled. His warm breath brushing my neck before he guided me backward onto the bed. The mattress dipped as he grabbed the waistband and tried to pull the pants down.

They barely moved.

Roman braced one knee against the bed and tugged harder.

"How the hell did you even get these on?" he muttered, straining as he yanked again.

With one final pull, the leather suddenly gave way, sliding free so abruptly he nearly lost his balance and stumbled back.

I let out the breath I'd been holding from sucking in my stomach.

"Crisco."

For a moment he just stared at me.

Then we both burst out laughing as the pants landed in a heap on the floor—finally off my body.

Roman shook his head, still smiling. "Would you like to take a shower?"

I nodded and reached for his hands. He pulled me gently to my feet and led me toward the ensuite.

Steam quickly filled the bathroom as the water warmed. When we stepped beneath the spray, the heat wrapped around us, washing away the lingering chill from outside.

Roman held me close under the stream, his hands resting firmly along my back.

"How are you after what happened tonight?" he asked quietly.

I looked up at him, running the sponge slowly across his shoulders and down his back while I decided how honest I wanted to be.

"Fine."

Even I could hear the lack of conviction in it.

"I got to spend good time with my friends. It was fun... until we got kicked out."

I glanced up at him, testing his mood.

He was working shampoo into my hair, fingers moving methodically through the strands as if he hadn't heard a word I'd said.

My head tipped back beneath the warm water as his lips brushed my neck, and a soft sound escaped me before I could stop it.

"Yeah," he murmured against my skin, kissing slowly along both sides of my neck. "All things considered... it was a pretty good night."

He was clearly trying to distract me.

And it was almost working.

"Except you kind of seemed like an attack dog," I said breathlessly before thinking it through. "Like someone let you off a leash."

He stopped instantly.

Then he straightened—almost too fast.

Great.

Maybe that comment should've waited.

"Do you know anything that could really hurt someone?" he asked suddenly, his tone serious.

The question caught me off guard.

"Yes," I said slowly. "Lots of things."

A worried look crossed his face.

"I thought you might," he said. "That's why I stepped in. You don't need to mess up your chances with that court hearing coming up."

He pulled me tightly against him, pressing my face against his chest as he exhaled heavily.

But was that really the reason?

"Okay, fine," I said, pushing back just enough to look at him. I cupped his face in my hands, forcing his eyes to meet mine even though his arms were still wrapped firmly around me.

"I need you to understand something."

I eased back a little more so he could see I meant it.

"I think the training Bruce is giving me is actually working. I feel... in control. Luke was definitely getting under my skin, but not enough for me to lose it."

Tanner, though... that might be another story.

The thought flickered briefly through my mind before disappearing again.

Roman's mouth curved into a small smirk.

"That's good to know," he said. "Hopefully we won't be hearing from him again."

"I guess he won't be mad anymore that I blocked him." I shrugged one shoulder and turned to step out of the shower. I was still a little uneasy about Roman's mood, and ending the conversation now seemed like the safest option.

Suddenly his hand caught mine.

He pulled me back beneath the spray and pressed me gently against the tiled wall, the water cascading over both of us as his body boxed mine in.

The look in his eyes had changed completely.

Heat. Hunger. Something raw and unrestrained.

And just like that...

We were definitely done talking.

His mouth found mine with a force that stole my breath, and every inch of him was solid and unyielding as he held me there. A current of heat shot through me, sharp enough to make my knees go weak. I couldn't tell if I should be worried or wildly turned on—except I was absolutely both.

I wrapped myself around him out of instinct, clinging to strength I trusted even when it felt a little combustible. He lifted me effortlessly, guiding us down onto the bench with a controlled urgency that sent a shiver down my spine. The moment he pulled me close, I gasped—everything inside me tightening at once. It was overwhelming in the best possible way.

He anchored me with his hands, steady and commanding, holding me exactly where he wanted me while the storm inside him worked its way free. His movements were intense, unfiltered, almost frantic with emotion—not careless, but close to something that bordered on surrender. I gripped his shoulders, trying to match him, trying to keep up, trying not to fall apart too fast.

The tension coiled tight between us until I could barely breathe. When he finally broke, releasing all that pent-up emotion into the moment, it pulled mine right out of me too. I collapsed against him with a strangled cry, trembling, gone, completely undone.

He held me there—strong arms, wet skin, heavy breaths against my neck—and for a long moment neither of us moved.

Only the sound of the shower and the echo of everything we'd just felt.

After drying off and pulling on a long T-shirt, I climbed into bed. Roman slipped between the sheets beside me and gathered me snugly into his arms before settling with his head in my lap.

I couldn't help running my fingers through his hair. He'd gone through a lot of mental gymnastics tonight, and I knew how exhausting that could be. As my fingers moved slowly through the dark strands, I felt his body begin to relax beneath my touch, the tension gradually draining out of him.

"Can I drop you off at brunch tomorrow?" he asked, not lifting his head.

I wondered how long he planned to stay in overprotective mode.

"Sure," I said. "I can have the girls bring me back afterward. Would that be okay?"

He nodded lightly against my lap.

A small sense of unease stirred inside me. I didn't like the feeling of asking permission. It reminded me too much of old habits I didn't want to fall back into.

"Oh, I almost forgot." He lifted his head slightly and looked up at me through sleepy eyes. "I scheduled the sleepover with the kids."

"What?" I blinked down at him. "Is that what you guys were doing tonight?"

Warmth spread through me at the thought. It was incredibly sweet of him to arrange a playdate knowing how much I loved spending time with them.

Roman looked rather proud of himself, and I found myself staring at him in quiet awe, almost forgetting everything that had happened earlier.

"I figured I might as well," he said. "I've been getting to know the guys better, and they'll be coming to our—" He paused. "I mean, my house."

Our.

Was that really a slip of the tongue?

"I'm learning things about you," I said softly. "I like it. I like that you and the guys get along—and that they're as comfortable with you around their kids as they are with me."

Chapter 17

ALEX

Oh yeah, there's that beach dream again. Nice relaxation and the sound of ocean waves. Why am I always alone in the dream though? I felt like there had to be some kind of symbolism there.

I rolled over and there was the most beautiful face staring back at me with a perfect smile. No anger or hostility anywhere to be found. Maybe it was the club and my ex and I should just let it go.

"Good morning," I said as I reached over, caressing his cheek with the back of my fingers.

"Yes, it is. Would you like to go for a run this morning?"

Nope definitely not. He was way too sexy right now.

"I think just a relaxing morning in bed might be nice." I inched closer to him and smoothed my fingertips over his amazing shoulders and arms, veering into every dip and over every mound, memorizing the definition. Those muscles alone made my eyes roll back in my head as my fingers fondled their way up and back.

He whispered in my ear, "That's the only kind of eye rolling I'm good with."

I groaned, and he pulled me closer, kissing me with a hunger that made my whole body tighten. One arm wrapped around my lower back, drawing me firmly against him, while the other slid along my jaw—his fingers brushing the side of my neck in a way that made my breath shudder. He tilted my head gently, deepening the kiss before trailing down my throat, across my collarbone, and lower, his mouth exploring with slow, deliberate intention.

Heat rippled through me, sharp and overwhelming, and I arched off the bed without even realizing it. His touch was everywhere—focused, impatient, and impossibly sure of my body. Every kiss, every pass of his mouth, every shift of his hands sent sparks racing through me until I was clinging to the sheets and struggling to stay grounded. The way he moved against me was purposeful, almost reverent, and yet filled with a kind of urgency that made my pulse thunder in my ears.

The pleasure built so fast my breath caught—and then there was nothing but release, powerful and consuming, pulling a cry from my throat before I could stop it. I barely had time to gather myself before he kissed his way back up my body, lingering in places that made me shiver, worshipping me with a tenderness that contrasted so perfectly with the fire he'd just set loose.

By the time his lips found mine again, I was still floating, barely tethered to my own skin. When he eased himself into me, it felt like being drawn into something I desperately needed. My my fingers laced through his short curls, my heart aching with how much I loved him in that moment. The way he touched me... the way he held me... the way he moved with me.

And all I could think—through the haze of heat and relief and everything we'd been through—was how grateful I was to have this back. To have him. To feel like this again.

Afterward we laid there together, fully sated. I simply admitted, "I'm happy." Euphoria spread across my face and the weight of the world left me, if only for this moment.

He sighed, "So am I."

Roman threw on some shorts and a t-shirt, kissed me quick, before leaving the room. I made my way into the ensuite to put on a long brown skirt and a white sleeveless button-down collared shirt with brown sandals. My hair was in long waves from last night's shower, and it didn't look too bad. I put on a little makeup to cover up the dark circles under my eyes then grabbed my sunglasses and threw them on my head.

Roman was in the kitchen making coffee. "You probably don't want breakfast, do you, since it's almost time to leave for brunch."

"I already had breakfast, thank you." I winked at him, and he shook his head and turned back around.

"You keep that up and you won't be going anywhere. I'll be having lunch and dinner right now." His gravelly voice sent shock waves of pleasure straight to my core. It left me breathless.

"I'm happy I didn't give up on us. In all honesty I would've driven myself crazy if you hadn't given in to me." The sincerity beaming from his eyes was enough to make me comply with whatever he would ever want or need from me. *Almost.*

I said jokingly, "And here I thought you gave in to me." He walked around the counter, sitting in the chair next to me and turned to face me. He pulled the chair over by the armrests and held me tight, with one hand around my waist and the other caressing the length of my hair as my legs rested between his muscular thighs. I placed my hands on his biceps for support.

"I mean, you were a challenge for me. I was wondering why I was chasing after someone who didn't want me. That's kind of a waste of time, don't you think? I'm not one to do that. I figured there had to be something else to it if I wanted to work this hard."

"You occupy more space in my head than my own brain does, that's for sure. Even when I had you confused, I somehow knew you'd come back to me," I said with a sigh, feeling my worry dissipate.

"Then why did you make it so damn hard?" He growled low as he kissed my forehead.

"I don't know, I guess maybe because I've always heard if it's too easy it isn't worth it. Maybe my head was telling me it was too good to be true. You know I have issues like that."

"That's funny because I usually expect it to be easy and this was anything but—however, definitely worth it." Weren't we a pair. Getting to know each other better should be our focus while we're living together for a couple of weeks.

We headed down to the car and suddenly I didn't want to let it go, "Roman, can we talk after brunch?" My worried expression returned.

"Of course. Is everything okay?"

"Mhm, I just wanted to talk about the next two weeks and what happens after that. Not too serious, but we got thrown into this and never had a chance to discuss anything." He kissed the top of my head and seemed happy I wanted to talk about that, in particular–except that was only part of it.

***

Sunday brunch, I thought with relief upon entering Sunny Side Up. I inhaled the delicious aromas that brought me so much happiness. This is where I come to decompress and truly relax or vent.

"Hello Ms. Kennedy, right this way. Mrs. Stevens and Mrs. Fletcher are already seated." I followed the hostess to the table to find Maggie still wearing her sunglasses in the restaurant.

I walked up laughing. "Lookin' good, Mags." I said and peered at Abby who was trying not to laugh.

She put her hand over her face. "I ordered a big freaking Bloody Mary this morning." Her voice was hoarse and low as she tapped a finger on top of her tall glass. I'm sure she was sporting a headache to go with those glasses.

I thanked the hostess and walked over to Maggie to say hi.

"I can't take you girls anywhere." I giggled and kissed the top of Maggie's head gently in case it really was hurting her.

Abby held it in as long as she could then erupted in laughter, tipping her orange juice in my direction and I tapped it with the mimosa she handed me.

Maggie blurted out, "So, Roman told Matt that you two are living together." She squinted over the top of her sunglasses. "Ouch" she mouthed and put her glasses back where they were. I rolled my lips to keep from laughing– knowing, now, her head must be hurting.

"I think Matt pressed him because he knew something was going on." She said.

"It's not a big deal. It's just for two weeks. He just figured Matt and Jack would need to know since they're my attorneys. Kind of need to know where the person they're protecting is staying, ya know?" I huffed through my nose before taking a larger gulp of my mimosa this time. "Ever since Friday I feel like I'm in the witness protection program or something. I really hate it— I just want to live my life. If Tanner comes after me on the street, I'll be ready." *Wouldn't that be poetic justice?*

Abby said, "Yeah, I believe you. I just wish you didn't need to be so prepared. Seems like a lot to go through because some asshole couldn't keep their hands to themselves. Maybe Roman will be with you when he does." Remembering the way Roman went after Luke was not a pleasant memory and I never wanted to see him do it again.

"That's what's bothering me so much though. I have a feeling that Tanner isn't harmless." I confessed. "I don't think it was a simple case of couldn't keep his hands to himself. I think he was out to hurt me." The girls gave a concerned look. I can only imagine how Roman would react if I told him that's how I really felt.

Maggie's face was overcome with fear. "Why do you think that?" She snapped and immediately her hands flew to her head.

Maybe I shouldn't say this because she seems really sensitive, but we've always told each other everything. But people can change. "I'm sure he'd been stalking me before that happened. I can't be the first person he's ever attacked, and I don't think I'll be his last if he's allowed to get out. They still aren't sure exactly what he drugged me with, just that it was some variation of rohypnol and fentanyl. The usual drugs are out of your system in twenty-four to forty-eight hours, and this shit put me out for four days. He wasn't messing around."

Abby started crying. "I don't know if this is pregnancy hormones or what, but I'm really scared for you now. He needs to go away for a long time." She choked through the sobs.

"That's how I feel too, but his brother has already stepped in to get him out on bail. Who knows if anything will happen to Tanner. I mean, I'm pretty sure the max is only ten years for what he did, and he'd be out in a year with our shitty system and his connections." I sat back in the chair and let my arms fall to my sides.

Maggie shook her head, "Well, do you know what you're going to do? I thought you said you thought it was Luke who was stalking you? Was that why Roman went after him like that?" She slammed her glasses on the table. I'm guessing she was feeling better after that Bloody Mary.

I grabbed both their hands to try and get them to relax. "I have an amazing legal team and the best support system a person in my position could ever ask for, so this week I'll have a better idea of what's going to happen in there. Plus, the guys put a sleepover together for me this Friday with the kids. They're staying Friday night and all-day Saturday, so nothing in this world will be bothering me then." I didn't think talking about the Roman and Luke incident on top of all this was such a good idea. I hope they didn't push it further.

***

ROMAN

Harrison lived in a trendy shotgun style house overlooking the river. It was a new development that we helped build. It was three stories with a balcony on every floor. It had three bedrooms, each with their own bathroom. One floor was all the kitchen and living room with a half bath. That's the floor we spent the most time on.

His style was more lived in than mine. He liked lots of color, but it was more sports and music memorabilia than anything. I mean, I liked sports too, but I didn't want to decorate my house with team merch, and I definitely didn't know stats the way he did.

I called before I came over in case Amelia was there. Her little white Mercedes convertible was in the driveway. Harrison's big jacked up pickup truck must've been in the garage. Amelia answered the door.

"Hey Roman, where's Alex?" Amelia looked behind me and moved out of the way to let me in.

"She's at brunch with Abby and Maggie."

"Oh, that sounds nice. We just made brunch ourselves. Would you care for some food and a mimosa?"

"Food, yes. Do you have any coffee?" I followed her to the kitchen.

"Coming right up... Damn I feel like I'm at work." She chuckled as she looked back over her shoulder.

"I can get it myself, you know. Where's Harrison?" I looked around and saw a lot of things that didn't look like Harrison's style.

"Shower." She pointed upstairs. "What's up with you today? Everything ok after last night?" She was casually talking while pouring the coffee and making a plate with some eggs and toast for me.

"Yeah, I think so. I feel like it's been a while since I've said that, but things are going really well. I'm not trying to jinx it." I don't know if she could spot a lie like Alex could, but I didn't need to explain anything to her.

She nodded with a smile and said, "I bet." I ignored the inflection in her voice that would suggest she may not believe me either.

After I finished eating, we took our drinks out on the balcony and waited for Harrison.

"This is me being nosy and it's none of my business, but do you and Harrison live together?" I arched an eyebrow and tried to read her expression before she answered. She was so private I didn't think she'd just come right out and tell me. If so, it would explain why she used Harrison's code for my elevator access and the woman's voice I heard in the background over the phone that morning after Alex woke up in the hospital.

"Yes, you are being nosy." She looked out over the river view not making eye contact.

"Ok, none of my business, I won't ask again." *I don't need to. I already have my answer.*

Harrison came out at the end of that conversation and said, "Despite it being none of your business, yes, we are living together now."

Confirmed.

"Ok, good. Maybe you'll get to meetings on time now."

He laughed but said, "Yeah, doubt that."

As soon as Amelia went back inside, Harrison asked, "Tell me, man, how is everyone with the court hearing coming up? I mean you all were on edge at the club last night."

"I don't know. This case seems like it's cut and dry, but Alex seems apprehensive about something, and I can't figure it out." I paused before I got into it with him about the ex-husband. "Luke was a separate situation."

"What's she so worried about? That dude wouldn't do anything stupid like coming after her, would he?" I shook my head while shrugging my shoulders.

"I don't know what he's capable of. It went from grabbing her ass and calling her names, to drugging and attempted rape. I mean, that escalated pretty quick."

"Yeah, sounds really messed up for sure. You be careful with all this, ok? I'll be in that courtroom with you. I'm pretty sure mom and dad are too." That's all she needed was everyone hearing all the sordid details.

"We don't need this turning into a circus either, though." I kicked my feet up on the ottoman and drank my coffee trying not to let this conversation piss me off.

"Dad's using this as an intimidation tactic. He thought he was done with that feud until this happened." This doesn't seem like some simple feud.

"What do you mean? Do you think the feud is the reason he went after Alex?" I sat up and turned to face him.

"Not sure but dad hinted at that, maybe."

I put my head back and let out a deep sigh and said, "Great, so basically, I've or we've or whomever, put a target on Alex's back because of our family bs?"

"Maybe I'm reaching. I don't know. I'm sure Alex had a hand in getting the target put on her own back with what she was doing." *Doing?* Nothing she did warranted that behavior.

"Like what?" I snapped. He put his hands up as if to say calm down. The anger was roaring to life again.

"Nothing bad, just wanting to help those people in that neighborhood and grabbing a guy by the balls..." That seemed to calm me down some.

I started laughing which brought the mood back down, at least somewhat. "Damn, can you imagine what she might've done to him if she'd been doing that MMA training back then." The thought came out before I realized it and his eyes grew wide.

"She hadn't even been training yet?"

"Nope, she was already fully capable of taking care of things herself." We laughed and Amelia came back out.

"Is the locker room talk over yet?"

"Whatever, you were doing your hair. You had no desire to come out here and listen to us." Harrison muttered.

She smiled and kissed Harrison on the cheek. "You are correct." She turned to me and gave me a wink.

Yeah, it's still weird to see them together.

After chatting with the two of them for a while a text came in from Alex letting me know she was on her way back to the penthouse. I told her to just text me again when she got in the elevator, and I would put the code in from the app on my phone. She said she had the girls with her and was going to give them a tour. I got in my car and headed home.

I noticed an eerie feeling in the garage when I arrived, just like she said, so I called the security office and had them run the tapes back to see if anyone had been in there at any time today other than the usual. I also sent an email to security asking that they keep eyes on the garage and all doors exiting and entering the building. When the elevator doors opened, I was pleasantly surprised by the three very happy faces that were sitting on the couch laughing hysterically.

Maggie waved while holding her breath and Abby said, "Hey Roman. Your place is amazing."

"Thank you. You ladies seem to be having a good time." I walked to the kitchen and put my keys on the counter.

Alex snorted, "Yes we were just naming the baby is all."

I shook my head and grabbed a water out of the fridge. I can only imagine what they came up with.

"What did you decide that was so funny?" I inquired but I was truly unconcerned, knowing that this was probably not the name they were thinking.

Maggie said with a bit of a slur, "We're going with Bloody Mary or Mimosa."

Someone's drunk.

I raised my eyebrows and played along, "What if it's a boy?"

Maggie replied again, "Well since they already have a Jack, it's going to have to be either Jim, Jose or Johnny."

Good luck to Matt when this one gets home.

"Well, if it's all good with Jack, go for it."

They started laughing again and I went over and kissed Alex on the head. I wended my way back to the bedroom to change clothes and process the conversation I had with Harrison as I tried to keep a level head.

Chapter 18

ALEX

After the girls left, I went back to the bedroom, to find Roman sitting on the edge of the bed with his head in his hands.

I walked over and sat next to him putting my arm around him and said, "Hey there. Wanna talk about it?"

He mumbled into his hands, "Yeah, I'm worried." *Oh no, what now?*

"About what? Me, the court stuff, what?" I said as patiently as I could because I was worried about him and his possible anger issues.

"No...about Abby's baby." I shoved him and he pulled me down onto the bed to kiss me.

I pulled away for a second. "Seriously, though, what's wrong?" I softened my face and looked him in the eyes, assessing his mood.

"Can we go sit in the hot tub for a bit? We can talk about it in there. I know you could probably use a nice soak anyway." I'd been sore all day but really felt it the second he mentioned it.

"That sounds like a great idea. I'll grab a suit real." I agreed and we left for the gym.

Steam curled up from the surface of the hot tub as I stepped down carefully, dipping one foot into the water first. The heat wrapped around my toes and the ball of my foot instantly, making me pause for a second before lowering the other one in. The warmth crept up my calves as I eased down another step, and by the time the water reached my thighs I could already feel a fine sheen of sweat forming along my forehead from the rising steam. I winced when the hot water met my midsection, the sudden temperature making me suck in a quick breath. For a few seconds it felt almost too hot, my skin prickling as my body adjusted. Then the warmth settled in, my muscles loosening as the heat soaked through me. I exhaled slowly and lowered the rest of myself into the water.

By the time I sank down fully, the tension in my shoulders had already begun to melt away.

We both turned so we were facing outward in the tub, our arms crossed along the edge with our cheeks resting on them, looking at each other while we talked.

"Ok, so tell me what has you so distraught?" I smiled hoping it would encourage him to be honest with me.

"Do you remember the first meeting about the Ellingtons at my office when you found out Tanner was the dude who...well was who he is?" Why are we talking about him? Maybe I don't want to do this after all.

"Yes. I'm not a big fan of that day." I inhaled deeply and could feel my pulse increase.

He smiled, reaching over to put his hand on my back, probably trying to relax me. I'm sure he could see the anxiety building just from saying his name. "Do you also remember thinking it was your fault they were coming after me. You know because of what you were doing in Burrow Township?"

I couldn't get a good read on him while he was trying to pacify me. "Yes." I said almost sounding like a question.

He paused, "Well, they may have been targeting you to get to me and my family. It may not have anything to do with what you were doing in that neighborhood. If they find out about Amelia, she'll be on the list too, I have no doubt. It was never your fault, it was mine. I should say it was their sick vendetta that caused all this trouble."

I was frozen. I couldn't even blink. I could feel my pulse in my eyes. What the hell was he saying? That these people are so sick, that they would go after me and Amelia because they want to hurt the Kings? That's just messed up. The Kings are such good people. *Fine.* Tanner wants to play this game, I'm definitely in the mood now. I shook the thoughts of him hurting Roman and his family out of my head, replacing it with him and I in the ring— MMA style.

"Don't worry about me and Amelia. I'll take care of Tanner in the courtroom. Matt and Jack can take care of Marcus in the legal and political arena." That was not at all what I had in mind for Tanner, but now I was determined to bring my plan to fruition.

***

ROMAN

After listening to her I had no idea what was going on in her head, but what I was feeling wasn't good. It was too intense to be the reaction she was giving me. She was hiding something from me, and it was bringing the anger to the surface again. The night she said she had something planned that I wasn't going to like was not just drunk speech.

"Alex, what are you thinking? I don't want you doing anything crazy."

She softened her face trying to placate me, I'm familiar with this routine. "Roman, I've got this under control. I have a whole team of professionals helping me. I promise I'm not going to do anything *crazy*." The emphasis she put on the word crazy had me thinking she and I have a very different idea of what that means. There's nothing I can do to make her tell me what's really going on in her head and I've got to control my temper. She's seen enough of that but she's testing me, for sure.

She reached over brushing her hand across my cheek as she scooted closer. She moved her hand to the back of my neck, kissing me almost forcefully. I could use a little of this. I let her take control and climb on top. She took my suit off while staring seductively at me and tossed it to the side. She reached into the water and my head fell back at her firm grasp, and I stretched my arms out on the side of the hot tub easing the tension from my body. She stopped and I opened my eyes watching her slowly pull the string on her bikini top letting it fall into the water and float to the other side. She slid her bottoms off, kicking them out of the tub. This I can handle.

I went to grab her hips and pull her to me. She caught my arms before my hands got to her with a devilish smile on her face, pushing my arms back to the side of the tub. As much as I wanted control of this right now, it seemed to be out of my hands and I was trying to let her see that the anger and aggression I showed last night is gone, at least somewhat. This distraction –and that's exactly what this is for both of us– couldn't be more welcome. She leaned in taking my mouth with hers sliding her tongue effortlessly between my lips— because, well, damn this is hot and I'm game.

Both of her knees were straddled tight to either side of my hips as she lowered herself down onto my lap. My head fell back with a groan as she worked the tension out of every inch of my body. Her hands were still holding my arms in place, her nails digging into my forearms making me wince, causing me to want to change positions. I'm not sure I'm into pain as much as I am pleasure. The heat from the tub and the jets bubbling up all around us is creating a sensory overload that I may not be able to contain much longer. Every time she adjusted her grip on my arms, she left a new more painful sensation than the first. I pulled my arms from her claws and wrapped them around her waist, flipping her around then grabbing her hands, securing them on the side of the tub. I leaned in taking her neck in my mouth, biting just hard enough to get a reaction and sliding in with a swift movement so strong it pushed her against the side. I was wondering if pain was her thing, maybe. She seemed to be rather fond of it as she pressed into me while I thrust into her harder keeping up with the rhythm. I let go of one hand and wrapped her hair around my fist, holding her in place as I channeled the anger, I felt into hammering her. She reached back with her now free hand and dug her nails into my ass but I'm too close to give a shit about the pain now. I could feel my release coming hard and fast as her insides trembled around me and her last dig with her freaking nails as she screamed at her own release, and I collapsed to the side of her. I pulled her onto my lap resting my head in the crook of her neck.

She whispered in my ear breathlessly, "I hope that helped." I knew she was distracting me from something, and it worked but I wasn't too fond of the claw marks I had up and down my arms. At least she didn't draw blood.

I squeezed her and said, "That was perfect..." almost "thank you." She smiled and I kissed her lips softly, wondering if I may have been too rough with her. She didn't seem to be too upset about it. I let whatever it was bothering me go, for now.

"Let's go, I'm cooking dinner tonight. We're going to relax, talk and get a plan going for this next couple of weeks. Sound good?" she asked as she grabbed my hands to help me out of the hot tub. We grabbed our discarded suits and threw on the robes we brought as cover ups and headed back to the penthouse.

***

ALEX

After a hot relaxing shower and throwing on some pajama like sweats, I started going through his fridge and pantry to decide what to make for dinner. *Hmmm, his pantry is as big as my closet,* I thought as I grabbed my phone off the shelf deciding I needed some music to drown out the thoughts of the court hearing for now. I flipped to a station that had a lot of Miley Cyrus on it. "Flowers" was the first song to play, and it had my hips gyrating so hard I felt like I was Miley in concert; in the pantry.

Even the music wasn't enough to stave off the anxiety completely, and I put my hands on my knees, taking one deep breath and then another. It's hard work trying to pull this off.

That's when I saw a bag of quinoa calling my name and some brown rice. Hopefully he had chicken in the fridge too. He did and some fresh broccoli. Perfect, now I can focus on dinner without getting distracted by the noise in my head. I shimmied all through the kitchen as I cooked and sipped on wine.

Roman was sitting on the sofa watching television, so I called over to him to see if he wanted something to drink.

He came over and sat on one of the stools at the kitchen island. "I'll have a glass of wine, your choice." He licked his lips as he looked me up and down stopping on my swaying hips.

I winked, pulling out the nice bottle of chardonnay I had open in the fridge and poured him a glass then topped off mine. He said he came over to watch me cook but that look would suggest he was just ogling me, probably remembering the hot tub, which was insane. I couldn't control my need to sink my claws into him and mark him, but I don't think he liked it as much as I did.

"What are you making for dinner, Chef Alex?"

"A yummy garlic chicken over brown rice and quinoa with fresh steamed broccoli."

He seemed excited and surprised.

"Damn, do I even have all that in my kitchen?"

I laughed. Why wouldn't he know what he had in his kitchen?

"Who bought this?"

He gave me a guilty look and said, "Amelia orders it and has it delivered."

"Well, she and I like the same provisions, that's for sure. We should have her and Harrison over one night for dinner this week," I suggested.

"Yes, we should. I would love that." He agreed and tapped his glass to mine. I was starting to feel domestic, and it felt weird. I bet it's just him rubbing off on me now that I'm trying to get him to stop worrying.

After dinner and a couple glasses of wine I announced, "We should discuss the next two weeks."

He said, without even a second thought, "Move in with me. Forget the next two weeks and just move in."

Um, excuse me? What!

I started getting dizzy and my breathing quickened as I stumbled to a chair. "I need to sit down for a minute." I put my head between my knees. He kneeled in front of me with both hands on the arm of the chair.

"Alex, that's where we're headed anyway," he insisted.

I shook my head. I couldn't even pick it up to look at him. "Roman, why did you do that? This was going to be an easy conversation. I don't even know what we are right now, and you want to move in permanently?"

"Why does everything have to be so damn complicated with you?" he yelled, sounding really pissed as he laid back on the floor covering his face with his hands to muffle his tone.

I'm complicated? I just wanted to discuss the next two weeks, not forever.

"I could say the same thing about you," I shouted back while squeezing the life out of the arm of the chair.

"I just know what I want." He sat up and moved toward me again like a predator about to attack its prey.

"Well, I don't." I threw my hands in the air in frustration.

"You can't say you haven't thought about it."

I need to steer this in another direction before I have a full-blown panic attack.

I got up and scrambled away from him. "Roman, I'm going to clean the kitchen and put my clothes in the spare bedroom."

He practically jumped up off the floor and grabbed my arm, spinning me around.

"Nope, not this time." He shook his head. "No more subject changes. We're talking about this, now," he demanded.

"Fine, I'm not moving in, the end."

He threw his head back and laughed and honestly it was a bit unnerving. *Is this that control freak stuff I was worried about?*

"Oh, so it's that simple now, is it? I don't think so. You told me you want to spend your life with me..."

I interrupted. "That was drunk me that said that. She says a lot of stupid shit." I tried to get out of his grasp, but he was holding me tightly and I was starting to sweat with nervous energy.

He had his arms wrapped around my waist and was looking right into my eyes. He started over, but this time spoke slower with a much deeper tone of voice that was almost hypnotic.

"You told me you wanted to spend your life with me and that if you tried to run away, I should chase you. This is me chasing you."

Oh my God, I did say that!

Now I don't know how to get out of this because it is what I want, but I don't think I can handle it. If he keeps pushing, it's going to freak me out, and I can see myself doing something stupid. I took a long deep breath to think for a minute on how to get out of this.

The aha moment I needed. It's the perfect time to talk about last night and find out if he has anger issues because I am not staying with him if that's the case. "Ok, but before I make a decision like that, I need to know something..." I looked back into his eyes, and I got the feeling he knew where this was going and his grip on me loosened.

"So, ask." He insisted as his jaw ticked, and his eyes narrowed.

"What happened to you last night? I mean, what was that last night?"

He didn't just loosen his hold on me, he let me go and dropped his arms to his side. I watched him as he walked over to the sofa, sat down and put his head down, running his hands through his hair back and forth.

"I told you I had other things to work on." he wasn't looking at me as he said that, and his hands were on his head gripping his hair tight.

"Yes, you did say that. Is that one of those things and if so, what exactly is it that you have to work on?" I carefully sat down next to him, fully expecting him to get up and move. I could feel the tension pouring out of him. This must be a big deal for him. I've never seen him like this before.

He patted me on the thigh and sat up with a halfhearted chuckle. "Wasn't it obvious?" I don't think he wants to come right out and name it so I will...

"Anger issues?" He nodded slowly and I realized I got it right but is that all?

"Among other things, yes," he said, leaning back to stretch out. It looked like he was trying to warm me up to tell me more. "I'm not really sure when it started. I was pretty young— got into a lot of fights. As I got older, as you can imagine, I worked with my mother to control the issue, but it never fully went away. It still rears its ugly head from time to time." I felt a sense of insecurity now wondering if he meant that it popped up randomly and I could be in danger of being on the wrong end of his fury.

"Does it just happen for no reason? I mean, should I be worried?" He laughed lightly, running his hands over his face.

"No, you're not in any danger from me..." His voice trailed off and I immediately felt like there was more to it than that.

"But..."

"But..." He hesitated, reaching out to rub my back gently, maybe letting me know he's in control right now and I don't have to worry, except I am worried and that's actually a problem. "I don't like people messing with you or trying to get between us."

"What does that mean?" Is it just jealousy?

"It means people like Luke and Tanner will always be on my shit list and I will have to try really hard to control how I react around them."

"Like, last night."

"Yes, like last night. I'm sure I scared you but unfortunately, I already had it in my head that I hated your ex-husband after talking to your brother and the little bit you told me."

I smiled because I felt the same way about my ex-husband and if he knew the way I felt about Tanner I'm sure his blood would boil. "I can't say that I blame you for what happened with my ex. He's had that coming from a lot of people. I wish it hadn't been you though."

"Alex, you have to understand, from the moment I met you, I've been protective as hell where you're concerned." The pained expression on his face reminded me of the day he brought that beautiful bouquet of flowers over and I ruined the moment by asking if he got them for my grave.

"Yes, maybe overprotective, wouldn't you say? Do you think I need to be protected like that?" I wanted to find out if he really did think I was a damsel in distress because I am no princess that needs saving.

"It doesn't matter what I think. It doesn't matter that you take training classes to defend yourself. It doesn't even matter that you *can* defend yourself. It only matters, in my mind, how I feel about you needing to. I don't like it, and I will always do everything in my power to make sure you don't have to."

Oh shit, will this work? Will he really lock me up and throw away the key?

"Were you like this with your ex-fiancé?" I'm not sure if I should throw her into the mix, he doesn't seem to like to talk about her.

"I got angry with her, that's for sure. Nothing like this. She had a very wrong idea about who I was. She tried to get her name on the business and the building for that matter. She used me to climb the social ladder. She wouldn't know love if it bit her in the ass All she wanted was money. Thank God for Amelia, apparently."

"Really, what did Amelia do?"

"She went to my mom who then had a long talk on the swings with me." I felt sad for him and leaned against him. He wrapped his arm around my shoulder. I wasn't afraid of this Roman. I was a little worried about Roman from last night, but it didn't seem to be directed at me.

"So, your mom was the one who talked you out of the engagement because of Amelia?"

"That's what I was told." he paused, taking in a few calming inhales and exhales. "Baby, I'm so sorry you witnessed that side of me. I can't take it back. I wish I could've just told you. It's been a long time since anything like that's happened. It's hard to say where my mind goes."

"Do I have anything to worry about if I somehow make you mad?" He laughed, tugging me onto his lap so he could look down at me.

"Alex, do you know how many times you've made me mad?" Hmm, good question.

"Who me? I've been a perfect little angel, so none." He laughed louder as he rolled me to my side and swatted my left butt cheek hard.

"Ow! What was that for?" I laughed through the fake reaction.

"That was for making me mad for the millionth time. I promise that you can't elicit that reaction from me honey. You hold my heart, Alex. If I think you're hurting from something I've done, it will break my heart."

Oh my God. If he did something to hurt me it would break his heart, but what if I did something to hurt him, would it break mine? Do I even have a heart to break, or does he have mine too?

"Do you think maybe we should hold off on living together until after the court hearing?"

"Why do we need to wait?" Because I could mess this all up and I'd rather not have to move twice.

"I just don't want to have too much to think about right now. I want to get court out of the way and then we can revisit this. Is that alright?"

He nodded and went to the kitchen to refill our wine glasses. I'm guessing that answer was not alright.

***

ROMAN

As we were cleaning up after dinner, I really felt the need to apologize. "I'm sorry for being so forward. I realize you've got a lot going on right now and this may have caused a little more stress, but I know this is right and it's what I want. I know it's what you want too."

"Are you just doing this so you can protect me, because I don't need protecting forever." She questioned my motives, and she might be right, but I'd like to believe it's because I just wanted her to move in.

"I'm not sure you even need it now, but it does make me feel better to know you're safe with me."

"If this is some kind of control freak attitude, you're going to be disappointed. If you start telling me what to do, I'll run the other way. You know this." I laughed watching her facial expressions. She's so expressive. She looks utterly crazed right now.

"As much as I'd like you to listen to me, I know it's not something I'll ever be able to control." She scrunched up her face.

"Of course I'll listen to you. I just won't be doing everything you tell me to do or not do." I shook my head, gathering her into a hug.

"Do you really think that's what this is about? We move in together and you no longer have a life?" She gave me an innocent look and shrugged her shoulders. "Alex, we have some work to do here. I have no desire to control you. I love you and I want you to move in, that's all. Being able to protect you and know where you are is just a little perk that would come with it."

I heard her let out a sigh before she said, "I don't know what a relationship is supposed to look like, that's why this scares me. Either I was in an abusive marriage or I was in something short lived. I have nothing really to compare this too. It's not like it's any easier. It's not like my parents displayed the best role models. I mean my mom treated my dad like crap and he just took it. I hated that he did that."

"Well, sounds to me like you need to see how people are supposed to treat each other in a relationship. Stop trying to compare this to that and just see what happens naturally. If I start to smother you or you think I am, then say something and I'll give you space. I'll do the same for you when you're giving me too much space." I winked at her, and she giggled.

"Oh my God this is going to be a shit show." I swear she has the most negative outlook on relationships. At least she's smart enough to know she needs therapy; a lot of it.

Chapter 19

ALEX

What's this, two alarms going off?

I reached over and flicked my alarm off, stretching my body all the way...

"Oh," I said, surprised when a hand touched my stomach.

"Good morning roomie," he said and I swallowed the lump in my throat feeling a little anxious about agreeing to this even if it's just two weeks.

"Good morning."

"Time to get up and go to the gym. I don't want you to think I'm hindering your routine." He said casually.

"Thank you." I said almost annoyed.

I wonder when the enthusiasm is going to wear off and he starts trying to get me to stay in bed.

"Well, as much as I like the gym, you motivate me to go more. So, thank you for that. I'm trying to focus on the things you do that I can benefit from. If that's okay with you?"

"Of course. If I didn't think I was so perfect and had everything under control, I would feel the same way."

He started laughing and rolled on top of me, kissed me quickly before he got off the bed, pulling me up with him. "Go get dressed and I'll make us a pre-workout drink and get a bottle of water together for you."

This isn't bad, but it could just be the move in 'starter package'. The complacent package comes next. Getting out of my head and going with the flow is what I should really be doing. He's always sweet like this, I just hope I don't make him crazy. The little plan I have could really screw all of this up.

I put on the workout clothes I packed and grabbed a swimsuit as I headed out to the kitchen. We went to the gym, and I got in a really good workout with some laps in the pool; a good stretch in the yoga room, and about fifteen minutes of relaxation in the sauna. I was surprised that Roman didn't meet me in the sauna. He seemed a little preoccupied, so I let him do what he needed to do. Maybe he's having second thoughts about moving in together. *Good.*

He barely said a word to me on the ride back up to the penthouse, so I had to break the silence.

"Roman, are you alright? What happened?"

He shook his head. "Oh, sorry, nothing. Just going through my meetings for this morning and some emails on my mind. I may have to go to Texas again this week, but I'm going to try and get out of it and send Harrison instead."

"You know you can go if you need to? I'll be fine." He gave me a weak smile.

"Yeah, I know, but it's a little too soon for me to leave you."

I didn't know what was going on, but I didn't think it was as simple as meetings and emails. He was entirely too distressed.

***

ROMAN

A lot of texts came through this morning—more than usual—and all before eight.

My phone had been lighting up since before the sun was fully up, buzzing across the nightstand like it had something urgent to prove. By the time I grabbed it, the screen was already packed with notifications.

Grant wanted a meeting.

So did Harrison.

And the Santoros.

My thumb hovered over the screen for a second.

The Santoros...I'd only met them once, and it hadn't been under normal circumstances.

Alex had been unconscious in the hospital. Tubes. Machines. The quiet mechanical rhythm of monitors keeping track of things none of us could control.

The room had smelled like antiseptic and plastic, the memory of it burning the back of my throat while I stood there staring at her, trying not to think about the possibility that she might not wake up.

That was when the Santoros arrived.

They didn't make a scene. They appeared in the doorway like they'd been there the whole time, composed and carrying themselves with the kind of quiet authority that made people instinctively step aside.

They asked about Alex like family would.

Only they weren't family.

Before they left, they told me something that had sat wrong with me ever since.

They said they were from a prominent family from Italy—a protected one.

Protected.

They didn't elaborate—didn't need to. The way he said it carried enough weight on its own.

I remember the way he studied me while he spoke, like he was deciding whether I was someone worth trusting with information that didn't belong in my world.

Under normal circumstances, I would've ended that conversation right there.

I didn't involve myself with people like that. I didn't even know people like that really existed.

But Alex had been lying in that hospital bed, unconscious, and something inside me had already started cracking under the pressure of it.

When they offered to exchange information, I agreed.

Even now the memory made my jaw tighten.

That wasn't a deal I'd ever expected to come back around.

Yet here their name was on my phone, seeming urgent.

I moved to my email next and saw several messages from Amelia. She'd already scheduled a handful of meetings for the week, all new, and one of them was a tentative trip to Texas. No details. No explanations. Just placeholders sitting on the calendar.

That was Amelia's way when she posted meetings before she got to the office. I knew she would fill me in when she got to the office but the lack of information was bothering me this morning.

What could be so urgent that this many people were trying to reach me before most offices even opened?

This wasn't normal.

Not for me anyway.

And definitely not with everything already hanging in the air.

With the Ellington chaos stirring up problems, every unknown was more trouble than it was worth.

By the time we made our way down to the gym, my mind was circling it even harder.

The space was quiet when we walked in except for the incessant inner monologue.

The gym's polished concrete, glass walls, and clean lines filled with rows of machines sitting in perfect order—treadmills facing the floor-to-ceiling mirror, free weights lined up on chrome racks, benches spaced with the kind of precision that should have held my attention and given me focus, but it didn't.

No music was playing to distract me. Just the faint hum of the ventilation system and the distant ripple of water from the indoor pool beyond the glass wall.

Alex barely acknowledged me once we stepped inside. She dropped her bag on the bench, pulled her hair up tighter, popping in her earbuds and stepped onto one of the treadmills like she already knew exactly how hard she planned to push herself.

Within seconds the belt started moving, the steady rhythm of her stride breaking the stillness of the room.

I let her have the space.

She looked like she needed it.

So I moved toward the weights.

The bar felt cool against my palms as I loaded the plates onto the rack. The quiet clink of metal against metal echoed more than it should have in the empty room.

I unracked the bar and lowered it slowly, focusing on the movement.

Down.

Press.

Up.

The muscles in my arms and chest tightened with the effort, the familiar burn felt good and necessary.

For a few seconds, my brain finally went quiet.

Then my phone buzzed on the bench beside me.

I ignored it.

Lower.

Press.

Rack.

The sound of the bar settling back into place bounced lightly off the concrete walls.

Across the room Alex's footsteps kept a steady rhythm on the treadmill. I glanced up without meaning to.

She'd already picked up the pace, sweat beginning to gather along her hairline, her breathing controlled but deeper now as she settled into the run.

I grabbed a towel and wiped the back of my neck before moving to the next set.

Rows.

Anything that required enough effort to keep my thoughts from drifting.

It didn't work.

Every few seconds my attention pulled back toward her.

She looked different lately.

Stronger.

More certain in the way she carried herself, like whatever had happened over the past few weeks had sharpened something inside her.

She didn't seem bothered either. At least not by anything going on this morning.

If she knew something about these meetings—or if they involved her in any way—she would've said something by now.

Alex didn't sit on information like this.

She was assigned to the Burrow Township relocation project now, so if any of this had to do with that situation, Grant would have looped her in.

He wouldn't go around her.

Grant respected her too much for that.

And Alex would skin him alive if he tried.

Which just left one question rolling through my head while I stared down at the phone buzzing again on the bench beside me.

What the hell does he want with me?

***

ALEX

Back in the penthouse, I didn't push for any more information. I got ready for work like normal. We quietly ate breakfast as I thought about our conversation from last night. *Should I really move in?* This court hearing is really going to test our relationship. Picking a fight with my attacker will sound completely mental. Not just to him but to everyone and there's nothing anyone can say to me to get me to change my mind.

With my mind already made up maybe the best test of our relationship is for me to agree to move in. If we can get past my plans for Tanner, I'm sure there's hope for our future.

"Roman, it's fine, whatever it is, but are you going to take me to work and pick me up or can we just stop at my place and pick up my car? I'd rather just do that." He seemed to snap out of whatever it was he was concentrating so hard on.

"Oh sorry, yes. We can stop and get your car. I mean, wait, I haven't thought about how I want to do this yet."

I was getting a little irritated with his protection plan, so I put my head on his shoulder and kissed his cheek as I batted my eyelashes at him.

"Take me to my car. I have shit to do and it's going to require me to drive around and look at properties. I'll have Darius with me, remember?" He still had a worried look on his face when he gave in.

"Okay."

He pulled me into a firm hug and nuzzled his head in my hair. He seemed to groan a bit also and I pulled away gently, looking into those beautiful, but tortured, eyes.

"Please stop stressing. Whatever it is, just stop."

"The problem is that I don't know what it is."

"Then it's nothing. Plus, I'm going to need you to be ready to listen to my first day back at work stories when I get home. Our home."

His eyes lit up and he said, "Seriously? Are you saying yes then?"

I nodded. I needed to get him out of this funk, and I knew this would do it.

"But we both have to have an out clause after the court hearing if things don't go well." He looked frustrated with me.

"Um, this is not a prisoner type deal so, yes, we can both get out of the arrangement at any time like a normal couple would if things don't work out. Why would we need a clause? Are we putting it into a contract or something?"

I snickered. "Habit, sorry. Always negotiating when it comes to housing." Thank God he laughed about it, because I was being dead serious. After this court hearing, he may not be too happy with me.

"How about after we take the kids back on Saturday, we go get some of my clothes? Or we can just wait until after the two weeks are up and decide then."

"Nope, the sooner the better."

Of course he wants everything now.

"Do you think I should sublet my apartment?" I wasn't ready to make a permanent decision.

He said, "Or, I can just pay your early termination fee, and we can put your furniture in storage. You can also do whatever you want to this place. I used a designer when I moved in, but if you want to change anything to make you feel more at home, go right ahead." I hadn't even thought about all my furniture. Even if things didn't work out, I was thinking about buying a house anyway. This way, I could save some money until I decided what I wanted and where I wanted it. Would we be buying it together or separately? Oh no, too many questions in my head, this isn't good.

"Alex, are you ready to go?"

Wow, that was overwhelming. Yes, get me out of here.

"I just need to grab a bottle of water and my things, and I'll be all set."

He kept his arm around me all the way to the garage and into the car. I noticed him looking around when we got into the garage though. Was he sensing that eerie presence too? In the car he leaned over and kissed me and said, "Thank you for saying yes to moving in."

"You may change your mind about that."

"We'll talk about the rules when we get home tonight."

What?

"Excuse me? Rules?" He turned his head away so I couldn't see his expression.

"Yes, the house rules. Your cleaning, cooking, and taking care of the man of the house rules. One rule is making sure you have my slippers and a martini ready when I walk in the door."

Clearly, he was kidding but playing along could be fun.

"Well, what if you get home before I do?"

"Then I'll be sitting on the couch naked waiting for my—you know." He smiled and winked as he looked down toward the front of his pants.

I burst out laughing.

"So, in the last five minutes you've completely lost your mind." He pulled into the valet, kissing me before I got out.

"I'm only kidding, but if you want to do any of that you're more than welcome," he said through the window as I was passing.

"You may get pleasantly surprised." I kissed those luscious full lips through the window. I gave him a wink and headed up to my apartment for a minute before having the valet guy retrieve my car.

Chapter 20

ROMAN

I didn't know she was going up to her apartment, I thought as I watched her get into the elevator. I thought she was just getting her car. I drove across the street and waited until I saw her leave. But as soon as I saw her at the valet, she called me.

"Thanks dad, all is good." I laughed and waved to her.

"Have a good day and I'll see you at home tonight." God, that felt so good to say to her.

I called Amelia on the way in to find out what these meetings were about. She said she didn't know, and she'd let Harrison talk to me about Texas. I drove to the office and once there, I stopped at Amelia's desk to get my schedule. I liked it on paper, so I didn't have to stare at a computer screen all day. I headed into my office with Harrison was right behind me.

"Hey man, good morning. I've got some crazy good news for you about Texas." Harrison said with excitement.

"Good news, huh? Like I don't have to go?"

"Sure, if that's what you want."

"Really? What happened?"

"You know how the zoning got fixed, right?" I nodded.

"I only know that it did get fixed but not how. I also thought we were waiting for the money trail."

He smiled from ear to ear and said, "I still don't know how it got fixed, either, but the money trail was found, and arrests were made. The project is ready to go again..."

I tried to say something, but he continued and said, "Hey, now wait just a second before you interrupt, I need to finish. The kickback money was returned. It's in an account down there being held by some financial advisor firm in the name of 'The King/Kennedy Project'."

I'm sorry, what? Who the hell?.. I looked at Harrison, confused.

He said, "I know, I know. We have no idea who did this. Like none."

That was unsettling.

"I can't touch that money without finding out where it came from." I stated matter of factly for Harrison's benefit. "I may have to go down there." I said under my breath.

Damn it! *What's going on?*

"How much money is it?" I asked curiously but dreaded the answer in the same breath.

"Approximately $500,000." I ran my hands through my hair and sat back in my chair.

I guess I don't have a choice. I'm not telling Alex about this right now. She'd freak not knowing who did this.

"Who would know Alex and would do this?" I asked more to myself than Harrison. My nerves were on edge now.

"No idea. I'll make the arrangements tomorrow for the jet. I'll go with you." I was shocked he wanted to be a part of this aspect of the deal, but he had been different the past couple of weeks. I thanked him and decided to call Grant and see where he wanted to meet.

Right before I dialed, the name Santoro scrolled across my screen. This ought to be interesting. I answered more formal than normal, "Roman King."

Mr. Santoro replied, "Roman, how are you? Alessandro Santoro."

"Alessandro, good to hear from you. What can I do for you?"

"Well, you see, we bought some property about thirty minutes north of the city to start a winery and we're going to need someone to do the renovations. I was wondering if we could meet here at the new place and talk about what that might look like."

Now that was interesting. I had no idea that they could do that since there was no commercial zoning. Had something changed, I wondered?

"You and Alex, both told me you couldn't get commercial zoning. Did you find something else?" My curiosity got the best of me.

He laughed and said, "No, we had our hearts set on this place and if you want something bad enough and it's meant to be, things always seem to work out. Don't you agree?" That made me laugh, thinking about Alex.

"You know, I'm going to have to agree with you on that."

"Do you think you and Alex could meet us on the property tomorrow afternoon and talk about the plans? Maybe stay for dinner?"

"I'll talk to Alex tonight and see if that would work. She's usually got some exercise classes going on several times a week, so I'll let you know." He agreed and I hung up and dialed Grant.

"Roman, sorry about the secretive message." He said after his greeting.

"No worries, what's up?"

"We need to talk. I'll text you the address and meet you there in an hour?"

"Yeah, does Alex…" He cut me off.

"Alex doesn't know about this, and I'd like to keep it that way for now."

"This sounds serious and a little shady. Are we on the up and up with whatever this is?" He chuckled.

"Yes, it's just information, but it's important and it can't be done over the phone or in mine or your office."

He texted me an address and we hung up. This was getting weirder by the minute. I plugged in the address. It was a very trendy expensive Italian restaurant. Well, that's fine because I'm hungry, and he can buy lunch for all the anxiety. I had Amelia block off an extra hour and asked her if everything else was okay. She said it was and that she had the plane ready to go for Texas in the morning, a hotel and got the other meetings rescheduled.

***

ALEX

If I was going to do this moving in thing with Roman, I needed to get some things from my place that were pieces of me. I took two pictures off the bookshelf. One was a family vacation shot, and the other was of me and the girls with their families at a birthday for one of the kids a couple years ago. I'd wanted to add a picture of me and Roman somewhere in there too, but for right now, I just needed this representation, so I didn't feel like I was living in his house.

When the valet pulled up my car I climbed in and inhaled deeply. I missed the smell she had that relaxed me and the dark tinted windows that concealed me from the craziness of the outside world. Damn it felt good to be driving Betty again. I never thought I would miss driving my car so much.

I had a meeting with Grant this morning We were going to conference call Matt so I could get the low down on where they were in the search for a relocation area for the Burrow Township residents. After thinking about the list of things I had to do today, I turned up the volume on my stereo to drown everything out until I got to the office. It was all starting to get bunched up in my head and it felt more like chaos than a to do list.

I stopped at the reception desk to say hi to our new receptionist Felicity. She seemed even more nervous around me now than the first time I met her. I wondered what that was about, as I made a mental note to engage more with her. I walked past Grant's office, but he was on the phone, so I waved and went down the hall to see Shay.

"Hey girl, how short is my schedule today?" My to do list might be long but I haven't been in the office in three weeks so I couldn't have that much scheduled.

"You have one meeting with Grant and Matt this morning and then you're picking up Darius Jackson and taking him to the District 5 area to scope out the neighborhood. You're supposed to be checking out a couple of places that Grant and Matt were looking at— to see what you think."

"Anything else?"

"Nope, not right now." This was good for my first morning back.

"Shay, make a date for us to spend the entire day together please. I'm going to bring you on these reconnaissance missions with me. You can have half of all the sales. I just think it's a lot more work than I can handle on my own...."

"What about answering the phone for you?"

"We can just have the calls transferred to your cell."

"That's going to be so much fun." She was bouncing in her seat.

"Don't get too excited, the fun I've had doing this so far hasn't exactly been anyone's idea of fun."

She looked solemn, then serious. "Am I going to have to carry a gun?"

I can't even imagine Shay with a gun. "No, not ever. Why would you say that? You'll be in good hands, I promise."

She let out a deeply held sigh, "Ok, good, because guns scare me, but I heard it's a bad neighborhood and was told I should carry a gun."

Good lord, who would tell this young woman to carry a gun?

"You know what? You can start today, and this is what we'll do until it's done. Does that work?" I smiled but didn't wait for a response since I had the answer already as Shay bounced out of her seat. "If you have other clients you want to work with, that will be fine also. I'll help you do whatever you want," she squealed, as I made my way down the hall and into my office to put my stuff down.

As I passed her again on my way to Grant's office I mentioned, "We're leaving in an hour." She was smiling and clapping like a little girl and all I could think was this woman has no idea where we're about to go. I don't think she's ever been out of the suburbs.

I knocked lightly on Grant's door as he was finishing up a call. He got up and came around the desk. It's always nice to get a welcome hug from Grant. "Thank God you came to your senses," he said and kissed my forehead.

"Yes, well at least there were senses left to come back to." I shook my head to forget all I'd been through.

"Grant, I'm so sorry for everything I put you and everyone else through. I just couldn't handle life after what happened."

"Ali girl, you have nothing to apologize for. I know you so well. I knew you would figure it out. When I first met you, you were married to that guy and all I could think was, 'she'll figure this out.' I knew Luke wasn't the guy for you. You looked defeated with him. I saw a fire in you that was being snuffed out."

We'd never had a conversation about this before. It was so strange to hear him talk so intimately about me.

"How about now? How do you feel about the guy now?" Everyone seemed to be on team Roman.

"Roman? I'm happy for you. He's a good guy. You should consider a commitment."

I laughed and said, "How committed do you think moving in together is?" His eyes widened.

"Did you move in with him?"

I nodded. "We're going to pick up some more things from my apartment on Saturday, maybe. I'm still a little nervous about it. What do you think?"

"I think you'll be fine, like I always do."

After that conversation we called Matt.

"Hey Grant, hey Alex."

"Hi Matt."

"Good to have you back on the project, Alex. Looking forward to dropping the kids off to you and Roman on Friday, too. So is Jack."

Grant interrupted, "Ok, first, I want to ask about something I heard from this weekend. Did Roman really lay out Luke at the club Saturday night?" Oh no, not the gossip again. Except the fact that three of the people that were there work here, but geez, keep your mouths shut.

"There was probably a slight lack of common sense due to alcohol involvement. I don't think he hurt him too bad though." Matt said as he tried to make less out of it.

Grant turned to me and said, "I knew if I asked you, you wouldn't give me the whole story."

"I think Luke got lucky it was broken up by the bouncers." Matt mentioned as I wondered if this is just a guy thing that Grant wanted to hear about something like this.

After we got that out of the way I moved us along, "Ok, now for the serious stuff please. What have you guys got for me?" I clapped my hands together, getting us back on track.

We went over everything that they'd been doing and where they'd been looking and the couple of houses that they found— the ones I was going to look at today. I'd been tasked with finding affordable housing that might not need too much work. The housing prices had gone up so much. It might be hard to find homes to replace what they had that didn't need total gut renovations.

"Grant, why didn't you tell me that Roman had gotten the zoning issue fixed with the Santoro's property? I meant to ask you about that the last time I was here?"

"Oh, I thought Roman would've said something to you." That's weird. Roman knew that was important to me.

"No, he hasn't mentioned it at all."

"Such a humble guy." Yeah, not really what I was thinking, but I'll ask Roman about it later. Now, however, I have to go grab Shay and head over to get Darius for his first day of work.

Chapter 21

ROMAN

I pulled into the parking lot of the restaurant. It was beautiful and damn busy for lunch time. I gave the hostess my name and told her I was meeting someone. She was staring so hard she barely got out, hello, before Grant walked up and tapped her on the shoulder. That's the only time being stared at like that is truly annoying.

"Roman, right this way." I followed him into a back room. There were a few tables in the room but no one else was in there. We sat down and a waiter came in from a door which looked like it led into the kitchen. He brought us both water and put some bread on the table. Grant shooed him out after saying thank you.

I looked at him curiously and he smiled. "I own this place. This is a private party room." He said it so nonchalantly.

"Nice. What's this information you have for me?" I was curious to know if Alex knew about this restaurant.

"First of all, I want to introduce myself. I'm Andrea DiGiovanni." He reached out his hand and I tentatively shook it.

"I'm sorry, what? What do you mean? I'm pretty sure we've already met, Grant."

"I've been able to keep this name out of the public eye since I moved to the United States fifteen years ago where I trained very hard to lose my Italian accent and roots. I worked for Alessandro Santoro and his family back in Italy. I was their consigliere to put it simply." My mouth hit the floor. I knew exactly what that meant and I also remember Alessandro's words "connected member of a very prominent Italian family."

Oh no! What the hell have I gotten myself into?

"Grant, should I call you Grant? What exactly is going on?" I clasped my hands and rested my elbows on the table.

"When I moved here it was because I was getting out of the business, basically going into hiding. Alessandro also got out of the business, and he sent me over here to set up a normal life. I helped him open the winery in California and in North Carolina. I had a..." He hesitated. "...layover in Cincinnati. I did a little research on the place and fell in love with it. I told Alessandro that he and his family would love it here. They weren't ready to leave Italy yet, but they came to visit, and we decided to get into real estate. I got my license and after a few years I opened my own office, and of course this place. You're not truly Italian unless you own a restaurant." He laughed but I wasn't in the mood.

"Well, I guess all that's good to hear, but how does Alex play into all this? I feel like you have a very vested interest in her. The Santoro's seem especially concerned about her as well." His smile was genuine, thoughtful even, when I said her name.

"Alex is special. When she came to work for me, she wasn't the girl you see today. She was sweet and maybe a little naïve. It took everything I had not to take care of that husband of hers." I swallowed thinking intently on what he meant by that. "I talked to her and tried to give her as much knowledge as I could about relationships and real estate to get her thinking for herself. She finally accepted her marriage was a sham, and her business wasn't. She got rid of the husband and I kept her busy with real estate while she went through, what she calls, *the dark times*. She's something else, isn't she? She told me she's moved in with you."

Now I was the one smiling even though my head was spinning from that information.

"I'm glad you were there for her during that time. I had the pleasure of meeting the loser over the weekend." I said.

He laughed. "Yeah, I heard." He paused. "Roman, Alex asked me about the zoning issue on Alessandro's property. I told Shay that King Construction took care of it not thinking it would ever come up again. She asked me why I never told her, and I put it back on you."

"You're going to tell me now though, right?"

"I'll tell you, but I want you to take the credit for it, for now. She's got enough going on with this court hearing and I don't think it would be a good idea if she found out who I was or who the Santoro's are."

I was on board with that. In fact, I didn't think it would be a good idea if anyone ever found out who they were.

"Grant, tell me about Texas." I figured he must be in on that too. He's the only person that would've known about Alex.

He laughed and said, "Oh. You found out already? Well, we obviously know who's doing this, the Ellingtons, so when we heard about what was going on in Texas we decided to talk to some friends. We relayed some of the shady antics they were pulling up here. It was nipped in the bud pretty quickly and people quietly got arrested and money was recovered. We decided the kickbacks would be put to best use in this relocation project, so we started an account for you and Alex to figure out what the best use for it should be. Do you agree?"

"That depends. Is the money clean?" I sat back, crossing my arms over my chest. I was having trouble being in this small room with him now. It was starting to close in on me.

"Roman, I'm not doing anything illegal." He chuckled. "I didn't even go to Texas. The money was just returned to its rightful owner, which was King Construction." Like it was no big deal. "I thought you might be good with putting Alex's name on the account too, so she could help with Burrow Township. She was planning to use her own money to help them. I know the Texas project doesn't have anything to do with displaced residents."

How did he know anything about the Texas project?

I took a deep breath. "That's actually a great idea. But you do have to see my concern in all this now though, right?" I grabbed the glass of water and gulped it down to get the desert out of my mouth. I thought I was going to have to ask him to open a door but clearly no one needs to hear this conversation.

"Of course I do. I promise you everything's fine. I'm not going to get involved with Burrow Township though, because I don't want anything to happen to Alex. She's like the daughter I never had, and I would do *anything* to protect her."

The way he said *anything* put me on edge even more than the conversation itself.

"She really makes you work for that one too, doesn't she?" He winked at me then started laughing.

I laughed with him only because I was almost scared not to. I don't know if I feel relieved or terrified at the thought of Grant watching over Alex.

"Thankfully," he continued "Alex wasn't in the picture when we dealt with the zoning issue for the Santoro's, so no one connected her to it." he informed me, which helped relieve some of my stress.

"Good to hear." *I wish I had a real drink now.* "How did you fix the Burrow Township issue?" I didn't know if he'd tell me, or if I should even be asking.

"Didn't have to. When the rep's brother got in trouble for what he did to Alex, he decided to pull out of the deal and focus on getting his brother out of that mess."

Great, that's all we need is Grant "taking out" the bad guy. Mr. Santoro said he thought someone needed to deal with these kinds of predators.

"I don't know if I should tell you this or not, but Tanner's out. Alex was advised to stay with me until the court case was over. She was really freaked out."

"Yes, I know. I saw her this morning she didn't mention anything. She doesn't like people to worry about her. I've got people keeping an eye on him, don't worry. We'll be running interference if he tries anything suspicious."

What? I got up and stood behind the chair. I needed to get some air.

"Grant, who's watching him?"

"Don't worry about it. You need to calm down. You'll never see them and they're there to protect you."

Don't worry about it? All I freaking do is worry. I felt the sweat beading up on my forehead.

"My weird eerie feeling was right, then? Tanner or your goons?"

He laughed.

This isn't even a little funny to me at all.

"They aren't goons. I hire ex-military. We don't do enough for the military vets here in the US." I felt better about that and absolutely agreed. I calmly took a seat and wiped my face with my hands.

"Well, Grant, thanks for the nightmares. I'm just a normal guy who thought I lived in a nice, safe bubble. I'd like to thank you and Alex for turning my life completely upside down." I snatched the linen napkin off the table and wiped my hands and held onto it with a vice-like grip.

"My guess is Alex has changed your life for the better. She's truly a gift and anyone who gets to be in her life is blessed. She's going to do great things so let's keep our girl safe."

I agreed with him there, but why in the hell is he so vested in her?

***

ALEX

I called Darius on the way to make sure he was ready for his first day. He sounded so excited. I was taking him to King Construction to fill out his paperwork. We got to the house, and I went to the back door as usual. Darius answered in a grey suit that may have been just a bit too big, but he paired it with a white button-down shirt and a blue tie that looked pretty old. He was also wearing some very clean white Nikes. He greeted me and stepped out of the way for Shay and I to enter. I said hi to Ella and she gave me a big hug and a thank you for giving her grandson an opportunity then reintroduced Ella to Shay.

Back in the car, I said, "Darius, I wanted to let you know that Shay will be working closely with us on this project." I glanced back through the rear-view mirror. He was nodding and taking notes with the pen and notepad he brought with him.

"And you've spoken to Amelia, correct?"

He continued nodding. "Yes, she's nice. She told me to come to the office and she'd have the paperwork for me to fill out." I smiled.

He had such an eager and excited look on his face, mixed with nervousness.

"Perfect, we're going to take care of that first. Then we'll head over and look at this neighborhood and a couple of houses there."

I pulled into the parking garage right next to Roman's car setting off straight to his office in the private elevator. I told Darius on the way up that I would introduce him to Roman and Harrison if they were around.

He looked a little nervous, so I assured him, "There's nothing to worry about. These two men are the nicest and smartest people you will meet in this business. They'll teach you a lot."

"This is just the first real job I've had, and I've never had to dress this nice. I don't want to mess it up."

"Well, I think that you'll fit in perfectly." He smiled and turned his head to look out the elevator window.

"Miss Alex?" he asked quietly.

I know it's a respect thing, but I felt like that's what little kids call their teacher, not their colleagues.

"Alex will be fine, Darius." I wanted him to feel like an equal with me. He had a lot to learn but I never wanted him to feel inadequate.

"Alex, I'm sorry for the way I treated you the first time I met you." I had a feeling we'd be discussing this at some point.

"Let's just move forward from that. What was happening to your neighborhood couldn't have been easy to watch. We know each other now, so it's a moot point." I probably would've lashed out at a stranger on my grandma's porch too if they had randomly been there.

"I know, but everything you've done for me and my family, I just want you to know that I'm sorry and I'll try to do better when I meet new people." Wow, that was such a mature outlook. I'm impressed.

"Darius, you're going to go far in life with an attitude like that. You have no idea how long it takes people to figure that out." He smiled.

"I look forward to working with you." I admitted.

We got out on the fifteenth floor, and straight to Amelia's desk. She was all smiles, but she was on the phone, so we waited. She came around and gave both Shay and I a hug, and she shook Darius's hand. "Nice to meet you Mr. Jackson."

"You, too." He stood eye to eye with her as he shook her hand.

"Amelia, where should we have Darius fill out his paperwork?" He was still staring at her a bit starry eyed.

"How about in the conference room? We don't have any meetings in there today."

"Are Roman and Harrison here?"

She grabbed my arm and pulled me aside.

"Yes, they're both here. Roman looks like he saw a ghost or something so Harrison is in there with him, right now," she whispered.

"Is he okay? Did something happen? He hasn't reached out to me for anything." I flipped my phone over to see if I'd missed a message from him. There was nothing.

"Not that I know of. He just got back from lunch."

"Well, I guess I'll talk to him first before we have this meeting. I'll get Darius started on his paperwork and have Shay help him if he needs it." I took Darius and Shay into the conference room.

"Miss, I mean, Alex?" Darius' eyes were following Amelia all the way back to her desk.

"Yes?" I rolled my lips trying not to giggle.

"Does everyone here look like her?" Oh, he's either intimidated or in love.

"No, thankfully. We'd never get any work done around here, would we?"

He laughed nervously and shook his head.

"I was just thinking I may not be dressed up enough for work. Do all the men dress that way, too?"

"They do but you fit right in, I promise."

I ushered Darius and Shay into the conference room and headed back down the hall.

I tapped on Roman's door and Harrison opened it with a smile. "Well, speak of the devil."

"Oh yeah, and what were you speaking of about said devil?" I put my hands on my hips and pursed my lips jokingly.

"My lips are sealed." Harrison made a zipper move over his mouth.

"Harrison, I have a new member of your team in the conference room. Would you mind going in there and introducing yourself to him. He's a little nervous and super excited." It was the quickest way to get Harrison out of here for a minute.

"Sure. Is it Darius? I heard we were hiring the first member of the new division of training. I'm proud of you for doing that." I didn't know this was a big deal.

"Harrison, I think that's the first time you've ever said anything to me that wasn't laced with condescension." I relaxed my arms and smiled.

"What can I say, you bring out the best in me." He tapped me on the shoulder before heading down the hall.

I closed the door behind him. Roman was sitting in his chair facing the windows.

"Hey, Roman, honey. All good?"

He turned around with a great big fake smile on his face.

"Could you say that again?"

"Say what again?"

"Honey."

I walked over and sat on his lap.

"Tell me what's wrong."

He shook his head and groaned, "Nothing's wrong. I have really good news for you."

Then why are you so growly? My imagination tried to come up with different scenarios before I reigned it back in.

"Like you getting the zoning fixed for the Santoros?" A weird look crossed his face, Amelia was right. It was haunting.

"Yeah, that. I just petitioned for it, and it happened. I was shocked that it was that simple." That didn't feel like the whole truth, but I didn't want to get into it with him. He didn't look comfortable talking about it.

"Okay, I didn't mean to interrupt. What's the good news or was that it?"

"No, there's more. Do you remember me telling you if I got any of the kickback money returned to us, I would use it to help the Burrow Township people?" He was leaning his head on my shoulder with his arms wrapped around my waist. His hands were clasped together.

"Yes."

"Well, down in Texas we got all the money back from the bad deals and I put it in an account in the name of the King/Kennedy Project. I want you to use it to relocate the residents. I don't know exactly what you're going to do yet, but whatever it is, I want you to use that money to do it." I couldn't believe what I was hearing.

"Roman, how much money is it?"

"$520,000." I stared at him in total shock. He wasn't even reacting. This news is amazing. Why isn't he more excited?

"Are you serious?" He nodded his head and handed me a piece of paper with all the information for the account on it.

I pushed away from him and said, "This just happened today?" He nodded but he was silent. Something didn't seem right.

"Is there something you're not telling me?"

"No babe, everything's fine. I was just really surprised how everything has suddenly started coming together." He faked another smile.

"It seems kind of magical honestly, but I don't want to look a gift horse in the mouth." Another saying my mom loved using. "Anyway, Darius is here, and I sent Harrison in to introduce himself. He's a little nervous to meet the owners of the company. I'm sure Harrison will be able to make him feel more comfortable but if you walk in there looking like this you may change." I warned him gently. There was clearly something going on he wasn't telling me.

"That bad, huh?" he said and I nodded.

"Give me a minute so I can return an email or two and I'll be right in," he muttered.

I gave him a sweet kiss and he embraced me tightly. I returned to the conference room.

***

ROMAN

I still had the trip to Texas tomorrow, but now that I knew what had happened down there, I didn't see a need to go. I'll send Amelia in my place. She and Harrison can stay down there for a few days and get a break from me and all this craziness. I think I'm going to have Alex work with me while their gone until I feel less overprotective. I don't know how to feel normal around Grant now, though. Oh lord, tomorrow we have dinner with the Santoros— that's going to be even more nerve wracking.

I leaned back in my chair, dragging my hands through my hair and down my face.

On my way to the conference room, I stopped by Amelia's desk and informed her "I'm not going to Texas tomorrow with Harrison. I'd like for you to go with him. How many days did you make the hotel reservation for?"

"Just two...Why does your hair look like that?" She looked at me with squinted eyes.

"Make it for three or four and just take a couple of days off." I smoothed my hair down not really caring what it looked like, but I still had to meet Darius. "I'm going to have Alex work with me here, so it'll be fine." I said that more to myself than for her.

"Does Alex know this?"

"Not yet, but I'm sure she'll be fine with it."

She laughed as she said, "Ok, whatever you say." I wasn't in the mood for Amelia's attitude.

"Amelia, are you cool with going to Texas with Harrison tomorrow or not?"

"Of course, if you can handle all the phone calls here. Do you want me to have them forwarded and bring my laptop?"

"Sure, you can do that. I know I won't answer that phone."

"Ok, well they're waiting for you in the conference room."

I walked to the door and leaned on the door jamb. Everyone was laughing and carefree. I wish I could join them.

***

ALEX

"Darius, don't listen to a word this guy tells you." I put my hands on Darius's shoulders and winked at Harrison.

"Harrison is a cool dude. I'm looking forward to learning about the money side of the business."

I shook my head slowly at Harrison.

"Thanks Harrison, but let's start with the basics." *I mean it's the kids first day.*

"Well, what if his basics are in the investment side?" Harrison would make a good recruiter.

"What is he investing in? Don't you think he should have a basic knowledge of the investment first?"

Harrison laughed. "Good point, but I still think he can learn both at the same time. He's a smart kid. I mean young man."

Darius had a look of pride on his face that I was just overjoyed by. I hope we can keep him this interested as long as he works with us.

"Well, just don't let too much of you rub off on him, we want him showing up to work on time." Laughter filled the room as someone cleared their throat at the door. I turned around to see a faint smile on Roman's face as he leaned against the door frame with his arms crossed.

Harrison grumbled, "Uh oh. Party's over folks. Dad's here." I shoved him when I saw the look on Darius's face. Now he looked nervous again. I shook my head at Roman, and he forced an amused look on his face. He loosened up his stance, walked over, said hi to Shay and patted her on the shoulder as he walked around the table and reached his hand out to Darius.

"It's nice to finally meet you, Darius. Alex speaks very highly of you." It was a little robotic for my taste, but it seemed to do the trick. The nervous look left Darius' face when he glanced at me and quickly stood up. He held his hand out to shake Roman's.

Darius seemed comfortable and eager to get out there and learn. I was eager to get out of here too, because the tension I could feel from Roman was intense. I wondered what all that was about. I knew he was heading to Texas tomorrow. *Is something else happening there that he isn't telling me?*

Maybe he'll tell me when I get home. *Home,* to Roman's house, now mine also, that was something exciting to focus on, not to mention weird, making my stomach roll.

After we finished all the paperwork, I walked to Amelia's desk to say bye.

"Hey, can you see Roman before you leave? He's got something to talk to you about," Amelia mentioned.

"Sure." I walked into his office with a smile on my face.

"Hey babe, we were just heading out. Amelia said you wanted to see me." He smiled and looked a lot better. He pulled me close then took a deep breath.

"Yes, I wanted to do that, first of all..." He said and leaned in to kiss my lips softly "...and I wanted to tell you I'm not going to Texas tomorrow. I'm sending Amelia with Harrison for a few days. They can handle all of that. I also wanted to ask you if you can work remotely for the next few days, with me, here at the office while they're away?"

I shot him a baffled look. "I can work remotely, yes, but I may need to leave the office to go look at properties. Can I have Shay here with me?" *Why in the world is he being so possessive?*

He said, "Yes, you can set up in the conference room, if that would work."

"Yeah, that'll be fine. I'll bring Darius in too and have him do some studying. Is there anything you'd like me to start teaching him to get prepared for the training program?"

He held me closer and said, "Let's talk about this more tomorrow in the office. What time are you done with work today?"

"Probably around four."

"Do you have any training or anything tonight?"

I shook my head. "Sunday, Monday and Friday are my days off from the studio."

"Oh, I almost forgot to mention. The Santoro's invited us to have dinner with them tomorrow night. They wanted us to come early to go over renovation ideas. They want me to do the work on their winery."

"I have a class from 4-5:30, but I can make it for dinner. Are we going to meet at their new house?" He nodded then kissed me with more desperation than "see you later." He seemed a little protective of me at the moment. I'm sure something happened that he's not telling me, or else now that we live together, I'm getting a look at the real Roman. Is he really an overprotective control freak? Oh Lord, I hope that's not the case, I will lose my mind.

Shay and Darius were waiting by the elevator, and I hurried over.

We rolled slowly through the neighborhood, the tires crunching over loose gravel and broken pavement as I eased the car along the narrow street. I checked the address again in my head, then glanced down at the directions on the console.

I wondered if this was really it, or if I'd gotten the directions wrong.

The place didn't look like the kind of neighborhood anyone would be investing in—not at first glance. Several of the houses sat dark and hollow, their windows boarded up or shattered, porches sagging under the weight of years without maintenance. Weeds had pushed up through cracked sidewalks, climbing over rusted chain-link fences and swallowing the edges of small yards that had probably once been neat and cared for.

A few homes still looked lived in—fresh curtains in a window here, a car parked in a driveway there—but they were scattered between empty shells that looked like they'd been forgotten.

It was the kind of street most people would drive through once and never come back to.

Grant and Matt had given me the information for a couple houses that were technically on the market. Properties someone had at least bothered to list, which meant there was a starting point.

But as I drove past another boarded-up place with a collapsed porch rail, my attention drifted to the ones that weren't listed at all.

The abandoned ones.

Those were the real question.

If half the street was sitting empty like this, someone owned them. Whether they were banks, private investors, or some absentee landlord who'd let them rot, it didn't really matter.

What mattered was finding out who.

I slowed the car a little more, studying the line of neglected houses as we rolled past.

Because if this neighborhood was ever going to stand a chance, someone was going to have to figure that out.

We had $520,000 to work with, and I still had no idea what the plan was yet.

I slowed the car again, letting it roll past another stretch of houses that looked like they had been abandoned for years. Paint peeled off the siding in long curling strips, roofs sagged under missing shingles, and a few porches leaned forward like they were seconds away from collapsing.

This neighborhood looked worse than the one the Burrow Township residents were leaving.

That thought sat heavy in my chest as I studied the street ahead of us.

I was trying to figure out what the point of this was when I caught the look Darius was giving me from the passenger seat.

Not curious.

Concerned.

The kind of look you give someone when you think they might've completely lost their mind.

"Is this the neighborhood y'all want us to move to?" he asked.

His voice pulled me out of my thoughts, and for a second, I realized I hadn't even processed the question.

I glanced over at him, then at Shay in the back seat. She was leaning forward slightly between the seats, her eyes scanning the row of run-down houses like she was trying to find something—anything—that would explain why we were here.

I didn't answer right away.

Because in that exact moment, something clicked.

It hit me all at once.

Like someone had flipped a switch in my brain.

I sat there staring out the windshield at the worst house on the block—a crooked little structure with boarded windows and a front porch that looked like it had given up years ago.

And suddenly it made perfect sense.

I pushed the door open and stepped out of the car so fast I barely realized I was moving.

The afternoon air was cool, carrying that faint dusty smell of old wood and empty buildings. Gravel crunched under my shoes as I walked a few steps toward the house, my mind racing ahead of itself.

Darius and Shay climbed out behind me.

"Alex?" Darius said cautiously.

I turned toward them, unable to stop the grin spreading across my face.

"Yes," I blurted out, almost laughing with the realization. "Yes, this is exactly where I want you all to move."

The silence that followed was immediate.

Both of them just staring at me.

Shay's eyebrows lifted slowly, her mouth parting slightly in disbelief.

Darius looked from me to the house, then back to me again like he was trying to decide whether I was joking or having some kind of breakdown.

The expression on both of their faces was the same.

You've got to be kidding me.

And that was when I lost it.

I started laughing.

A full, sudden burst of it that caught even me off guard.

I stepped forward and wrapped an arm around each of them, pulling them both into a quick hug right there on the side of the road in front of the ugliest house I'd ever seen.

They stood stiff for a second, completely confused while I laughed like a woman who had just stumbled into something brilliant.

Because somehow, standing there in front of that falling-apart house, I was starting to see exactly what this place could become.

Chapter 22

ROMAN

I left the office at four o'clock when my phone started ringing. Alex's name flashed across the screen in bright white letters, cutting through the dim, quiet room like a warning flare. My heart kicked hard—too hard—and for a split second the air began to suffocate me.

"Alex, are you alright?" I answered too fast and too sharp without thinking. The panic was right there in my voice, and I winced the second it left my mouth.

Great. Perfect. Exactly how to freak her out—good job, Roman.

She paused. "Hi... yeah, everything's fine. Should it *not* be?"

I scrubbed a hand down my face, trying to shake off the adrenaline. "No. Sorry. Just... used to strange things happening lately."

She laughed, the sound soft and genuine, easing some of the tension coiled up in me.

"So, I just dropped off Darius and Shay and I'm headed home. I have the most amazing idea, and I need to know if what I want to do is going to be feasible."

Ah yes. Her ideas.

The last time she came to me excited about an idea, I practically scorched the hope from her world. Hopefully this time I'd actually be useful.

"I'm all ears."

"I'm kind of excited about it, so I'll tell you when I get there so I can focus on driving."

"That's a great idea. I'll see you when you get here."

"Thank you, babe. Love you and I'll see you in a few."

Everything in me went still.

She hasn't said she loves me since the day Tanner turned our world upside down. Hearing it again hit me like oxygen after being underwater too long.

"I love you too," I said quietly, meaning every syllable.

There's nothing like loving someone who loves you back—genuinely. It settles into your bones. It rewrites the wiring of your heart. It steadies things you didn't realize were shaking.

A minute later, Amelia called to check in before her flight.

"Are you sure you'll be okay without me here for a few days?" she asked, suspicious, probably picturing me pacing the office until she returned.

"Yep," I said, popping the P. "Alex is going to be using the conference room as her office. She's bringing her whole team. You'll still be answering phones remotely. I don't see any problems, do you?"

"I don't. But I'm not sure I believe you."

"I'm sure it'll all be fine eventually."

"I'll call you when we board and when we land. I'll send you anything important, otherwise you'll get the usual emails."

"Thanks, Amelia. Keep Harrison on time."

"Will do."

We hung up at the same time, and that's when the elevator dinged.

I was leaning against the wall, arms crossed, trying to look relaxed when the doors slid open—and there she was.

The reason my pulse had been jittery all afternoon. The reason my shoulders finally dropped out of my ears.

I stepped inside, not even trying to slow myself down; I wrapped her up in my arms, pulling her tight against me, breathing her in like she was the first air I'd gotten all day.

She laughed against my chest. "Hey there... it's really nice to see you too."

I cupped her cheeks, thumbs brushing the warmth in her skin, and kissed her like I hadn't seen her in months, not hours. She kissed me back immediately, arms sliding around my waist, fingers curling into my shirt, and suddenly the elevator felt too small, hot, and full of electricity.

The doors opened and we nearly stumbled into the penthouse still tangled up.

"Sorry," I said breathlessly. "I just missed you today."

She laughed, pink rising to her cheek bones, hopefully a little flattered. "You saw me *twice* today already."

"I know. I'm just excited about you moving in."

That part wasn't an exaggeration. At all.

"Me too." she said.

I shrugged off my suit jacket and tossed it over the back of one of the island chairs. The room was quiet except for the faint hum of the fridge and her light footsteps moving across the floor behind me. The penthouse smelled faintly of cedar from the candles Mary burned throughout the day and the coffee I'd made earlier, but her perfume—light, warm, familiar—was already taking over the space and I inhaled deeply.

I grabbed a beer from the fridge because it was quicker than a bourbon, turned around, and caught her staring at me like she was trying to read my mind.

"Want a glass of wine?" I lifted the bottle of cabernet sitting on the counter.

She smiled, nodded, and slid onto one of the stools.

I poured the wine, set the glass in front of her—

—and then she abruptly slammed both hands down on the marble countertop.

The sharp crack echoed across the kitchen.

My spine went straight.

Her eyes locked onto mine, wide and alert.

"What's wrong?" she demanded.

***

ALEX

"Nothing," he said, shaking his head. "I'm gonna take a shower."

"Not so fast, no subject changes." I threw his own comment back at him.

He tipped his drink back then smirked at me while trying not to laugh.

"Touche" He managed to mumble after swallowing half a bottle of beer.

I raised an eyebrow trying to figure out why he's been so upset and anxious.

"I can tell you need to talk about this. Whether it's with me or a professional." He had a weird pale look to him. Maybe he just needed a minute. "Fine, go take a shower..." I conceded, "...I don't know what's going on, but you look ill." I figured he'd talk about it at some point. I watched him practically drag his feet all the way down the hall.

Instead of continuing to worry about it, however, I sent Grant a text expressing my excitement about the neighborhood, and my phone rang.

"Grant, that neighborhood is perfect." I didn't bother to say hello. I knew he knew exactly what I was talking about.

"That's my girl. Tell me what you're thinking."

"Where do I start? It's like a fresh canvas just waiting for its artist."

He chuckled.

"I know that it's going to take a little bit of work, but I know you're that artist, with Roman's help...have you told him yet?"

"No, he's been acting really weird today, so I haven't had a chance to tell him anything."

"What kind of weird are we talking about?"

"I don't know, he looks sick—like he's seen a ghost or something."

"Is there anything I can do to help? Want me to talk to him? Maybe it's a guy thing. Maybe it's the moving in together."

There's a thought.

"No. I'll just talk to him and see if that's it. And my ideas for this place are amazing and guess what?" I bounced up to my knees on the sofa.

"I'm all ears."

"They got all the kickback money back from the zoning fraud in Texas and Roman put it in an account for me to use on this relocation project. $520,000. I don't even know what to say, it's like a miracle."

"Well, now that is good news. Baby girl you're going to do great things, I just know it." I don't think he's ever called me 'baby girl' before, but it sounded so fatherly and warm.

Grant had always been more than just a mentor. In many ways, he'd been the steady parental figure I needed when life had been unraveling years ago. I honestly don't know what I would've done without him during that time.

I loved my own dad dearly, but he was the mellow, laid-back kind of father who preferred peace over confrontation. When things got messy in my life—when the stories got heavy and complicated—he would listen for a moment before admitting he didn't really know how to help. He cared. I never doubted that. But he didn't have the tools for the chaos I was walking through.

Grant did.

Somehow he always seemed to know what to say. And when he didn't, he still stayed on the line, letting me work through things without ever feeling alone.

"I've been thinking about the neighborhood," I said into the phone, pacing slowly across my living room. "Not just patching things up... I mean renovating the whole place."

Grant didn't interrupt, which meant he was listening carefully.

"My thought is to see if the residents would be willing to use the money they get for their homes toward the purchase of the new ones. The money coming from Texas could help fund the renovation side of it."

I paused for a moment, staring out the window as the rest of the idea formed more clearly the longer I talked.

"I still have a good amount saved myself," I added. "Enough to help get things started. But what I really think this needs is a nonprofit. Something that could raise money to rebuild neighborhoods like this... not just here, but in other areas that have been neglected."

There was a quiet moment on the other end of the line.

Then Grant chuckled softly.

"Alex," he said, "I think that's a fantastic idea."

Relief settled into my chest.

Grant had always been the person who could tell me honestly if I was chasing something impossible. If he thought this could work, that meant something.

"Well," I said, letting out a small breath, "now I just need to see if Roman agrees."

***

ROMAN

The quiet after Alex stopped talking about everything was a relief I hadn't expected to need so badly.

I stood under the shower longer than I normally would, letting the hot water pound against the back of my neck, hoping it might wash some of today out of my head. It didn't.

Talk about paranoia.

I wasn't going to be able to walk out of this building again without scanning every corner, wondering who was standing there to protect and who was there to hurt. Before today, the only person I had to keep an eye out for was Tanner and whatever revenge fantasy he was chasing.

That was already more than enough.

Now Grant had casually introduced the mafia and some militia group into the equation like it was just another detail in a construction contract.

Perfect.

I ran both hands through my hair and dragged them down my face, the heat from the shower still clinging to my skin. My brain kept circling the same questions over and over again, none of them with answers I liked.

When I finally shut the water off and stepped out, I wrapped a towel around my waist and leaned over the sink, bracing both hands on the counter while I hung my head.

Just breathe.

I stared at the marble for a minute, trying to pull myself back into something resembling normal.

Then my phone started ringing.

I groaned and lifted my head.

Ugh. Not the damn phone.

Who the hell is it now?

For a second I considered ignoring it, but the screen lit up again. Whoever it was clearly wasn't planning to give up.

Grant.

Or Andrea.

Or whoever the guy actually was.

My stomach twisted as I grabbed the phone, already feeling sick before I even answered.

"Yup."

Grant chuckled on the other end like we were catching up over coffee.

I'm glad he thinks this is funny.

"I just got off the phone with Alex," he said. "She thinks you're sick. I told her you might be having some moving-in-together jitters."

That was a decent excuse... except for the small detail that I had practically begged her to move in here with me and she'd only agreed after a considerable amount of persuasion.

I groaned.

"Did she call you," I asked, rubbing the back of my neck, "or did you call her?"

"She reached out to me. She's really excited about the new neighbor-hood renovation."

I frowned.

"What new neighborhood renovation?"

There was a pause.

"I guess you two haven't talked about it yet then?"

No, Grant. We definitely haven't.

I closed my eyes, trying to mentally shove everything he'd told me earlier into a locked box somewhere so I could function like a normal human being again.

"Nope," I said. "Definitely haven't been able to concentrate yet. It's weird. Ever since lunch I've been... preoccupied with some new informa-tion."

I hoped he could hear the sarcasm without thinking I was trying to start a fight.

He laughed anyway.

"Yeah, sorry about that," he said. "I never wanted to have to tell anyone, but I trust you with that information... and I trust you with Alex."

That sentence alone made my stomach tighten again.

"One day I'll have to tell her," he continued, "I know that. But right now, it's not in her best interest." He trailed off before saying, "I heard you two are having dinner with the Santoros tomorrow night."

I slowly lowered myself onto the closed toilet lid and leaned forward, resting my elbow on my knee while my hand held up my head.

"We sure are," I muttered. "They asked me if I'd do the renovations for their winery."

Another introduction I could've happily gone the rest of my life with-out.

"That's great," Grant said warmly. "I know you'll do an amazing job. I've seen your work. It's impressive. The first time Alex was at your penthouse she sent me pictures. I didn't know it was yours at first—I thought she was listing it."

He laughed.

Right now I was wondering if I should list it.

Sell the place.

Disappear somewhere quiet for a few years.

"She really seemed to like it," I said. "That's for sure."

I rubbed my face again and forced my thoughts back to Alex.

"I'll talk to her about this new idea she's got," I said. "Maybe I can help her out this time."

Grant sounded genuinely appreciative.

He seemed like a good man.

Which only made everything he'd told me earlier more unsettling.

In all fairness, he hadn't said he'd done anything illegal. Or immoral. He'd just... explained things. The kind of things most people didn't casually admit to over lunch.

So maybe I should focus on that.

We wrapped up the call a minute later.

The apartment felt too quiet when I set the phone down.

I pulled on some clothes, ran a hand through my still damp hair, and headed back out toward the living room.

Time to hear all about Alex's newest idea.

***

ALEX

I took a slow sip of my wine, staring out across the living room while the music drifted through the space, letting myself imagine what that neighborhood could look like when it was finished. Not just new houses, but something that actually helped the people who lived there rebuild their lives. The more I thought about it, the more certain I became that this was something worth fighting for.

A few minutes later I heard the bedroom door open.

Roman made his way down the hall wearing a pair of gray sweats and a simple t-shirt, his hair still damp from the shower. He looked tired, the kind of tired that had more to do with whatever was going on in his head than anything physical.

Without saying a word, he walked over to the couch and stretched out, settling beside the chaise before laying his head in my lap like it was the most natural place in the world to land.

I smiled down at him, setting my wine on the table.

"Do you feel better now?" I brushed my fingers back and forth lightly through his damp hair, and he sighed and snuggled close. "Tell me what happened today that's got you so, I don't know... not you."

He mumbled into my stomach, "It's nothing really. I think it's just everything that's going on and then trying to get you to move in with me. You said yes, and now I'm going to have to share my closet and dresser and bathroom—"

I started laughing and said, "You're such a bad liar." He buried his face in my lap further and moaned.

"I know, but I'm serious, there's just been a lot going on this week, that's all."

I didn't really buy any of this.

"Okay, if that's all it is."

He nodded with his face still nuzzled where I couldn't see it.

"Now for the exciting news I've been wanting to tell you since I got home. I found the neighborhood where we can relocate the residents."

He rolled over and looked up at me with a smile on his face.

"Are you sure I don't already have a bid on it?"

I picked up a pillow and held it over his face.

"If you do, you won't." He started laughing and I thought I heard him say 'the apple doesn't fall far'.

He hurried to cover it up by saying, "I don't think I do, though."

"Well, it's a neighborhood in Matt's district that he and Grant were re-searching. Since neither of them said anything to me about anyone having any dibs on it, I doubt you do either."

He sat up and got comfortable as he started to really pay attention now.

"Tell me what your plans are, and we'll see if there's anything I can do to help you with it."

The moment I started thinking about it again, the excitement came rushing back.

"I want to start by talking to all of the residents," I said, my fingers still moving through his hair while I spoke. "I want to see who would be willing to take the money they get from selling their homes and use it—or at least part of it—to purchase a home in the same community."

Roman shifted slightly but stayed where he was, listening.

"The houses are rundown," I continued, "but they're not unlivable. What I'd like to do first is take the money you already allocated for the project and renovate those homes first. That way the families who live there would immediately have a nicer place to live."

The more I talked, the clearer it became in my mind.

"Then after that," I said, leaning forward a little, "I want to start a nonprofit and use it to renovate the rest of the neighborhood. Not just the houses, but the whole area. I'd love to put in a community garden and maybe a park. Somewhere people actually want to spend time. I want it to feel like a safe place to live... more friendly, you know?"

Roman lifted his head slightly, looking up at me with a surprised expression.

"Well, damn," he said. "That really does sound like a great idea."

A small smile pulled at my lips.

"I know I told you I usually only take on big projects and not home renovations," he continued, "but this is an entire community. That's different. It's something I've never done before, but I'd love to help you with it."

His tone was thoughtful now, like he was already running the logistics through his mind.

"I've got a great architectural team," he said. "And a few newer architects who would probably jump at the chance to work on something like this. It'd be a good experience for them."

Then he shrugged casually.

"I could donate some money to help you get the nonprofit started too. And I can introduce you to a few investors who might be willing to contribute."

I stared down at him for a moment, my chest tightening a little at how easily he had stepped into the idea.

Not just supporting it.

Helping build it.

Now this was the reaction I had hoped for the first time I'd gone to him with one of my ideas.

Before I could stop myself, I slid off the chaise and climbed onto his lap. "Oh my God, Roman, this is everything."

I couldn't contain the excitement bubbling up inside me. I kissed him, and in the next second he had me pulled down onto the couch, his arms wrapped around me as we both laughed like a couple of teenagers who'd just gotten away with something.

A few minutes later we were stretched out on the couch, naked, facing each other, the room quiet again except for the music still playing softly in the background.

"I can't wait for the next project we do together." He said as he kissed my forehead stroking his hand up and down my spine.

"I need to take a shower," I said finally, pushing myself up from the couch. "Then we can either eat dinner here or go out and celebrate."

That worried look crossed his face again.

"How about we stay in and celebrate," he said. "I'll cook." He rolled over placing a hand behind his head.

I tilted my head at him for a second getting a good look at his impressive physique before reading too much into what he was saying.

Maybe he was still thinking about Tanner being out there somewhere. That would make sense, even if the tension still felt a little unlike him.

Still... Roman cooking?

That was never something I was going to complain about.

"I'll be out in a jiffy."

I leaned down, kissed him quickly, grabbed my clothes, and ran down the hall toward the shower.

Chapter 23

ALEX

This might be the best decision I've made in a long time.

Why in the world did I fight this for so long?

Every time I blink, the memories from last night replay with this warm, quiet glow around them—like scenes from a film I'll love forever. I can feel them more than I can remember them.

Roman helping me with my project like it was the most natural thing in the world.

Roman cooking dinner—actual dinner—not just ordering in, but making something beautiful and setting it out like we were at some five-star restaurant. And then the two of us sitting there in our sweats, completely mismatched with that elegant room...

God, that room. Formal, breathtaking, like it was meant for silk gowns and sparkling wine—not me barefoot and cross-legged at the table. Somehow, it still felt perfect.

But dessert...

Dessert is what I'll never forget.

We didn't even stay in one room. We somehow turned the entire penthouse into a trail of half-finished kisses and breathless laughter. Dessert in the living room. Dessert pressed up against the hallway wall. Dessert on our way to the bedroom—where, honestly, I'm not sure we slept at all. The night blurred into this seamless stretch of heat and softness and being wanted in a way that made every part of me let go.

And then dessert for breakfast at two in the morning, because of course we did.

Because everything about last night felt impossible to slow down.

It all felt... right.

Roman rolled over and grumbled, "Good morning. How'd you sleep?"

"Not sure I did, but I'm so excited that I need to work off some of this energy at the gym."

"We could workout in bed," he winked.

I laughed and gave him a little shove. "I have a team coming to the office this morning and I don't want to be late or unprepared, so it's gym time, shower time then work time."

"Okay, okay. I'm going to try out your schedule for a few weeks to see how it goes." Is he excited or am I excited? This can't only be my energy I'm feeling.

As he was heading into the bathroom I asked, "Babe, are you excited about all this?"

He groaned, "Of course I am. I love getting up at 5:00 am after three hours of sleep and going to the gym."

"Maybe not that part, but us?" I said a little louder since he was in the bathroom now. He came back over to the bed and grabbed my face, planting a kiss on my lips.

"This is the best thing that's ever happened to me—so yes."

I smiled to myself as he said it, knowing I had my answer. Everything suddenly felt lighter. The idea, the support Roman had given me, the possibilities ahead of us—it all had my energy running so high I could practically feel it buzzing through my body.

But I also knew myself well enough to recognize the warning signs. At some point this rush was going to crash, especially if I kept running on excitement and very little sleep.

And I still had training tonight.

Today was definitely going to be a short day at work.

I didn't think Shay or Darius would mind if I cut out early. They both had plenty to keep them busy, and honestly, they'd probably appreciate the quieter office for a few hours.

Maybe I could even see if Roman had something they could help with today. Shay might have other clients she needed to work with anyway, and Darius never seemed to run out of things to do.

Either way, the day suddenly felt full of possibility.

I made it to the office by eight to get everything set up in the conference room. I had to make a plan for this neighborhood and figure out where we're going to start.

Roman came in and asked me if I'd like some coffee.

I jumped up from the table. I needed something mundane to do to calm me down and making coffee seemed like the perfect distraction. "Yes, show me where it is and I'll get it."

"I was just being polite because Amelia's not here today." He nudged me with his shoulder.

"Oh no? Where is she?" Why does that sound familiar? Did I know she wasn't here?

"I sent her to Texas with Harrison, remember? I think they'll be back on Friday."

Of course, how could I forget.

"That's right. That was nice of you to give them some alone time."

He laughed. "They live together. I don't know how much more alone time they need."

"When did that happen? Is that why you asked me to move in with you, because they moved in together?" I started laughing but I really wondered if that's why he did it. He was the family minded one— Harrison was the playboy. Yet here he was already shacked up. I bet there was some sibling rivalry involved in this arrangement.

"No." He responded with a smirk that told me everything I needed to know.

"Roman, I forgot to ask you if you had something for Darius to concentrate on today. I'm going to go over my idea with them, but I really need to get out of here around two so I can rest before training. It's at four, then we have dinner with the Santoros."

"I almost forgot about that. I'll rest with you. I have to be at their house by four to go over renovation ideas for the winery." He put his head back with his hands covering his face. I doubt we'll be staying up that late on a work night again.

"Then I guess this is a short day for everyone. We can pick up where we leave off tomorrow. But I seriously need to take a nap, so if you're planning on coming up there to rest, you better mean nap and nothing else." I put my hands on my hips and gave him my most serious face without laughing.

He did laugh. "Yes, I really mean rest. I'm tired right now." He admitted. "Let me show you where the coffee is."

I followed him to the coffee machine, and he spun me around. "I've always wanted to have an office romance by the coffee machine." His gaze was searing. I knew he was serious.

"That's funny, so have I." I teased in response. He lifted me up to sit on the counter and stood between my legs and I wrapped them around his waist.

"You're going to make my job so much harder. Maybe you should go back to your real estate office." He smiled then pulled me close and put his lips to my ear. "But not this week." he hummed in my ear. I got the chills all over and seriously considered letting this happen.

"There will be people here in fifteen minutes and I really don't think this would be a good impression for the new guy."

He reluctantly agreed. "Coffee it is, then." He smacked my hip and made the coffee.

Damn, we should've gotten here earlier.

***

ROMAN

"Are you going to go home first to shower and change after the gym?" I asked as I poured my coffee, trying to sound casual even though I already hated the idea of us going separate ways.

"I didn't think about that. That's a lot of driving. Maybe there's a shower at the gym—I've never needed it, so I didn't notice. I'll call Bruce and find out."

I nodded, but something tightened in my gut. I trusted Bruce. I trusted the training. What I didn't trust were my own nerves. Watching her spar last time damn near put me through the roof. I couldn't go back in there; I'd end up interfering. And she didn't need to fight two people.

I had to let her go alone plus my meeting with the Santoros coincided with her training.

Amelia had already rescheduled all my meetings to next week after I emailed her about leaving early today. I justified it by slotting a renovation walk-through at four, so technically I wasn't bailing on work—but I also wasn't pretending this afternoon was anything other than what it was. I wanted to be home when she got there. I wanted to know she was safe.

I stayed in my office most of the day, pacing more than I worked, until Alex called me into the conference room to go over her idea with Shay and Darius. I liked watching her like that—focused, certain, in her zone. She came alive when she had a plan, and this one was good. Better than good.

We were actually going to work on a project together. I didn't realize how much I'd wanted that until she started talking and I caught myself smiling like an idiot.

She had a vision for the "new" Burrow Township—revitalization, opportunity funnels, income streams designated directly to the community, long-term stability instead of a band-aid fix. And Darius was on board; confident he could get the neighborhood behind it.

I told her I had a contact—one of the best in the nonprofit investment world. A guy who could map every infrastructure, legal angle, and long-game payout model they'd need.

She lit up. I don't think she even realized she did it. I did.

I also had the auditorium on the 16th floor—floor-to-ceiling glass, black acoustic panels, tiered seating, the works. Perfect for a community meeting once the time came. We'd have to wait until after next week, though.

Next week.

The hearing.

My stomach clenched. The second I thought about it, an unnamed panic started climbing up my spine. A week from today. One week. I needed to keep my head screwed on straight for her. She didn't need my nerves; she needed my strength.

I looked over at her—animated, confident, explaining a logistics flow to Darius with her hands—and I forced my brain to settle.

Focus, King.

She needs you steady.

But the thought kept circling like a vulture at the edge of my mind:

In seven days, she's going to have to sit in a room with the man who terrorized her.

I swallowed hard and pushed it down.

I have to stay focused.

For her.

No matter what.

"I can go door to door and talk to everyone and see how they feel about this. I know they like Alex a lot and trust her, so I don't think it'll be too hard to get everyone to at least come to a meeting and hear where this could go."

Darius leaned forward as he spoke, elbows on the table, eyes sharp with purpose.

He'd clearly been turning this over in his mind long before we sat down. Good. That neighborhood would listen to him in a way they don't listen to anyone else because he was from the neighborhood.

"Darius, that would be great, actually. I need to make a trip to your house soon anyway to visit your gram," Alex said, the warmth in her voice unmistakable.

Ella.

As soon as Alex said her name, her whole expression went soft—fond, protective and anchored. Ella wasn't just a part of the project to her. She was a symbol for everything Alex was fighting for. Everything she refused to let be destroyed.

Darius chuckled. "Yeah, she doesn't want you to forget about her just because I work with you now."

Alex burst into a genuine, unguarded laugh. Her entire face brightened. You'd think someone pulled open shutters in a dim room. Every time she talked about Ella or that street, something inside her came alive.

"Oh, I could never forget about her," she said. "She was my first favorite person in your neighborhood."

I watched her with a quiet sort of awe.

This work fit her. Not just the business side—this was personal for her in a way I was still learning to understand. It wasn't a job or a project to her; it was a moral responsibility.

And she was damn good at it.

I leaned back, letting the conversation flow, but the weight of my own thoughts settled hard. She really was transforming everything. Not just Burrow Township. Me.

I'd written checks for years, thinking that made me philanthropic—thinking money equaled impact. I didn't see the holes I left behind or the families uprooted after we cut their compensation checks. I didn't ask where they'd go next or how they'd rebuild.

But Alex saw every detail. Every face. Every ripple that happened long after the papers were signed.

And now all I could see—painfully clearly—was how shallow I'd been.

Damn.

When I step back and look at it honestly, I've been an asshole, haven't I?

Not malicious—just careless. Detached. The exact kind of businessman I never wanted to become.

But this?

This project?

This partnership with her, with Darius, with Ella's neighborhood?

This was redemption.

Not in a sappy philosophical sense but in a practical, brick-by-brick, we're-actually-going-to-fix-something sense. And I wanted to pour everything I had into it.

All the resources. All the connections. All the leverage I've built over the years.

Alex deserved that.

They deserved that.

And maybe—just maybe—this was the legacy I'd want tied to my future family. Not the money. But this. Doing actual good and knowing the people involved by name and story.

I glanced at Alex again. She was talking animatedly with Shay and Darius, already spinning her wheels into a dozen next steps.

Yeah.

This is exactly where I'm supposed to be.

And she's the one who put me here.

Chapter 24

ALEX

Oh. My. God! What the hell is that alarming noise? Is the building on fire or something?

Roman yelled, "Turn that damn thing off already."

I started laughing when I realized that was the timer for my alarm. Holy crap that thing is loud.

"Sorry, geez, not oversleeping with that, are we?"

"Why is that your alarm sound? That's absolutely horrible." He still had his hands over his ears.

"You woke up, didn't you?" I gave him a playful tap on his arm.

He reached over and said, "Give me that thing right now, I'm changing it." I laughed as we fought for supremacy of my phone.

"Nope, not going to happen."

He took a shower to help him wake up and I packed a bag of clothes to change into. Bruce said they had a place to shower and change, so I was all set to get ready after training.

Roman met me out in the living room dressed in a nice white button up shirt, gray slacks, a brown belt and brown shoes. I was tempted to skip training tonight, looking at the man in front of me. I hope this feeling never wears off. That was always my fear getting into a relationship, the honeymoon phase. Although, Roman and I have already gone through so much drama that I'm sure there was no room for a honeymoon phase. We skipped right over that.

"So, you seem to be fine with me going by myself to training."

He smiled but still looked a little weary.

"Well, I don't really have a choice and I'm damn sure not watching you train again. I think you'll be fine in your car, plus we're connected on life 360."

"Ummm, when did this happen?" I stared down at my phone thinking it was now a tracker, and it was freaking me out. Can someone really do that to your phone without their knowledge?

"Sorry, I did it yesterday when you were in the shower. Not because you moved in or because I'm trying to control you, but...I'm just kidding, you should see your face." I reached out and smacked his arm then took a deep breath of relief that he didn't actually do that.

***

I warned Bruce I might not be at a hundred percent today after another night of almost no sleep.
He didn't care. Naturally.

"Your opponent doesn't care how much sleep you've had, and neither does the defendant," he said flatly, adjusting the wraps on his hands. "In fact, he's hoping you're not at a hundred percent. Just be aware of that."

Good.
That's exactly what I needed—someone who wouldn't tiptoe around me because my life is imploding. Someone who reminds me that Tanner doesn't care if I'm exhausted, distracted, or unraveling. He'll take whatever advantage he thinks he can get.

So no, I didn't need gentleness today.
I needed fire.

I climbed into the ring and let myself disappear into the movement. Punches, pivots, breath work, counter-moves—Bruce pushed me hard, and I pushed myself harder. Within minutes I forgot about sleep, forgotten wounds, everything except the clarity of the fight. My body remembered what my brain tries to forget: I'm not weak. And I'm not helpless.

When training was over, I was drenched, shaking, and strangely calm.
A hot shower helped too.
I changed into a black long-sleeved maxi dress with wedges—simple, comfortable, appropriate for a family dinner. I sat beside Bruce on the bench outside the ring to thank him.

"You're welcome," he said, no warmth, no softness—just Bruce being Bruce. "I'm not sugar-coating anything for you in here. This isn't cardio hour at the Y. You walk into that courtroom unprepared, he wins."

"I know." I exhaled. "I don't want to be complacent. I need focus. Control."

He nodded, expression stone-cold. "You'll be strong in that courtroom. You've got a whole damn army behind you. Don't let him or his attorney get a reaction out of you."

I swallowed hard.

My plan flashed in my mind—the piece no one knows about.

Not Roman.

Not the attorneys.

Not even Lisette.

Bruce might understand it.

He might be the only one who could hear it without trying to stop me.

But not today.

One secret at a time.

I pushed open the gym door, stepped into the warm evening air, and headed to the car. The sky had that burnt-peach glow of almost-sunset. I turned up the radio on the drive just to drown out my thoughts.

Halfway there, I texted Roman.

ME: *Hey babe. I'm on the way but I'm sure you already know that ;)*
ROMAN: *HA HA. :) I'll see you soon.*

I rolled my eyes and smirked.

He really is a pain in the ass.

My pain in the ass.

***

ROMAN

I followed the GPS to an address about thirty minutes from home to a very long tree lined driveway. It felt like the first time Alex and I went to Lookout Park and I thought about all the terrible things that could have happened to her in such a hidden, desolate area. Yep, all those feelings are back, only this time I'm worried about myself. The drive didn't help calm me down after all.

But wow, this house is incredible.

I climbed the enormous stone stairs and rang the doorbell. Someone dressed in a tuxedo answered the door and said in a thick Italian accent, "Good afternoon, you must be Mr. King. Please, come in. Mr. and Mrs. Santoro are right this way." This is the life Alex thought I had. I laughed. My family would never live like this. A butler was a little too much for us.

I felt like I was in old world Italy. It reminded me of the places my parents used to take us when we were kids. It really was incredible though. The ostentatiousness of my parent's house had nothing on this place.

Mrs. Santoro was the first one to greet me with a hug and a kiss on each cheek. She made sure I called her Lucia. I shook Mr. Santoro's, Alessandro's, hand then we sat down and had a glass of wine from one of their other vineyards.

"Roman, I feel like you have to have a connection to what we do before you can truly get on board with the vision. What do you think?" Just then Lucia excused herself to the kitchen.

"Well, I guess that depends what connection we're talking about." He raised his glass and tipped his head at me.

"I like you Roman."

My eyebrows were raised as I considered how I felt about that. "Grant called me yesterday after you spoke. I'm guessing you're feeling a little apprehensive about us now?" Now my nerves were on edge, and I was starting to feel trapped. I also felt like they weren't who I thought they were...anymore.

I said, hesitantly, "Yes, I'm having some trouble with the information Grant gave me yesterday." I took a rather large gulp of wine. I wish I had something stronger.

"Well, you showed up today, so it couldn't be that bad, right?" I could tell he was trying to make me feel better— I didn't know if it was working as I shifted uncomfortably in my chair. My clothes were even making me feel a bit confined.

"You know, I'm just a normal guy who builds things. I'm really kind of boring. I thought stories like this only existed in the movies. After yesterday I realized my nice little boring bubble was about to pop. My girlfriend, on the other hand, would probably think it was cool."

"Yes, Alexandra is an amazing young lady, isn't she?" He was beaming as he talked about her. It was almost like they knew her. "Grant introduced us to Alex, and we absolutely fell in love. She has a very special place in Grant's heart."

I thought that was kind of weird, honestly.

"I noticed he was very protective of her. Said he thinks of her as the daughter he never had. Is there something else I should know?"

He smiled but there was something behind his eyes that I may not really want to know.

"We all have stories we can't seem to share. I believe Americans say, 'Skeletons in the closet?'"

Hmmm, what other skeletons could he possibly have in his closet worse than what he already told me?

"Alessandro, you have an amazing home. Truly remarkable. How do you all like living in Ohio? It couldn't possibly be anything like Italy." *Good time for a subject change*, I think. I sat back in my chair taking a deep breath and another sip of wine to relax.

"We love it so far. It's so peaceful and quiet. No one bothers you out here." All I could think as I scanned the view of the parts of the yard I could see, was that it looked like a nice place to bury the bodies.

We finished going over his renovation plans, and he told me once Alex arrived, we'd walk the property so he could show me where he planned to build the winery.

Lucia came back with the kids and introduced them. There were four of them, from the ages of ten to sixteen. Two boys, Alessandro Jr. sixteen, Luca ten, and two girls, Anna twelve and Valentina fourteen. Then a big white dog came bounding through the house. That's when we decided to go outside. The dog gave me a quick sniff and was out the door.

Luca said, "That's Sage. She's my dog."

"That's a great name, Luca." Alex was pulling into the driveway as we came outside. I've never been so happy to see another person in my life. The dog was the first to greet her. It looked like an old friend saying hello. Alex not only attracted children, but apparently, she attracted dogs too. This dog was all over her. The kids were trying to rein her in, but it seemed Alex was loving every second of it. I had no idea she was a dog lover. Her dad has a dog, but she isn't crazy over her like she is with this dog.

When the kids got the dog to calm down Alex waved to all of us and finally made her way over. She looked beautiful. You couldn't tell she'd just spent an hour and a half in the ring with an MMA beast getting beat up. Or maybe she was doing the beating up, either way, she looked fantastic. She introduced herself to all the kids while she walked over, winked at me and went straight over to Lucia first, then Alessandro. Finally, she found me and gave me a nice hug and kiss. I didn't want to let her go.

"Wow, this place is amazing at sunset." She had an awestruck look on her face as she stared into the glow.

"Yes, it is. Come." Alessandro motioned for us to follow. We walked to the backyard, and it was like a whole other world.

***

ALEX

I held Roman's hand as we walked toward the backyard. The second we stepped outside, the sun hit that perfect line between horizon and sky, painting everything in a wild explosion of reds, oranges, pinks, and golds. One of the Santoro kids shouted for all of us to turn around so they could take a picture, and we stood there, framed by the kind of sunset you only ever see in movies.

Then the lights came on—strings woven through trees, path lights glowing along the stone walkways, soft uplighting illuminating the landscaping. The whole yard shifted from beautiful to ethereal in an instant. It felt enchanted. I loved it as much as I loved Roman's parents' home, which was saying something. This place was a dream

Of course, I got lost in it.

Again.

Roman nudged me gently back to reality.

"Sorry," I said, blinking hard. "It's a habit apparently."

Everyone laughed.

Alessandro asked, "So, Alexandra—were you envisioning something?"

"A little," I admitted. "I was just wondering what else you could possibly do to make this any more wonderful."

"Roman," Alessandro said, turning to him, "any ideas?"

Roman was staring at me—not the view. My stomach flipped.

"Actually, I do," he said, winking. "This place is already gorgeous, but you're planning a vineyard too, right?"

"Yes," Alessandro replied.

Roman nodded toward the hills. "You'll need open space for the vines, but you can keep them past the rolling slopes. And you'll need a winery—probably where that other building is." He pointed. "Was that an old barn or stable?"

Alessandro's eyebrows shot up. "I'm impressed, Roman. Do you know anything about vineyards?"

I straightened a little, curious too.
Since when did Roman know anything about wineries?

"I've been to my fair share," he said casually. "I enjoy them."

That little flare of jealousy crept into my chest before I could stop it.
Wineries.
Plural.
Memories.
Possibly with women.

He must've sensed it.

"My mom is a connoisseur," he clarified quickly. "My dad isn't into wine, so they used to take us when we were younger. When I got older, it became a thing she and I did together—wineries in the U.S., Europe, Australia."

Ah.
That I could handle.

Lucia smiled warmly. "You must bring your mother one day. She should taste our wines."

"I will," Roman said. "She'll love that this place is so close. She adores Italian wine."

We walked and talked as the sun dipped lower, the sky deepening into lavender. Dinner was served on the stone patio overlooking what would soon become a vineyard—candles flickering on the table, the scent of rosemary and grilled vegetables drifting through the air.

"Roman," I asked, "do you have an architect who knows anything about vineyards?"

"I have an architect for just about everything," he said, taking a sip of wine. "But I plan to be hands-on with this one."

His excitement lit something warm within me.
This place was magical and I couldn't wait to see what he did with it.

After dinner, the kids went inside, leaving the four of us to finish our wine under the string lights. Eventually we said goodnight and got in our cars. Roman made me talk to him the entire drive home—part sweet, part aggravating. I knew we'd have to discuss it. I like music when I drive, not feeling like I'm reporting in.

I pulled into the garage behind him, and we rode the elevator up together. As soon as we stepped inside the penthouse, I kicked off my wedges and dropped my purse by the door.

"Okay, buddy," I said, pointing to the couch. "Have a seat. We need to talk."

His head dropped immediately, shoulders shaking with suppressed laughter as he walked over to the sofa.

"Oh no," I warned. "This is not a laughing matter. This is serious. You have officially lost your mind." I threw my hands up.

He tried to stop, but the laughter broke loose anyway.

"I'm sorry—don't hurt me," he managed between breaths, still laughing.

"Roman, you cannot possibly think this is cool," I snapped. "You can't keep doing this. I don't need a chaperone. I don't need a bodyguard. I don't need another dad. I absolutely do not need a tracker, and I hate talking on the phone while I'm driving."

My hands were balled into fists at my sides. I was furious.

He kept laughing.

What in the actual hell was going on with him?

***

ROMAN

"Honey, I really am sorry." I let out a breath I'd been holding as the laughing drifted off. "I'm sorry for the ride home. That was my fault. I had too much to drink, and I probably shouldn't have been driving. I needed you to keep me focused so I could make it home."

She walked straight toward me—quiet, steady—and slapped me.
Hard.
The crack echoed through the room.

She ran down the hall before I could speak.

My cheek stung, but the shock hit harder. I stood there, stunned, jaw tight, every nerve fired awake.

If I wasn't sober before, I sure as hell was now.

I followed her to the bedroom and found her on the floor—knees pulled in, back against the side of the bed, hands trembling. Her face was blotchy and wet, and she looked both furious and terrified.

My irritation dissolved instantly.

I lowered myself to the floor beside her and touched her chin gently. "Alex... look at me for a minute."

She lifted her head, and the anger in her eyes nearly undid me. Tears streamed down her cheeks in steady tracks.

"You should've left your car at their house," she hissed through clenched teeth—then covered her face, shoulders shaking as a sob tore out of her.

"I know," I said quietly. "You're right."

Before I could say anything else, she grabbed me—arms locked tight around me, as if she was afraid I'd disappear. The air punched out of my lungs from how hard she held on.

"I don't want to lose you," she cried against my shoulder.

Lose me?

I wrapped both arms around her, pulling her closer. "You're not going to lose me."

She sucked in a shaky breath. "That's how I lost my mother, Roman."

Everything inside me went still.

I closed my eyes, pressing my cheek to the top of her head as her sobs grew louder, rawer, heartbreak spilling straight out of her. And suddenly the slap made perfect sense. The fear underneath it. The grief. The panic. All of it.

And all I could think was—

What was I doing?

How could I be so careless with the woman who trusts me more than anyone?

A slap wasn't enough for what I did.

I held her as close as I could, whispering apology after apology into her hair. "I'm so sorry. It won't ever happen again. I swear it. Never."

I knew why I drank—trying to numb everything I had bouncing around in my head—but that didn't excuse a thing. Not with her. Not ever.

I didn't know how to fix it tonight.

But I knew we couldn't unravel any further.

I brushed my thumb along her tear-damp cheek. "Come on," I whispered. "Let's just go to sleep."

Chapter 25

ALEX

I woke up right before the alarm, heart already heavy, and slipped quietly out of bed. He was still asleep, sprawled on his stomach, the sheets twisted low around his hips. Normally, that sight would pull me right back under the covers with him. Not today.

I wasn't ready to talk to him. Not when the fear still sat like a stone in my stomach.

So, I went to the gym alone.

The slap lingered in my mind like an echo I couldn't escape. I couldn't believe I'd actually done that—an instinctive, uncontrolled response that didn't even feel aimed at him. Maybe it was something I had wanted to do to my mother and never could. Another topic for Dr. King, for sure. I couldn't just go around hitting people because they made bad decisions.

I drove myself hard that morning.

Weights.

Cardio.

A dozen fast laps through the pool.

Then the sauna—heat pressing in on all sides, pulling sweat and tension out of me in steady, slow rivulets until I could almost breathe again.

I leaned back against the cedar wall, eyes closed, letting the heat blur everything.

Then the door opened with a soft hiss.

Roman stepped in quietly, like he was entering a church. He didn't say a word. He moved to the lower bench and sank down in front of me, sliding his arms around my waist with a gentleness that broke something inside me.

He rested his forehead against my chest, his hair still messy from sleep, breath warm against my skin.
Guilt poured off him in waves.

My fingers lifted on instinct, combing through his hair, soothing him even though I was still hurting too.

"I'm so sorry about last night," he murmured, voice low and hoarse. "I was drunk. It won't happen again."

"I'm not going to excuse your behavior," I said softly. "But... I'm sorry for slapping you. I still can't believe I did that."

His arms tightened around my waist, and he let out a rough groan.

"You should've hit me harder."

A laugh almost escaped—but the truth of it still didn't sit right with me. I was just grateful nothing happened. Grateful he was still here. Grateful I could still feel his heartbeat pressed to my ribs.

And for the first time since last night, the fear eased—just a little—as I wrapped my arms around him and held him close.

***

This morning was the deposition, and I was already fraught with anxiety, so I really didn't need all this extra drama. It was quiet in the house as we got ready with each of us thinking about the events of last night and what's going to happen next Tuesday at the court hearing when things get real.

"Alex, this is just you going to tell your side of the story to the officers. No one else is going to be there. This is not at all like court." I smiled and nodded, knowing he was trying to make me feel better, but I hated the thought of telling this story again and then reliving it on Tuesday.

He pulled me to him placing his hands on my shoulders holding me in place as he looked deeply into my eyes and smiled, bringing my attention back to the present.

"I know. You're right. I just need to relax and get this over with." My mind was telling me that was the right thing to do and say but my heart was not following suit.

Roman held my hand all the way to the police station as I stared out of the window contemplating telling my attorneys what I had planned since they were bound by attorney client privilege and wouldn't be able to tell anyone else. If only to find out if they thought, it was a good idea or if they thought I was out of my mind. I didn't notice we stopped until Roman gave my hand a gentle squeeze and said, "Alex, we're here baby."

I released his hand before we entered the police station and shoved them in my pockets to hide the shaking. I had no idea what to expect here and the anxiety had me glancing sharply from left to right trying to see if maybe Tanner was here giving his side of the story as well. I can't imagine they would do such a thing, but you never know with all the crazy shit that's happened in my life. The station was just as I pictured it in my mind, stale and monotone. The clicking of keyboards, the smell of bad coffee and no one taking a real interest in anything going on around them. I can hear a few people talking and laughing probably at the expense of some poor soul who made a bad decision.

I closed my eyes trying to will away the negativity. I had no idea what they were laughing at and my recent interactions with CPD's not so finest has left a bad taste in my mouth. Two deep breaths later and I was able to open my eyes and concentrate on the person in front of me at the desk.

"Hi, I'm Roman King and this is Alex Kennedy. We have an appointment with DA Martin and Detective Lewis for a deposition." Roman took the initiative to introduce us, knowing how hard this was going to be for me and any other time I may have condemned such an action but today I welcomed it and was grateful.

The officer nodded and punched our names into the computer to pull up our appointment as he pointed to a bench next to the desk. "Please have a seat and I'll let them know you're here."

I managed to grumble out a thank you and Roman guided us over to the bench with his arm possessively placed around me, not letting go of me after we sat down. He leaned in placing a kiss on my temple and whispered, "I'm right here baby, it's going to be fine, I promise." How can he promise that? He has no idea what's going to happen, not here and not in the courtroom. I know he means well, but this is out of his control, but hopefully within a realm of control that I can convey in other terms at a, to be determined, date.

"Thank you for being here with me. I truly love you for that." I melted into him taking a deep breath of his scent to calm and soothe my broken soul. Oh, how I wish he knew how much I needed him for that, but I don't even want to admit that to myself most of the time. The thought of needing someone so desperately is scary as hell and it makes me want to run away with the same desperation.

"Mr. King, Ms. Kennedy? Come with me please." The officer took us into a room with a big mirror and a long table with chairs all around us. It looked like an interrogation room, and I felt a sense of dread wondering if this was the room they brought Tanner to after he attacked me. The officer left us alone after asking if we would like anything to drink. We both declined and I sat staring at my hands, wringing relentlessly in my lap.

Roman wrapped his arm around my shoulder and I shrugged him off when I heard the door handle jiggle, and my guard went up. He nodded, knowingly, pulling his arm away then rested them both on the table clasping his hands in front of him. I needed some space to get my mind wrapped around what I really wanted to do. Do I tell the officers or my attorneys about my plan or do I keep it all to myself and carry this burden on my own? It's heavy and it's consuming, and I don't know if I can do it alone but it's something that has to be done and the one person that can't know and would try to stop me with everything he had, is Roman.

"Alex, Roman. Good to see you both." Matt reached out his hand keeping the whole thing professional. Jack as well, followed by the DA and the Detective.

"Alex, the first thing we are going to do is put the two of you in different rooms. Is there anyone in particular you would feel more comfortable doing the interview with?" DA Martin asked. I didn't know what to expect but I guess it was to make sure no one tainted the story or the evidence having us in separate rooms and not having Roman in the room would help me make my decision about telling someone what I was up to.

"I'd like Matt and Detective Lewis if that's ok?" Jack always tried to bring the temperature of the room down and Matt would be more likely to let me get it all out. I've known both of them since college and being like brothers to me, I knew which of my own brothers I felt more comfortable talking to as well.

"Ok, Roman, DA Martin and Jack will be interviewing you, so if you'd please follow them so we can get started." Matt gestured with his hand to the door and Roman looked at me a little apprehensive but nodded and followed them out of the room without complaint. I smiled at him as he turned to look at me before he left the room, but I could tell it never hit my eyes, and he didn't reciprocate a smile in return.

"Alex, this is a deposition, and we want to hear again what happened, as much as you can remember, but we also need to prep you for the courtroom. It's coming up fast and we need to be prepared. We have to know what we're dealing with going in there. I know you enough to know that if they push the right buttons, you're going to lose your shit, and we can't have that." This is why I chose Matt over Jack. He doesn't hold back and says it like it is, no beating around the bush. Maybe I will be able to tell the officer and Matt my seriously deranged plan floating around nonstop in my head. In fact, the closer we get to the court date the more concrete the plan becomes and the more palatable it seems.

"I'm ready for whatever you need." I said, wondering if I honestly meant that or if I'm running on some sort of autopilot and only saying what I think everyone wants to hear.

"Ms. Kennedy, could you please tell us what you remember about that night." Detective Lewis asked. My mind started to scramble as it tried to go back to the worst memories it's ever had to experience, never wanting to actually go back there again. The thought of drinking a glass of wine to suppress them was battling for supremacy and my hands started to tremble. I clenched them into fits, releasing them a couple of times before I could get the urges under control. I took a deep breath closing my eyes, opening them when I felt ready and monotonously reliving the events of that night the best I could, which wasn't much since the drugs took most of the memories from me. At the end of my rendition of that night I let out a long exhale, feeling much better, like I'd be safe telling my plan to the two of them. Just as I was about to let them in on my secret, Matt asked a question so formal and cold I wasn't really sure what he was doing, so I hesitated long enough to rethink that decision.

"Ms. Kennedy. What were you really drinking that night?" Excuse me? What? Really drinking? What the fuck is he doing?

"Water, I already told you that." I snapped.

"I don't need any more than a straight answer Alex. When I ask you a question, I don't want you to give me any more than a yes or no or a one-word answer to the best of your ability, alright? No explanations." What is going on?

"Now, let's try this again. Are you sure you didn't have one drink, not even one at your house for happy hour?"

"No...I specifically..." Matt cut me off with the sharpest tongue I've ever heard him use.

"I thought I just said do not answer anything other than yes or no." My eyes went wide, and I nodded feeling a tightness in my chest trying to figure out if he's ever spoken to me like this before and if so, did he really mean it or was he kidding.

"Who made your drink?" I thought about how to answer this with as little words as possible, scanning my memory for who actually made the drink for me, and did I notice since it was only water.

"Umm, I don't know..." Matt looked to the detective and back at me.

"What do you mean, you don't know? Didn't you order it from someone?" Is this part of the questions he wants me to be vague about or is this something he really needs to know. I cautiously gave a more informative answer.

"The barback handed it to me, I didn't actually see who made it. It was just water, I wasn't too concerned with how it was made, I guess." Tears started welling in my eyes as I realized it didn't matter what my drink was, someone wanted to hurt me, and they did it with water. I looked at Matt who was looking to the detective, and she was writing notes in her notebook that she always had with her.

"What are you writing, is that important?"

"It's fine, it's just information that we didn't have before. Let's continue."

"Ms. Kennedy. What were you doing that you didn't notice who made your drink?"

"What do you mean? I just told you I didn't think water needed eyes on it." However, clearly it did, and I felt a tear glide down my cheek.

"Alex, just answer the question, do not ask questions back."

"Then let me know when we're pretending to be in court and when you're asking me a legit question, damn it." Matt snapped his head up and glared at me as the detective reached over and calmed him with a hand on his forearm.

"Would you like me to continue the questions, Mr. Stevens?" Detective Lewis calmly tried to defuse the situation between Matt and myself, but I knew he wouldn't allow her to take his place.

"No, detective, she doesn't need coddling right now." Matt said through gritted teeth not taking his eyes off me. The detective didn't seem phased by the interaction, so I let it go and didn't give Matt the piece of my mind that was right there on the tip of my tongue.

"Texting. That's what I was doing?" I moved on from the tension in the room and back to the task at hand so I could get the hell out of here. The anxiety building in my chest was raging to the surface and I sure as hell didn't want to take out this uncontrollable anger on the two of them and possibly get myself thrown in jail.

"Who were you texting?"

"Roman." Now I'm starting to see the importance of short answers and the need to not bring up the plan with Matt or Detective Lewis.

"Roman who and who is he to you?" I smirked and huffed out a breath of air thinking this is so weird pretending when I know they know the answers to these questions already.

"Roman King and he is...was my boyfriend." Is he my boyfriend again? I don't even know the answer to a question as simple as that at the moment.

"Was? Why is he not now? Aren't you living with him? Do you make it a habit of cohabitating with men you're not dating?" Matt shot each question right out of the cannon as if I were the one on trial and I lost my senses about why I was here.

"Excuse me? I think you of all people know why the fuck I'm living with him." Something snapped and I didn't know how to rein it back in. I stood up and slammed my hands on the table, frustration replaced by anger.

"Alex, I'm not asking as your friend, I'm asking as if I were his attorney." Matt's face was unsettled, and he stood up towering over me, placing his hands on the table to lean in, bringing him down to my height. The urge to reach out and slap him was almost more than I could bear. I flopped down in the chair wrapping my arms around me, digging my nails into my biceps to control my temper and keep my hands to myself.

"You can't behave this way in the courtroom, Alex. No matter what they ask you, you have to be in control and just answer the fucking question." His nostrils were flared, and I knew I'd pushed too far this time. Definitely not exposing the plan to either of them now.

***

ROMAN

I followed the DA and Jack to another room just a few doors down the hall from where I left Alex. I sat down in the chair they directed me to, as they sat across from me.

"Roman, we've been getting some rather strange messages from the defendant's attorneys about them filing charges against Alex for assault. This court room drama is going to be a lot on her. Can you tell us anything that could help us keep her under control in there?"

"Like what? Maybe if you could keep it out of court that would help immensely." They looked at each other and smiled, probably thinking the same thing.

"Don't think we haven't been pushing for that but he's really playing this bullshit up. Has she said anything about that night that we can use to help her case? The whole not knowing what happened and thinking it was you, isn't really the nail in the coffin we need."

"She hasn't talked about that night with me other than to tell me she has nightmares about it. She said something recently that has me worried, but she said it was just because she had too much to drink. She said I wasn't going to like it. I still don't know what, if anything, she was talking about."

"Well, we can't use what we don't know, so let's not worry about it now." I pushed it to the back of my mind hoping it was nothing.

We finished talking about the case and thinking about ways to help Alex remain calm in the courtroom and we concluded that it would all be in Alex's hands once we were in that room. I shook both of their hands and thanked them for their time and what they were doing for Alex and led the way out of the room.

"Fuck off Matt. You should've warned me about what you were going to do here today. That was bullshit." Alex sounded pissed as she came charging out of the room, they were in, with Matt hot on her heels and the detective trying to grab Matt's arms while he jerked them away. I started towards Alex when Matt yelled back at her in a tone, I've never heard from him. It was alarming to say the least.

"Sure Alex, it's me that needs to fuck off, right! I've been trying to help you. To make sure you don't lose it in there. If you do...if you behave like that, out of control, they won't take you seriously and he'll win. Do you fucking understand me?" I started over towards them to get him away from her and Jack shoved me out of the way, getting right in between Alex and Matt.

"What's going on here? Both of you back down right now." Jack's tone was more level but still on the verge of aggressive. Alex sure does know how to rile up the crowd, doesn't she? Alex swatted Jack's hand away from her and I took a few steps in her direction trying to gage how contemptuous she was and at the same time not wanting to become a target myself.

"I'm fine." She said as she put her hands up, taking a step back into the wall, closing her eyes tight.

"Baby, it's me. Let's go home." I gently took her hand, feeling the tension in her grip, watching as her face went from red to a more natural tan again. Her eyes opened slowly— I could tell she'd been crying. She nodded then threw a nasty glare at Matt and I got her out of there as swiftly as I could. I'll have to talk to Matt later and find out what happened. Right now, I just want to forget about what I just saw.

Chapter 26

ALEX

It's too late for me to care what they think now.

My mind is already made up.

No matter what happens in that courtroom, I'm going after Tanner my way. He'll get what he deserves—every last piece of it.

Despite Wednesday's detour to the police station, my team and I still made progress. By Friday, Amelia and I had put together invitations for the Burrow Township residents to attend the District 5 renovation meeting in two weeks. That gave us enough time to get through the hearing and have Roman's auditorium ready. Amelia was good at this sort of thing—Roman told me she was a natural planner—and she happily took the lead.

By the end of the day, the only things on my mind were what we needed from the store for dinner... and our plans with the kids tonight.

I walked into Roman's office, and for the first time all week, he actually looked relaxed; leaned back, laughing into the phone. When he saw me, he winked and patted his lap as an invitation. I crossed the room and sat, and his arm slid around my waist before he hung up.

"Who was that? Must've been a good conversation."

"It was Matt," he said, amused. "I was getting some info on the kids for tonight. He basically said you're their favorite person in the world and I shouldn't bother trying to compete."

That made me giggle. My relationship with Matt had become the emotional equivalent of fighting with one of my brothers—heated in the moment, forgotten as soon as everyone cooled off and remembered the anxiety was never actually about each other.

"You know what? He might be right," I teased. "But I'll try to convince them you're not so bad."

I poked him lightly in the chest, and he grabbed my hand before I could pull it back.

"Hey, I meant to ask you something," he said.

"Oh? What's that?"

"When we were at the Santoros' the other night, that dog was all over you, and you were totally fine with it. Do you really like dogs that much, or were you just being polite?"

I laughed at the unexpected question.

"That's a weird thing to be curious about, but no—I love dogs. I love dogs and I love children. I just... feel like I'm too selfish for either right now."

He frowned, thinking that over.

"At your dad's house, you don't really engage Sadie," he said carefully. "Is there something about her?"

I winced at the memory. "Sadie's old. I love her, but when she gets too excited, she gets hurt. The last time we played the way I played with Sage, she blew her knee out. So now I just try to keep her calm. It feels awful ignoring her, but it's better than watching her be in pain."

He wrapped his arms around me, kissed the side of my head. "That's music to my ears," he murmured. "Maybe we could get a dog. To start."

"To start what?" I asked, playing coy even though we both knew exactly what he meant.

He gave me that soft, steady smile—the one that warmed my heart. "Our life together."

"Maybe someday," I said, brushing my thumb over his jaw. "Right now, we need to make sure we have everything we need for a kiddie sleepover."

He nodded.

"Let's not talk about the future right now," I said, lifting my hands slightly in a quiet plea. "Let me get through next week first before I even try to think about dogs, families, or anything that requires long-term planning. We're going to have a houseful of kids tonight, so I want a little time alone with you before they get here. I think we've got plenty of snacks and food, and we can turn the living room into a pillow-fort campground with popcorn and movies."

He took my hand practically pulling me into the elevator. The moment the doors closed, he was all over me—warm, familiar, steadying and overwhelming at the same time.

Then he paused, took a breath, leaned against the glass, and pulled me close.

"Did I say something wrong?" he asked quietly.

Stop trying to ruin the moment.

"No," I said softly. "I just want you alone for a bit before the chaos begins. Once those kids get here, we won't have a minute to ourselves."

He still didn't look convinced, but his shoulders relaxed a little.

So I reached down, slipped off one of my heels, dangled it in my hand, then let it fall to the floor. His eyebrows rose. Then I took off the other shoe and—in a very deliberate, very obvious subject change—tossed it straight into the penthouse as soon as the doors opened.

He laughed, shaking his head.

"You coming?" I called behind me as I kicked my second shoe deeper into the room, dropped my purse on the island, and took off down the hallway with him close behind.

And honestly—

that rush?

That was incredible. Much better than the heavy conversation he had clearly been trying to initiate. I always said I wanted him to "chase" me figuratively, but apparently the literal version worked just fine too.

He caught me halfway to the bedroom and tossed me onto the bed with a kind of wild, playful urgency that made my heart flip. It wasn't anger—just pent-up energy and adrenaline that matched mine perfectly. It made me laugh, breathless, amazed at how quickly he could shift my mood.

We probably needed moments like that more often. It released tension the same way training did—only without the bruises.

Afterward, he pulled me from the bed with a grin. "Come on. We need a shower. We have visitors in an hour."

Later, in the kitchen, I asked, "Are you nervous?"

"Not really," he said casually. "It's something I've wanted to observe."

"Observe?" I raised an eyebrow. "What exactly are you planning to observe?"

"The way you are with the kids. I've seen you with them at their house, but I'm curious to see it here."

Ah.

Research.

For his imagined future.

I thought about my ex-husband for half a second and shuddered internally. If I'd observed him with kids before marrying him, maybe I'd have avoided that entire disaster. Roman, on the other hand... the thought of him with children made something warm and complicated twist in my chest.

"Research, hmm?" I teased.

"Maybe," he said with a playful shrug. "But even if I thought you might eat your young, I'd probably still keep you."

That made me burst into laughter. "That's reassuring and a little disturbing."

He wrapped his arms around me and murmured, "I can already tell you'll be a wonderful mother someday."

My breath caught. The room tilted just enough that I had to steady myself on his forearm.

"Please stop," I whispered, gentler than he expected. "Talking about kids and dogs right now... it's a lot. I can't process all that with everything else going on."

"That's what I was trying to figure out."

"What do you mean?" I asked.

"You tend to dodge anything that feels too big or too emotional. I wasn't pushing you—I just wanted to know where your head was on those topics. That's all. I'm not in a hurry."

I exhaled, feeling the truth of it.

Communication... not exactly my strong suit.

He wasn't pushy—thankfully—but he also wasn't always direct, which meant I often didn't realize he was trying to get clarity until I was already overwhelmed.

Something I needed to work on.

Preferably before either of us had another meltdown.

***

ROMAN

"What time is it, babe?" I called from the kitchen, moving things around on the counter.

"They'll be here in about thirty minutes," she shouted back. "So we've got time to get snacks out and turn the living room into a pillow-fort par-tay."

"What snacks?"

She rattled off a list—berries, cut veggies, crackers, chips, popcorn—while she came bounding down the hallway with an avalanche of pillows and blankets stacked in her arms, I pulled the pizza from the freezer and set it on the counter.

My phone buzzed in my hand. Matt's name lit up the screen.

"Hey Matt, you guys on your way?"

Maggie's voice answered instead. "Hi Roman, it's Maggie. Yes, we're all coming together. Is it okay if we have a drink at your place before we head out? We can talk about what the kids might need."

"Of course," I said. "We'll see you all when you get here."

Alex came down the hall again with another leaning tower of pillows covering half her face. "Who were you talking to?" she mumbled through the cotton mountain before dropping everything onto the sofa.

"Matt and Maggie. They're on their way. They're all riding together and want to stop in for a cocktail first."

She blinked. "Okay, but why did they call you and not me?"

"No idea. Did you check to see if they called you?"

She grabbed her phone. "Sorry—they did. I missed it. I was a little... distracted."

Yeah. She was definitely territorial about her friends. It was cute, though she'd never admit it.

"So," she said, regaining her upbeat tone, "what should we have out for everyone to drink?"

"Let's just open the bar and let them pick," I said.

She nodded. "Perfect."

"Want something now?" I asked.

She shook her head. "I'll just have one with everyone when they get here. But nothing after that. Not with all the kids here."

I liked hearing that more than I expected. Responsible. Grounded. Another point in the mental list I was keeping—pros and cons, though so far I hadn't found a single con.

The elevator dinged, and the doors opened to a thunderstorm of small voices.

"AUNT ALI!!!"

Three kids launched out of the elevator at full speed, racing straight to her as if I didn't exist. They wrapped around her legs, arms, waist, whatever they could grab.

Matt stepped out behind them with a grin that could only be described as smug. "Hey Roman, you sure you're ready for all this?"

"By the looks of it," I said, watching Alex drop to her knees and get swallowed by tiny hugs, "it'll be like I'm not even here."

They all laughed, and I ushered the adults toward the bar.

***

ALEX

"So... what's it like living together?" Maggie asked, swirling her wine as she leaned her hip against the counter like she was settling in for a show.

"It's already had its adjustments, if you know what I mean." I let out a long breath and rolled my eyes toward the huge windows, watching the last bit of sunset reflect off the river.

Abby raised an eyebrow, reading between my lines instantly. "You mean he's gone from whatever he was before... to full-on overprotective?"

"Exactly." I pressed a hand to my chest, exaggerating the exhaustion, earning a snort-laugh from her.

The penthouse felt loud and warm with everyone inside—kids squealing, toys being tossed around. The scent of popcorn was already drifting from the kitchen, mixing with the sweetness of the dessert candles Roman insisted on lighting for ambiance. The girls were perched on barstools beside me, knees turned in, glasses clinking lightly as they shifted to get closer. It felt like one of those cozy girl-talk circles where you know you're about to get grilled.

Right then Jack called across the kitchen. "Hey, Alex—congratulations!"

It was like someone hit a switch. Both girls swung their heads toward me so fast the air moved.

I held my hands up like I was under interrogation. "I was going to wait to tell you on Sunday. And it's not... really a congratulations thing."

Abby narrowed her gaze, her dangling earrings swinging as she leaned forward. "Well then what is it?"

I glanced—no, glared—at Roman, who suddenly found the fruit bowl extremely interesting as he busied himself rearranging grapes like he was filming a cooking show.

"I agreed to move in permanently," I said under my breath, though the words still seemed to echo off the high ceilings.

Maggie's jaw actually dropped. "What? Are you two officially together now?"

I gave her shoulder a shove. "Stop."

Abby dissolved into laughter, almost spilling her drink. "This is wonderful. Are you happy?"

Heat crept up my neck. I took a slow sip of wine, letting the cabernet settle warm on my tongue before I answered.

"Yeah... of course. Otherwise I wouldn't have done it. Right?"

But they kept staring. Maggie squinted like she could see something written across my forehead. Abby tilted her head, studying me like I was a puzzle she was halfway through solving.

Outside, thunder rumbled softly somewhere in the distance, and inside, the kids' voices rose and fell in excited waves. Roman glanced over at me from across the room—gentle, hopeful—and that made everything twist a little tighter.

I shook my head, waving the girls off with a little laugh. "Brunch. We'll talk at brunch, okay? I have kids to play with."

And with that, I slipped off the stool, letting their suspicious stares burn into my back as I walked toward the living room where the kids were already building a mountain of pillows. The air smelled like buttered popcorn and comfort and chaos—exactly what I needed to hide in for a minute.

Chapter 27

ALEX

It turned into a long, joyful night with the kids—the kind of evening that left the whole apartment buzzing with energy. The sounds of squealing and shrieking bounced off the tall windows of the penthouse while little bodies tumbled into piles of pillows on the floor. Every few minutes another round of giggles would erupt. It started with one child and spread to the others until none of them could stop laughing.

Roman and I eventually surrendered to the chaos.

Pizza boxes were spread across the coffee table while the kids argued over which slices had the most pepperoni. After dinner we curled up together for a movie, bowls of popcorn balanced carefully on little laps. No sugar tonight—Roman and I had silently agreed on that one. If we loaded them up with sweets, none of us would sleep before sunrise.

Tomorrow they could have all the sugar they wanted.

Their parents could deal with the consequences.

By the time the movie ended, the living room had transformed into something that looked like a tiny campsite. Dining chairs were pulled together with blankets draped across the backs, creating little tented spaces underneath. Pillows were stacked everywhere like miniature mountains, and the fireplace glowed quietly nearby, its colors cycling through soft pastels that washed the room in warm, gentle light.

Roman and I stayed on the sofa instead of joining the fort. It gave us the perfect vantage point if any of the kids woke up confused in the middle of the night.

Watching Roman with them might have been my favorite part of the whole evening.

He was a complete natural.

The boys climbed all over him like he was some kind of human jungle gym. At one point both of them were riding on his back while he crawled across the rug pretending to be a horse, snorting dramatically while they steered him by the shoulders. When they finally "defeated" him, he collapsed onto the carpet in exaggerated slow motion, letting them celebrate like they'd just conquered a giant.

Sophia and I kept ourselves busy in a quieter corner of the room.

She wasn't the glitter-and-lip-gloss type—Maggie had made that very clear—but sometimes she just wanted girl time, and I loved those little moments with her. Maggie always joked that Sophia should've been my kid.

I never knew whether to laugh or feel secretly flattered or sorry for poor little Sophia Grace.

Thank goodness the couch was comfortable, because Roman and I didn't fall asleep until almost two in the morning.

And of course the kids were bright-eyed and full of energy again by six.

Roman and I shuffled into the kitchen like a pair of zombies, quietly making coffee while the kids brushed their teeth and changed clothes down the hall. Soon the apartment came back to life—the soft chatter of Saturday morning cartoons playing from the television, the smell of bacon sizzling in the pan, eggs scrambling while the coffee brewed.

Little feet ran back and forth across the hardwood floors while the kids argued over which cartoon character was the best.

I stood at the counter sipping my coffee and mentally mapped out the day.

First the park.

Then lunch.

Ice cream, obviously.

And if everyone still had energy left... the aquarium.

But that part made me hesitate.

If the aquarium was packed, keeping track of three excited kids in a crowd could get tricky. Between my own protective instincts and Roman's recent overprotective streak, the last thing I wanted was for either of us to feel overwhelmed. The children's museum might be calmer.

Still...

I really wanted the aquarium.

Once breakfast was finished and the kids were fully hypnotized by cartoons, Roman and I slipped away to shower and change.

"Roman," I called from the closet as I pulled on my jeans, "do you want to go to the aquarium or the children's museum today?"

"Either one is fine with me," he answered from the bathroom.

I leaned against the doorframe. "I'm just worried one might be more crowded."

A moment later he stepped into the doorway with a towel draped over his shoulders.

"Okay."

That was not helpful.

I crossed my arms and stared at him.

"I mean for watching the kids," I clarified. "Less crowded might be better."

One eyebrow lifted.

"Am I making you anxious?"

I couldn't help laughing.

"Yes—but I get protective about these kids too."

His expression softened and he walked over, brushing his fingers gently down my arm.

"Either place is doable," he said. "We just tell them everyone holds hands, and no one wanders off without an adult. How does that sound?"

The tension that had been sitting in my chest immediately eased.

"That sounds perfect."

I smiled.

"Aquarium it is."

Roman smiled back, and together we walked out into the living room to deliver the news.

The kids erupted into cheers like we'd just announced Christmas was happening twice this year.

And suddenly I felt that excitement again too.

I could already picture it—the glow of the tanks lighting up the dim hallways, the soft echo of water moving behind thick glass, the way the kids would press their faces against the exhibits while stingrays glided past like underwater birds.

Today was going to be magical.

***

ROMAN

We pulled into the parking lot of the MMA studio, and the moment the car rolled to a stop, the calm I'd managed to hold onto all afternoon vanished.

Just like that.

My stomach tightened the same way it had earlier in the day, like my body knew something my mind was still trying to ignore. The building looked exactly the same as it always did. Lights glowed through the front windows, and the faint thump of music and movement pulsed through the walls. People came and went through the front doors like any other evening.

But tonight it felt different.

Too exposed.

Too public.

I cut the engine and stayed there for a moment, staring through the windshield while Alex unbuckled beside me. The parking lot lights cast long shadows across the pavement, and every movement out there seemed a little sharper than it should have been.

The whole day had been easy.

The park. The aquarium. The kids racing from one thing to the next, their laughter carrying through every space we stepped into. For a few hours I'd almost forgotten everything Grant had dropped in my lap this week.

Watching Alex with the kids had a way of doing that.

She moved through the world with this natural warmth that people gravitated toward without even realizing it. At the aquarium she'd been surrounded the entire time—Sophia Grace holding one hand, Cameron tugging on the other, questions flying at her faster than she could answer them. She never seemed overwhelmed by it. If anything, she lit up under the attention.

At one point I'd stood back and watched her in the dim blue glow of one of the giant tanks while Sophia asked her about the fish swimming past.

And I'd caught myself imagining something I thought I'd lost. A family—kids.

A life that looked a lot like today, settled somewhere deep within before I even realized I was thinking it.

But now we were here again, and reality had a way of showing up whether I wanted it to or not.

Alex turned toward me, already halfway out of her seat, her energy still riding high from the day.

"You coming in?" she asked.

I forced a small smile and pushed my door open.

"Yeah," I said. "I said I'd try."

The evening air hit me as I stepped out of the car, and before I could stop myself my eyes moved across the lot. I scanned the rows of cars, the sidewalk, the small group of people walking toward the entrance.

A few vehicles.

Two guys heading inside.

Nothing out of place.

Still, the tension didn't leave.

Alex slung her bag over her shoulder and fell into step beside me, completely unaware of the storm running quietly through my head. She bumped her shoulder lightly into my arm as we walked.

"You survived the kids today," she said. "Training should be easy after that." She grinned, clearly amused with herself.

A short laugh slipped out of me.

"If getting kicked by professional fighters counts as easy, sure." I mumbled and pushed open the door to the studio.

The sounds spilled out immediately—gloves striking pads, muffled shouts of encouragement, the heavy rhythm of people moving across the mats.

I followed her inside, trying to ignore the tight knot sitting just under my ribs.

Maybe it was nothing.

Maybe my brain was just running wild after everything Grant told me.

But the closer we walked toward the training floor, the more my instincts refused to settle.

Something about tonight didn't feel right.

Chapter 28

ROMAN

Alex was in the ring talking to Bruce, her shoulders loose but her stance alert, the way it always was when she slipped into training mode. Felix waved to me from across the room. I lifted a hand in return, though my eyes stayed fixed on Alex.

I wondered—not for the first time—if he'd ever sparred with her. But even if he had, Bruce was in there now. If anyone could keep her safe, it was him.

Except... why was Bruce stepping out of the ring?

My pulse kicked.

Another fighter climbed in—bigger, broader, heavier in every sense than Felix. His expression was unreadable, but something about him sent a warning straight down my spine.

Bruce dropped onto the bench beside me.

"Hey, Roman. Didn't think we'd see you again."

I barely blinked.

"Mm-hmm. Me either."

He might've laughed, but all I could hear was the blood rushing in my ears.

"I told her Tuesday's class is canceled," he said. "So today's the last one before the hearing."

That snapped me out of my trance.

My head whipped toward him. "Right. It's almost here."

He shouted toward the ring, "What are you waiting for? Get to it!"

The moment I looked up—Alex hit the mat.

Hard.

I was on my feet before the thought even registered. Bruce blocked my chest with one steady hand, firm as a wall.

"Roman, listen," he said calmly. "This is what I've been training her for. I told Raphael to rile her up and push her. He won't hurt her. I promise. But I need to see where she is mentally. Raphael is close in size to Mr. Ellington, and he's not afraid to take a hit."

My stomach twisted.

Mr. Ellington.

Everything in me recoiled.

Bruce kept going, his tone unshakably steady.

"She came in the other day worried she was too tired to fight. She's told me what happened. She's scared it could happen again. She needs to feel capable. I'm trying to take that fear away. So stay calm. Watch."

I lowered myself slowly back onto the bench. My hands pressed to my knees as I took a long breath, then another. I wasn't sure if it was helping.

When I finally forced myself to look up, what I saw nearly brought me to my feet again—but for a different reason.

She wasn't being overwhelmed; she was meeting him head-on.

Her movements were sharp, calculated. Every time Raphael lunged, she found an answer—pivot, block, counterstrike. She dropped him. Twice. Then blocked two blows in rapid succession.

She looked... furious. Focused. Alive.

I'd never seen her like this.

After about fifteen minutes, Bruce stood.

"That's good. Water."

Raphael tapped her head in some mock gesture of approval. She swatted his hand away, aggressively annoyed.

Bruce spoke quietly to her, and she nodded, still bouncing lightly on her toes, still biting her lip the way she did when adrenaline mixed with nerves. He guided her to sit and drink.

The intensity in the room eased just enough for me to breathe.

A woman with her gloves slung over one shoulder came over at Bruce's signal. She slid onto the bench beside me.

"Hi, I'm Jules."

I huffed a humorless laugh.

"Are you my next distraction?"

She grinned. "Yep."

"It's nice to meet you. I'm Roman."

"Oh, we all know who you are," she said playfully.

I groaned. "That bad, am I?"

She laid a hand on my shoulder. "Roman, I've been doing this for years. She's a natural. You really don't need to worry about her."

"That doesn't help," I muttered. "Telling me she's naturally good at fighting makes me wonder how much anger she's been carrying around."

Jules blinked in surprise.
"Alex? She's one of the least angry people here. If I told you some of the stories in this room, you'd lose sleep for a month."

I swallowed hard. I already had enough nightmares of my own.

"You... aren't planning to tell me any of them, right?"

She dipped her head, shoulders shaking in silent laughter.
"No. I'm just saying—she's not alone. This place is a family. Think of it like sibling rivalry."

"Makes sense." I politely agreed while the unease tamped down some—but not much.

Harrison and I never fought like this often—he preferred pranks and tattling—but the concept was familiar. A structured outlet. A safe one. Not like the things I used to struggle with before empathy became a curse and a compass at the same time.

Jules stood, patting my arm. "You just needed perspective."

I thanked her, and she jogged back to her training group.

I finally felt steady enough to lift my gaze back to the ring.

***

ALEX

Okay, cute jerk. Let's see what you got.

He wasn't playing around. He came at me, and it was everything I could do to fight back. I held my own even when he had me on the ground. I fought my way out and took him down. He was not going to lay another hand on me, and he didn't.

I knew I'd taken a beating out there, but I couldn't feel a thing right now. My insides were vibrating and sweat was pouring off me— I was ready to go again even though Bruce wanted me to calm down.

He pulled over a stool and made me sit, directing me to look at him. I tried my best to stay engaged with him as he spoke and I drank the water.

His hands were heavy on my shoulders again. "Deep breaths." He said. I followed his direction and could feel my body start to relax.

"How did that feel?" He asked.

Like someone else was in control. I thought seriously.

"I don't really remember what I did or how I did it, I just know that after he took me down for the third time, I wasn't going to let him do it again."

Bruce laughed and said, "Atta girl. That's exactly how I want you to feel in that courtroom. He's not going to touch you ever again."

I smiled at Bruce and asked, "How's Roman?" I couldn't get a read on him during the sparring, so I wasn't sure if he was okay.

He snorted. "I had to restrain him, but I sent Jules over to help out. She's got a way about her that calms the nerves. All things considered; I think he's good. I don't think he liked what I had to tell him about this match up, but he understood it."

Ugh, he's probably a mess.

"Raphael was mean. You've never matched me with him before...any particular reason why?"

Bruce nodded. "I picked someone about Tanner's size and made sure he wasn't afraid to say something nasty to you."

"Well, it worked. I wanted to tear his head off. That was a lot of anger I didn't know I had in me."

"I'm looking forward to hearing what he has to say later about how you did. If he says he was going easy on you, he's lying."

It didn't feel like he was taking it easy on me.

"He's not going to be mad at me, is he?"

He laughed. "He'll get over it. Don't let your guard down with him in this ring for one second."

That was the last thing Bruce said to me after the break. I guess I forgot for one second and that right hook I just got to the face is going to leave a mark.

I finished with some conditioning and punching bag exercises. I did a bit of jumping rope and rope climbing as a cool down. When training was over, Bruce asked me to come over where all the fighters were. They had a good luck card signed for me, and I got a hug from everyone, including Raphael who said, "That dumbass doesn't stand a chance against you."

I was choking back tears as I smiled, nodded and hurried to the front door— walking right past Roman.

***

ROMAN

Okay I can watch this stuff. Jumping rope, rope climbing and hitting something that won't hit her back. This I can handle. The guy that was in the ring with her, came over to me and looked me up and down like I was some punk.

He said, "Your girl is dope."

What does that mean?

"Thanks, I think."

"Not to piss you off, but I didn't hold back much on her so if y'all get in a fight, I'm betting on the girl." If we get in a fight like that, things have taken a turn for the worst between us.

"Thanks for the heads up. I'll be sure not to piss her off."

He laughed, reaching out his hand to me in a gesture of peace it seemed. I reluctantly shook it thinking he might sucker punch me too, but he said good luck and went back over to the group of people around Alex. Next thing I know she's running out the door with tears streaming down her face.

"Alex. Hold up baby." I grabbed her hand, and she spun around, and she buried her face in my chest.

"Hey, what happened?"

She took a deep breath before looking up at me and said, "I did it."

"Did what?"

"I conquered my fears."

I was confused. What fears was she talking about?

"I don't understand."

She stood there catching her breath before she stammered out, "I was so scared of this court hearing on Tuesday. It was consuming me. I was afraid of Tanner coming after me again. Now, I'm not."

"So why are you crying?"

"Just emotional is all. This whole place has my back. I have so much support behind me, there's no way I can lose."

I hugged her, hoping that this was the plan she didn't think I'd like, because I definitely didn't like this.

"Can we go out and celebrate tonight? I just want to be normal and go out to dinner and not be worried and looking over my shoulder."

She seemed relieved. *This I feel good about.*

"Absolutely. Are we dressing up or down, your choice?"

"Let's dress up."

On the ride back to the penthouse, I called one of my new favorite restaurants and made a reservation. You usually need at least a couple months ahead to get a reservation for this place, but knowing the owner has its perks. When we arrived at the penthouse, Alex headed in to take a shower and I got a text.

GRANT: *"You'll get the best table in the house tonight."*

ME: *"Does she know you own a restaurant?"*

GRANT: *"You know, I don't think she does."*

ME: *"Is that a secret, too?"*

GRANT: *"No, I just own a lot of things."* Then the phone started ringing and I picked up.

"Hello Grant."

"Hey, Roman. It seems you might be more at ease with me since you've decided to bring her to my restaurant."

Nope, not really.

"Yeah, or I was trying to impress her by getting a reservation at the only restaurant in town that has a two-month long waiting list." I don't know if I'll ever feel comfortable around him again actually.

"I hear your meeting and dinner with the Santoros was a good one."

"It would've been better had I not known what I know."

He laughed then asked, "Is this a special occasion?"

"Yes. Alex said she conquered her fears, and she wanted to celebrate. I figured I needed to conquer mine and celebrate at your restaurant."

His chuckle was at my expense. "Roman, that's exceptional. Dinner is on me tonight. I'll have a nice bottle of Dom chilling for you when you get there and whatever you want is all yours. I may stop in to say hi to the two of you."

I hope he knows I'm not coming there so he'll pay the bill. We hung up and I went to get ready.

She came out of the bathroom wrapped in a towel and said, "What time is our reservation?"

"When we get there." She looked at me with that don't start face, hands firmly set on her hips.

"Another one of those 'I know the owner' favors?"

I laughed and said, "Yep!" She rolled her eyes and walked past me. I grabbed her by the arm.

"Oh no you don't. You don't get to roll your eyes at me whenever you feel like it." She rolled her eyes again only with more exaggeration.

"That right there is what I'm talking about." I pulled her in close and kissed her lips, then her jaw and neck. When I looked up at her face, she rolled her eyes again, and I whispered in her ear. "That's when it's okay."

I let her go and jumped in the shower.

"If I can't roll my eyes, you can't peck and run." She said as we got dressed.

She was laughing, breathless, one hand fumbling with the fabric of her dress as she tried to pull it into place. Her cheeks were flushed from laughing...

I tugged my shirt straight, still chuckling.

"What exactly is a 'peck and run'?"

She narrowed her eyes in that mock-offended way that never failed to make me grin.

"You know exactly what it is. You kiss me, get me completely derailed, and then you walk off like nothing happened."

Oh. That.

Yeah, okay—I deserved that.

I couldn't help laughing as the memories flickered through my mind—every time I'd brushed my lips over hers and walked away just to feel her stare burn into my back. I hadn't realized she'd named it, but of course she had.

She fixed me with a tired but earnest look.

"It's not funny. It's actual torture."

"Well," I said, lifting my brows, "feel free to get me back anytime you want."

And honestly—yes, please.

Her expression softened, amusement lingering in her eyes as she leaned back against the wall. "How did you get a reservation at this place so last minute?"

She asked it casually, but I could hear the curiosity underneath. She'd been trying to get into this place forever. What she didn't know was that tonight wasn't about luck—she just didn't realize she was the reason the doors opened.

"I didn't," I said. "You did."

Her brows pulled together in confusion.

"What do you mean I did? I've never even been here because I'm not waiting two months for a reservation."

"Maybe you should've tried harder."

She blinked at me like I had completely lost my mind.

I grinned. "Babe, don't worry about it. You'll see when we get there."

When we stepped inside, the same hostess from lunch, the day I met Grant, recognized us immediately—her smile just a little too bright, her attention lingering a little too long. Something about her rubbed me the wrong way.

"Mr. King, Ms. Kennedy," she said, greeting us before I could even open my mouth. "Right this way."

I shot her a polite but questioning look as we followed her through the dimly lit dining room. I'd remember her tone later. Something felt... off.

Alex glanced at me sharply, nearly whispering, "What's going on?"
Her hand hovered near my arm as though she was ready to bolt.

I laughed quietly to reassure her.
"I didn't do this. I promise. Nothing to worry about."

She didn't look convinced.

Her eyes moved across the room, scanning every table, every wall sconce, every shadow like she was bracing for a surprise proposal or an ambush.

Good grief.

Was she really that worried I was going to pull out a ring at dinner?

They led us to a small round table tucked beside a stone fireplace—warm light flickering over the walls, washing everything in soft amber and gold. The heat from the hearth made the air feel calm and intimate, like stepping into a private world far from the city outside.

The servers were already waiting for us.
Two flutes of champagne appeared as if on cue.

As we sat, the waiter offered a polite bow of his head and said simply, "Enjoy."

And the moment his hand left the champagne bottle, Alex turned to me with wide, unsteady eyes—half nervous, half overwhelmed, half... something else entirely.

Whatever she was imagining—it wasn't the truth.

Not yet.

***

ALEX

I looked around the restaurant again, scanning every corner, every shadow, every table. The low sensual lighting from the sconces made the whole place glow like candlelit honey, and it only made everything feel more surreal. Were people... watching us? Waiting?

This had all the markings of a surprise party, except I couldn't imagine what for. It wasn't my birthday, it wasn't an anniversary, and Roman had insisted—multiple times—that this wasn't his doing. I didn't know if I should believe him or not.

My stomach fluttered with nerves, and not the good kind.

He lifted his champagne glass toward me, the firelight catching in the bubbles.

"Cheers to no more fears."

I laughed—more out of confusion than anything.

"I'll drink to that. But you're going to have to tell me what's going on."

He just checked his phone, smiled like he knew a secret, and slipped it back into his pocket.

"You'll find out in about five minutes."

"Why five minutes?"

He shook his head, maddeningly calm.

"You can wait five minutes."

My eyebrows pulled together.

"...Why don't we have menus?"

"Hmm..no idea." he said, letting out a breath right as the waitstaff appeared with warm bread and herb-infused olive oil. The fragrance filled the small circle of space around us—rosemary, cracked pepper, a hint of citrus—which only heightened my already-frayed nerves.

Another waiter stepped up, hands folded politely.

"Is there anything else you'd like to drink?"

Yes.

Something strong. My mind rushed immediately to liquor.

"A Grey Goose martini, up, with blue-cheese stuffed olives, if you have them."

His answer made me freeze.

"If we don't, we'll make them for you, Ms. Kennedy."

"Please don't go to any trouble," I said quickly.

He offered a warm smile.

"For you, Ms. Kennedy, it will be no trouble at all."

Why was he talking to me like that?

Why did half the staff seem to know my name?

I turned to Roman, wide-eyed.

"You've got to tell me what's going on. I feel like I'm on one of those prank shows."

He laughed into his champagne and muttered something under his breath.

"Now you know how I feel."

"What did you say?"

He shook his head.

"Nothing."

Then took a very long sip.

By the time my martini and our appetizers arrived, I was fully spiraling.

"Five minutes is definitely up," I whined as I picked up my glass.

That's when I felt a tap on my shoulder.

Before I could turn, I was pulled into a tight, familiar hug—a hug I knew by heart.

I gasped and pushed back just enough to see his face.

"Grant?"

He was grinning like he'd known this moment was coming all along.

"Did you do this?"

My voice was half-breathless, half-accusatory.

"I did some of it," he said with a shrug. "Roman did the rest."

He leaned in and kissed my cheek, keeping his arm slung comfortably around my shoulder.

"How could you have known?" I asked confused, wondering if Roman had called him.

Grant burst out laughing. Roman took a very healthy swallow of champagne and stared at the fireplace like it suddenly needed his full attention.

Grant finally said the words that made my brain short-circuit.
"This is my restaurant."

I blinked. Then blinked again.

"Your what?"

He smirked.

"My restaurant. I own it."

I stared at Roman, then at Grant, then at Roman again.

"What—like you own-own it?"

"Just like that."

He laughed as though this were common knowledge.

"I didn't realize you didn't know."

My jaw dropped.

"How did I not know? And how did Roman know before I did?"

Roman stayed very still, very silent.

Suspiciously so.

Grant answered for him, because of course he did.

"We had a lunch meeting here one day. Roman called me this afternoon and asked if we had room for my girl—and the answer will always be yes."

My girl.

Somehow hearing it from Grant made it hit differently.

I glanced at Roman again, giving him a half-accusing, half-fond look.

"Grant, would you like to have dinner with us?" I asked, partly because I wanted him there... and partly because I wanted answers.

He shook his head, smiling.

"How about a drink, and then I'll leave you two to your night."

I hugged him again, warmth blooming in my chest.

"This is amazing. Thank you both for always being so good to me."

And for the first time since we'd walked in, I felt myself settle—just a little—into the magic of the moment.

***

ROMAN

Grant stayed for the one drink. He was relaxed—exactly the energy Alex needed. The three of us laughed and told stories, and for a few minutes it felt like the weight of Tuesday drifted somewhere far away.

Between the conversation and Grant's talent for distraction, we managed to keep Alex's curiosity from circling too close to one single question: Why didn't she know anything about his restaurant?
She didn't press it, but I knew the curiosity was still there, hovering under her smile.

When Grant finally left, the table felt quieter without him. Alex smoothed her napkin over her lap, took one more sip of her martini, and then looked at me with an expression that was both hopeful and hesitant.

"Could we maybe go somewhere close to home and walk to a place where we can have a nice after-dinner drink?" She tucked a strand of hair behind her ear. "I just want to do something I used to do after dinner with my friends. I feel like my old life is so far away, and I miss it a little."

The vulnerability in her voice caught me off guard. She wasn't asking for nightlife—she was asking for normalcy. She was trying to build courage in small, manageable pieces.

"I know just the place," I said gently.
There was a quiet bar next to my office—dim lighting, soft jazz, tucked away from the rest of downtown. I used to go there after work when I needed silence. Solitude had been my comfort.
Until Alex.
Now too much solitude felt dangerous.

"Did we pay the bill?" she asked, brows pinched with worry.

I smiled. Her mind never stopped moving.
"Do you think Grant is letting us pay in his restaurant?"

She blinked, caught between delight and discomfort.
"Really? He took care of the tab?"

I didn't want to open the door to the deeper conversation—the one that might lead to the things Grant confided in me. That wasn't my story to tell.
"Yes, he took care of everything," I said simply

She still looked a little stunned, as though she wasn't sure whether to smile or dig deeper. I slipped several bills under the charger plate as a tip—the staff deserved it after pulling off a flawless last-minute arrangement.

"What are you thinking?" I asked, trying to read her face, to see if she was drifting back toward thoughts of Tuesday or staying fixated on Grant.

"That there are things I don't know."

Not the answer I was hoping for.

I exhaled slowly. Maybe I shouldn't have asked.

"Grant owning a restaurant?" I tried to keep my tone light, making it sound like it wasn't something worth spiraling over.

Her eyes stayed locked on mine.

"Yes, like that. And he said he owns a lot of other things. I've never even been to his house, and yet I've always felt so close to him. It seems like he's keeping something from me. Do you think he is?"

Ah.

There it was—Alex slipping into detective mode. Old Nancy Drew, alive and well.

I needed to tread carefully. Grant's life wasn't mine to unpack for her, and I wasn't going to ruin whatever trust he had in me. But I also knew she needed reassurance, not deflection that felt like a lie.

"I don't know," I said calmly. "You'll have to ask him, I guess."

That was the safest truth I could give her without crossing lines.

She nodded slowly, though I wasn't sure the thought had left her mind. And with Tuesday only three days away, I prayed she wouldn't keep digging.

We had enough to face already.

Chapter 29

ROMAN

What?...what?...nooo...!

I jolted upright, heart pounding, breath caught somewhere between my lungs and my throat. Thank God—it was only a dream. A nightmare, really. I'd never had one like that before. Alex was somewhere ahead of me, screaming, fighting, reaching—and no matter how fast I ran, I couldn't get to her. Then she vanished, swallowed by darkness, and I was standing alone.

Now I was awake, sweating, chest tight, trying to shake the echo of that fear.

I rolled over. She was right there, asleep beside me, her breathing slow and steady. Peaceful. Completely untouched by the chaos that had thrown me out of sleep. I watched her for a moment longer than I probably should've—just letting the certainty of her presence settle my heartbeat.

I eased closer and wrapped an arm around her waist. She made a soft, sleepy sound but didn't wake. I hoped I could fall back asleep too.

Eventually, the alarm clock blared its shrill cry. She shut it off quickly, already stretching.

"Would you mind if we set that for six, at least on the weekends, instead of five?" I grumbled. Considering I'd barely fallen back asleep, another hour would've saved my sanity.

She didn't even turn her head. "I would mind. I like my routine. I like waking up at five."

"Fine," I muttered, dragging a pillow over my face.

She stood up, tying her hair back. "Are you going to the gym this morning?"

I moaned dramatically, making sure she could hear it.

"No," she said, "but I *am* going running. Would you care to join me?"

Of course, the one morning I didn't want to move was the one morning she wanted me at her side. But I wasn't going to let her run alone—not after that dream.

"Absolutely," I said. "I'd love to."
I mashed the pillow to my face and mouthed a silent groan.

She laughed. "Yeah, I've heard that one before...Mr. Club Guy." She swatted me with her pillow and headed for her shoes.

We jogged down toward the river with earbuds in. The early morning mist was still rising off the water, and the sky was pale, soft, barely awake. When the path opened to the riverwalk, we took the earbuds out. The quiet sound of water lapping against the stone wall made everything feel calmer.

"Is it as pleasant running with me as it is running alone?" I asked, slipping an arm around her shoulders and pulling her close long enough to kiss her temple.

"I think it is," she said. "How do you like it?"

How did I like it? I'd follow her anywhere. There weren't many things I wanted to do without her...she just happened to be the one who craved solitude.

"I mean...it's fine," I teased. "But I can think of better people I'd like to run with."

"Oh really?"
She shoved me off the path. I grabbed her wrist and gathered her back into me, leaning in to kiss her as she tried (and failed) to push me away.

We passed the bench swings and I slowed down, pointing. "Want to sit for a minute? I have something to talk to you about."
My legs were grateful for the rest, and honestly, my nerves were too.

Her smile faded. "Is this serious?"

"Maybe...but not too serious."
For me and the others, it wasn't serious at all.
For her? Anything involving her friends was practically life-or-death emotional territory.

She looked uneasy. "What is it?"

"No one wanted to bother you this morning, or make a big event out of it...but Matt asked if it would be okay if we all went to brunch today." I kept my tone soft. "Just a little get-together before the hearing. A show of support. The girls asked me to ask you if you'd be comfortable with that."

Her expression softened instantly. "Really? I think that would be great. I love the support, and I feel like I could use it before..."

Before *what?*

There it was again—another half-sentence that didn't match the look in her eyes.

She stared down at the ground, her legs gently swinging. "Alex," I asked quietly, "before what?"

"Oh—nothing. Just before I have to see him again."

Too quick. Too rehearsed.

Not at all what she'd been about to say in my opinion.

The uneasy feeling crept back in, curling around my ribs.

Something was off.

And whatever it was...she wasn't telling me.

***

ALEX

My mind drifted back to the nightmare I'd had last night—the one that shook me awake before dawn. Maybe I needed a vacation. A real one. Somewhere with warm sand beneath my feet, a crystal-clear ocean stretching endlessly across the horizon, a good book in my hands, and a cold bottle of water beside me.

Why water and not wine or vodka?

I actually laughed out loud.

Right—because even in my imagination, my subconscious was trying to behave. In real life, if I'm anywhere near a beach, there's definitely wine involved. Sometimes vodka.

"Roman, did the girls get a table for six this morning?" I asked, slowing my legs to a mild back a forth motion as we swung gently. We had a standing reservation for three on Sundays, and those tables went fast.

"I think Maggie reserved one just in case you said yes," he replied.

Just in case.

That wording tugged at something inside me.

"Good," I murmured. Then, after a beat: "Do I seem fragile to you?"

He wrapped his arm around my shoulders and pressed a kiss to the side of my head.

"Not in the least, honey."

I didn't buy that.

Not fully.

"Then why did the girls ask you instead of me about brunch? They keep going to you first lately."

I sounded like a spoiled teenager hearing her friends hung out without her. I hated that.

He didn't flinch. "Maggie said they wanted to make sure all the guys were on board before asking you. The other day when I took the call, it was Maggie using Matt's phone because they couldn't reach you. Alex, you're everyone's favorite. From me to the kids. I promise."

I couldn't help but laugh, picturing the kids bursting through the penthouse yelling my name.

He wasn't wrong.

So why was I reacting like this?

Probably because deep down I knew I was about to do something on Tuesday that no one—absolutely no one—would approve of. Maybe picking a fight now would soften the blow when they found out. Maybe part of me was bracing for them to be disappointed in me.

Roman was right: I couldn't overthink this.

We stopped at our usual coffee shop. The smell of freshly ground coffee beans, the low hum of early conversation, the warm ceramic cups—it all calmed me. We talked about everything and nothing. Silly things. Happy things. Roman teasing me about whether the guys at brunch would get any "juicy info." I reminded him they'd be sitting right there, so no.

After coffee, we ran the rest of the way home.

We slipped into the shower together, letting the hot water wash away whatever tension lingered. Then we got dressed, sat in the living room, and spent an hour reading with soft classical music playing in the background.

It felt like a life I could easily fall into.

A rhythm.

A safe place.

Then we walked to brunch.

We were the last to arrive. Everyone was already settled with Bloody Mary's—except Abby, who held a Virgin Mary with her usual flair. We ordered ours when the waitress circled back. The moment I lifted the glass, the cool stem resting between my fingers, I felt my shoulders loosen.

This—these people, this table, this little moment of normalcy—was exactly what I needed.

But beneath that, something else pressed against my ribs.

A quiet ache.

A fear I dreaded but couldn't stop.

After Tuesday, everything could change.

I could lose all of this—my friends, Roman, the fragile sense of belonging I'd found. And I couldn't tell a single person why. No one would under-stand. No one would ever tell me this plan was a good idea.

That's why I was meeting with Roman's mom tomorrow.

I needed someone grounded. Someone I trusted. Someone who could help me work through my emotions without prying too deeply into what I was planning.

Because Tuesday was only the beginning.

The hook.

And for my plan to work, he needed to take the bait.

And considering who he is—arrogant, careless with consequences, and always convinced he's untouchable—I didn't think that would be a prob-lem.

Not at all.

***

ROMAN

The conversation was good, light, and thoughtful. No one mentioned the hearing—not even once. I kept catching glimpses of Alex across the table, her smile bright, her laugh free of tension. For the first time in days, she looked like she wasn't carrying the weight of the world.

Then Abby leaned in and squinted at her.

"Alex, you have a bruise on your face. Did you know?"

She darted a quick look at me, and Maggie drew in a loud gasp.

"Oh my goodness! Roman, did you hit her? I mean—she probably deserved it—but still!"

The whole table burst out laughing.

All except me.

Because I had watched that bruise form.

Alex answered smoothly, "Abby, I know it's there. And no, Roman didn't touch me. I got it at training last night. But you should see the other guy."

She gave a playful wink, and again the laughter rolled. She made light of it. I couldn't.

Matt raised a brow at me. "So how'd you do? I'm guessing you're not a fan of watching her fight."

I swallowed the tightness climbing my chest.

"Not remotely. I was there when she got that particular bruise."

Alex gave me a careful smile, silently asking me to let it go, and the conversation shifted to safer topics.

A few minutes later she turned toward Matt and Jack.

"You two need to start taking kickboxing with us. Roman said he'll do it if you both do. One night a week. We do Wednesdays now, but after the hearing I might rearrange my training, and then we could switch to Saturdays."

They exchanged a look.

"I'm in," Matt said with a shrug.

"Same," Jack echoed.

I nodded toward Alex. "Count me in too."

Her excitement was immediate. "Yes! We needed something fun to do together."

Brunch ended on a warm note. We said our goodbyes and started the walk home. A few blocks in, she turned to me with an eager grin.

"So... what do you want to do today?" I said.

I myself hadn't thought that far ahead.

"Can we go shopping? I want to get something to wear for the hearing." She asked and I groaned internally.

"Of course. Where?"

Please not the mall. Please not the mall.

"The mall will be fine," she said cheerfully. "I hate shopping, but I want to wear something special on Tuesday. Something that feels... new."

Well, that settled that.

I took her hand gently.

"The mall it is."

We didn't even bother going upstairs—we got straight in the car and headed out. And if I was lucky, we'd be in and out before the mall swallowed the whole day.

***

ALEX

We must've gone into ten stores, looping through racks and displays until my feet ached and Roman's patience looked like it was losing structural integrity. But in the very last store, I finally stopped. There it was.

A dark gray pantsuit—clean lines, sharp shoulders, quiet strength. I paired it with a white collared bodysuit underneath and found a pair of gray closed-toe heels that matched perfectly. The color felt symbolic. Somber. Storm-colored. Appropriate, considering I was preparing to bring a storm with me.

When we got home, I realized I'd never even unpacked my things. The suitcase was still sitting exactly where I left it. I stared at it for a long moment, wondering if I should even bother unpacking before Tuesday. Wait. See how life looks after everything falls where it will.

But I did hang the suit in the closet. One lonely outfit suspended inside a massive walk-in—its double doors opened like an empty stage around it. It looked symbolic and sad. Very sad.

Roman had his laptop out at the kitchen island, scrolling through emails he'd probably ignored all weekend. I had calls I needed to make too. And after today, I definitely needed tomorrow off

I called Shay first, told her I wasn't coming in Monday. She could use the real estate office if she needed it, and if she thought Darius could help with anything, he was free to work with her. She understood and said she'd see me Tuesday.

After I hung up, I thought about who else might be there that day. And that's when I decided to call my father.

"Hi, Dad."

"Hi, Ali Marie. What are you up to today?"

He sounded fine. Relief loosened the built-up tension.

"Nothing much. Just calling to ask if you were going to be at the hearing on Tuesday."

Silence stretched across the line—long enough for me to brace myself. "I'm going with Edward," he finally said. "He said he wanted to be there."

His voice no longer sounded fine.

"Well, don't let him get all worked up in there," I said, knowing full well that was wishful thinking but my dad was my main concern.

He let out a deep laugh. "No promises. I'm not sure how I'm going to be in there when I see that man."

"You and half the room," I said quietly.

"Good," Dad replied. "I'm glad you don't have to do this alone."

We said our goodbyes, and I called my brother next.

"Hey," Edward answered instantly, like he'd been waiting for it.

"Hi. I talked to Dad. He said you're coming Tuesday. Do you know if Patrick is too?"

"He said he can't. Doesn't want to hear what happened to you."

I expected that. Patrick wasn't sensitive—he just cared too much and handled emotion like a grenade with the pin halfway out.

"Well," I said softly, "I don't even know what happened to me. Just what I've been told."

The truth of that always lit something hot at the base of my skull.

"I'm sure they're going to say a lot of things in that room. And it's not going to be comfortable," he warned gently.

"I know."

A breath wavered through me. "I feel good about Tuesday, though. I've got a lot of support, and I've been training hard. I want to stay in my head and not let Tanner get to me. But I want to warn you—they're going to say things to try to make it look like my fault. I didn't say anything to Dad, but... it's not going to be pretty."

"I figured," he said. "Just don't let any of it get in your head."

"I won't. But make sure Dad knows to expect it. Tell him it's all perfor-mance—just political theater to get Tanner off."

"I'll do my best. And Alex... if Dad leaves the courtroom, don't let it bother you."

A tear slipped down my cheek before I could stop it. If my father walked out, it would only be because something inside him broke.

"Right," I said quietly, swallowing the lump forming in my throat.

We hung up and before I could set the phone down, Roman's arms wrapped around my waist from behind. His head rested gently on my shoulder—solid, warm, and grounding—right when I needed it most.

***

ROMAN

"Everything okay?" I asked gently. "I feel like I ask you that a lot, don't I?"

She let out a breathy laugh—thin and strained. "My dad's going to be there Tuesday. Edward just warned me he might not be able to handle it is all."

I turned her toward me, pulling her close. Her eyes were glossy, on the edge of spilling.

"I understand how he feels," I said quietly. "It's going to be hard for me to hear things too. But I can only imagine what it'll be like for your father to hear how his daughter was attacked."

She swallowed, looking away for a moment. "Not just that... but what they're planning to say about me."

I hadn't even considered that part. God help us—especially her father.

"Is he going by himself?" I asked.

She shook her head. "No. Edward's going with him. But Patrick isn't."

"Do you think they'd want to sit with my family?" I offered.

She lifted a shoulder, unsure. "Would you mind introducing them? Just in case? Your mom might be helpful. Your family is going, right?"

I nodded.

My entire family seemed unusually determined to show up. They had their own history with the Ellingtons, but even with that, their reaction to this felt intense.

"They want to show a united front."
If that's really all it is.

She told me she was taking the day off work tomorrow and planned to see my mom. I asked if she wanted me to go with her, but she shook her head. She wanted to talk to my mother alone, come home afterward, relax, and go to bed early. Honestly, that sounded perfect.

I took a deep breath, held her close again, and kissed her before heading back to the kitchen counter then diving back into work.

My Monday schedule wasn't heavy—just enough to keep me busy. I needed to pull the training committee together, check in with the architects about the winery project, and make sure everything with the riverwalk project and the apartment builds were still on schedule.

She walked into the bedroom and closed the door softly behind her. I figured she needed a moment alone—time to breathe as she processed all the unknowns.

And for once, I didn't follow.

I went to the fridge and grabbed a beer then turned the TV on as Harrison's name scrolled across the phone screen.

"What's up, Harry?"

He didn't laugh and said with a rather irritated tone, "Really?" I laughed to myself.

"Sorry, what's going on?"

"Do you want to come to dinner at mom and dad's house?" That's right, we missed dinner at their house this weekend.

"Not tonight. Alex wants to stay in. The calm before the storm, you know?" I think I needed the calm as well.

"How are the two of you doing, anyway?"

"I think we're good. For once." So far, anyway.

"Do you think you'll be able to handle this courtroom drama on Tuesday?" Probably not. I thought honestly.

"Sometimes I feel like I'm going to be fine, and other's I think she's got something up her sleeve that she isn't telling me."

"What do you mean? What could she possibly have going on that you don't know about?" No telling. Especially when it comes to her.

"Good question, but she said something to me one night that I can't get out of my head. Granted she was drunk at the time, but something about it hasn't sat right with me since."

"What did she say?" Maybe Harrison can help me get over this.

"She said she had something planned that I wasn't going to like."

"You did say she was drunk when she said it, right?" Everyone keeps telling me it's nothing, but I know it's not nothing.

"I just have a feeling it's more than that."

"Well, did you talk to her about it?"

"I did and she assured me that it was nothing. She said it could've been anything."

He laughed. "I don't doubt it with that one."

It's not the nothing part that's bothering me so much. It's the something.

"I'll be in the office tomorrow, so let's talk about Texas and a couple new projects I want to get started on. I'm going to need some investor help on one of them." He sounded excited and we said goodbye.

***

ALEX

I needed to talk to someone about what I had planned. Everyone is just too protective of me. Who would listen without being judgmental, or tell anyone else?

I sat quietly, listening for anything that might sound like an answer—something from above, or wherever it was supposed to come from.

I've got it!!! BRUCE!

I found his name in my contacts and hit the call button. Hopefully, Roman was too busy to come back here and check on me.

"Hey slugger, what's up?"

"Bruce, I need your help." My palms were so sweaty. I needed someone to know who's going to support my decision. Please let Bruce be on my side.

"What's up? I don't think I have any more classes for you to take." He was so good at helping me relax, I couldn't help but laugh.

"I don't think I can handle another one of your classes. This is serious though, and as much as I want to talk to you over the phone about it right now, can I come see you tomorrow at the studio? Do you have time?" I couldn't chance Roman overhearing me.

"I've got time in the morning around nine, would that work for you?"

"Yes, thanks." I felt like that would help, unless he tells me I'm crazy and decides to rat me out. Ugh, more stress.

I finally made my way back out to the living room where Roman was now sitting on the couch drinking a beer.

He looked up and said, "Hey, babe. I was wondering if you wanted to set up an office in the house?"

"Sure, but do you have any room for another office in here? Your decor isn't really my style, I don't want to mess anything up."

He grinned and shook his head.

"I already told you to do whatever you want to this place. I want it to feel like your home too. I have plenty of rooms we can turn into another office. Let's go look around and see if there's one you like best. I don't think I've shown you mine yet."

You know what? I realized as we started up the stairs, I didn't think I had ever actually seen the whole place when I wasn't exhausted or worried about something.

Every other time I'd been here, something dramatic had happened, or it had been late, or I'd been too tired to care about anything beyond finding a bed. Seeing it now, in the middle of the day with a clear head, suddenly felt like a little adventure.

"This will be fun," I said, half to myself as Roman led the way up the stairs.

The second floor opened into a wide hallway that stretched across the length of the penthouse, the same clean, modern aesthetic continuing everywhere I looked. Roman pushed open the first door and stepped aside so I could look inside.

Guest room number one.

It was beautiful, of course—sleek and immaculate like the rest of the place—but it looked almost exactly like the rest of his home. Everything was black and white. Not a hint of color anywhere. A large platform bed sat perfectly centered against the far wall with crisp white bedding tucked tightly into the corners. Above it hung a large black-and-white abstract photograph that looked expensive enough to belong in a gallery.

Across from the bed was a massive television mounted neatly on the wall.

The kind of television that made you wonder if anyone actually watched it or if it was just there because the room looked incomplete without one.

I stepped farther inside, peeking into the walk-in closet before wandering toward the bathroom. The guest bath was just as polished as the rest of the house—large glass shower, smooth stone countertops, perfectly folded white towels stacked like they belonged in a luxury hotel.

"Wow," I murmured, stepping back into the hallway.

Roman opened the next door.

Guest room number two.

It was almost identical to the first. Same platform bed, same abstract artwork, same sharp black-and-white palette that seemed to define the entire penthouse.

I glanced around, amused.

"Do you own stock in black and white?" I teased.

Roman smirked but didn't answer.

The third door he opened revealed the laundry room, and I actually stopped in the doorway for a second.

It was enormous.

Not just a washer and dryer tucked into a corner like most homes. This was an entire room devoted to laundry. Two machines sat side by side beneath a long counter that stretched across one wall, with wide tables for folding clothes. Along the opposite side were rows of hanging rods, enough to dry half a department store's inventory.

I slowly turned in a circle.

"Roman..."

He leaned casually against the doorframe while I stared around the room.

"I have a question."

He crossed his arms, already looking suspicious.

"What?"

"Do you actually do your own laundry?"

His brow lifted.

"Sometimes."

I looked back around the room again, trying to picture him standing in here folding shirts.

"Because," I said, gesturing around us, "why in the world would one person need a laundry room this big?" I just had to ask, "Do you have roommates I don't know about?"

He laughed and mumbled out with his head down, "No roommates. I do have a housekeeper. She cleans and does the laundry."

"Why have I never seen her?"

"I gave her a week off so you could get moved in and settled before I introduced you. My parents aren't like that, but I'm not into cleaning and doing laundry. She does the grocery shopping too. It got to be too much for Amelia with all her other responsibilities."

"Why didn't you just tell me that to begin with?" I murmured.

He looked embarrassed. "I didn't want you to think I was pretentious."

"I wouldn't have turned you down because you don't like to clean, grocery shop, or do laundry." I never saw that coming though, for some reason.

"So, you don't mind if my housekeeper comes back tomorrow?"

The poor woman hasn't worked in a week because of me. I hope he paid her for her time off.

"Nope. Does she live here?" He shook his head.

"No, she comes Monday, Wednesday and Friday."

"I have some things to do tomorrow, so I won't be in her way. What's her name so when I get back, I won't be surprised? Does she know I'm living here now?"

"Yes, she knows. Her name is Mary."

This explained why the place was always so clean. "I'm looking forward to meeting her."

"Cool. What things do you have to do tomorrow?"

Just give him basic information.

"I'm going to talk to Bruce in the morning and then go see your mom, Dr. King."

He squinted and asked, "Are you taking another class?"

"No, I'm just going to talk to him." That was honest. "I'm going to take this week off. I don't know what's going to happen on Tuesday, so I don't want to have anything else scheduled. I feel like the amount of people who are going to be called to testify is going to drag this out." He pulled me into one of his calming embraces, so I let the tension dissolve right out of me.

He whispered, "I love you."

I hope that he still does after the hearing.

I hugged him tighter and said, "I love you too."

I didn't want to let go.

Chapter 30

ALEX

Hmm... I stretched my arms out wide, eyes still closed, the silky sheets gliding over my skin as I worked the sleep from my body and loosened the last of the tension in my muscles. The faint scent of Roman's citrus body wash lingered close, warm and familiar, and I reached for him instinctively—only to find nothing but empty space. My eyes opened. He was already up. Probably in the kitchen making coffee or mixing our pre-workout drinks.

I headed out to the kitchen in just his tee shirt, and I screamed when I opened the door. Startled by the petite older woman, with a vacuum in the hall.

I started laughing and went over and hugged her and said, "Oh my goodness you scared me. You must be Mary." She looked a little frightened and taken aback by the hug and shook her head.

"Yes, you must be Alex." She stepped around me still holding the vacuum.

"That's me. I'm sorry if I scared you. Roman didn't tell me you started so early."

"I always start around seven." I shook my head thinking it couldn't be after seven and marched out to the kitchen to find out what was going on.

He was already dressed and ready for work.

"Did you turn my alarm off again?" I asked indignantly. "You've got to stop doing that."

Why is he so controlling?

He turned around and said, "Good morning to you, too." He came over and hugged me, kissing my forehead as I stepped back, crossing my arms over my chest.

"I didn't go in your phone but, I did turn your alarm off, only because you didn't wake up and do it yourself. I asked you if you wanted to go to the gym and you said no, so I let you sleep."

Ugh, what the hell. I guess I needed the sleep. Oh well, no gym this morning. I can go after I see Dr. King.

"Ok, sorry. I think I scared Mary. I know she scared me."

"I'm sure she'll be fine. I made you some breakfast. Do you want anything special for dinner tonight? I can just order something if we don't want to cook."

So, this is what a real domestic relationship is supposed to look like.

I smiled and envisioned our life together.

"I'll think about it and let you know later. Thank you for breakfast. Have a good day." He handed me a coffee as he left for the day.

I sat in my car in the parking garage, running through what I was going to say to Bruce. How was I supposed to keep him from freaking out and still convince him to go along with this? I turned on the music and cranked it up, letting it fill the space in my head until there wasn't room for doubt. By the time I pulled into the studio, I had it. I knew exactly what I was going to say.

I got out quickly, moving before I could second-guess myself, and headed inside. Bruce looked up, smiling as he waved me into his office. I stepped in and closed the door behind me.

"What the heck are you so excited about?" he laughed. I was practically bouncing up and down.

"Bruce, please don't get mad at me and don't tell me no." I was almost out of breath. He sat back in his chair and crossed his arms.

"I promise not to get mad, but I do not promise I won't say no until I hear what it is."

"Fair enough. Tuesday is the big day. I want to provoke Tanner." My hands were balled up in fists and I was biting my bottom lip.

He raised his eyebrows with a look that was more confused than surprised. "What? What do you mean, provoke him? Why do you want to provoke him?"

I had everything running so fast through my head.

"There's a reason I wanted to learn how to fight. It wasn't just to get control of my emotions. I have control of them, I promise."

He leaned forward and put his arms on the desk. "Oh shit, you want to fight him!"

I just smiled and nodded, waiting for him to say something else.

"Tell me your thoughts. I'm intrigued."

Fantastic. Now I can get it off my chest and finally relax a bit.

"He's planning to have his lawyer spin the whole thing making me look like I somehow did this to myself or asked for it. I just want to give him a chance to finish what he started, fairly." Or try to, I should say.

He sat back and clapped his hands together and said, "Only a dumbass would want to fight you. What do you need from me?"

Oh my god, I can't believe he's really going to help me. My heart was racing so fast now.

"Well, first I need to get him to take the bait. When his lawyer starts interrogating me and trying to make it sound like I'm some kind of de-generate, I plan to make a personal attack of my own against him. I want him to sue me." When I say it out loud, it sounds completely mental.

"How do you plan to get him to sue you?" He sat back in his chair. This was such a rush having someone to talk to about this stuff.

"Well, he's quite the arrogant SOB, so I'm going to take everything he did to me and say he needed the drugs for a fake yes."

Bruce was laughing now.

"I'm sure that's not everything you plan to say in there. What if they object to what you're saying and make you stop?"

Good question. I think I know what to do though.

"Well, I've thought about that. I guess I just keep going until they threaten me with jail time." I don't need or want to go to jail for any reason because of this guy.

"And what if they convict him and he gets jail time?"

"That would be awesome, but as far as I'm concerned, nothing they give him will be enough and that's where you come in."

He looked sideways at me and asked, "Where exactly do I come in?"

"If he sues me, which I believe he will, there will only be one way to prove it's not defamation. He would need to fight me. I want to do it here. I want there to be lots of media, a total circus. I want to humiliate the guy beyond repair, and the deal will be that he spends an extra five years in jail with no chance of early release."

"Do you think a judge would really go for that?"

I hope so, I thought, or this is all for nothing.

"I don't know, but I'm going to try." They'd be nuts to say yes to it, but I'm going to be as compelling as I can.

"You're a crazy girl, but you have my support. What does Roman think about this?" I put my hands on my head and took a deep breath.

"Roman doesn't know. No one knows. Not my friends, family or my attorneys."

He sat back again and let out a deep breath. "You're going to scare the hell out of a lot of people. Are you ready for that?" That's the only real fear I have.

"I'm worried, I have to admit, but I'm not just doing this for me. I don't ever want to feel like a victim again and I want other women to know that they don't ever have to be victims either."

"Can I ask you something?" He sounded cautious.

"Sure, absolutely."

"When this is all over, would you consider teaching a self-defense class and talking to victims of domestic violence?"

I hadn't thought about it, but I would like to do that.

"Can I circle back to that after court is over. I just want to get my life back. This has been so consuming, and I don't think I could really help anyone right now." I hope someday I can be more helpful.

"Of course. Yes, let's revisit this after the hearing and whatever comes after that. I've got your back no matter what, and the rest of the team here does too."

I hugged Bruce and then headed over to see Dr. King.

***

ROMAN

I arrived at the office to find Harrison and Amelia being all lovey-dovey at her desk. It was such a weird thing to witness, but she didn't like anyone seeing them like that, so she switched to professional mode as soon as she saw me.

"Good morning Mr. King."

Just stop calling me that. Is that too much to ask?

"Seriously? Do you call him Mr. King at the office too?" I pointed at my brother.

She smiled and got ready to say something when Harrison interrupted.

"Do you really want to know what she calls me?" She smacked his arm, and I shook my head and walked into my office.

Amelia followed me in laughing. "Sorry about that. Here's your schedule for the day."

"Thanks. Are you two going to be like this every day?"

She shrugged her shoulders.

"Kind of annoying, isn't it?" she said as she smirked. I nodded. "Yeah, that's how we feel around you and Alex." She winked at me.

"Please stop calling me Mr. King. I feel like an old man when you do that."

"Fine. How's Alex? Is she coming into the office today?" Amelia asked standing one foot in and one foot out of the space.

"No, she's taking the day off and going to see my mom."

"I'll be at the office all day tomorrow manning the phone and the computer, if that's cool." She mentioned.

I'd hate it if I had to shut the place down for this crap.

"Yeah, that's perfect. I feel like this is going to be a shitshow tomorrow and I wish so many people weren't getting involved in it."

"You know Harrison's going, right?"

"Yes, with my parents." I rubbed my hands quickly over my face and tried to focus on something else.

"I'll shoot Alex a text and let her know I'm thinking of her."

"Thanks." She closed the door as she left.

I had a few meetings about current projects and then at three I had the meeting with the architectural team about the winery. I invited Harrison to come to that meeting as well.

I met Harrison at the door.

"Here we go. You're stepping into the life." He joked as he slapped me on the back.

"Shut up. I'm doing a renovation, that's all." I was in knots about it as it was.

"That's what you think. You'll become family, symbolically and then...you're in." I shook my head.

"You're an idiot. Let's go make some money." I firmly pushed him on the shoulder and ushered us out the door.

The team sitting around the conference table that morning was the same one I'd used to renovate the breweries. If there was a group I trusted to take something with character and turn it into something extraordinary, it was them. They understood how to build something new without stripping away what made a place special.

The glass walls of the conference room overlooked the city, the morning sun reflecting off neighboring buildings and spilling across the polished table. Coffee cups sat beside tablets and notepads while I spread the photos of the Santoros' property out in front of them.

The moment they saw the first image, the room went quiet.

"This is the place?" one of the architects asked.

"Yeah," I said. "That's it."

The main structure didn't look like a typical winery at all. It resembled a large Italian villa, the kind you'd expect to see perched in the countryside outside Florence. Tall stone walls, arched windows, and a square tower that gave the whole place a subtle castle-like presence. The color of the stone shifted in the light, warm and aged without looking worn down.

I slid another photo across the table showing the surrounding buildings scattered across the property.

"These aren't dilapidated," I explained. "They're just not currently being used for anything."

Several smaller stone structures dotted the land around the main villa—long rectangular buildings that looked like old storage houses or barns that had once served some purpose years ago. Their roofs were solid, their stonework intact. They simply hadn't been touched in a while.

One of the team members leaned closer to the table, studying the layout.

"So the idea is to incorporate everything that's already here?"

"Exactly," I said. "Nothing gets torn down unless it absolutely has to. We build the winery into what's already standing."

Another photo showed the land beyond the buildings. Rolling hills stretched across the property, the ground sloping gently in wide, open curves that seemed made for vineyards.

"That's where the vines will go," I said, tapping the image. "Those hills are going to carry the vineyard itself."

The room slowly shifted from quiet observation to focused energy.

Now they were leaning forward.

Now they were seeing it.

One of the architects rested his elbows on the table, tracing the layout of the buildings with his finger like he was already walking the property in his mind.

"This could be incredible," he said.

"That's what the Santoros are hoping," I replied.

We started talking through the early vision—how the large outbuilding could serve as the central tasting space, where production areas might be built into the surrounding structures, how the vineyard rows could follow the natural curves of the land instead of forcing straight lines across it.

It wasn't going to be a simple renovation.

This was building a winery from the ground up using the bones of something that already existed.

Which made it far more interesting.

After about thirty minutes of discussion, sketches, and rough ideas bouncing around the table, I gave them the tentative start date and the timeline the Santoros were hoping for.

Then I stepped toward the window and pulled out my phone.

"Let's get everyone on the same page."

They answered on the second ring.

I explained that the team had reviewed the property photos and was excited about the project. Within a few minutes we had a time scheduled for the entire group to come out, walk the grounds, and sit down with the Santoros to discuss their vision in person.

When I hung up, the room felt different.

Everyone could see it now.

Not just a winery.

A place that looked like it had been there for centuries, even though we were about to build it from the ground up.

As we exited the meeting, I asked Harrison to come back to my office to talk about some investment strategies.

"What can I do for you? By the way, that's going to be an awesome project. Mom's gonna go nuts over that winery." That's exactly what I thought, too.

"I know, I mentioned to them that mom would love it and they're very excited for her to come visit."

"Are you trying to bring the whole family into their world?" He leaned back in the chair with his arms behind his head.

"Harrison, I'm not bringing anyone into any life, shut up already. Plus, you agreed mom would love it." I let out a deep breath and threw my head back. I'm not trying to think about what or who I'm dealing with when it comes to this winery project.

"In all seriousness, what's up?" He was relaxed and ready to listen.

"Alex wants to start a non-profit for renovating rundown neighborhoods." I scrolled through my emails as I talked.

"Yeah, I heard about that neighborhood she chose for the relocation, and I about fell out of my chair. It's a shit hole."

I snickered a little because that was true. Even Alex said so.

"From what I heard, she left Shay and Darius thinking she lost her mind, but she has some amazing ideas, and we have a big meeting with the residents of Burrow Township to come in and hear what she's got to say."

I leaned forward and put my arms on my desk.

"Do you need me to pitch an investment to some investors about the non-profit then?" he asked.

I clasped my hands together and nodded.

"That would be great. I think after the hearing would be best, but if you can get some of your people together and set up that meeting, at least we'll have that on the books."

***

ALEX

Lisette was at the door as always when I pulled into the drive.

I waved as I was getting out of the car, "Hi, Dr. King." I said as I followed her to the office. She gave me a quick hug and put both hands on my shoulders, looking me up and down.

"Let me look at you. You look fantastic. I may have to start taking your classes." She was always so encouraging and sweet to me. I hated what I was about to do.

"Roman and the guys are going to take kickboxing classes with us, you should definitely join." Keeping things light should help with whatever emotions I might be feeling.

"I'm going to look into it. Could be something fun for me and Fitz to do together," she agreed.

"That's the same thing I thought. Couples' kickboxing should be a thing."

After our initial chit chat, Dr. King asked calmly, "Tomorrow is the start of the hearing. How are you feeling?"

I held her gaze, thinking about my level of stress as it pertained to this hearing and stated confidently, "I feel really good."

She relaxed her position on the couch and crossed her legs.

"You know what? I believe you." I was glad for that because I did feel good about it, but maybe not everyone else would.

I got right to what I wanted to talk about because I had so much nervous energy. "What do I do if I say something that someone may not like hearing? There's going to be a lot of people in there and we already know his lawyer is going to spin this whole thing back on me. I'm going to have to defend myself. My dad's going to be in there, my brother, Roman, you and Mr. King..."

She interrupted. "Alex, we're all going to be in there by choice, if we don't like it, we can leave." That was about as matter of fact as it gets, it was just hard to think why my dad would be leaving.

"That makes me feel better, maybe. I still might feel uneasy about having to talk about this in front of everyone." Now I was wringing my hands and bouncing my knee.

"What is it that you may have to talk about?" This was a little weird, but I felt like honest communication was the way to go.

"Dr. King, I'm afraid they're going to talk about my past behavior. Not that it's actually a big deal, honestly. But..." My eyes shifted downward as I tried to think of how to put this where I didn't sound like a complete floosy.

She uncrossed her legs and sat up a little straighter. I couldn't tell if she was uncomfortable or just getting ready to run out of the room.

"Without getting into detail, what kind of past behavior do you think might make people uncomfortable?"

Where the hell should I start?

"How shall I say this? Short relationships?" The heat of embarrassment rose to my face.

She started laughing and said, "Like one nighters?"

I put my head into my hands and muffled out, "Oh my God, how embarrassing. I thought I was over humiliating myself." She reached over and grabbed my hands off my face.

"Alex, we all have a past. If you have open, honest communication with people and they're fine with the relationship, however short or long it may have been, then there's nothing to worry about. Who are you afraid to upset in there?"

My face fell. It's not like anything happened in those relationships but I went on a lot of dates. The only one I took further than a date besides Roman was the one who started all the sordid rumors, leaving me with a lot of trust issues.

"My dad." I could feel the tears prickling my eyes as I said the words, but I blinked them away and tried to concentrate on her response.

"Ahh. That can be a little nerve racking. Is he the type that would be bothered by it?" she inquired, while still holding my hands.

"Most definitely. He couldn't have any kind of personal conversations with me growing up and I'm daddy's little girl." She released my hands and just oozed sympathy at that point.

Maybe I should just convince him it's better off if he doesn't come. Yeah right, he'll never not be there for me. I wrestled with the thoughts.

"You should give him a heads up," she said.

I slumped onto the sofa. "I talked to my brother and let him know what they were planning to do. He told me not to worry if dad had to leave in the middle of it." The more pain I see in my father's eyes the more I will inflict on Tanner. Maybe having my dad in there won't be so bad after all.

She nodded. "It sounds like your brother's going to be taking care of your dad. I think you should just concentrate on what you're going to be doing in there and that's being truthful." I thought about what I was going to be doing in there— being truthful and vicious.

"As always, Dr. King, you've helped me get over a hurdle. I wish this wasn't happening and I'm sorry for whatever you hear in there that affects you."

"Alex don't worry about me, I'll be fine. I'm there if you need me after as well."

I said, "Thank you." I popped up from my seat and practically ran out of there.

My ride back to the penthouse seemed to take forever. I changed for the gym and tried to decide what I wanted for dinner while I was working out. By the time I was finished I was starving. I went all through the fridge and the pantry and couldn't decide on anything, so I decided to order Chinese food. But what the heck would Roman want? I realized I had no idea what he likes to eat. All this time together and we really haven't gotten to know each other. We've just been dealing with so much outside interference.

As my nerves start to get the better of me, my mind races to do something to calm down, like take a shot or have a drink of something.

"No" I argue with myself, that's a bad idea with court in the morning. I need to be on my game.

I'll order food and then go take a nice hot relaxing soak in the tub. I slipped into the warm bubble bath, adding lavender oil then lighting a candle. I put my earbuds in and listened to calming meditation music. The water was soothing and just what I needed.

I punched in the code for the delivery guy to come up. My eyes popped when I saw what he brought.

Oh lord, I may have over ordered.

I stood there looking at all the food spread out on in the kitchen and thought, who the heck was going to eat all this? I jumped when the elevator doors opened.

"Do you think I ordered too much food?" I blurted. My brows scrunched hard.

He nodded as he plastered a chaste kiss on my cheek and headed down the hall to change.

"You must've been starving." Roman said when he came back out of the bedroom wearing his sweats. He rested his chin on my shoulder.

"You have no idea. I forgot to eat lunch. I was just trying to keep my mind occupied." I was starting to feel the exhaustion in my body now, however.

"Yeah, I know. I've managed to keep most of it out of my head today. Had a lot of meetings and talked to Harrison about getting with his investors about your non-profit." I squealed with delight.

"Oh my God. Are you serious?" He nodded then caught me when I hurled myself into his arms.

"Have you eaten yet?" He was trying to get me back on track. He knew I was distracted.

I shook my head. "No." I was so nervous but I'm also starving so it's good to have the voice of reason here with me.

"Then let's eat!" He grabbed some plates, kissing my cheek as we plated up the food.

***

ROMAN

I didn't think I'd ever have to remind her to eat, but she barely touched anything until I nudged a plate toward her. She must really be distracted by the hearing. Still, once she started tasting the food, we sampled everything together and kept the conversation light—mundane topics, gentle humor, anything that felt normal.

But then she shifted, as her expression turned uncertain.

"What if you hear something in there you don't like... or aren't comfortable with?"

She reached out, cupping my cheeks with both hands, her eyes scanning mine with quiet worry.

Honestly, I'm not going to be comfortable with *anything* that's said in that courtroom, but there's not much I can do about it.

"Like what?" I asked, hoping she might give me a glimpse into whatever she was keeping from me. I took her hands gently from my face, stroking along her knuckles with my thumbs, letting her know she was safe.

"Well... like when they start asking me questions about before we met."

I almost laughed—not because it's funny, but because I've heard stories, and as much as I don't care to hear them said out loud, none of it changes how I feel about her. Not one thing.

"Do you want me to tell you stories about *me* before we met so you can feel awkward and we'll be even?"

She laughed, shaking her head dramatically, then shoved my shoulder.

"But I'm serious. What if you hear something that bothers you?"

Too late for that. I've already heard enough to last a lifetime.

"Look," I said, "nothing in there is going to bother me more than what's already happened. So don't worry about me."

She slid closer, looping her arms around me and tucking her face into my chest like she was trying to anchor herself.

"Thank you. I'm sorry."

"Babe, you have nothing to be sorry for. I'm a grown man and you're a grown woman. We just weren't lucky enough to find each other before wasting time on a bunch of useless relationships."

She held me tighter and burrowed into my shoulder like the words hit her somewhere tender.

"For getting you and everyone involved in this," she mumbled.

"Look, it's going to work itself out. You'll have a lot of support in that courtroom. I hope it's over tomorrow. But whatever happens, I'm going to be there for you."

"I hope so," she whispered.

I wrapped my arms around her, and let the movie play while she drifted off—completely out within minutes, breathing softly against my chest.

When the credits rolled, I carried her to bed, easing her down gently so I wouldn't wake her. Then I headed to the kitchen to clean up the mountain of leftover food. We were definitely going to be eating this for days.

I was glad she fell asleep early. She needed it.

I only wished I could do the same, but my mind wouldn't shut off.

This hearing...

Whatever she isn't telling me...

Whatever's about to be said in that courtroom...

I had a bad feeling we were all going to need to be on our A-game.

And I had an even worse feeling that tomorrow was going to change something.

I just didn't know what.

Chapter 31

ALEX

That was a restful night's sleep, but how did I get to bed? Must've been the angel next to me. I had that great dream on the beach again too. His eyes fluttered open and a smile followed.

"Hi. Thanks for the lift to bed." I murmured.

"You're welcome. How did you sleep?" He mumbled as I focused on the most beautiful sleepy brown eyes then watched him yawn.

"It was perfect. Just what the doctor ordered. How about you?" I stretched over and rubbed my hand lazily up and down his arm.

"It took me a while to go to sleep because I was perfectly content watching you sleep so soundly. Did you want to go to the gym?"

I nodded in agreement, "But I just want to sit in the sauna and meditate after I do a little yoga. I need to get my mind in a calm state. I've been so hyped up and today is game time." He inched closer to me, hooking his arms around my waist, closing the distance between us.

"I have something that will calm your mind." There was a hot, searing look coming out of those eyes now. He kissed my lips and my jawline, working his way down. He was right— this was definitely calming.

After a lovemaking session we went to the gym for some yoga and meditation.

Breakfast was quiet until the phone rang. Matt's name scrolled across the screen.

"Hi Matt. I have you on speaker, Roman's here."

"Hey you two, good morning. Jack's here as well. We're heading to the courthouse. Just wanted to let you know that we'll meet you outside and walk in together."

Roman asked, "Is that usual practice? Is something wrong?"

I scrunched my brows together and looked at Roman, who now looked somewhat nervous. It had me wondering why he would think that was a big deal or that something might be wrong.

Jack said, "It's not a big deal at all. We just got wind that there's a bunch of reporters waiting there to make this a zoo and thought it would be better if we all walked in together." I could feel the anxiety welling up in my chest.

"What the hell for?" I sounded panicky and agitated.

"Just part of his shady defense, nothing to worry about." Jack's voice was calm and reassuring but I felt neither calm nor reassured.

Oh lord, I'm going to hyperventilate.

"I can only guess who started that bullshit. What does that mean, now?" I realized I had a death grip on Roman's sleeve. I looked up at him, taking a deep breath and released his arm. He put a hand on my back, and I know he was just trying to calm me down but I'm not sure anything is going to be able to do that for me today. I'm going to have to get a grip before all hell breaks loose.

Matt reacted sternly. "Nothing. It means keep your mouth shut when we walk in the building no matter what they ask or say to you, do you understand me?" He sounded pissed but Jack and Matt knew me as well as their wives, how I would react to getting harassed.

"Alex, we're serious this is not going to be the time for you to tell anyone how you feel, that's what the courtroom is for." I'm sure Jack was trying to figure out how to diffuse the tension that builds between Matt and myself since the deposition.

I was gritting my teeth when I said, "I hear you loud and clear. No telling anyone to fuck off." I shook my head, leaving my phone there as I stormed across the room to get some air and think. I heard Roman say thanks to the guys, before hanging up the phone.

As he was walking toward me, I addressed my fears. "I knew this was going to get worse, I just knew it. He's such a piece of shit." I was pacing back and forth— the nausea was creeping in.

"Matt and Jack are right. We just go into the building and ignore the media. You can say everything you need to say in the courtroom." Roman tried to be as comforting as possible. I mindlessly nodded my head ruminating over the plan of what I was actually going to do to that son of a bitch in there.

"If this is all over the news, what's going to happen to my business? This is insane. If they make shit up about me for ratings or to sell news, everything I'm trying to do for those residents will get destroyed." That's my biggest fear. Everything I've worked so hard for, ruined.

"That's not going to happen. Those people know you." Roman tried to reassure me but my focus was elsewhere.

"Maybe, but what about the investors?" They sure as hell don't know me but they will soon enough. I'm sure I'll be known as the loose cannon after this.

"They know me and Harrison. They don't care about things like this, I promise."

I was trying to stay calm but all the yoga and meditation this morning was washed clear from my veins and replaced with anxiousness and fury.

"Court is at nine. What time is it now?" *Time to get this over with.*

"It's eight."

"We should leave soon and get there early. I have to let everyone know what's going on, so they're not blindsided."

I called my brother to let him know about the reporters. I told him to maybe come in a little later with dad, but he said they were already on their way. He didn't seem to concerned.

Roman drove while I called the girls to get some motivation and text Shay to update her on the situation in front of the courthouse.

ALEX: *"Hey girl, just a heads up that there are reporters outside the courthouse. Don't talk to them, just come on in."*

SHAY: *"Thanks. Are you hanging in there?"*

ALEX: *"Doing just fine, girl. See you soon."* I hated to lie to her, but it helped me lie to myself as well.

I called the girls on a three way.

Maggie said, "Hey, girl!"

Abby said, "Alex, you've got this."

I laughed and said, "Maggie, I'm going to need you to stomp the fuck out of the eggshells right now." I needed as much fuel as I could get for this showdown.

Maggie obliged, "In that case, good morning, Jerkface. We're on our way."

I said, "Thank you girls. I wanted to make sure you knew about the reporters outside the courthouse."

Abby said, "We know. He just wanted to make trouble. Marcus apparently did it trying to feed the flames."

It was Marcus too huh? Nice. I just shook my head hoping Roman didn't get too upset about it.

"Let's get this over with." I said trying to end the conversation.

Roman chimed in because I had them on speaker. "Maggie, Abby, Good morning. Why don't you sit with me." They both agreed and we parked the car.

Here we go.

***

ROMAN

I was gripping Alex's hand tighter than I meant to as we walked in step toward the courthouse. Matt and Jack were waiting off to the side, arms crossed, each wearing an unusually serious expression. I'd never seen either of them look that rigid before. Maggie and Abby had driven separately, and I spotted them now, weaving through the crowd to reach us.

"I still don't get this," Matt muttered, shaking his head. He wasn't wrong. The whole thing felt exaggerated and wrongfully sensationalized.

"This is personal," I said. "He's going after my family... and anyone connected to us. They'll use whatever they can to hurt the company and ruin our reputations." That's the only thing that made sense.

Jack snorted. "Sounds like a couple of sore losers to me."

Alex looked nervous—her shoulders tight, her jaw set—but Maggie and Abby flanked her instantly, talking to her in low, steady voices. Hopefully grounding her. The closer we moved to the steps, the more her breaths shortened. I leaned in, lowering my voice so only she could hear.

"All the important people know the truth. Don't let this rattle you. Remember everything you've worked so hard for."

She turned to me with a look that landed somewhere between cold and disconnected. Her nod was slow, sharp. "I'm fine. Tunnel vision. I promise."

But her tone carried an edge that unsettled me. And her eyes... her eyes were too calm. Not peaceful calm—numb calm. The kind you get before walking straight into a storm.

Matt sent her a quick wink. She smiled back, but the expression never touched her eyes. Something else had taken root behind them—something determined and unsettling.

When we reached the steps, Matt and Jack moved ahead, carving a path through the reporters.
Questions flew immediately—loud, sharp, invasive.

Alex flinched at a voice from the crowd shouting something ugly at her. I felt her twist, almost pivoting to respond, but I wrapped an arm firmly around her waist and kept her facing forward. Her breath hitched; I felt her ribs tighten under my hand. She made it up the last step, through the doors—

And as soon as they closed behind us, she tore her arm free and stepped back from me.

I lifted both hands, giving her space, knowing forcing closeness right now would be a mistake. She wasn't calm. She wasn't even close.

Matt stepped in immediately, intercepting her at just the right moment. "Don't let them get to you. Take Maggie and Abby to the bathroom. Splash some water on your face, breathe."

Her expression was furious—eyes bright, chest rising and falling too fast. Maggie and Abby ushered her toward the bathroom before she could unravel further.

"Thanks," I told Matt quietly. "She seems better when you handle her." It annoyed me more than I expected.

"I've known Alex since she was eighteen," Matt said, voice softer now. "She was a sweet girl before she married Luke. That marriage changed her. We lived through all of that with her. You've basically stepped into Luke's old place in her life—and even though you're nothing like him, she's not far removed from that divorce."

So I was walking around with a ghost on my back. Fantastic.

"I should've taken that into consideration," I muttered.

"You've gotten in her head," Jack said. "Don't back off. We're all seeing glimpses of the sweet Alex again. The girls are grateful. So are we."

"I don't think we'll see that version of her today," I admitted. "She keeps needing space from me... and I don't know how she'll get that living together. She hasn't even unpacked her things yet."

Matt clapped a hand on my shoulder. "She'll get there."

I wasn't so sure. The real question was—*where is she going before she gets there?*

***

ALEX

The girls snagged me by each arm, practically shoving me into the restroom. I'm not even sure if they pushed me into the women's bathroom.

Maggie said, "No name calling right now. This is serious. You need to pull your shit together. You can't go into that courtroom with that look on your face."

"What look is that, Maggie?" I spit out placing my hands aggressively on the sink before looking at the crazed wild eyes staring back at me in the mirror.

Abby growled uncharacteristically, "Calm down."

I whipped my head around in her direction and said, "Don't tell me to fucking calm down. There's not some lunatic having a whole battalion of reporters call you a psycho bitch whore."

Maggie and Abby were silent, holding their breath before we all burst out laughing and Maggie said while gasping for air, "What... is... a... psycho... bitch... whore?"

I put my hands on my face, doubled over and screamed into my hands to muffle the noise I really wanted to make. When I came back up, the girls had gained their composure, and all the anxiety seemed to be out of my system for the moment. I turned back to the sink and patted some cold water on my face then dried it. I calmly fixed my hair taking a deep breath and motioned the girls back to the hall.

Matt asked, "All good?" *Not yet*, I thought, but it will be.

I nodded and snarled, "Yep, let's go send this asshole to jail." I smiled contemptuously as I walked in front. I was going to use this adrenaline to my advantage now. Abby and Maggie hurried to keep up.

At the door to the courtroom my dad, brother and Roman's parents were already there. Matt and Jack said they would be inside and to meet them at the table with the DA. I gave dad and Edward a hug and waved to the Kings. Roman ushered his parents and Harrison over to meet my dad and my brother.

He introduced our families, "Hank. Edward. These are my parents Lisette and Fitz. This is my brother Harrison." My family shook hands with everyone, and I suggested they sit together. They agreed and out of the corner of my eye I saw Grant, Shay, and the Santoros. I started to get an uneasy feeling about all these people hearing these horrible things said about me.

Roman turned around and said, "Shit." Why does that bother him? He should be happy I have so much support even though I'm a little agitated with all these people here.

I looked at him questioningly. "What?" He looked nervous and agitated himself. I reached out, taking hold of his hand and his palm was sweating.

"Nothing, it's fine." It didn't seem fine, and his vibe was just as complicated as his words.

As soon as they came over, we started the introductions but apparently Roman's dad already knew Grant and the Santoros. I didn't have time for this new revelation. I needed to get in the courtroom and get ready for war. Mrs. Santoro hugged me and told me everything was going to be fine just before I grabbed the handle of the door. I thanked her then Abby, Maggie and I walked into the courtroom.

Abby whispered, "Who were they?" I ignored her, scanning the room zoning in on the defendant's seat for Tanner. I spotted him staring at me, creepily, with a shit eating grin on his face. I immediately looked for Jack and Matt who were ushering me forth keeping my focus on them.

Unspoken words "Don't look at him just look at us." The girls sat in the seats right behind us saving a spot for Roman. I took my seat in between Jack and the DA.

The DA instructed me, "Alex, I don't want you to look at the defendant at all during this unless someone asks you to point him out." The rest was kind of a blur of telling me what I should and shouldn't say or do to the point I tuned them all out. I knew what I was going to do; common sense told me that it was going to be a disaster.

***

ROMAN

What are the Santoros doing here?
Why would Grant bring them?

The nausea crept in as I wondered why the mafia needed to be present for this.

This is going to be a circus.

I decided the only sensible move was to introduce everyone and pretend none of this was unusual.

I introduced Alex's dad and brother first. Edward moved his father into the courtroom quickly, guiding him away from the crowd, probably trying to shield him from too much stimulation. I turned to introduce my parents next—only to realize my dad was already locked into a conversation with Grant and the Santoros. Hugging them. Talking as if they were long-lost friends.

Meanwhile my mother stood stiffly beside him, hands clasped so tightly her knuckles were pale. She looked anxious, not at all eager to meet anyone.

Harrison shot me a suspicious look from across the room.

I shrugged. I was as lost as he was.

Time to remove myself from whatever that was and get into the courtroom. I could ask Dad later how in the world he knew them.

Inside, I spotted Tanner sitting up front, eyes locked on Alex. Thankfully she wasn't looking in his direction. Abby and Maggie were waving me up to the seat directly behind her, and that's when Tanner snapped his head around to glare at me.

The expression he wore... cold, hostile.

I met his stare head-on as I slid into the bench beside Abby and Maggie.

Alex was whispering with her attorneys, so I didn't get a chance to speak to her before the bailiff announced the judge's arrival. Everyone rose.

The courtroom was packed with support for her—rows and rows of people. Tanner, on the other hand, seemed to have only a handful behind him. His brother Marcus sat rigidly in the front row, eyes sweeping the room like he was cataloging threats. When his attention finally collided with mine, his stare sharpened with something that felt calculated.

He flicked his gaze toward the back of the room.

I followed it.

He was watching Grant and the Santoros.

My stomach tightened. Of course they stood out—Grant always stood out—but something about the way Marcus focused on them felt... intentional. Familiar. Like he recognized them.

Maggie leaned in and whispered, "What are you thinking about? You're starting to look like Alex."

I smirked, pulling myself back to the present. She was right. The energy radiating off Alex was bleeding into me. I was truly grateful that I couldn't feel anyone else's emotions at the same intensity.

When the hearing began, the witnesses were called first, and that portion moved quickly. Tanner's attorney barely attempted to cross-examine anyone. Not a single witness seemed shaken by him. If his strategy was to unsettle us, he failed.

When the court broke for lunch, we considered walking across the street—but the reporters were still swarming outside like they'd been waiting for fresh prey. None of us wanted to deal with that. We settled for vending machine food and gathered in a conference room to talk strategy.

Jack and the DA led the conversation. Matt leaned back in his chair, calmer now, and said, "It's going well in there. They haven't pulled anything unexpected."

Alex, who'd been silent up until now, murmured under her breath, "They're just waiting for me."

Her voice was flat. Her face unreadable. She stared at the table as if she could drill a hole through it.

Jack nodded slightly. "Maybe. But based on the witness list, they don't have anyone else. They'll have to put Tanner on the stand if they want his version on record. And if they do... anything he says about your character is hearsay. If he brings up the assault, he's going to have to explain what actually happened."

He leaned back and added, "I doubt he wants to recount the story of the young woman who put him on his knees."

Everyone laughed—except me and Alex.

She lifted her eyes to mine, something tight and apologetic in them, something I didn't understand.

And the closer we moved toward her taking the stand, the more certain I became:

She was planning something she hadn't told anyone.

***

ALEX

I could hear Matt and Jack talking strategy beside me, but their voices were distant, secondary. I was filtering for anything important, anything that should alter my plan—but nothing did. My mind was fixed on the step I was about to take. I'd spent too long feeling powerless. Today, I was reclaiming something. Not just for me but for every woman who'd ever been cornered, blamed, or talked over.

Tanner was counting on his silence to save him. There was no world in which he climbed up on that stand and allowed my team to question him. He wouldn't survive it. So, of course, their only play was to turn this into some twisted "mutual situation."
They were going to try to reshape what happened.

And I was going to make sure they failed.

When everyone laughed at the idea of Tanner testifying, I glanced toward Roman. I wished he would laugh too—to just follow the moment and let it lighten him. But no. He was staring straight at me, eyes tense, expression sharp. He knew. He was piecing it together.

It's too late now, love.
I have to do this.

Bruce was sitting quietly in the back of the courtroom, ready to drive me home if everything went sideways. My home. The apartment I hadn't fully moved out of, the apartment I claimed I was "too busy" to dismantle.
Maybe on some level...I knew I'd need somewhere to land after today.

When the break ended and it was time to go back inside, I took Roman aside as everyone returned to the courtroom. I needed those last seconds with him. Needed him to hear me—truly hear me—even if he didn't understand what I was about to do.

I placed my palms gently against his cheeks.
"I love you. I want you to know that."

He smiled, but it was strained, almost pained. The worry in his eyes looked like it was physically hurting him.

"I do know," he murmured. "I love you too. But... please. Tell me what's going on. Just a little honesty right now."

"You'll find out soon."
I lowered my hands, forcing space between us so I wouldn't break. If I held on any longer, I'd falter. I needed focus. I needed fire. Not fear.

He gripped my shoulders, squeezing and letting go like he was trying to hold on without caging me.
"Alex, I have a bad feeling about this. Should I get Matt and Jack before you go in? Just to talk? Something's off—"

I shook my head slowly. Deliberately.

"No one can stop what's about to happen," I whispered. "No one knows except me. This is for me—"

My throat tightened.

"—and for a lot of women who deserve better than feeling like victims."

His breath hitched. I could see it—his instinct to stop me, to protect me, to pull me away from that courtroom and shield me from everything inside. It tore at me.

"I need you to stay calm," I continued softly. "And I need you not to say a word."

He didn't like that. His jaw clenched, his eyes pleading.

"I don't know if I can do that if I don't know what's coming. Just tell me so I can brace for it."

I couldn't.

If I told him, he'd tell them.

And they'd try to stop me.

Before he could say anything else, Maggie stepped back into the room. "Alex, they just called you to the stand."

I gave Roman one last look—one that held apology, love, and something resolute beneath it—and hurried out before I saw the heartbreak in his eyes bring me to my knees.

I'm sorry, baby.

More than you know.

***

ROMAN

"Maggie... she's planning something." My voice dropped as panic closed around my throat. "Something no one knows about. Did she say anything to you?"

We followed after her with hurried steps. Maggie shook her head quickly. "What did she say to you?"

"That she wanted me calm. That I wasn't to say a word. And that whatever she's about to do is for women who don't want to feel like victims."

Maggie's eyes widened. "You don't think she'd actually—attack Tanner, do you?"

Did I?

"I don't know," I whispered. "It sounds like something she'd do if she made up her mind."

We slid into the pew just as Alex placed her hand on the Bible, right hand lifted. My stomach dropped.

Oh no. What is she about to do?

Abby whispered, "Where were you two?"

I groaned under my breath. "Getting ready for the main event."

"What does that even mean?" Abby hissed. Maggie shushed her sharply.

Maggie leaned close. "Alex has had something up her sleeve this entire time. We're about to find out what it is."

I fixed my eyes on Alex.

She didn't look nervous.

She didn't look scared.

She didn't even look present.

She looked vacant—cold—like all her emotions had been locked behind some internal steel door.

They ran through her name, occupation, basic questions. Matt and Jack handled the direct examination, and she was flawless. Calm. Controlled. Almost unnervingly so.

My knee bounced so hard the bench vibrated. Maggie placed her hand on it, grounding me for a moment. It was the same anxious bounce Alex did when she was trying to hold herself together. Only this time... she wasn't bouncing at all. She was utterly still.

Then Tanner's attorney rose.

I felt my pulse shoot into my throat.

He didn't even look at her.

He looked at his paper—like he was reading a script he'd been rehearsing for weeks.

Attorney: "Ms. Kennedy, is it true that you frequent Sebastian's Bar on a regular basis?"

Alex: "Yes."

Attorney: "Ms. Kennedy, is it true that you've met men there before?"

Alex: "Yes."

Attorney: "Ms. Kennedy, is it true that you've had intimate relations with men you met there?"

Alex: "Yes."

I felt heat crawl up my neck. These weren't questions—this was an ambush.

Maggie leaned in. "Roman... what is she doing?"

"Telling the truth," I muttered tightly. And hearing it like this burned far more than hearing rumors ever did.

"She hasn't blinked once," Maggie whispered. "Not once."

I swallowed hard. She was using something Bruce taught her—some kind of mental lockdown.

Stone.

Unshakeable.

Unreachable.

The attorney continued.

Attorney: "Ms. Kennedy, isn't it true you've had so many encounters at Sebastian's you can't remember all the men's names?"

She blinked. Finally. A sign of life. Her expression shifted like she was analyzing the wording, searching for the right angle.

Alex: "I don't know, maybe. Is that what you want me to say? You know, that's a good question. But honestly, no. I remember names very well. It's one of my talents."

Ah. There she is. My Alex—sharp, wry, in control. But where had she been hiding?

Attorney: "Ms. Kennedy, please answer yes or no."

Matt whipped his head up, alarm flooding his eyes. He shook it—barely noticeable—warning her to stay steady.

Alex stared the attorney down.

Alex: "Then don't ask stupid questions that don't deserve yes or no answers."

The room exhaled a collective gasp.

Matt's expression twisted—concern, surprise, maybe even fear. Something was off.

Judge: "Ms. Kennedy, there was no question pending. Please refrain from speaking unless counsel asks one. Counsel, proceed."

The attorney didn't hesitate.

Attorney: "Ms. Kennedy, isn't it true that you and my client have already had sexual relations, and you simply didn't care to know his name?"

Everything fell silent.

Then—

Alex laughed.

Not a nervous laugh.

Not a startled one.

A cold, deliberate, unsettling laugh that echoed off the walls.
And every hair on the back of my neck stood up.

Chapter 32

ALEX

Sexual relations? He grabbed my ass, and I crushed his balls! That's what he calls sexual relations. I couldn't help it, I laughed, full on hysterics. All the questions this guy was asking were vapid. My dad already left the courtroom, so I don't care anymore how bad this gets.

I looked straight at Tanner exactly as my counsel instructed me not to do to fuel the anger. "Sexual relations?" I hissed. "Is this a joke? He grabbed my ass in a crowded bar. I grabbed his balls and dropped his pathetic ass to his knees and listened to him cry like a fucking baby."

It got loud in the courtroom and the judge started hitting his gavel. I was chewing my bottom lip so hard I thought it might be bleeding. I calmed myself down enough to release it.

The judge quickly turned to me and sternly warned, "Ms. Kennedy, you will not use that kind of language in my courtroom. Now if you need a minute, let me know and we can take a recess but do not continue using that kind of language or I will hold you in contempt."

I took a deep breath and gained some of my composure back.

"I'm sorry your honor..." I looked to the judge for just a second "...I won't do it again. I apologize." I mean I wouldn't laugh again, probably.

The judge said, "Let's continue." I returned my focus to Tanner to see he wasn't smiling anymore, which made me smile.

Attorney: "Ms. Kennedy, are you admitting you assaulted my client?"

Whatever the little predator wants to call it, I guess.

"I'm saying I defended myself from any further assault on my person." I corrected the attorney as I cocked my head, thinking how could someone ever defend a piece of shit like Tanner.

Attorney: "Just answer yes or no please."

"Yes or no, please!" *You get what you give, fucker.*

Matt jumped up and barked, "I object your honor, the question has already been asked and answered. She already said she grabbed the defendant by his testicles." Matt winked at me and rolled his eyes because he knew he couldn't stop anything that I was about to do but he could at least help a girl out. The judge said sustained and the questions continued.

Attorney: "Ms. Kennedy, the night you were allegedly drugged, isn't it true that you actually have a drinking problem, and you were just drunk and since you had already had a sexual encounter with the defendant, you willingly went into a private room with him and were engaging in an aggressive sexual act?"

I wish I couldn't feel my heart beating in my eyes right now. How do I get control of this? I honestly felt like attacking him right now. Concentrate. Move, countermove. *Get a grip Alex.* Take a deep breath this is it. Don't look at Roman.

"No. I've never had a sexual encounter with Mr. Ellington. I was assaulted by Mr. Ellington after he put drugs in my water. I was drinking water that night. If I do have a drinking problem, however, I'm pretty sure I would never drink enough alcohol to go home with a pathetic loser like Tanner Ellington. Plus, alcohol doesn't put you in a coma. Doctors are generally smart enough to know when someone has alcohol in their system, and they still haven't identified what it was he used on me. On top of that, he's such a pussy that he had to drug me to force sex on me. Tanner would never have been able to do that to me unless he drugged me. I would've kicked his fucking ass. Even if I slept with everyone in Sebastians or everyone in the town for that matter, I still never would've wanted to sleep with a pathetic rapist like Tanner Ellington."

I guess I never heard the judge or anyone else for that matter because Matt and Jack were both up at the stand telling me to shut up.

***

ROMAN

In one breath she went on the offensive—calling him a coward to put it mildly, a predator, announcing she could take him down herself. It didn't even sound like her. Her voice was sharp, cutting through the quiet like a blade. Maggie and Abby clung to my arms with white-knuckled grips. Matt, Jack, the other attorney, the DA—everyone was trying to get her to stop, but she didn't hear a single one of them.

It was like she'd disappeared into some internal firestorm and only one person existed in her line of sight.

Tanner.

Not until the judge threatened her with jail for the third time did Matt and Jack rush the stand and physically intervene. By then the courtroom had erupted—voices, movement, people trying to understand what they'd just witnessed. The judge slammed his gavel repeatedly and ordered everyone except the attorneys and their clients to leave.

Out in the hall, shock covered every face.

Harrison wandered up first, shaking his head but grinning. "That was great. She didn't care what happened as long as she said what she needed to say."

He wasn't wrong. But I couldn't stop thinking about what it meant.
Why she chose that moment.
What it was building toward.

"It was satisfying," I admitted. "Tanner finally got hit with something he deserved."
But the unease in my chest kept tightening. Something about her outburst didn't feel random.

Maggie stepped in with full solidarity mode. "She took her power back. That's what that was."

Maybe. Or maybe it was something more dangerous than empowerment.

Grant came over and patted my back. "She can handle herself, can't she?"

I pulled him aside. If anyone knew what was really happening beneath the surface—it would be him. "She's provoking him, isn't she?"

Grant's jaw flexed. He nodded once. "It looks that way. I don't know what she's trying to trigger. But I doubt she's doing it alone."

"It isn't you, is it?"

His expression shifted—offended, almost. "I would never put her at risk."

Good. I probably shouldn't be questioning a man with his reputation, but I had to know.

"Do you think she's in danger now?" I asked quietly.

"Yes." The answer was instant. "The Ellingtons aren't predictable, and they aren't harmless. Tanner being provoked publicly—especially with his brother here—puts her at risk. We need to protect her."

This was the first time I fully agreed with him.

I rejoined the group and pulled my mother aside, hoping she might've sensed something, but she shook her head nervously. No answers there.

I scanned the crowd—dozens of people who loved Alex, all equally confused. If she'd confided in someone, they were hiding it well.

I found Edward. "How's your dad?"

He snorted. "Alex really let Tanner have it. Dad's outside. Thank God he wasn't in the room for that mess."

He looked almost proud of her—proud in a way that didn't help the unease crawling up my spine.

I nodded. I couldn't imagine what it felt like for her father to hear any of that.

"I think she planned it," I admitted quietly. "I don't know what her endgame is—she won't tell me anything—but I'm almost certain she was provoking him."

Edward rolled his eyes. "That doesn't shock me at all. After her divorce... she didn't care what anyone thought. I had no idea how deeply she'd been affected by all of it."

That divorce again.

I'd heard it repeatedly now—this invisible wound she never fully got over.

My mother once told me, *"A divorce isn't the same as a breakup."*

She was right.

I'd never lived it personally, but watching Alex unravel and rebuild herself in real time... I was beginning to understand exactly what she meant.

***

ALEX

Okay, sorry. No. Not sorry at all. I stood as tall as my five-foot four-inch stature could and planted my hands firmly on my hips.

Matt yelled, "Alex, what the hell were you thinking?" I rolled my eyes and looked away before answering.

"That I was going to stand up for myself." I threw my arms down to my sides aggressively— fists clenched tight. "This is my life, not the rules of the court. I don't care if they fine me or arrest me. I'm going to say what I have to say to that asshole. Everything I said was the truth. Just because no one liked the words I used doesn't make it any less true." I snapped back.

Jack was more controlled but still loud as he threw his arms in the air. "Well, you have a $500 fine to pay and you're lucky that's all. The DA is going to talk to the judge and claim PTSD or something."

Who gives a fuck about $500?

"I don't care about the fine, like I said." I was calmer now, stretching out my fingers as I looked at the nail marks in my palms.

"Well, you may have screwed up your case. Tanner could get off on a technicality," Jack informed me. I laughed. I never thought he was going to get charged with anything in the first place.

"What technicality? Hurt feelings? Emasculation? If he gets off it's because his brother got him off. The doctors can attest to the drugs in my system. Bruce can attest to his assault. Steve can attest to the fact that I was drinking water that night. I'm going to make sure the bastard goes to jail." My breathing was so labored that I could barely catch my breath, and I was still seeing red.

Matt looked at me like I was crazy. "Oh yeah? How're you going to do that? They may never let you testify again!"

Yep, don't care about that either.

"I don't want to testify again. Don't need to." I crossed my arms with an indignant look on my face. I needed to get out of this room and away from Tanner is what I needed. Part one is done. I needed air and space.

"Alex, what are you up to?" Matt gently took my arm, turning me toward him.

I shook my head, trying to contain the tears that I knew were starting to pool in the corner of my eyes as the adrenaline was beginning to filter out. "I'll tell you when I ask you to represent me." I managed to choke out.

Jack looked at me confused and stated the obvious, "We represent you now, Alex."

"As a defendant." I whispered. They looked at each other with more worry than concern.

"Alex, please tell me you aren't planning on doing something stupid." Matt inquired anxiously.

Doesn't get much stupider than this, I thought.

"Don't you think I already have? The ball's in his court now." I blinked away the tears before they could fall. The confused look on their faces was going to have to stay that way until the time comes.

The DA came back over and said, "The judge is sympathetic to you Alex, but you made a mockery of his courtroom and he's angry about that. He told the attorneys that he's going to recommend five years if it goes to trial unless we can come to a plea agreement now. But he said if it goes to trial and you pull something like what you just pulled, you'd be removed from the courtroom, and you wouldn't get to defend yourself and he'd get off. Knowing that, how do you feel about him taking a plea?"

"What's the plea? If he's not going to get five years, what's he going to get?" I needed to know what the options were before this would really work.

He said, "He'll get one year. He'll probably serve six months and do community service. He'll need to enter a rehabilitation program for sex offender's and register on the national sex offender's list."

Even though I wanted to say he could go screw himself, I didn't want to go through a trial and that was exactly what I was looking for. I wanted him to come after me, one way or another. I know he will too. I could see it in his eyes. I heard the vial things he was saying to his brother about me. The only focus I had in that courtroom was on him. I had tunnel vision on him alone and I zoned in on his every word. I could feel his anger and his vengeance. That's all those two seem to know. I got out of my head for a second, looked square at the DA and replied, "Yes, offer him the deal."

Chapter 33

ROMAN

I'm so sick of waiting.

Every second feels like someone tightening a cord around my throat. Where *are* they?

What's going on behind those doors?

I keep replaying possibilities in my head — all of them bad.

Did she get arrested?

Did she provoke Tanner into something and the courtroom erupted? Did she lunge at him the way it looked like she wanted to?

Did *he* do something?

I don't know, and the not-knowing is torture.

I walk circles around the lobby, deliberately separating myself from the clusters of people talking quietly. The air feels thick in here — stale courthouse air, faintly metallic from old pipes and overworked vents, with the buzz of fluorescent lighting like static against my nerves. Every footstep echoes off stone tile. Every cough feels too loud. Every muffled voice behind those doors makes my heart kick like it wants out.

Mom and Dad eventually wander over, breaking through my pacing. Dad slips an arm around my shoulder.

"You're going to have your hands full with that one," he murmurs, half-amused, half-cautioning.

I let out a rough, sardonic laugh — more forced air than actual humor. "I don't even know what I *have* with her right now. She did all of this on her own."

I scrubbed a hand over my face.

"Should I be worried?"

I looked to my mother — if anyone can read someone's motives, it's her. She studies me with soft eyes before glancing at the closed courtroom doors.

"I don't know," she says honestly, surprising me. Her voice is calm, thoughtful. "She reminds me of those mama bears. Sweet, gentle, easy to love — unless someone threatens her pack. Then she's fierce. Controlled, but fierce. I don't think she's as out of control as people assume."

I frown.

Protecting her pack?

"What pack?" I ask aloud. "This wasn't about protecting anyone. This was revenge."

Mom shakes her head slowly and touches my arm — grounding, steadying.

"No, honey... her pack is women. All women. She did what she did to protect them."

The words hit harder than I want to admit.

Because it sounds exactly like what she told me in the conference room — that this wasn't just for her.

Before I could think further, the courtroom doors open with that heavy wooden thud, and Matt steps out first. His expression is unreadable, which is never a good sign. Jack follows, then the DA... then Alex.

She's smiling.

Not wild, unhinged or shaken.

A calm, almost mischievous smile — the kind she uses right before she reminds me she's two steps ahead of everyone—like she was today.

"Roman, did you bring your wallet?" she asks lightly. "I'll pay you back."

Everyone laughs — probably out of nerves or relief or both — and I pull her into me, inhaling her vanilla scent like it's the only oxygen left in the building. My chest loosens a fraction.

"Yes, sweetheart. I have my wallet. Let's go pay your fine."

Her shoulders relax, and for the moment, I let myself breathe.

Later at my place, the penthouse is full in a way it rarely ever is. Full of voices, bodies, comfort. The kitchen smells like hot pizza, garlic, and the deep, fruity notes of the wine the Santoros brought. The lights are warm, the skyline glows behind the windows, and the atmosphere feels thick with aftershocks — a shared understanding that something big just happened, even if no one's naming it.

Alex's dad declined to come up — overwhelmed, I assume. Edward took him home.

Amelia arrived around five, still in work clothes, hair pinned neatly.

Bruce stopped in only briefly, clapped Alex on the shoulder, then left for the studio.

The Santoros mingled in the living room with my parents, gracious and composed despite everything I know about who they truly are.

On the other side of the room, there's the sound of Maggie's laugh, Abby's teasing commentary, Jack's eye-rolling, and Matt's booming chuckle. Harrison is in the middle of them, eating it up like he's at a dinner party instead of decompressing from a courthouse showdown.

And then there's Alex — radiant, animated, talking with Shay and Grant. Her hands move when she talks, her eyes light up, and she looks... free. More free than she's looked in days.

I stand at the kitchen island, nursing a drink I'm not even sure I'm tasting, my eyes drifting from group to group. The conversations blend into a low hum — laughter, clinking glasses, the rustle of people settling into couches and bar stools.

But my brain refuses to settle.

Who knows what she planned today?

Someone must have known.

Someone must have helped her.

She doesn't do reckless things lightly — there's always intention under her chaos.

Grant?

He's loyal to her, but he swore he'd never put her in harm's way. And I believe him.

My mother?

If she knew Alex was walking into danger, she'd have shut it down instantly — or shut Alex down entirely until she promised not to go through with it.

Jack and Matt?

They *are* her attorneys. They'd be bound by privilege even if they did know something.

Or maybe — maybe she really did do this alone.

Maybe that's the part that terrifies me.

I rub my hand down my face, trying to push the storm out of my head. The view of everyone laughing and relaxing should be comforting — should make me believe the worst is over.

I force a breath, push off the counter, and decide to join the nearest conversation before I spiral myself into madness.

***

ALEX

That wasn't as terrible as it could've been.

No one stormed out. No one disowned me.

They weren't thrilled about my courtroom outburst, but they also weren't angry with me — a bigger relief than I expected.

Once everyone left, I poured another drink. The warmth hit me fast, and with it came the sharp awareness that if I wasn't careful, I'd say something to Roman I'd regret.

Roman dropped onto the sofa beside me with a heavy exhale. "Finally," he muttered. "I thought they'd never leave."

I smiled faintly. "I'm just glad they still want to be around me."

He turned his head, studying me. "Why wouldn't they? Because you lost control today?"

His tone wasn't light. It wasn't teasing. It was edged — irritated in a way that made my stomach dip.

"No," I said softly. "Because I let him get to me."

Roman let out a short, rough laugh. "You didn't lose control. You knew exactly what you were doing. Everyone else was caught off guard — you weren't."

That hit harder than I expected, and I managed a small, uneasy laugh. "I'm sorry for all of it."

He didn't smile. If anything, his expression darkened.

"Sorry for what?" he demanded. "Not trusting me enough to tell me what you were planning? Alex, I know you have trust issues, but this... this isn't healthy."

There it was — the Roman I'd been expecting hours ago.

"I *do* trust you." My voice sharpened before I could soften it. "I trust you to protect me and love me. But if I tell you something like this, you'll try to stop me — and I can't have that. I need you to trust *me* enough to let me handle what I need to handle."

I swallowed and forced myself to stay steady.
"You need to be like my dad," I added quietly. "If something feels too hard to hear, you step back. You don't interfere."

Roman stood abruptly, went to the fridge, grabbed a beer, and shut the door harder than necessary. I followed but kept the island between us. The emotional distance was already enough.

"Alex," he said, pressing his palms into the countertop. "Why do you put people through this? Why do you shut everyone out?"

I reached toward him on instinct, but he pulled away, leaving my hand suspended in the air before I lowered it and twisted my fingers together instead.

"Right now, there's nothing to tell," I said gently. "You're getting upset over something that doesn't exist yet."

"That's not true."
His voice was low and tight.
"You stood in that courtroom and admitted you provoked a dangerous man on purpose. And I'm supposed to believe I have nothing to worry about?"

His eyes were tired. Frustrated. And clouded by the alcohol he'd been steadily sipping all night.

I spoke calmly, softly — the opposite of how he was speaking to me.
"As of now, he's agreeing to a plea deal. Jail time. Community service. He has to register as a sex offender."

Roman lifted the beer to his lips and took a long drink, then lowered it with a cold, humorless smile.

"Six months and community service," he echoed. "A light punishment, considering what he did. Congrats."

The sarcasm stung, but I took it. It was better than shouting.

"Roman," I said gently, "just come sit with me, please."
I tilted my head toward the sofa, softening my expression. "I'm actually feeling better now that the hearing is over. I'd like to just... be done with it for the night."

He hesitated — then rounded the counter, took my hand firmly, and tugged me toward the bedroom.

His grip wasn't angry.
Just worn down.

Afraid.
And trying not to show it.

Chapter 34

ALEX

The rest of the week I pretended everything was fine.

It was the only thing I could do.

Deep down I knew I was in a waiting game. Something was coming—I could feel it hovering just beyond the edge of everything—but there was no point in staring at the sky waiting for lightning to strike. Life had to keep moving in the meantime.

So I stayed busy.

I had the week off from training and classes, which left me with more time than usual to throw myself into work. Strangely enough, work had started to feel different lately. More purposeful. Less like something I did to stay afloat and more like something that actually mattered.

The nonprofit idea had taken on a life of its own.

I sat in on several meetings with potential investors, explaining the vision for the organization and how it would help fund the Burrow Township relocation project. Some of them were cautious, others genuinely excited, but at least they were listening. Roman had brought his team into the conversation as well, and together we started mapping out what it would actually take to make the project happen.

Logistics.

Costs.

Phases of construction.

All the practical pieces that turn a hopeful idea into something real.

The only part we couldn't control was the people.

The residents.

Without them agreeing to the plan, none of it would work.

Thankfully Darius had been incredible. Over the past week he'd managed to track down most of the families and explain the proposal well enough that many of them had agreed to attend the meeting Amelia had scheduled. It was going to take place in the auditorium at King Construction in just a few days.

That thought alone kept me focused.

I had spent hours working on the presentation—organizing the numbers, the visuals, the timelines. If we were going to ask people to trust us with something this big, we needed to show them exactly how it would benefit them.

The work kept my mind occupied while I waited.

Waited for the other shoe to drop.

Saturday morning felt different the moment I woke up.

It wasn't anything obvious—nothing dramatic—but the atmosphere in the house had shifted in a way I couldn't quite explain. The quiet felt heavier somehow, like the walls were holding onto something unspoken.

I found myself wanting to get out of the house.

Do something normal.

Fall was just beginning to creep into the air, and that had always been my favorite time of year. The mornings felt cooler, the sky seemed sharper somehow, and the sunlight carried that soft golden color that only showed up for a few weeks before winter took over.

Lookout Park immediately came to mind.

I loved going up there when the leaves started changing. The view stretched across the entire valley, the hills turning shades of gold and crimson while the air carried that crisp, earthy smell that only came with autumn.

A picnic sounded perfect.

Simple.

Peaceful.

Exactly the kind of distraction I needed.

I stood in the kitchen for a moment, wondering if Roman already had something planned for the day. Lately it felt like we had been moving around each other instead of with each other.

Since the hearing, something about him had definitely changed.

He'd been going to bed later than usual, and we hadn't been going to the gym together like we normally did. When he was home, he used to sit at the kitchen island working while I moved around the apartment doing whatever needed to be done.

Now he kept disappearing into his office and closing the door.

This morning he hadn't gone running with me either.

And for the first time in weeks, he hadn't seemed concerned about me going out alone.

I leaned against the counter, turning that thought over in my mind.

Maybe he thought everything was finally over.

Maybe he believed I was safe now that Tanner was going to jail.

I knocked on his office door and heard him say, "I'll call you later."

"Come in," he said in a tired, raspy tone.

I cautiously pushed the door open. Now I know what it feels like to walk on eggshells. It's awful.

I tried to sound as pleasant as I could. "Hey, good morning. It's beautiful out there today."

He looked up quickly and dismissively. "Hi, good morning, yep."

I took a deep breath and tried to be cordial but he was making it difficult. "Would you like to have a picnic at Lookout Park today?"

He still didn't look up as he mumbled. "Mmm." It sounded like he had no desire to go.

"Roman, why are you working on a Saturday? I thought you only did that when you needed to distract yourself?" *Let's see if I'm his problem.*

He smiled and looked up at me. "That's what I'm doing."

I see. This is where we are now.

"Distracting yourself from what? Me?" I couldn't help instigating what I knew to be the beginning of an argument.

He nodded and let out a long breath.

"Yes, Alex. I can't stop trying to figure out what you're up to, so I thought I'd work. Except all the extra work involves you, so for whatever reason it's not working."

I laughed and came around the desk and sat on his lap.

He didn't put his arms around me so I put my hands on his face and said, "Please stop. This isn't healthy." I thought a little of his own medicine would help, but I probably didn't think that through.

He was smirking but nothing in his face told me he was happy. "Being worried about you isn't healthy, you're damn right. What should I be when my girlfriend provokes a rapist to come after her? I don't know what you're up to, but you don't seem to need or want my help, so why do you want to spend time with me? That's what I've been thinking about."

I guess I'll be going on that picnic on my own today then. I got up and walked out of the room. He didn't bother to follow and I didn't want to make things worse.

The drive up to the lookout was beautiful—clear sky stretching endlessly above me, a soft breeze slipping through the open windows and brushing against my skin like it was trying to calm something deeper than the surface.

I should probably use this time to think. Really think.

About us.

About him.

About what this is turning into.

He needs space—that much is obvious. And if this... whatever this version of him is... is what I'm going to keep getting, then maybe I need space too.

My apartment is still exactly how I left it. Untouched. Waiting. The fridge is empty, but that's easy—I can order food, fill the silence with takeout containers and background noise if I have to. I've done that before.

Still... this isn't how I pictured today going.

Not even close.

But if I'm being honest with myself—really honest—I think some part of me always knew we'd end up here eventually.

I got in the car and called Roman. It rang once... twice... then went straight to voicemail.

Of course it did.

I kept it short. "Hey... we need to talk when I get back."

I dropped the phone onto the passenger seat and pulled onto the road, my fingers tightening around the steering wheel as the quiet settled in too fast, too loud.

Ten minutes later, my phone lit up.

Roman.

I answered on the first ring. "Hi."

A pause. Then, steady and controlled, "Hi... I think you're right."

And just like that... there it was.

The thing I never said out loud, but always kept tucked away somewhere in the back of my mind—an exit. An out clause. A quiet understanding that nothing ever really stayed. Not for me.

The irony wasn't lost on me. For so long, I'd been the one who didn't want the relationship. The one with one foot already out the door before anything even had the chance to matter.

But this time...

This time, I thought he was it.

I swallowed hard, trying to keep my voice steady, but the pressure in my chest cracked something open anyway. My vision blurred, the road in front of me smearing into streaks of color as I blinked too fast, too hard.

"Okay... see you soon," I managed, the words barely holding together before my voice gave out.

I ended the call before he could hear it—before he could hear me breaking.

The tears came anyway, hot and relentless, slipping down my cheeks as I drove the rest of the way home, one hand gripping the wheel, the other pressed against my mouth like I could somehow hold it all in.

But I couldn't. Not this time.

***

ROMAN

I went to the gym while she went running. I needed some space. Some time to think. She was being so careless with this situation and she wouldn't let me help her— clearly she didn't trust me. I know she's been working with my mom, but even my mom can't help her with whatever this is. She isn't going to get better until she decides it for herself. She's been drinking every night just to calm down, especially when she thinks I'm not looking.

I got back to the house before she did, took a shower, and changed. Then I headed into my office to make sure Alex would be ok without me. I called Grant and told him to keep an eye on her. I told him that it was just too much for me and she'd be in good hands with him. I told him we both had plenty to focus on with work and that whatever she had planned was going to have to be on her. He agreed and gave me his sympathy. I called my mom next.

"Good morning, Roman." I'm sure she could tell what this was about.

"Hi mom." I knew she could hear the sadness in my tone.

"Oh Roman, what is it honey?"

"I can't do this anymore." I breathed out.

She sighed, "What happened?"

"She's so obsessed with whatever this plan of hers is that she's scaring me. This isn't the woman I wanted to be with."

"She may have some more serious things she needs to work on. The timing may not be right for either of you right now." I shook my head and felt the tightness in my chest. I didn't want her to agree with me. I wanted to hear how I was overreacting and needed to give her a break.

"Mom, this feels worse than the last time." I had my face in my hand just trying to hold it together.

"I'm sure it does, Roman, because this time you want it to be over, but you still love her." I've never loved anyone like I love Alex.

"What if she doesn't want it? What if I send her over the edge?" She seemed so fragile even with whatever this crazy plan was of hers.

"What have I told you about the things we can and can't control?" I leaned back in my chair, running my hands through my hair.

"I know I know. I can't control how anyone else feels, thinks, acts or reacts. I only have control over myself." She laughed because she's made me say that so many times.

"That's right. In Alex's mind she's doing what she has to do. By not telling you, she thinks she's protecting you. It doesn't matter that you don't feel the same way, because that's just the way she thinks. Now she's telling you you're better off not knowing. She has a very protective nature about her. She doesn't really like being protected though. I don't know what it's going to take to change that. It's something she may have to figure out on her own." I took a few deep breaths to keep the tears I never saw coming from spilling over.

"You're right, I just need to let her go." I exhaled deeply. "Hey mom? Can I go to church with you and dad tomorrow?" God knows I needed something. Maybe I just needed God.

"Of course, honey. We'd love that."

I got a lot of prep work done for the week ahead then decided to call Harrison and see if he and Amelia were going to mom and dads for dinner tonight.

"Yeah, we're going around five. You ok?" Harrison sounded concerned. Am I okay? Probably not but I'll be fine someday.

"Sure." But I'm definitely not fine right now.

"Is Alex coming with you?" Right then Alex was calling, so I sent it to voicemail.

"I don't think so."

"I guess we'll see you tonight then." I hung up and took a few minutes to get myself together, listening to the voicemail that said we needed to talk.

"Hi, I think you're right." I said as I called her back then shuffled to the kitchen and grabbed a bottle of water. I didn't want to get in the habit of going straight to the liquor cabinet like she's been doing lately. I was sitting on the couch when she came in. She was smiling but I could tell she'd been crying. Damn, this was going to suck.

***

ALEX

I had already packed it all up in my head—every drawer, every hanger, every piece of me that had started to feel like it belonged there. I'd moved myself out before I ever stepped through the door, so when the conversation was over, it would just be logistics.

Clean. Quick. Done.

The elevator felt like it was dragging its feet on purpose, each floor slower than the last. As I looked out over the greenspace inside King Construction—lush, controlled, perfectly maintained; a calm, curated world that felt completely at odds with the chaos sitting in my chest swallowing my nerves.

There was nowhere to hide in here. Nowhere to look but straight ahead at the faintly reflected image of myself in the glass—eyes still glassy, skin flushed—trying to hold it together just long enough to get through this

The doors finally slid open.

And there he was.

Sitting on the sofa... still... quiet... carrying a kind of sadness I had never seen on him before. Not controlled or guarded. Just there, written all over him.

It hit me harder than I expected.

I was silently grateful I'd grabbed a bottle of wine before leaving on my picnic. A little liquid courage to steady the nerves threatening to unravel me. I needed it. I needed something to keep me from falling apart before I even said a word.

My stomach twisted as he lifted his hand and patted the cushion beside him.

An invitation.

Or maybe a goodbye.

God... I hoped he didn't try to stop me.

I'd told him once to chase me—to fight for me—but not like this. Not when everything already felt like it was slipping through my fingers. I didn't have it in me to be pulled back just to break all over again.

I swiped at the last of my tears with the sleeve of my sweater, pressing the fabric under my eyes until I was sure nothing else would fall.

Then I walked over... slowly... cautiously... like one wrong move might shatter whatever fragile thing was left between us.

And I sat down beside him.

The first thing he did was envelope me in a hug. I couldn't contain the tears or the sobs at that point. This hurt so much, feeling his own pain mingling with mine. He laid his head on top of mine and I know I felt a tear land on my cheek that didn't belong to me.

His voice cracked when he choked out, "Alex, I'm so sorry. I'm sorry for everything that's happened to you. I'm sorry that I couldn't be there for you and help you. I know, now, that it's not my place. You have to do that on your own and until you do, there's no place for me."

I sniffed and looked up into his eyes. He was breaking up with me. I wanted this, didn't I? I should feel grateful that this is what's happening right now.

Why do I feel like shit? Why does this hurt so much?

"I'm going to get my things and go." I didn't know what else to say and I tried to get up, but he pulled me back down and kissed me.

"Just remember, I love you and nothing will ever change that." I've never seen him so sad and knowing that it was me that made him that way ripped a hole through the place where my heart should be but felt empty. I nodded and hurried down the hall to pack my things and I left.

I don't remember getting back to my apartment. I hadn't been there in so long I almost forgot what it looked like. It seemed so cold and lonely. It was cold because it was time to turn the heat on, but it wasn't what it was before. My place always felt lived in and cozy. Roman's place was the one I felt was more antiseptic and lonelier. I guess it's not the decor but who's there with you. I felt like an empty vessel right now, just like my apartment. I'm the one who's antiseptic and cold. He was the one who was lived in and cozy.

My phone was ringing, and Matt's name was scrolling across the screen. "Hey Matt." I answered without any enthusiasm at all.

"I think you got what you were looking for," he said accusingly.

I was too busy being in my head to comprehend what he was saying.

"What are you talking about?" I rolled my eyes at his annoying tone.

He laughed but it wasn't a funny, ha ha laugh, it was more pissed off than that.

"You forgot already, huh?" He stopped laughing and spit out with irritation as he continued, "You've been served."

Okay this is what I've been waiting for.

"Oh that. What does it say?" I was chewing my lip trying to prepare myself for what I was about to hear.

"I think you should come over and we can go over it with Jack. I'm not going to be able to represent you on this one because of my political involvement, but Jack said he'd do it. And Alex, this is going to cost you." It's already cost me. My thoughts went to my mother and then to Roman.

"I'll be over in about an hour, okay?" I stared blankly at the wall trying to mentally prepare myself for whatever this was.

"Sounds good. Alex, I'm sorry about all of this. You didn't deserve any of it, but I don't think what you did was helpful at all."

"Thanks for everything you've done Matt. You know I appreciate and love you all." Please just tell me I haven't lost them.

"I know. We love you too." That's what I needed to hear.

When I got there, I was scared. I didn't really feel like I would have the support I needed to do this from my friends and family, so I needed to make a quick call to get my strength back.

The phone rang and Bruce picked up, "Hey Alex. How are you?"

"I'm nervous. What I wanted to happen has happened, and I don't think anyone is going to support any of it." I knew they weren't. Roman breaking up with me was proof of that.

"I already told you we've got your back here. Call me when you know." Thank God for the gym or I don't know if I'd be able to do this.

"Thank you, Bruce." I took a few deep breaths and knocked on the door. Maggie answered it and immediately hugged me.

"I don't know what to say Alex." I got some distance, wiping the tears from my face as I left her with a faint smile before walking past her to the kitchen where Matt and Jack were waiting with the summons.

***

ROMAN

I got to my parents' house and headed straight out back where everyone was having cocktails before dinner. I tried to pull myself together before I went out there, but I knew mom was going to feel it all, so I didn't even bother. I went straight to the bar, poured a bourbon and drank it like a shot. Then I poured another one and sat down. I took a deep breath before I even looked up at anyone and finally said, "Hey."

Mom was the first to say something. She said, "Hi, honey." Harrison, Amelia and my dad all said hello, then they went back to talking to each other like I wasn't there. Is this how it's going to be now? I'm going to be invisible with nothing to say because I'm obsessing over her. Screw this.

I abruptly confronted my father, "Dad, how do you know Grant and the Santoros?" Everyone's head popped up quickly. I'm so pissed about all the secrets.

He answered without hesitation, "I did some work for Grant about ten years ago, why?" I know who they are, so what fucking work did he do for them?

"What kind of work?" I snapped. I'm sure my tone was not going over well.

"What kind of work do you think?" His face was a little angrier than I was expecting and it felt like he was hiding something.

"I don't know, that's why I'm asking." My mood felt destructive.

"Son, I built him a restaurant and a real estate office. What's going on with you?" He's going with the most obvious answer then— bullshit. Why didn't I know about this? I've worked with dad for a long time and even before I worked there, I was with him at the office a lot.

"How did I not know this?" I accused.

"Why would you know this? You didn't work for me ten years ago. You don't know every job I've ever done or know every person I've ever met."

I'm being such a jerk right now, but his tone is frustrated and irritated with me. I know there's more going on.

Harrison yelled, "Chill out, dude."

I lashed out and spat, "Screw you, Harrison."

I turned abruptly back to dad and said, "That explains Grant, but what about the Santoros? Mom didn't seem to know them." Mom came and sat next to me and put her arm around me. What is she trying to protect me from? Information or myself?

"Roman, what's with all the questions about these people? The Santoros funded the projects for Grant. It's been a long time since I've seen any of them. I was surprised to see them at Alex's hearing. They told me you were doing the renovations on their winery. I thought that was great that they brought business back to King Construction."

That seemed legit. I didn't need to hear that my dad was part of some secret underworld life. I couldn't handle any more of this craziness. I wanted my normal, boring life back. I had a feeling I was never getting that again, though.

"Sorry dad. Sorry Harrison. I need to go for a walk and get some air." No point in trying to open this can of worms up right now.

I somehow made my way to the swings and sat down. I didn't even realize mom followed me back there.

"I'm losing it, aren't I?" I said as she sat in the swing next to me. She chuckled.

"How could you not lose it a little? This has been a rollercoaster ride for you, honey."

"Why was she the one? Why did I choose the one who pushed me away and put herself in harm's way? Does that really sound like something I'd do?" She reached out and grabbed my hand. I tried to breathe deeply so I didn't get angry, but all I wanted to do was punch something.

"Why do you think you chose her?"

Because I've lost my freaking mind, that's why.

"Besides the obvious, beautiful, smart, successful...I guess because she wasn't like the rest of them." She's not like anyone I've ever met. She's like a drug.

"And what do the rest of them look like to you?"

"Needy and superficial." Easy and safe.

"What did Alex have that they didn't?" The interrogation swings are in full force now.

"She was independent. She clearly doesn't need me or anyone else for that matter, maybe to a fault. She told it like it is from her point of view, anyway. She was just real." I ran my hands down my face.

"Real isn't perfect, Roman. Real can get ugly. Real can hurt. But it's also genuine and what you see is what you get. We all have skeletons in our closet. Demons that we're fighting that sometimes we keep to ourselves, so we don't burden others. It doesn't mean it will be easy knowing that, it just means sometimes we must make sacrifices in order to deal with those demons. It's best to fight demons with angels. I'm glad you're coming to church with us tomorrow."

I guess Alex was going to have to figure out a way to fight her demons without me. I guess all I can do is pray she finds an angel to help her fight hers.

Chapter 35

ALEX

I got to the kitchen and looked around for the kids, but they were nowhere I could see. I was hoping they would be because I could use some of their calm energy right now. Since this wasn't a normal social visit it's probably a good thing they aren't.

I felt all these judgmental eyes on me but for now I had to tune it out.

"Where is it?" I asked not wanting to fake pleasantries. Abby looked at me and came over, giving me a hug.

She whispered in my ear, "Are you okay?"

I hugged her back and nodded. Matt handed me the summons and it was exactly what I'd been hoping for. He was suing me for defamation.

I looked between Matt and Jack. My eyes wide as saucers as I skimmed over it.

"Is this a joke?" I shouted as I flailed the paper with my hand.

"No and it will never make it into a courtroom." Jack answered— doing most of the talking.

Maggie and Abby looked confused, and I shook my head and started laughing, "What sane person would sue someone for saying they could beat them up? That they wouldn't need drugs to have sex with them, that they could overpower them. It even calls me a little girl with a big mouth." I was now laughing hysterically.

Matt and Jack weren't laughing when Jack demanded, "He's trying to bankrupt you, Alex. He can play this game until you have nothing left." I laughed again and had that moment of clarity and calm.

"I don't think so." I simply stated while staring right at Jack.

"How do you plan to stop him?" He asked.

"By proving what I said was true." Sounds easy enough.

"Oh yeah, and how do you plan to do that?" He snapped. I think I broke Jack.

"By taking it to the ring. I want to fight him fair and square. Prove that he absolutely needed to drug me to overpower me. Prove that I could not only take him down but neutralize the threat." They were all looking at each other like I was crazy. Abby and Maggie's mouths were on the floor.

Jack's voice raised even more than before, "How in the hell do you think we can make that happen?"

"Petition whatever judge is going to throw this bullshit out. I want to have stipulations that say when I win, he gets five years for what he did and no chance of early release. There will be no rules for the fight. No one gets in trouble for any injuries caused and no one can step in to help unless someone is rendered unconscious— then that ends the fight anyway. If he wins, he can get whatever he's asking for monetarily in this lawsuit." Maggie and Abby's mouths were still agape, and Matt was turned around trying not to laugh.

Jack voice cracked, losing all control. "Do you really think a judge will go for something like that? This isn't the movies, Alex. This is real life. Judges don't allow fighting to the death as acceptable alternatives to court proceedings."

"I also want the media there. I want it to be a fucking zoo."

He yelled, "Alex, did you fucking hear me?" I smiled thinking I've never heard Jack yell before much less use the f word.

"Yes Jack. I hear you. I see you. I know what you're saying but this is what I need you to do for me. If you can't, I'll get someone who can. I only need a body in the room with me that calls themselves an attorney to do this because this lawsuit is bull. I just need to be able to plead my case. He's an arrogant scum bag who would love a chance to beat up a woman and I want to give him that chance."

He looked terrified at the prospect of not at least trying to protect me— probably from myself.

He said, "Alex, the guy is twice your size. Do you really think you can win this?" There is nothing else that I've wanted to do since this whole thing happened.

"No doubt in my mind." He let out a sigh as his head fell forward. Matt and Jack were like brothers to me, and this could not make them feel good at all.

"Fine. I'm going to take this on. Meet me on Monday at my office and we'll go over the details. No more talking right now."

Maggie screamed, "Are you crazy?"

I said, "We'll find out soon enough I guess." I didn't want to get into a fight with my friends. I just wanted this over with.

Abby mumbled through tears, "Alex, the guys don't want us hanging out with you, you know brunch and kickboxing, until you figure this out." I smiled as the tears welled up in my eyes, but I had a feeling this was coming.

"It's okay. I need some time to focus on this."

Maggie went to reach for my arm but I politely moved out of her reach and she asked, "What does Roman think of all this?"

I winked and said, "Roman who?"

I saw the sad eyes again. I felt the tears getting ready to fall so I hugged the girls fast and got the hell out of there.

***

ROMAN

Let go and let God. My new mantra, I guess. The penthouse wasn't the same without her in it. At least it was quiet. That gave me the perfect opportunity to sit quietly and talk to God for the first time in, I don't know how long. I just needed him to watch over her and if it was meant to be it was meant to be.

My phone was ringing. Maggie's name was scrolling across the screen. Maybe it's just Matt from Maggie's phone I wondered.

"Hello." Maggie sounded like she was crying.

She sniffled and whispered through sobs, "Roman, she's lost her mind." I just looked up and thought, *"Good luck up there, God."*

I sympathetically responded, "Maggie, she needs to figure this out on her own."

"Do you know what she's getting ready to do?"

No idea.

"Nope and I don't know if I want to. She moved out. I told her I need space from her craziness."

Maggie laughed and said, "Smart man. Doubt you'd be able to watch this shitshow. If you really don't want me to tell you I won't, but if she gets her way, you'll find out."

"Do you think I need a head's up?" Surprises are not my thing lately.

"Probably," she murmured.

"Ok, what is our very special girl up to?" I sat and listened without saying a word as Maggie told me everything Alex had planned. At least now I know who she was working on this with— it had to be Bruce. I couldn't believe he would go along with something like this, but he trained fighters, and from what Jules said they all had a past— most of them worse than hers.

"Maggie, you're right, that's going to be a real shitshow. I really hope it goes her way." I agreed as I tried to swallow the lump that now formed in my throat.

There was silence on the other line. "You ..you're not going to try and st..stop her?" She stammered.

I laughed through the frustration. "Seriously? You think anything I say to her will help? She lumps me in with the rest of the men who've jilted her." *Why does everyone think she'll listen to me?*

She was sobbing loudly now. "Sh..sh..she doesn't but I understand wh ..why you'd feel that way." That's when I caught a glimpse of her photos on the shelves in front of the sofa. Oh, dear God help her.

I met Mom, Dad, Harrison, and Amelia at the steps of the church, and we walked in together.

I paused just before the doors, drawing in a slow breath, telling myself every prayer I said inside would be for Alex.

But the moment I crossed the threshold... something shifted.

It wasn't what I expected.

The air felt different—still, grounded and steady in a way I hadn't felt in a long time. It settled over me, quiet and undeniable, and for the first time since everything started unraveling, the noise in my head eased.

I thought I was there for her, but I wasn't.

I was there for me.

And somehow, that realization didn't feel selfish. It felt... necessary.

A calm worked its way through my heart, loosening something I hadn't realized I'd been holding so tight. For the first time, I believed she was in good hands.

And maybe... so was I.

If only I could get her here. If she could feel this—just once—maybe she'd understand. Maybe she'd see that the path she's on... isn't the one meant for her.

I sat beside Mom, leaned forward, resting my elbows on my knees as I clasped my hands together and bowed my head.

"Please give her peace," I prayed silently, the words forming slower, heavier. "She needs it... more than she lets anyone see."

I swallowed, my jaw tightening as the next part came harder.

"Protect her... because I can't."

That truth sat heavy and brutal.

Then I shifted, just slightly, letting the prayer turn inward.

"Guide me. Put me where I'm supposed to be. Give me the strength to walk that path... whether she's on it or not."

Mom's hand came to rest against my back—warm, steady—and she didn't move it when I finally lifted my head. She just stayed there, supporting me, reminding me I wasn't carrying this alone.

And just like that... the weight started to lift.

Not all at once, not completely—but enough.

Enough to breathe.

Enough to stand.

Enough to know I wasn't supposed to carry all of this by myself.

I knew I'd still see her. With everything we had tied together, there was no avoiding that. And it wouldn't be easy.

But something had changed.

I wasn't holding on the same way anymore.

I'd given it to God.

And somehow... that made the idea of letting go feel possible.

I still believed she was special. Still believed she was meant for something bigger than even she understood.

It just... might not be with me.

And for the first time, I was okay with that.

After church, I pulled out my phone and texted her.

***

ALEX

No brunch Sunday.

The thought landed heavier than it should have.

What am I even supposed to do with my morning now?

I could get ahead on meetings for the week... go over notes, prep, stay productive. Or I could finally go to the grocery store like a normal person and not live off takeout and whatever I can piece together last minute. I could sit down and read through that ridiculous lawsuit again—

No.

Absolutely not.

That was the fastest way back into my head, and that's the last place I needed to be right now.

I needed quiet. I needed space.

I needed... out.

The gym.

Of course.

It had always been my go-to—something physical, something that forced everything else to fade into the background, even if just for a little while.

Thankfully, it wasn't crowded. I didn't have to think about anyone else, didn't have to make small talk or pretend I was fine.

I swam laps first, letting the rhythm take over. Stroke, breathe, turn. Stroke, breathe, turn. The repetition steadied me, pulled me out of everything I didn't want to feel.

Then the sauna.

I sank into the bench, the warm, dry air wrapping around me, sinking into my skin, loosening the tension I hadn't even realized I was still carrying. My muscles softened, my thoughts slowed, and for a moment... everything just went quiet.

Peace.

It surprised me.

The feeling was familiar in a way I wasn't ready for, settling in deep, almost instinctive. It reminded me of being wrapped in Roman's arms—safe, grounded, held in a way that made everything else feel distant.

I exhaled slowly, leaning back against the wall.

For once... I was glad he didn't have to deal with me anymore.

The thought came without resistance, without the usual pushback or second-guessing.

I'm honestly shocked it lasted as long as it did.

And there it was.

Acceptance.

Not sharp. Not painful. Just... there. Like something that had been waiting for me to finally stop fighting it.

Roman and I weren't meant to be.

Maybe we never were.

And maybe... that was okay.

I reached for my phone before stepping into the shower, more out of habit than anything else.

One message.

Roman.

"I went to church this morning. I prayed for you."

I stared at the screen for a second, then felt something soft pull at the corners of my mouth.

Of course he did.

My eyes closed briefly as it settled in, that same quiet calm from the sauna lingering, deepening, making sense now.

So that's where it came from.

***

I was in Jack's office at 9:00 am Monday morning to go over the counter-suit.

"I managed to get a meeting with the judge for you to plead your case in his office rather than in a courtroom, since we all know it's ridiculous." I can't believe it even made it out of the clerk's office to be honest.

"When is that?"

He laughed and said, "He thinks the lawsuit is nuts and wants to throw it out immediately, so he'd like to see us all ASAP." Hopefully the judge will let me talk.

"Does he have time right now?"

"He told me to bring you in as soon as you got here."

That's what I want before I'm too nervous to say what I needed to.

"Good, let's get this over with."

We got to the judge's chambers and Jack whispered in my ear, "Tanner's here too. I don't want you losing it or doing what you did in that court-room here." I could feel my pulse in my eyes again just knowing he was nearby. I took a couple of deep breaths before I responded.

"I promise I'm only going to sit there and let you do the talking. Please ask him for everything I told you to."

"The judge is going to want to talk to you. I want you to be respectful and not take an attitude with him. If you want things to go your way you have to ask nicely."

I was biting my lip because I was just ready to rip this guy's head off, but I knew Jack was right and I had to make this happen before I could do that. I took another deep breath.

"I promise." I balled my hands into fists to hold in the tension as much as I could.

"Then I promise to ask for everything you want." He reached over and patted my shoulder before entering the judge's chamber.

The first person I saw when Jack opened the door was Tanner and Jack placed his hand on my lower back to guide me to the opposite side—furthest from Tanner.

The judge looked at us and said, "Mr. Fletcher, how are you today?"

Jack responded, "I've been better your Honor." The judge laughed. I couldn't even bring myself to react. I was concentrating too hard.

"I can imagine you have. These are some unorthodox matters before us." He looked over at Tanner and his lawyer and continued, "Mr. Robino, did you really have your firm draw up this garbage?" I was kind of shocked the judge talked to them like that, but it was a bunch of garbage.

Then he continued before the other attorney could even respond. "I'm not even going to give this any consideration. I'm going to throw..."

I looked at Jack for help.

Jack interrupted the judge and said, "Excuse me your Honor. Before you do that, my client would like me to ask something on her behalf." The judge looked at me curiously, but I could tell I had no expression on my face right now and would be hard as hell to read. All I was trying to do was hold in the anxiety I knew was trying to escape.

He cautiously asked, "What would that be Jack?"

First name basis, huh? Is that a good thing or a bad thing? It sounded like sympathy.

Jack continued but shook his head a little and proceeded to explain. "Your Honor, my client is concerned that Mr. Ellington is going to keep harassing her with lawsuits to try and bankrupt her. My office is not the cheapest in town. If she has to continually pay legal fees and court costs, just to get these thrown out, it could end up costing her a lot of time and money. She runs a very successful real estate business and is now starting a nonprofit to help people in underprivileged circumstances. She's seeking a permanent solution to the problem."

Jack is damn good at his job and a good friend to boot.

The judge asked intently, "What would a permanent solution to the problem be for her?"

Jack cracked his neck and let out a deep sigh before saying, "She would like to prove that the lawsuit is bogus and that there was no defamation."

"And how the hell would she be able to prove that?" I liked that the judge was assuming what everyone was assuming, that I couldn't do this and that it was nuts. I smiled and waited for Jack to continue. I love being underestimated.

He forced the words out, "Well, she would like to fight him." His head dropped right after he said it.

The judge laughed and looked at me and said, "You've got to be kidding, right?"

I laughed a little and so did everyone else in the room.

I calmly stated, "No, your honor. It's not a joke." Jack reached over and put his hand on my arm as the room went silent.

Tanner blurted out, "Absolutely. The answer is yes."

The judge glared at him and said, "You will speak when I speak to you. Do you understand me Mr. Ellington?"

He sneered, "Sure."

The judge raised his voice without yelling, "The correct response is 'Yes, your Honor.' Not sure."

I thought Tanner was going to growl at him when he huffed out an irritated, "Yes, your Honor." I acted unfazed, even though I wanted to smile, but now I felt like the judge might be a little more sympathetic to me.

The judge looked at Jack and said, "Mr. Fletcher, this is highly unusual. Why would you even suggest such a thing to your client?"

Jack's face pinched up in pain. He frustratedly explained, "Oh no your Honor, I didn't, and I wouldn't. You see Ms. Kennedy has been a family friend since she was eighteen years old. She's like a sister to me and to my wife, and she's the godmother to my child, soon to be children. We all did everything we could to talk her out of this. She threatened to go to another law firm, and I don't trust my family with just anyone, so here we are." My heart swelled but I held it together the best I could. I knew I was going to get my turn to talk, and I needed to be ready.

The judge looked at me and said, "Ms. Kennedy, do you know how lucky you are to have such good people in your life? Why would you want to do something like this?"

This is what I was hoping for. And of course, I know I have good people in my life or else I'd never be able to do this.

I looked over at Tanner, scrutinizing him from head to toe then turned back to face the judge. "Your Honor, I'm sorry for bringing this on everyone. Trust me, I know what I've done to people in this whole process. But men like Tanner can't keep going around thinking there's no consequences for their actions. I understand that the legal system only has so much authority and the law is what it is. I want Tanner and people like him to know that there's people like me out there who aren't going to allow this behavior. I want women to know they aren't powerless to men like Tanner. If they want to fight back, they can."

The judge looked at me and said, "You think getting into a ring with a man twice your size to prove you can hold your own is what women need to see?"

Hold my own? That is not my plan at all. I sat up straight and blew out a breath.

With a smile on my face I said, "No, your Honor. I'm not going to hold my own. I'm going to win. I'm going to prove that there was never a time where Mr. Ellington could've done to me what he did without drugging me. In return I want him to have a five-year sentence with no chance of early release on top of all the things he was already assigned."

I couldn't get distracted so I didn't even look in Tanner's direction, but I could hear him chuckling and whispering to his attorney.

The judge said, "Where shall we have this little brawl, right here on Fountain Square?"

I mean, I would but I don't think that would be a good idea. Honestly, right here right now in this office is fine but I want him humiliated.

"No, your Honor. The gym where I take kickboxing classes and is also an MMA studio— they have a ring."

The judge shook his head and said, "I can't even believe I'm considering this. Mr. Ellington, how do you feel about what Ms. Kennedy is suggesting?"

I knew he would lose points if he said he wanted to do it. No real man wants to hit a woman, and no real man would go along with a man hitting a woman.

Tanner said, "What do I get if I win?"

The judge looked at me wondering the same thing, I'm sure.

"I'll pay whatever restitution he's asking for in this lawsuit."

Tanner was now laughing hysterically.

He choked out, "You'd pay me two million dollars if I beat you up in that ring?"

I turned my head slowly in his direction and glared with the heat of the sun. "Absolutely."

The judge seemed rather irritated with Tanner as well. "Okay, I'm going to sign this. How much time do you need to prepare for this Ms. Kennedy?"

"Honestly, I'm ready to go right now, but I think Saturday would be best so I can work this week. I have a lot going on with the relocation of an entire community thanks to Tanner and his brother Marcus."

The judge asked, "The Representative from the Burrow Township district?"

"Yes, your Honor. Marcus revoked a historical preservation assignment to make millions of dollars and didn't care about the entire community he was displacing." The judge shot Tanner a glaring look.

"Okay, Saturday at 10:00 am. That will give me time to get there." I looked at Jack who was trying to be cool about this, but I could tell he wanted to get out of that room because he couldn't believe this was going to happen. As soon as the judge signed the paper, he handed it to his clerk to get it filed and Jack and I went out to the hall to wait for a copy.

We went out to lunch and talked about what just happened and I told him I wanted this to be a circus.

He said, "I know you're all pumped up about this, but do you really, in all honesty, think you can win?"

"Jack. I'm betting $2,000,000 that I can."

Chapter 36

ROMAN

I stayed out of most of the meetings she held this week. After the news of the fight on Saturday, I couldn't look at her without wanting to kidnap her and run away. What the hell was she thinking? This is insane. Why would a judge agree to something like this? How is this even legal?

Well, I'm not watching it, that's for sure. I don't care how powerful I make her feel. She's insane. I know she had an appointment with my mom this week but that wasn't going to help do anything. I need to find out if I can get any information about what was going to happen there so I decided to call Grant.

"Hello, Roman."

"Grant. Have you heard the news?" He sounded tired.

"Yes. It's all over the TV and social media." I shook my head.

I asked, "Why is she doing this?"

"She thinks it's for the betterment of women. To let them know they aren't powerless against these predators."

But why does she have to be the one to do this?

"I get that, but do you think this is a good idea? This guy is dangerous."

"Yes, he is. If you don't want to hear this, you should hang up now."

"Why stop now, just tell me." *Fuck do I really want to hear this?*

"Tanner's been arrested on multiple occasions for abuse against women. Physical and drug related. He's gotten off every time because of his brother. This time the woman didn't back down. That's the only reason anything happened to him. Alex is the one who took the plea deal for the lower sentence. She knew she'd have to go through a trial to get the five years and they'd just let him out early, so she decided to bait him so she could ask for more severe terms."

Well, damn, she's a smart girl, isn't she. Except for the part where she's going to fight a violent abuser. I laid my head down on the desk.

"Grant. Do you think she can beat him?" I mumbled into the desk.

Grant laughed. "You don't? I thought you knew her better than anyone?"

I thought about that and watching her fight in the ring at the gym. I guess I was only paying attention to the times she got hit over the times she was doing the hitting. Maybe she can do this.

"Well, you'll have to let me know how it goes." How can I possibly watch that when I can't even watch her with people who didn't want to hurt her.

"I'll do that. Don't worry about our girl, Roman. She's going to figure this out."

Two more days till show time. The door to my elevator opened and in walked Harrison and Amelia.

"Hey guys, how are you?" I'm sure this is just more feeling sorry for me and worrying about Alex.

Amelia responded, "We're fine. How are you? I'm sure you've seen the news and social media and know what's going on, right?"

"I did, yes." I leaned back and stretched my arms out on the back of the sofa.

"Are you going to try and stop her?" Harrison demanded.

Why do people think I have any power to stop this? "Why would I do that?"

"I don't know, maybe because she's getting into the ring with a psycho?"

Not sure which one of them was more psycho, to tell you the truth.

"You know she did this, right? She got a judge to agree to this."

Harrison commented, "That can't be true. No judge would ever do something like this, would they?" Apparently, they would.

"I mean, I know she's been training and working out or whatever, but this is dangerous. Why would a judge turn this into some kind of hunger games?" Amelia sounded alarmed to say the least. I shook my head. That's a damn good question. Maybe this judge should be looked into also.

"I don't know, I wasn't there, and I won't be at the insane spectacle either."

Harrison seemed a little uncomfortable when he said, "Well, I'm going to support the girl. Too many people are calling her crazy and insane..." He tipped his head directly at me and I smiled "...and I don't want that getting in her head, so Amelia and I are going."

"Thank you." After they left, I stayed up a little while longer trying to extend this day as long as I could.

***

ALEX

I kept myself busy all week with work.

It was easier than listening to everyone argue about me.

Everywhere I turned, someone had an opinion. Half the people online thought I was reckless. The other half thought I was lying. I couldn't win the argument, and I had no interest in fighting with strangers on the internet who had already decided what they believed.

So I shut it all off.

Social media disappeared first. Then the news. I stopped checking my phone for anything that wasn't directly related to work. When reporters started lingering outside my apartment building, I simply walked past them without answering a single question.

Grant stepped in quickly.

He made sure the ones waiting outside my office stopped bothering me, and he promised he'd work on the ones hovering around my building too. I wasn't sure how he planned to pull that off, but if he could make them disappear, I wasn't about to ask too many questions.

Peace and quiet suddenly felt like a luxury.

When I was at King Construction for meetings, I didn't interact much with Roman either. Not intentionally—there was just too much happening. My time there was spent buried in planning sessions and strategy meetings as the nonprofit began to take shape.

Harrison had pulled in several of his investors to help get it started, and the momentum behind the project grew faster than I expected. The idea that had started as a hopeful conversation was quickly becoming something real.

The Burrow Township meeting was the moment everything shifted.

Amelia had organized it in the auditorium, and by the time the residents started filing in, the room was packed. I stood at the front with my presentation ready, my heart pounding harder than it had during most fights.

But once I started talking, the nerves disappeared.

I walked them through the plan—how the relocation would work, what the homes would look like, how the renovations would happen in phases, and what the nonprofit would do to support the rest of the neighborhood over time.

By the time I finished, the energy in the room had changed.

Almost everyone was on board.

A few families chose not to participate. They believed we were relocating them to a dump, and honestly I couldn't blame them for feeling that way. The area wasn't beautiful yet.

But I had a vision.

And if we followed through, they would eventually see it.

Even better, Shay and Darius had become so familiar with the project that they could practically run the presentations themselves. That had been part of my plan from the beginning. I didn't want what was happening in my personal life to overshadow the project or slow the work down.

If something happened to me tomorrow, the plan would still move forward.

Every afternoon after work, I went straight to the MMA studio.

Bruce made sure I stayed focused.

Training had become my escape from everything else—the noise, the tension, the waiting. When I stepped onto the mats, the rest of the world went quiet.

Raphael had become my new sparring partner.

He pushed me harder than most people had before, correcting small things I hadn't noticed in my own technique and forcing me to sharpen instincts I already thought were solid. Every session left me bruised, exhausted, and strangely calm.

By the time Friday rolled around, I felt ready.

The whole team surprised me that night.

When I walked into the studio after work, the mats had been cleared and tables were set up along the walls. There were balloons tied to the chairs, homemade dishes spread across the tables, and a stack of cards sitting near the center like a small tower of encouragement.

A potluck.

It seemed like the entire gym had shown up.

Some of them hugged me. Others slapped me on the back and joked about how badly I was about to scare whoever stepped into the ring with me.

But what mattered most was the support.

Standing there surrounded by people who believed in me felt reassuring. I was ready.

On the way to my car, my phone started ringing. It was Harrison. I answered, since it was probably something to do with the non-profit.

"Hey Harrison. What's up?"

"Alex, I know Roman doesn't want to be there tomorrow, but I do. I want to make sure you know you have the King's support. All of them."

I knew I wouldn't be able to hold back the tears for too much longer after hearing that.

"Thank you, Harrison," I managed to choke out.

He said, "I talked to your brother Edward after he reached out to Roman, and he's going to be there too." Now the tears are flowing. My brother never called me to tell me he was coming. I just figured they thought I was nuts too and wouldn't want to see it. I could barely get out another thank you.

"See you tomorrow." I sat in my car and cried.

When I got home, I took a long hot shower, changed into comfy sweats, ate dinner and cried some more. This was the loneliest feeling in the world without Roman, and he wasn't going to be there tomorrow either. I sent out one text before I decided to go to sleep for the night.

ME: *If you pray for me, that will be enough to know you're with me and support me.*

I waited for what seemed like forever for a response, but it was only about a minute...

ROMAN: *Always.*

Thank God.

***

The alarm scared me this morning. I thought I was in the ring, and it was time to fight. Tanner seemed even bigger in my dream. I needed to wipe the sweat off my head and get in the shower.

My phone was blowing up with texts, but I only looked at two of them. The one from Jack telling me to meet him at his house so we could ride together, and the one from Bruce telling me to meet him in the office as soon as I got there.

I threw the phone in my purse and didn't look at it again. I had to stay out of my head, and I didn't need anyone telling me not to do this. There was something I did need, however. I ran back to my bedroom and grabbed that gold cross Mrs. Santoro gave me out of my jewelry box and threw it in my bag.

Jack and I pulled up to the back door of the studio and entered there. We went straight to Bruce's office. We didn't want to get caught up in any questions from reporters.

Bruce asked without pretense, "Alex, are you ready?" I took several breaths as I thought about what I was about to do.

"I guess I better be."

Jack said, "I'm going out there for a minute to see who's here."

As soon as Jack was out of earshot, I confessed, "Bruce, I'm going kill this guy."

The look on his face seemed almost fearful.

"What do you mean? Like literally?"

Yes. My hands were shaking, and I could barely breathe.

"I don't know. I've never felt rage like this in my entire life. I don't think it's good. I need to know someone'll stop me if I go too far." He grabbed both of my hands and first told me to calm down and breathe.

"What if you're just fighting back?" He tried to reassure me.

Self-defense is definitely not what I'm talking about right now.

"If he's still fighting, then that's not what I mean. I mean if he's out cold and I keep going."

He started laughing. *Not helping at all.* Does he think I can't knock him out? Right now, I know I can.

"If he's out and you're still going after him, I'll make sure to stop you, since the only rules are the fight ends if someone is out or gives up."

I let out a deep breath before someone knocked on the door. I turned around and Roman's mom was standing in the doorway. My heart sank. I didn't think she would want to see this.

She came right over and hugged me. "You be careful in there. I know you can do this, but I would've never wished for it."

I held the emotions back and said, "Lisette, will you still help me when this is over? I have something to ask you, after." She put her hands on my face.

"Of course I'll help you, as long as you need me to." Now I can do this.

I grabbed the gold cross from my bag, held it in my hand, closed my eyes and simply said, "God Help Me" then put it back in my bag. I don't know if there is a God right now, but what the hell could it hurt.

As I was getting ready to walk out, Bruce stopped me at the door.

He held my shoulders, and I felt like Rocky as he instructed me, "Put your blinders on right now. It's packed out there. It's loud, it's obnoxious and not everyone is rooting for you. They aren't important. The only person you're doing this for is you. Whatever noble reasons you have for doing this is great, but right now it's all about you and getting the job done. Nothing else matters." I took a deep breath, bobbing my head. I pushed all the other thoughts out of my mind and let all my rage and anger for what Tanner and his brother have done totally consume me. My body was shaking so badly on the inside that I almost didn't think I'd be able to go out there. Then I remembered to get control and focus and a calm like before a storm, came over me and I knew I was ready.

Bruce walked out with me, staying close enough that I could feel his presence without him saying a word. He'd been right about the blinders.

I needed them.

The place was packed—wall to wall with people, the air thick with noise and heat and anticipation. Cameras flashed from every direction, bursts of light cutting through the chaos like lightning. It was loud, overwhelming... alive in a way that pressed in from all sides.

I wanted a circus.

I just didn't realize it would feel like this.

I narrowed my focus, forcing everything out except the path in front of me. One step. Then another. Just get to the ring.

That's it.

I caught sight of Tanner just outside it, surrounded by his people, talking like he didn't have a care in the world. That smug smile was already on his face, like he'd decided the outcome before we even stepped in.

He just knew he had this in the bag.

A slow smile pulled at my lips.

I can't wait to prove his ass wrong.

My attention shifted to my corner, and the tension in my chest eased just a fraction when I saw Harrison and Edward standing there with Raphael, deep in conversation like this was just another day, not... this.

Not everything riding on what was about to happen.

I climbed into the ring, still in my sweats, the canvas firm beneath my feet as I crossed straight to my corner.

My corner.

The memory hit me as soon as I got there.

The Sharpie.

My initials still marked the padding, a small, defiant reminder of the first time I'd been laid out right there. At the time, it had felt like claiming something that had tried to break me.

Now... it almost made me want to laugh.

But there was nothing funny about this moment.

Not in here.

Not tonight.

I rolled my shoulders back, letting the humor fall away as quickly as it came, my focus sharpening into something harder... steadier.

This wasn't about what had already happened.

This was about what I was about to do.

Edward reached out his hand and I grabbed it immediately. He smiled and said, "That is one dumb dude over there. Make sure everyone else knows it too."

I laughed and Harrison said, "Who created this zoo?"

I smiled acknowledging that it was me.

He said, "You better fucking win then!" while shaking his head. I nodded, but I couldn't talk right now. My only thoughts were about what I was planning to do in the ring— this fight was between me and Tanner.

Raphael climbed into the ring and whispered in my ear, "I'll let you punch me in the face next time we spar, if you win."

I laughed and mocked, jokingly, "Let me?"

He smirked and said, "Of course I'd have to let you. Not like you could do it on your own."

I shoved him away and nodded. I knew he was trying to keep my head in the ring. He didn't want anyone giving me soft inspiration. I looked over at Matt and Jack who were talking to the judge. They all had their arms crossed and their faces were full of serious expressions. I couldn't think about that though. I needed to stay right here in this ring full of rage. I looked in the only direction I needed— right at Tanner. Just his face was enough to enrage me. I could feel heat rising through my body. I couldn't hear anything else going on around me other than the blood rushing through my ears. He was talking and smiling to his attorney and his brother. So, Marcus the politician showed up to watch his brother beat up a woman. That's probably not going to look good for his next political campaign. I'll have to make sure I get a hit in for him, too.

I decided not to look around anymore until Bruce came into the ring followed by Tanner. No one else was allowed in there. I was still wearing my sweats— Tanner had on a tee shirt, shorts and gym shoes. I was wearing my normal training attire, which was a sports bra and short spandex shorts underneath. I was trying to provoke him as much as possible.

Bruce looked at Tanner and treated him like any other fighter, not some sick predator and said, "Are you going to wear those shoes in the ring? I would suggest taking them off, so you don't trip on your laces." Tanner rolled his eyes and huffed out a laugh then walked to his corner, taking his shoes and socks off.

When he came back over, he snarled, "Better?"

I don't know if I would take an attitude with Bruce. He might be a professional, but I'm sure Tanner remembers being manhandled by him already.

Then Bruce said, "Yes, now what about your shirt? Do you really want your opponent to have that kind of leverage against you? She could use your own shirt as a weapon." He darted his eyes at me and licked his lips. Bile came up in my throat, but I forced it back down.

"She's wearing a sweat suit. I think it's fair, don't you?" With that I removed my sweats and watched his eyes get predatorial. That's exactly the reaction I was trying to invoke. He smiled and licked his lips again as he removed his shirt.

God, he makes me sick to my stomach.

"Should I take my shorts off too? Maybe we should just do this naked." He mocked.

He's one sick mother and all these people watching. I could feel the evil intent coming off him. *Deep breaths.* I could tell Bruce didn't like it, but he was trying to keep things fair.

Finally, Bruce growled out in his burly deep voice, "I think this is good. Now the rules are that the fight's over when one person taps out or becomes incapacitated. We have all kinds of security in this building and paramedics if necessary. I'm not going to say keep the fight clean, because the premise of this was dirty from the beginning, so don't kill each other is all I'm saying. When I leave the ring, you won't start fighting until I ring the bell. Do you both understand?"

We nodded our heads while staring into each other's eyes. His had nothing but blackness behind those blue eyes.

As soon as Bruce was out of the ring, I was standing toe to toe with Tanner. I had to look up to see his face. He was smiling, creepily at me, and he leaned down to whisper in my ear.

"I'm going to knock you out and then assault you right here in the middle of the ring, right in front of your boyfriend hiding on the back wall back there."

Oh my God, Roman's here.

I whipped my head around to see him and as soon as our eyes locked, I felt this searing pain on the side of my face. I went down to my hands and knees. Then another pain in my side and then a loud smacking sound and a sharp pain right on my ass.

***

ROMAN

Oh, damn babe, I'm so sorry!

I needed to get up there. My mom grabbed my arm, and someone pushed me up against the wall.

Raphael was right in my face and curled his lip. "Stay the hell away from that ring. He just used you to distract her. What do you think would happen if you go over there now? Let her work this out. I told you she can take a hit. He ain't no fighter, he's a weak ass punk who hits women."

I was shaking mad now, but he was right, I was only going to distract her more. My mom had tears in her eyes when she saw what had happened. It was everything I could do to look up again and see the rest of this.

Raphael patted my shoulder and said, "Take a deep breath and just watch. I've trained her all week."

I don't know if that should make me feel better or worse. I knew Raphael didn't take much pity on his opponent or even his sparring partners. I watched him punch Alex in the face too.

But then she was up with that eerie look in her eye.

Now, babe, go get him!

***

ALEX

Ow, I think he broke my ribs. I should've known he was going to freaking cheat, Bruce didn't even ring the bell. He's pleased with himself right now, so that's a good distraction. I think I heard Harrison ask if I was okay and my brother ask if I was going to let that creep do that to me.

It's fine, I'm fine.

I'm not going to let anyone do anything to me. I'm not going to let Tanner touch me ever again.

Tunnel vision was back, and I couldn't feel any more pain. I stood up and shook myself off. At this point it was just a game. Do I screw with him and make this a good show, or do I take him down fast and fierce? I think a little embarrassment would be good for him. I could taste blood in my mouth, and I looked right at him, as he smiled. I smiled back, wiping the blood away. I tuned out everyone else in this place; now it was just me and him.

I said with a nasty smirk on my face, "So, you have a thing for my ass, huh?" The thought made me want to vomit.

He laughed and said, "I can't wait to do it again."

"I bet you can't, except the next time it will be your ass, and the hand will be attached to a guy in your jail cell named Moose." That wiped the smile off his face, and he came at me. I moved just far enough to slap his face and trip him at the same time. He went flying down to the mat and jumped up fast, putting his hand to his face like he couldn't believe that just happened.

I held both hands out to the side and said, "You like to hit women? Here I am, come get me."

He ran at me again and this time I moved to the side and kicked him right across his stomach. He doubled over. I slapped his ass as hard as I could before pushing him over with my foot. I didn't take my eyes off him or listen to anything else going on around me. I was going to finish this as soon as he got back up.

He stood and turned around with pure evil intent and said, "I'm going to be between your legs in the middle of this ring, bitch. In front of all these people including your boyfriend."

I don't think so, you sick freak.

"Oh, you'll definitely be between my legs, but I don't think you'll like it," I spit out then gave him a wink.

"I'll definitely like it. I'll make sure you can't walk for a week."

I laughed. "Do your worst." I felt sick having this conversation, but I needed to keep him focused.

The last thing I saw in Tanner's face was hatred—sharp, blinding, coming straight at me with nothing held back.

Then the world narrowed.

One second he was moving toward me... the next, I had him.

My legs snapped into place on instinct, muscle memory taking over before thought could catch up. I locked him down, one leg tight across him, the other anchoring as I pulled and twisted, isolating everything I needed. My grip tightened, my body braced, every muscle engaged with precision.

I felt it before I heard it.

The strain.

The resistance.

Then the shift.

A sick, subtle give under pressure—ligaments stretching past where they were meant to go, the joint no longer holding the way it should. The sound came a beat later—low, wrong—followed by a sharp separation that traveled up through my hands and into my arms.

The bell started ringing.

Again.

Again.

Again.

It echoed over everything, loud and urgent, but distant at the same time, like it was happening somewhere outside of me. His body slackened beneath mine, the fight draining out of him, his weight heavy and unresponsive.

That should've been it.

It was over.

I released, pushed myself up, breath coming fast, heat pouring off my skin—

And then I saw his face again.

Something snapped.

Not clean. Not controlled. It cracked open all at once.

Before I could stop it, I was back on him, straddling his chest, my knees digging into the mat on either side of him. My fists came down hard, the impact jarring through my knuckles, up my arms, each hit landing with a dull, sickening thud.

Again.

Again.

Again.

The canvas shifted under us, the noise of the crowd swelling into something chaotic and sharp, but I couldn't separate any of it. I was locked in—focused and completely out of control at the same time.

Each hit fed the next.

Each impact pulled more out of me.

I couldn't stop.

Hands grabbed at me—voices shouting—but they didn't reach me. Not fully. Not enough to break through what had taken over.

Then arms wrapped around me from behind.

Strong. Unmovable.

Bruce.

He hauled me back, dragging me off him, but I fought it—twisting, straining against his grip, my body still driving forward like it hadn't gotten the message that it was over.

That I'd already won.

That it needed to end.

I tried to break free, to get back to him, to finish something that didn't even need finishing anymore. My chest burned, breath ripping in and out of me, my pulse pounding so hard it blurred everything at the edges.

It took everything Bruce had to hold me there.

And even then... I wasn't ready to let go. I wanted him dead.

***

ROMAN

I pushed away from Raphael, the movement sharp and instinctive, and took off toward the ring. My shoes hit the floor hard, fast, my pulse already pounding before I even got there.

By the time I reached it, Bruce had just gotten inside, his arms locking around her as he dragged her off Tanner.

Alex was still fighting him.

Not struggling—fighting.

Her body twisted against his grip, every muscle engaged, breath tearing out of her in sharp, uneven pulls. There was nothing controlled about it. Nothing measured. It was raw... volatile... like she hadn't come back from wherever she'd just gone.

Tanner lay flat on the canvas, his body at an angle that didn't look right. One arm was positioned wrong—too loose, too disconnected—and his chest barely moved. The mat beneath him was scuffed, damp with sweat, the air thick with heat and something metallic that sat heavy in the back of my throat.

Voices erupted around me.

His brother.

The lawyer.

They were shouting—loud, frantic, their words cutting through everything else.

"If he dies—"

"This is on you—"

"We will sue—do you understand me? Permanent damage—"

My jaw tightened as I stepped closer, the noise pressing in from every direction.

Permanent damage.

I almost laughed.

Was he talking about the same kind of damage Tanner walked in here planning to do to her?

The accusations kept coming—sharp, desperate, reaching for anything they could grab onto.

"She cheated—"

"She's trained—this isn't a fair fight—"

"She knew exactly what she was doing—"

Yeah.

She did.

That was the point.

The paramedics rushed in, their bags hitting the mat with a dull thud as they dropped to their knees beside him. The sound of Velcro ripping open cut through the chaos, followed by clipped instructions and the steady rhythm of hands assessing, checking, stabilizing.

"Stay with me—"

"Get his arm—careful—"

"We need to immobilize—now—"

I barely heard them.

My focus snapped back to her.

Mom was in the ring now, moving straight to Alex, her voice low but firm, hands coming up to her shoulders, then her face—grounding her, pulling her back.

"Breathe... Alex, breathe..."

Alex's chest rose and fell too fast, her eyes wild, unfocused, like she was still in it—still swinging, still trying to get back to him. Bruce kept her locked in place, his arms like steel around her, holding her there no matter how hard she pushed.

I could feel it from where I stood.

The aftermath.

The energy still crackling off her like a live wire.

Out of the corner of my eye, I caught movement—Jack and Matt cutting across the floor, purposeful, controlled in a way everything else wasn't. They headed straight for Marcus and Tanner's lawyer, not alone.

An older man was with them—sharp, composed—and behind him, a small group followed, including a few uniformed officers.

That shifted things.

Fast.

The shouting faltered, just for a second, tension snapping in a different direction as attention turned.

But I didn't move.

Couldn't.

I stayed locked on her, watching as she stood there in Bruce's grip, trying to come back to herself, the fight still lingering in every breath she took.

And all I could think was—

I definitely didn't know that side of her.

Oh Shit. Were they there to arrest Alex?

Harrison grabbed my shoulder as I was headed toward them and said, "Hey there. I didn't know you were coming. I think you need to wait right here." I pulled out of Harrison's grip and Edward came over and stood in front of me.

He said, "Roman, this isn't the time. Let them handle this." I calmed down and turned around.

"You're probably right. I wasn't even supposed to be here." Maggie and Abby came over and each gave me a hug. I couldn't stand this. I was just pacing in a circle.

Maggie said, "I'm speechless. I knew she was mad, but I never expected something like that. That was scary."

Abby said, "She needs help dealing with whatever it is she's got going on in that head of hers."

That was for damn sure.

"I know. We broke up Saturday because of it." They seemed to have already known by the look on their faces.

Maggie said with tears in her eyes, "We had to cut her off too until she figures this out."

Abby said, "I don't want to lose my friend." They both had tears streaming down their faces.

When the place started clearing out and Tanner was on his way to the hospital, I saw the paramedics working on Alex's ribs. I guess that kick to the side must've done some damage. I started walking over toward her, but my mom and Bruce stopped me.

Mom said, "Roman, she's going to the hospital in a minute to get some x-rays. Let's wait until she's been looked at and comfortable. The hospital is going to keep her overnight in case she has a concussion, and she said she'll take visitors then. She doesn't want to talk to anyone right now. Especially you— those were her words."

I guess I can understand that.

"Can I go over with you later?" I still wanted to make sure she was okay.

"I'm going with her right now and I'll text you later if she wants to see you."

At least my mom will be with her. I nodded and went back over to talk to Harrison and Edward. I wasn't in the mood to talk to Bruce. I felt like he egged this behavior on when he agreed to help her.

Jack and Matt came over and Matt said, "Hey Roman. I didn't think you were coming."

I shook my head and said, "Maybe I shouldn't have."

Jack said, "Good to see you man. She was probably glad to have you here."

Really, she doesn't want to see me.

"I don't know about that. I'm probably the reason for some of that damage." I admitted, "Was the older gentleman someone important? I noticed he was watching intently."

Jack said while rolling his eyes. "He's the judge who signed off on this pit fight."

So a judge really did agree to this.

"Who would do that?"

He huffed with a smile on his face while shaking his head, "He did his best to talk her out of it. Basically, he said it was nuts, but I think Tanner pissed him off and Alex was very compelling in his office. You know she told the judge she wasn't in there for herself. She was in there for all the women who didn't think they could get justice against a 'predator' like Tanner. He didn't even blink after that. He grabbed his pen and signed on the dotted line."

"Damn, she's a determined lady, isn't she?"

A voice behind me said, "Yes she is." I turned around to find Grant and Alessandro. I nodded and shook both of their hands.

Jack said, "While I've got all of you here. I just wanted to let you know that Alex won't be dealing with any legal action from this fight, so the only kind of worrying you need to do is about her state of mind. It's not good. We nipped the legal stuff in the bud, but she's got some work to do on herself. The judge already said the paperwork he signed from this nonsense will prohibit either party from suing."

Well, that was a breath of fresh air. Alex sure did go to extreme measures to make this happen, didn't she?

After Alex and my mom went to the hospital, we all decided to meet at Maggie and Matt's house to wait and see if Alex was up for visitors.

***

ALEX

Bruce's arms were still tight around me like a vice grip but someone was holding my hands. When I got focus again I saw that it was Dr. King. That's when I let out my breath and a horrific cry, letting go of the rage and anger. Bruce let me go and I collapsed onto the mat. I was hyperventilating and crying. That was awful. I could've killed him and I would have if someone hadn't stopped me.

Oh my God, what have I done?

Bruce was telling me it was ok, that Tanner was going to be fine. I couldn't breathe.

Dr. King said, "Alex, we're going to have you looked at by the paramedics now." I nodded but couldn't stop the gasping. I became the monster I was fighting. I was still choking on sobs when the paramedics came over and asked me the usual questions if I was hurt and I shook my head until one of them touched my side and I flinched. They told me they thought I had at least one broken rib and would need to go to the hospital to be looked at.

Finally, the tears dried up. "Dr. King, will you go with me to the hospital? I need to talk to you." She nodded and I pleaded, "Please tell Roman not to come. I wish he hadn't seen any of this. In fact, I don't want to see anyone right now, Ok? Maybe later but not right now." What the hell would I say to anyone?

Bruce and Lisette left me with the paramedics and that's when I could feel the adrenaline leaving my body and the actual pain creeping in. I thought I was going to pass out. My jaw and my side were on fire.

I hoped all these people saw what a monster Tanner was, and the power of popular opinion would keep him far away from Cincinnati when he finally got out of jail. I also hoped that other pieces of shit just like him knew they were on notice, because I planned to teach self-defense classes at Bruce's studio. If I can arm every woman in this city with the ability to take on an attacker, I will.

They helped me out of the ring, their hands firm on my arms, steadying me as my legs tried to decide if they were still mine. The noise followed me—shouting, movement, the sharp beeping of equipment—but it all felt distant, like it was happening somewhere behind a wall I couldn't quite see through.

The lights overhead were too bright.

Too white.

Too much.

They guided me toward the gurney, the metal frame cold when the back of my legs brushed against it.

"I'm fine," I said automatically, even as my voice came out thinner than I meant it to.

"You're going to the hospital," one of them said, already reaching for the straps.

"I don't need—"

"You have to be secured for the ride."

Of course I did.

I exhaled, short and controlled, and let them help me sit. The padding dipped under my weight, the paper crinkling beneath me as I leaned back. My body felt heavy now—drained in a way that settled deep in my bones, replacing everything that had been there just minutes ago.

They pulled the straps across me—tight across my chest, my waist, my legs—locking me in place. The pressure grounded me, even if I didn't like it.

"I need my doctor," I said, turning my head slightly, searching through the blur of movement. "Dr. King. I want her with me."

There was a pause. A quick exchange of looks.

Then someone nodded.

"Go get her."

The doors of the ambulance opened with a sharp pull, the outside air rushing in—cool against my overheated skin, carrying the faint smell of rubber and pavement and something sterile that clung to everything medical.

They lifted the gurney, the sudden shift making my stomach tighten as the wheels locked into place inside with a solid click.

Everything felt smaller in there.

Closer.

The doors shut behind us with a heavy thud.

A second later, she climbed in.

Dr. King.

Relief hit me harder than I expected.

She didn't say much—just came straight to my side and took my hand, her grip warm and steady, anchoring me in a way nothing else had managed to.

I held on.

The engine started beneath me, a low vibration rolling through the frame of the ambulance as it pulled away. The siren kicked on, sharp and loud, cutting through everything as we moved.

I kept my eyes on her.

On the calm in her expression.

On the way her thumb brushed lightly over the back of my hand like she was reminding me—without words—that I was here.

That I was okay.

And she didn't let go.

On the way there I said, "Lisette, I'm so sorry for hurting Roman. None of this felt like me. It felt like a part of me had broken off and had a mind of its own. I felt like I was going crazy."

She just nodded and listened.

I said, "I need to be locked up."

She smiled and said, "I don't think you need to be locked up. I do think you need a break, though. Let me talk to a friend of mine. They own a retreat in Indonesia. In Bali."

I smiled and said, "That sounds like a vacation for nutjobs."

"Kind of. There are no padded walls. In fact, there's not a lot of walls at all."

"Is it like 'Naked and Afraid'? I get dropped off in the middle of nowhere and fend for myself?" She laughed, and for the first time in a long time, I genuinely laughed too.

She said, "No. It's a place with no alcohol, no electronics, and no self-deprecating behavior. You just have to spend time with you."

"How long is this rehab?" I let out a much-needed cleansing breath.

"Forty-five days," she said, so matter-of-factly, I realized she must have some serious knowledge of this place. Must have sent a lot of her nutty patients there.

"When do you think I could get in?"

The sooner the better. I needed to get on with my life now.

"I'll talk to my friend and see if I can get you in immediately. In the meantime, I want you to stay in the hospital on the psych ward. I'll admit you. There's a nice private room that I use for my special patients. Only you can allow visitors. You'll need to give me the list of those you choose. I'm going to have some exercises for you to do while you're waiting for your place at the rehab center."

Lisette had called ahead and had the room reserved. They took me straight to x-ray and got that over with. I had two cracked ribs and a fractured cheekbone.

Nice work, Alex.

I mean who would do that to themselves. What I did was sadistic, I have to admit.

As soon as they wheeled me back to the room, I changed into the hospital gown then sat in bed and wrote out the list of visitors that I would accept and when. Lisette had gone to call the rehab center to see when they could take me. My list consisted of my dad, my aunt, my brothers, Abby and Jack, Matt and Maggie, Shay and the boys, Ella and Darius, Grant and the Santoros, Bruce, Harrison and Amelia could come any time. Roman was on the list too, but I wasn't ready to see him yet so I indicated that I would let Dr. King know on that one.

She came back and said, "Alex, you're all set for a week from Monday. Can you get everything in order before then?"

I nodded and thought about how this must be the reason I worked so hard with Shay and Darius to get them ready to take things on without me.

"Thank you, Dr. King. You saved my life." She came over and hugged me tight.

"No sweet girl, it wasn't me." She kissed the top of my head and left.

If it wasn't her, who was it?

Chapter 37

ROMAN

Apparently, this fight was big news, and it was all over the TV and social media. At Matt's house that night he had the TV on outside and we watched the highlights. It was just as scary on TV as it was in person. I took my beer, turning around and walking away to the edge of the patio.

Matt and Jack came over and Matt asked, "How are you, Roman?"

Like I want to drink an entire bottle of bourbon, so probably not too good.

I shrugged and said, "Who was that girl? That wasn't Alex in that ring."

Jack said, "Not at all. That wasn't the girl we knew from college."

Their wives joined us and Abby said, "Do you think she's going to be okay? I don't know what to tell Jax about his aunt Ali."

Maggie said, "Yeah, I just told Sophia and Cam that she wasn't feeling well and couldn't come tonight. I don't want her around the kids like that. It's one thing to be a badass woman, it's another to be whatever that was."

Abby said, "You mean a killer. I hate to say it, but that's what she looked like out there. I didn't recognize that person. She scared the hell out of me."

I knew how they felt. My phone rang and I saw that it was my mom, so I excused myself and walked into the yard before I answered.

"Hi mom, how is she?"

She said, "Well, all in all, she'll recover. She's in a lot of pain. Emotional, mental and physical. She's scared and she knows she frightened everyone, including herself." I started breathing heavily through my nose and my chest was tightening. I needed to see her.

"Can I come there tonight?"

She was silent for a second and I knew that Alex didn't want to see me.

"Roman, that's not going to be possible. I've checked her into my room. She's going to be there until she goes to rehab in about a week. She's asked that you not come see her right now."

I nodded and said, "What kind of rehab are we talking?"

"The kind she needs, honey. I'm not at liberty to tell you anything else." Doctor-patient confidentiality. More serious than I thought.

"Can you tell me how her ribs are?" I hope she can at least tell me that much.

"She has two broken ribs and a fractured cheekbone. She's comfortable. I'm sure she'll want to talk to you before she leaves." That sounds promising, I guess.

"Mom, how long is she going to be gone?"

She said, "I'll let her tell you everything when she's ready." I shook my head, and we hung up, and I went back over to say goodnight to everyone. I just needed to be alone right now.

As I walked up to say goodbye I said, "Well, she's okay, I guess." She isn't dead, so there's that.

Maggie asked, "Who was that?"

"My mom." I smiled and corrected myself, "Dr. King. She said she has a couple broken ribs and a broken cheekbone. She's in a special room for my mom's patients." Everyone knew my mom was a psychologist, so they knew what that meant.

"She's going to be in there until they release her to go to a rehab center, but that was all the info I was allowed to have." I smiled the best I could before saying, "Goodnight, everyone."

***

ALEX

The hospital allowed me to set up my office in the room so I could do zoom meetings and have Shay and Darius come in so I could get them ready to be the front runners for the project soon. I had seen everyone except Roman. I knew that I'd be leaving soon to go to Bali and spend forty-five days letting go of anger and resentment and trying to find myself again. I know I'm in here somewhere. I can't imagine that Roman would want to see me after everything that happened, but I wanted to at least say goodbye and thank him for being there to support me even though I knew he hated every second of it.

I've hurt a lot of people, and I needed to say I'm sorry. I lost so much of the trust I had from my friends and family. I don't know how I'm going to get that back, but I hoped I'd figure it out at this retreat. My friends didn't want me anywhere near my godchildren, and that was breaking my heart the most, but it was all my fault, hoping to repair the damage upon my return.

All the days blurred together in here.

Morning. Afternoon. Night. The same walls, the same quiet, the same steady rhythm of machines and footsteps in the hallway. Time stopped feeling real—just something that passed without asking me if I was ready for it.

On Friday, my dad and my aunt came to see me.

The moment they walked in, I knew.

They'd seen it.

Apparently, the fight had made national news. Of course it had. Of course my worst moment—my complete loss of control—had been broadcast for everyone to see.

My aunt didn't even try to hide it. She was furious. Her voice was sharp, her eyes locked on me like she couldn't believe I would put myself in that kind of danger.

And the worst part?

I agreed with her.

There was nothing to defend. Nothing to soften.

So I told them everything—where I was going, why I was going, what this next step was supposed to be. My voice stayed steady, even when theirs didn't.

They cried.

They hugged me.

And somewhere in the middle of all of it, the anger faded into something softer. Concern. Love. The kind that doesn't disappear even when you make choices they don't understand.

We talked for a while after that. Real conversation. Honest. Grounded.

It felt... good.

When they left, the room felt quieter than before.

On Sunday, I told Lisette I was ready to see Roman.

The words sat heavy in my chest, but they didn't shake. Not like they would have before.

Maggie and Abby had gone to my apartment and packed a suitcase for me.

Lisette explained that the rehab would have everything I needed. Clothes, essentials, structure... all of it provided.

But I could bring whatever made me feel like me.

I needed that.

Something familiar.

Something that reminded me of home... so I didn't lose myself completely in a place I'd never been, doing something I'd never done.

Because if I was being honest—

I was scared.

I'd never been alone like this before. Not really. Not without an out, not without a distraction, not without something—or someone—to keep me tethered.

And this time... it was just me.

Sunday afternoon, I sat on the edge of the bed, a loose tee shirt and yoga pants, my hair twisted up into a messy bun. My laptop rested beside me as I worked through the last of my emails, trying to tie up whatever I could before everything changed.

A knock sounded at the door.

Soft.

Measured.

It opened slowly, and before I even looked up—

I knew.

I felt him.

Roman stepped inside cautiously, like he wasn't sure what he was walking into, like he didn't want to push too far, too fast.

But when our eyes met—

He smiled.

And it wasn't the tight, controlled smile I'd gotten used to. It wasn't weighed down by worry or frustration or all the emotions I seemed to pull out of him whether I meant to or not.

It was... easy.

Real.

And before I could stop it—

I smiled back.

I think it was the first time in a long time that seeing him didn't feel like something I had to brace myself for.

He looked calm and relaxed.

I said, "Hi" then moved the laptop off the bed, placing it gingerly on the table.

He slowly walked over and gently sat on the bed like he was trying not to jostle me and mumbled, "Hi, how are you?"

"Sober and bruised." He put his head down with pain written all over his face and nervously chuckled.

"I'm sorry it's not funny. I think I was just trying not to cry." I nodded and held my own tears in.

"I know. Me too." I was barely able to get out. I just wanted him to wrap me in his arms, but I know I didn't deserve it.

"I hear you're going away for a while."

"Yes. Extended vacation."

He smiled and it hit his eyes and that warmed my heart and kept me from full on sobbing.

"Thank you for waiting to come. I needed to release some things and detox before I saw you. I'm pretty sure I was drinking too much along with holding in a lot of anger." The smile left his face and tears pooled in my eyes again.

"You're welcome. I didn't realize you felt you were drinking too much. I kind of thought you were, but I didn't want to say anything."

I wouldn't have listened, I'm sure.

"Yeah, it's easier for us to admit what's wrong with other people than it is ourselves, huh?" I chuckled a little in hopes the tears would be fended off.

He laughed with me and said, "I guess I can take this time to admit my issues too." I shook my head. I didn't want him to compare apples to oranges. He was nothing like me. He is such a good, wonderful person.

"Nah, you're perfect to me." He hugged me and I wrapped my arms around his waist and just breathed him in. I needed that soul connection one last time before I took this journey on my own.

I pulled away, taking his hands in mine and said, "I'm sorry. I'm so sorry for all the pain I caused you. I'm sorry for scaring you. I don't know why I couldn't just love you and let you love me..." Tears silently fell as I continued, "I'm hoping I can figure that out while I'm gone. The girl who lands you will be truly blessed. I just don't think it's me, and I don't want you to wait for me."

He smiled and said, "Don't tell me what to do."

I laughed through the tears.

"Will you stay with me tonight? I know I have no right to ask for this, but I had to." I pleaded. I needed one more night of calm and he was the only one who could bring that to me right now.

"Yes, and I'm going to ride with you to the airport tomorrow. I'm letting mom use the plane to fly with you to your retreat. I don't want you to do this alone and when you're ready to come home, mom, I mean Dr. King, will be there to fly home with you as well."

I swallowed back the sobs threatening to come again, "You know where I'm going then?"

"I know all about mom's exclusive retreat. She's gone there before. Can you imagine listening to everyone's shit day in and day out and not having to take a break from it? Especially a person like my mother, who feels things so deeply."

It wasn't just a place for her patients. Lisette was a patient too.

"I never thought about how I could be affecting her with all this craziness. Damn. Here I was thinking she was this rock who couldn't be affected by anything, but she could fix me."

We both started laughing and then he concurred, "Yeah, that would be one hell of a superpower wouldn't it?"

I don't think he and I have laughed this much ever.

***

ROMAN

Morning came too fast.

Dad had dropped Mom at the hospital early, and by the time I pulled up, Alex was already standing near the curb with her discharge papers in hand. She looked pale but steady — that quiet, worn-out calm people get after days of running on adrenaline. We didn't say much on the drive. The sun hadn't even fully risen yet, the sky a washed-out blue, and the world felt strangely muted... like everything was holding its breath.

The sun was just beginning to rise, making the whole city feel half awake. The streets were nearly empty, and for a few minutes it felt like the world was paused just for us.

When we arrived at the private airport, the jet was already waiting and ready to go.

I walked around to the back of the car and lifted Mom's bags from the trunk, carrying them toward the plane. The cool morning air still hung over the runway while the first streaks of sunlight began touching the metal of the aircraft.

I opened the cargo hold and loaded the bags carefully inside before closing it again.

Mom spoke quietly with Alex, the two of them already shifting into whatever rhythm they would have for the long trip ahead.

Once everything was set, I walked back over then I turned to Mom.

She reached up and held my face in both of her hands the way she used to when I was younger, her palms warm against my cheeks.

"Safe travels," I told her. "And thank you... for everything you've done for Alex. When I asked you to help her, I didn't expect... all of this."

I paused, trying to find the right words. "I know it put you in a tough spot. That's a lot to carry, and I'm grateful."

Her eyes softened the way only a mother's can — regret and strength woven together in a quiet understanding.

Mom added with a wry smile, "And I'm going to stay a few days myself before flying back. They have the best rest-and-recharge setup anywhere. Might as well take advantage."

I pulled her into a hug, and she kissed my cheek before boarding.

When I turned, Alex was standing a short distance away with her hands clasped in front of her — fingers laced, thumbs fidgeting, eyes glued to the ground like she was deciding whether to stay rooted there forever. The early morning light haloed off her hair, giving her a glow she didn't realize she had.

I walked over and said quietly, "So... here we are."

She didn't look up until I lifted her chin with my fingertips. Her eyes were big, tired, but clearer than they'd been in days.

"Yep. Here we are," she echoed softly. "This is so weird. I don't know how we even got here. One minute we were talking about empathy... and the next I'm on my way to a tropical looney bin."

Her attempt at humor pushed a small laugh out of both of us.

I gently embraced. She fit herself against me immediately, no tension, no hesitation. For once I didn't feel that tight, aching pressure behind my ribs that always came with worrying about her. And for once, she wasn't carrying that shadowed sadness in her expression either.

"Yeah, well," I murmured against her hair, "you and the coconuts have fun."

She smiled up at me — a real smile, unlike the brittle one she'd worn for weeks.

"Roman, I'm so grateful to you. And your mother. And your family." She paused, looking suddenly shy. "I hope when I come home... you'll get to meet the real Alex."

I cupped her cheek with my hand.

"We all have a dark side and a light side," I said. "Both are real. I love *all* of you, Alex. Not just the easy parts."

She took a breath. A soft, sincere one.
"Same," she whispered.

I kissed her — slow, deep, trying to store enough of her in the moment to last the next forty-five days without her. When she pulled back, she squeezed my hand once, walked up the ramp, and boarded.

And just like that... she was gone.

***

ALEX

I watched him the entire time the plane taxied, rolled, and finally lifted off the ground—Roman growing smaller and smaller through the window until he faded into the blur of clouds and distance. Only when I couldn't see him anymore did I let my eyes close. The exhaustion hit fast. I drifted under before the plane even leveled out.

When we landed in Bali, the warm air rushed in the second the cabin door opened, soft and humid like someone wrapping a warm towel around my shoulders. Two attendants took our luggage, loading everything into a small car while Lisette stayed close, gently guiding me like she knew I was running on fumes.

The drive to the retreat was quiet and surreal. Lush green everywhere. Flowers the color of sunrise. The ocean flashing turquoise through the trees like it was winking at me.

The retreat itself was… unreal. All the bungalows were open-air, the kind you only see in movies—tall thatched roofs, wide wooden beams, draped white fabric moving with the breeze. Everything smelled like saltwater, jasmine, and warm teakwood. A tall fence wrapped around the property for privacy, but every bungalow opened toward the ocean like the entire place was built to breathe.

Today the sky was crystal blue. The sun warm but soft. Like it knew I needed gentleness.

Lisette helped me check in and introduced me to the staff, all of whom had this calm, centered energy that made me feel like I'd entered a different world. They told me my official itinerary wouldn't begin until tomorrow. Today was for unwinding. Releasing. Simply arriving.

Lisette touched my arm. "I'll come get you before dinner. We'll walk together."

I nodded, grateful for her steady presence. This place even had a beautiful name—almost poetic:
"Wisdom by the Water Wellness Retreat."

I changed into my bathing suit, grabbed a book off a wooden shelf in my bungalow—something about healing from addiction, titled *With Wisdom Comes Water*. It was written by the founder of the retreat. Someone who'd fought their own battles and won.

Book in hand, I wandered down the winding path toward the beach. The sand stopped me in my tracks — powdery white, warm under my bare feet. The ocean was so clear it looked unreal; every shade of blue layered together like brushstrokes.

Several lounge chairs were already set up along the shore, each one cushioned and inviting. I sank into one, the soft fabric hugging me, and inhaled the clean, salty air. My whole body unclenched.

"Excuse me," a voice said gently.

I looked up. A young man stood there, offering me a bottle of water with a kind smile.

I accepted it. "Thank you."

The moment I wrapped my fingers around the cold bottle, something clicked. A slow, quiet recognition. I looked around — the sky, the chair, the book, the water.

This was my dream.

The one that had kept coming back. The one where I woke up on the beach with only a book and a bottle of water.

Except this time... I wasn't dreaming.

And instead of wine bringing me wisdom, it brought me wellness.

I tilted my head back, looked up at the endless blue sky, pressed my palms together, and whispered, "Thank you."

Acknowledgements

With Wine Comes War is where everything surfaced.
This was the point where the pain, the anger, and the trauma could no longer be contained. It didn't come out quietly or in measured pieces—it detonated. What had been buried for so long erupted all at once, bleeding into everything and everyone in its path. Relationships were strained, some were broken, and what remained in the aftermath felt like devastation.
This story is raw because it had to be.
But even in the destruction, there was something else—something I didn't expect at the time. There was beauty in the ashes. Because once everything is exposed, once the pain is no longer hidden, it creates the opportunity for something new to begin.
Healing.
Not the kind that happens overnight, and not the kind that comes without effort. But the kind that begins the moment you realize that surviving isn't the same as healing.
For most of my life, the path was simple—fight or flight. And for me, it was always fight. I didn't run. I didn't back down. I pushed forward, often swinging, often defending, often reacting.
But what I came to understand is that I was fighting against everything... and not necessarily fighting for anything.
And that realization changes everything.
Because sometimes the strongest thing you can do isn't to keep swing-ing—it's to step back, regroup, and choose what is actually worth fighting

for. To heal. To rebuild. To move forward with intention instead of reaction.

That shift—learning the difference between fighting against and fighting for—became one of the most important lessons of my life. And it lives in every page of this book.

To my children: you are who I fought so hard for and how I learned the difference and eventually rebuilt and healed, moving forward in love instead of war.

To my readers, thank you for walking through this part of the journey with me. It isn't always comfortable, and it isn't always easy, but it is real.

And if this story impacted you in any way—whether it challenged you, stayed with you, or made you feel something you didn't expect—I would be so grateful if you left a review. Your words help these stories reach the people who may need them most.

Love, always,

JJ

About the author

JE Johnson
Just a believer who loves to write about extraordinary circumstances
wrapped up in highly dramatic fashion with a hard fought for happily ever
after bow— because a love worth having is worth fighting for!
Cheers!
https://www.jejohnsonauthor.com/